HOSTILE TAKEOVER

LUCY LENNOX

Cover Art by: Natasha Snow

Cover Photo: Michelle Lancaster

Editing by: Sandra at www.OneLoveEditing.com

Beta Reading by: Leslie Copeland at www.LesCourtAuthorServices.com, May Archer, and Molly Maddox

KEEP IN TOUCH WITH LUCY!

Join Lucy's Lair
Get Lucy's New Release Alerts
Like Lucy on Facebook
Follow Lucy on BookBub
Follow Lucy on Instagram
Follow Lucy on Pinterest

Other books by Lucy:
Made Marian Series
Forever Wilde Series
Aster Valley Series
Twist of Fate Series with Sloane Kennedy
After Oscar Series with Molly Maddox
Licking Thicket Series with May Archer
Virgin Flyer
Say You'll Be Nine

Visit Lucy's website at www.LucyLennox.com for a comprehensive list of titles, audio samples, freebies, suggested reading order, and more!

This book is dedicated to the incredible May Archer who not only improves my writing with invaluable feedback but also makes my life better in more ways than I can count. May, your friendship is a treasure.

PROLOGUE
ELLISON

"Ponder and deliberate before you make a move."
~ Sun Tzu, *The Art of War*

"... or not."
~ Ellison York

"Okay, York, here's the dare." Kirby Heath's eyes were a little cloudy from drinking too many shots with dirty names and a little mean from being born into the kind of wealth and privilege most people only dreamed of. "The next server who comes into the room gets the Ellison York treatment in the storage closet. You up for it?"

"Uh... What's the Ellison York treatment exactly?" I asked, stalling for time.

Already, Drake Lou and Will Dinsmore had taken their turns, bringing back some cute tennis girl's pink panties and a lipstick kiss in Corinne Knight's signature red lip color right above his belly button, respectively. And now, apparently, it was time for me to uphold the honor of the York family name by taking mine.

Nothing good ever starts with a drunken dare. I was just sober enough to know that much.

But the final night of the father/son golf tournament at the Crosbie Golf and Country Club in Greenwich, Connecticut, wasn't known for being a time when intelligent decisions were made. It was known for being a time when fathers passed down their tendency to overdrink, tell blatant lies about conquests on and off the golf course, and salivate over the bar bunnies in the member-only area of the clubhouse.

It also happened to have coincided with my very overdue, very public dumping by my long-term girlfriend, Nessa, who felt that senior year of college meant moving on from relationships that were "outdated" and "not representative of who we were now" or whatever.

"Dude, I should not have to spell this out for you," Kirby said with an eye roll. "You take this person in the closet, you do a dirty deed, and you bring back proof."

"Photographic or physical proof," Drake clarified, lifting his shot of tequila. "We won't take your word for it."

The drunken guys around me—men I'd called my friends since elementary school, through our years at Choate, and at Yale, too, for a couple of them—laughed out loud at the very idea of taking some-one's word for something. If there was one thing our fathers taught us at a young age, it was that honor was mostly for the middle class.

I was starting to think Nessa had a point about outgrowing certain relationships, because the pretentious snobbery of the people around me had started getting old years ago.

The familiar clack of the billiard balls punctuated the indrawn breath Drake took when the fiery tequila hit his throat. In the nearby dining room, I could hear the low rumble of voices from our various fathers and grandfathers as they shared drunken recol-lections of particularly good shots from the day's golf cham-pionship.

"Stop overthinking shit. You should be thanking us," Will said.

"This is a total gimme. Did you see the body on that server with the red hair? Mm. Besides, she's been eyeing you all night."

I thought of the server who'd brought our last round of beer. She was gorgeous. Thick red hair pulled back in a braid that nearly hung down to her ass and a figure that totally did it for me. She'd flirted with me in the past when I'd been here with Nessa, so maybe she'd be fine pressing a kiss to my stomach for fun.

Kirby handed me another shot—my fourth Buttery Nipple in an hour—which meant I was well past buzzed and on my way to sloshed, but I slammed it back anyway, repressing a shudder at the butterscotch flavor. It was easier just going along sometimes.

"Never be the man who ruins another man's good time, son." My father had told me this on multiple occasions.

It definitely didn't pay to ruin Warren York's good time. One didn't argue with my father unless one wanted to be punished severely. He was a ruthless, egotistical businessman who'd inherited the wealth acquired by hundreds of years of Yorks who came before him but acted like he'd earned it all himself.

Sadly for my mother, my sister, Gigi, and me, he wasn't any better at home than he was in the office. My father's favorite brand of punishment involved tightening the purse strings, not on the offender, but on someone the offender loved. When I upset my father, he punished Gigi or my mother.

And there was nothing my father cared about more than keeping up appearances.

"Yeah," I agreed. "I'll do it."

Suddenly the room went oddly quiet. I glanced up and noticed a server had, in fact, entered the room. But it wasn't the redhead.

It was Grey Blackwood.

The kid from the projects who'd caddied at the country club for years.

The business student prodigy who'd landed himself a full ride to Yale.

The guy in my calculus class last semester who'd leaned over and asked to borrow my graphing calculator, and whose unique scent—

coffee and limes or some shit—had made my dick move when it had never, ever moved for a guy before.

The gorgeous man I'd low-key been obsessing over every day since then, which accounted for all the times I'd hung out at the country club this summer, hoping to catch a glimpse from afar, and for all the soul-searching I'd been doing about my sexuality.

My heart beat so fast I thought I might faint right there.

Grey strode over to one of the high-top tables on the far side of an empty pool table and began loading dirty glasses onto a tray. When one of the guys made a crass comment about one of the female servers, Grey's jaw tightened. I wondered if he felt as uncomfortable here as I did, as frustrated by the pretentious bullshit as I was.

I felt everyone's eyes on me as I watched Grey focus on his task. As soon as he left the room again, the guys around me burst into noisy chatter all at once.

"Dude, obviously we meant a chick," Drake said with a laugh.

"What?" I asked, still trying to shake off the haze I seemed to get when I was around Grey Blackwood.

Someone slapped the back of Drake's head. "Don't be a homophobe. What's wrong with the dude? It's just a kiss in the closet, for fuck's sake. C'mon, York. You got game either way, right?"

Several of the guys hooted and high-fived, but Drake seemed upset about it. "For real, guys. I meant a girl. Obviously."

Tanner Young rolled his eyes. "You saying there's something wrong with kissing a guy? Do we need to have a conversation right now?"

Tanner had been out of the closet since our last days of Little League. Or at least it had seemed that way. Drake's foot was fully in his mouth. He looked at me in slight panic. "Not what I'm saying at all. It's just—"

"It's fine," I said as nonchalantly as possible. Inside, I was a nervous wreck. Somehow, I'd agreed to kiss Grey Blackwood in a closet on a dare? Was I dreaming? "I'll do it. No big deal."

Maybe it was the liquor speaking, or maybe it was the bi-curious asshole in my head, who seemed to have taken over my better judgment. Either way, I wasn't one to shirk a dare, even if I hadn't known exactly what I was agreeing to.

Besides, this was like permission from the universe to do the thing I'd been dreaming about for weeks. The perfect excuse had just been handed to me on a silver platter.

Someone asked Kirby, "Isn't that the scholarship kid who's going to work for your dad after graduation? They doing charity work now or something?" Several other guys laughed.

"Yeah, dude, but supposedly he's hella smart," Kirby said. "Better him than me. I'd rather earn my money the old-fashioned way, you know?"

A chorus of voices sang, "Inheriting it," before breaking into laughter again.

I ignored them and slid off the stool, barely catching myself before stumbling. Great. If I could *find* Grey and then *find* the storage closet, I'd be golden. "Be right back, yeah?" I said, once again trying my hardest to act not-drunk and not-overly-interested in the dare.

Everyone cheered me on and slapped me on the back as I made my way out the open doorway and into the hall. I glanced toward the dining room, hoping like hell Grey wasn't in the process of serving drinks to my father.

"You lost?"

I whipped my head around in the other direction and saw the man I'd been looking for.

"Yeah, um. No? I mean... no?" Super. This was off to a stellar start.

Grey's eyebrows lowered. "You okay, man? Need the men's room?"

I met his eyes. They were fucking gorgeous. Clear blue-green and intense as shit. "Um." I swallowed. "No. No, I need..."

You. This. Us.

I cleared my throat. "I want..."

He frowned and approached me, reaching out to clasp my elbow. "Come with me. I'll get you a glass of water."

Good. That was good.

"Can we... can we go somewhere private?" I asked, forgetting about the guys and thinking only of Grey Blackwood and finding out what it would be like to be alone with him for only a minute. My head spun with images of what it would be like to kiss him, to touch him. Belatedly, I remembered this was his workplace. "I don't want to get you in trouble."

He chuckled. "My supervisor's smoking weed outside. You're good."

Within seconds, he'd pulled me down the hallway to a closed door. Once he opened it, I saw the storage room everyone talked about. Shelving reached all the way to the ceiling, and most of it was covered in pristine club hand towels folded into neat stacks. A large ice machine hummed in the corner, and right next to it was an old-fashioned water cooler.

Grey grabbed a paper water cup shaped like a cone from the stack on top of the water cooler and filled it before handing it to me. I sucked it down greedily, if only to get that godforsaken butterscotch flavor out of my mouth.

"Thanks," I mumbled before moving forward to refill the cone. I brushed my shoulder against his chest as I stepped past him. Suddenly, the room seemed much smaller than it had before. The scent of coffee and laundry detergent surrounded me, but it was over-laid with the barest hint of apple shampoo.

I turned my head to see if that smell was coming from him, but at the same moment, he turned his head toward me to ask me some-thing. The words died on his tongue as we found ourselves nose-to-nose. From this close, I could see his hair was hundreds of different shades of blond. A hank of it had fallen down over one eyebrow. It made him look vulnerable, unlike the proud man who seemed to have his shit together on the golf course and in class.

"Hi," I breathed.

"What are you doing?" he asked in a weary voice. The air between us was thick and heavy. If I'd been any more sober, I would have chickened the fuck out and run out with my tail between my legs.

But I wasn't sober.

"I just... I..."

"Ellison." He spoke my name like a warning.

"You're smart as shit," I said stupidly.

"I know," he replied, meeting my eyes in challenge.

"Why do you work here with all these rich assholes around you? It's unbearable."

His face widened in a reluctant grin. "Spoken by one of the self-same rich assholes."

I frowned, and Grey's eyes followed the movement of my lips. My cock liked that. A lot.

"Why?" I repeated breathlessly.

"Good money, better connections. I want to be an investment banker, and the only way to do it well is to work for one of those rich assholes one day. The men in that room control eighty percent of the country's investment capital. I want a piece of it."

"But—"

He cut me off with the barest brush of his lips against mine. It was so light, so *nothing*, he could have written it off as an accident, but it was enough of a spark to light the whole damned stack of fireworks between us.

I lunged for him with both hands, grabbing his face and smashing my mouth against his. He grunted at the impact, but then Grey's arms came around to hold me tight while he kissed me back.

He kissed me back.

I could barely breathe. It wasn't enough. My heart hammered in my chest with something like panic. What if he stopped? What if this all stopped and I couldn't have it anymore? This awkward, grappling kiss was everything. *Everything.* And I knew right away it was only the beginning.

I wanted more. I wanted him. I wanted to be naked and ready for whatever came next. My dick was out of fucking control right now, and I couldn't even figure out how to go about getting off. I just knew I wanted to get off with him. With Grey.

"Whoa, whoa. Slow down," he said, pulling back a little. I grabbed his shirt and fisted it to keep him from pulling away.

"No. Stay," I begged, not giving a shit how desperate I sounded. "Please."

He studied my face for a moment before bringing his hand up and running a thumb across my cheek. "Fucking gorgeous," he murmured before leaning in for another drugging kiss. He pulled back again and met my eyes. "You're drunk."

My brain spun with all the things I wanted to do to him, with him. "Let me suck your dick," I blurted. The words floated fat and weird between us. Finally, he smiled. It was kind and held an uncomfortable amount of pity.

"You don't want this. You're just upset. I heard about your girlfriend."

"Ex-girlfriend," I corrected. "And I'm not upset. I'm horny. For you." I let out a little laugh after that since the idea of being horny for this guy, for *any* guy, was a little crazy. But it was the truth.

His skepticism was clear as day. "You're bi?" he asked.

"What? No," I said without thinking.

His lips widened in that same grin, the one that went to my dick but also made me feel a little like an errant child.

"Then I guess we're done here," he teased. "Since you're straight and all." He deliberately shifted so his hip brushed against my straining cock. The noise that came out of me was embarrassingly desperate.

We continued to stare at each other.

"Please," I breathed. Apparently, my ability to retain a single shred of dignity was gone. And, honestly, I didn't much care in this moment. Part of me knew if I didn't take this one chance to touch him, to experiment with this newfound desire of mine, I'd regret it forever.

"On your knees, then," he said gruffly, calling my bluff.

I dropped to the ground before he took another breath, before he could change his mind.

His eyes lit up with shock, but I wasn't sure which one of us was more surprised.

Grey grabbed me under the arms and yanked me up, shoving me against the wall and muttering something about being an idiot and going to hell for sure. My head spun, and my dick throbbed. Before I knew it, he'd opened my pants and fisted my cock.

"Oh fuck," I said on a gasp. "God, please."

He dropped to his knees and licked my cock, starting with the tip before slathering the shaft with saliva and then sucking the entire thing into his hot, wet mouth.

I let out a long groan of disbelief and pleasure. This was... this was unbelievable. Incredible. Mind-fucking-blowing.

I grabbed his hair but tried not to pull. Nessa used to throw a fit if I dared pull her hair. But, god. This... this was so different. He wasn't hesitant at all. Grey Blackwood knew exactly what he was doing.

I shoved my free hand into my mouth to keep from screaming. The whole thing was over in seconds. The incredible sensations had built and crested before I knew what was happening. I bit into my fist and choked on a scream, horrified at the possibility of drawing attention from the guys awaiting my report.

This was way, way more than a dare.

And I would never tell a soul about it, no matter how much shit it earned me from Kirby and the other assholes.

I looked in his eyes, desperate to see... something in them. Pleasure? Approval? Satisfaction? But Grey was hard to read. His eyes were intense as hell, but I couldn't tell what he was thinking.

"Your turn," I said, switching places with him and trying to act way braver than I felt. I wasn't one for one-sided hookups, but I also didn't want to humiliate myself in front of him by trying something new.

Sure enough, what came next was horribly humiliating. My fumbling at his belt, his endless patience, the sounds I made when I revealed his dick, the way my hands shook when I reached for it.

I glanced up at him as if asking for permission. The look in his eyes was oddly vulnerable, so unexpectedly exposed that I hesitated a beat before he quickly shuttered it.

"Suck me."

I leaned in and tasted him, squeezing my eyes closed and trying to ignore the entire room spinning around me. His hand was gentle in my hair, caressing my head softly as if with affection. I hadn't been expecting that. I'd assumed he'd grab me, control me with a strong, maybe even painful, grip.

But he treated me like brittle glass, as if the mishandling of this moment would result in disaster.

And it did.

"What the actual fuck?"

Everything happened so fast. The open door, the barked questions in multiple masculine voices, the bright light of a camera flash, the snickering laughs and singsong taunts, the feel of Grey's hand as it brushed against my face before quickly tucking his dick back in his pants and zipping up.

The sound of my father's stern voice promising to ruin Grey Blackwood for corrupting his son. The sound of Kirby Heath's father revoking Grey's job offer. The snickering of my supposed friends calling me the king of dares. The surprised squawk of someone promising Grey was no longer an employee of the Crosbie Golf and Country Club.

And the deafening sound of my drunken, confused self saying nothing at all.

1

GREY - 15 YEARS LATER

"Attack him where he is unprepared. Appear where you are not expected."

~ Sun Tzu, *The Art of War*

"Must you always go in there looking like the Doom-Bringer?"

My personal assistant had a lazy drawl despite being one of the hardest workers I'd ever met. I shot him a look. "In this case, I am literally a doom-bringer. Do you expect me to go in there with pompoms and a cheerful chant about the joys of acquisition redundancies?"

We were striding down Ninth Avenue toward the Gallin building for my last and the ultimate takeover in the plan I'd concocted after that night at the Crosbie Country Club fifteen long years ago. York Capital was finally mine. It had taken me ten long years of planning and surreptitiously buying up stock here and there as the market and my own liquid capital allowed.

But it was finally here. The day I got to walk in and tell Warren York where he could shove it.

"Not cheer exactly, but you could at least fake a tear for all the people who will be losing their jobs through no fault of their own."

I glared at Marcel out of the corner of my eye. "I am nothing if not generous with severance packages."

He sighed. "That's not what I mean, and you know it. It just seems like the only time I see that fire in your eyes anymore is when you're telling someone you've ruined their life."

A lanky teen with giant headphones almost clipped me on a skateboard. I grunted and stepped to the side, trying not to bark out a complaint about him not watching where he was going. "When did I ever have fire in my eyes for something besides work?"

Marcel skipped to catch up with me. His shorter legs often had to work harder to keep up with my pace, but the younger man had boundless energy, so I didn't worry too much about it.

"When you helped those kids in Queens find a place to practice their music. When you donated a truck to the family rescue group. When you visited your mom for her—"

I cut him off. "Stop. If this is your way of buttering me up for some other do-good project, it's unnecessary. I told you to go ahead and fund whatever causes you want. That's the purpose of the Blackwood Giving Program. Just submit your request to Dara, and she'll assess it."

"You're deliberately misunderstanding me, which is incredibly uncharming." He grabbed my elbow to stop me from walking into a moving car, but as soon as the car passed, we continued. "You've become so focused on building the business, I feel like you've forgotten how to have fun."

"I've never been fun," I corrected.

He fisted his hands and shook them in the air while letting out a sound of frustration. "That's what I'm trying to say! God, Grey. You're going to die of a heart attack before you're forty. What's the point of all this financial success if you don't have some fun? Take a break, for god's sake. You did it. You finally finished the corporate acquisitions you've been working on for a decade. Go to the Mediterranean, ride a camel in the desert. Hike the Appalachian Trail. Do something.

Something other than studying the market and jumping at every opportunity that comes your way."

"The point of financial success is to ensure I never have to worry about money ever again," I informed him. "To make sure my mother doesn't have to clean up another puddle of vomit or get groped by a patient on pain meds. To make sure everyone who ever doubted me, ever stood in my damned way, knows I succeeded despite the obstacles. To help others. That's the point."

"Yes, fine. I know. I get it. But it's done now." He grabbed my arm again to stop my forward progress. "Let me book you into that resort I told you about in the Caribbean. Just for a week. You can get massages, drink umbrella cocktails, and maybe find an island man in a tiny bathing suit to keep you company."

"Remind me again why I keep your bossy self around?" I grumbled.

"Because my charming smile lights up your life. Also, because my very rich, very muscular husband would frown on you firing me."

I rolled my eyes. We both knew that wasn't why.

His suggestion did sound good, and after the satisfaction of seeing the look on Warren York's face today when he realized he no longer owned his family business, it might be nice to go revel in it with a quasi celebration.

"Hypothetically speaking... is there Wi-Fi at this resort?" I asked.

Marcel rolled his eyes. "Even if there wasn't, I know you have a sat phone and a satellite hotspot. Remember when I thought you were out of service on that safari and you still managed to send me a week's worth of contract work that needed to be done overnight?"

"That contract couldn't wait. If I hadn't gotten the necessary signatures before leaving Tanzania, the deal would have fallen through."

"Tell that to my husband," he muttered. "It was his birthday."

I shot him a look. "Pretty sure Luca didn't mind when I made up for it by buying him a motorcycle."

He snorted. "It was an electric scooter. Hardly a motorcycle. And I'm not complaining. *Much.* You know I enjoy working for you, otherwise I wouldn't. I'm only saying there's no such thing as you being completely off the grid. No matter where I send you to relax, you're still going to do work. Even more reason to go ahead and let me make the reservations. You can work *and* relax."

"I'm not sure those things are as compatible as you think," I grumbled. "If I'm working, by definition, I'm not relaxing."

"Well, at least work in a place with a view," he snapped. "Jesus. I've never heard of someone griping at the idea of a week on a private island."

"Bring Luca and come with me," I said, realizing I could get more work done if Marcel was there. "You can even force me to swim every once in a while. You'd enjoy being able to boss me around like that. Admit it."

He tapped his lips. "True. But I can't. Luca's mom is having a baby shower for Luca's sister, and it's a command performance."

"Then let's put a pin in the resort idea until I see how today goes. I may need to stick around and supervise the transition. I'm still not sure if we've found the right person to install here, and I might want to transfer some of the company's holdings out before handing management over to someone else anyway."

Marcel made a note in his phone. "How did I know you were going to come up with an excuse?"

I ignored him. "Contact Lita Henley and arrange a dinner. Maybe I can lure her away from Eastmann and Secura. Even if she doesn't want to jump ship, I can ask her opinion about the European realty holdings."

He continued to tap his phone until we arrived at the entrance to the building. "Showtime," I said under my breath.

Marcel looked up and up and up at the shining tower. "You always sound so gleeful on takeover days. It's a little creepy."

"If you'd worked as hard as I have to acquire one of the world's largest privately held investment holdings, you'd be gleeful too." And, honestly, "hard work" didn't even begin to describe it. After the shit that had gone down that night in the Crosbie Golf and Country Club, everything had changed. Every single contact in this business I'd been carefully cultivating for five summers on the golf course had ghosted me, and the coveted first-year associate job at Heath and Kelty Investments had disappeared in a puff of smoke. After losing my job at the club, I'd almost lost the ability to afford returning to Yale for my final year, even with the scholarships.

But I'd done it. I'd worked as many jobs as I could manage and barely slept. I'd developed relationships with my business professors and had managed to turn one of them into a longer-term advisory role, so I had someone to help guide me through that first year of starting my own investment company.

I glanced from the shiny exterior of the building down to my nearly pristine Tom Ford brogues. It wasn't that long ago I hadn't known what the hell brogues even were. I'd grown up calling them "fancy men's shoes." It was one of a million examples of how I still never felt like one of them.

Like the old money families who owned this city and managed all of its money.

I was an outsider, a kid from White Plains who'd spent more time being raised by my apartment building neighbors than my mom. Those neighbors hadn't had a clue about things like proper business attire, appropriate wine pairings, and so many other little details that still separated me from the men and women I'd always aspired to be.

I followed Marcel through the doors and across the large open expanse of the lobby. Marcel had already arranged security passes for us, so we made our way directly to the elevator that rocketed us up to the executive floor of York Capital.

There was a unique kind of quiet in an elevator in the city. Suddenly, there were no horns honking, no people chatting in various languages, no pinging of phone notifications. Marcel tapped softly on his phone screen while I took a deep, centering breath.

This was it. Finally.

I tried not to think of Warren York's son, the cowardly asshole who'd fucked me over. After setting me up that night in the clubhouse storage room, Ellison had simply walked away as if his fake seduction hadn't ruined my fucking life.

Even though I wasn't one to get nervous—at this point I had nerves of steel on acquisition day—part of me wondered what it would be like to shove this takeover in Ellison's face. I wanted him to see his precious father's reaction to losing their family business.

I wanted them both to suffer.

Marcel walked ahead of me to the minimalist front desk and spoke softly to the attractive receptionist. The woman glanced up at me with a tiny wrinkle between her eyebrows and responded with a question. The interaction went back and forth for a moment until she picked up the phone, presumably to ask someone higher than her for permission to allow us back to the inner sanctum.

"That won't be necessary, Nikki," I said, half remembering and half guessing her name from the Human Resources rolls I'd scoured early that morning. "Just direct us to the largest conference room and call an all-hands meeting of upper management. Thank you."

Her eyes widened in surprise. "And you are...?"

"Grey Blackwood. The new owner of York Capital," I said calmly, shooting her a wink. "And your new boss."

"Uh... let me get Mr. York on the phone," she said, even though she still held the phone to her ear.

I made eye contact with Marcel. "Let's go."

This wasn't our first takeover, and it wouldn't be our last. We moved toward the hallway, which led back to the executive offices. Nikki squawked behind us, but I ignored her.

Luckily, there seemed to already be a meeting in progress in the first large conference room we came to. I entered through the glass doors and made my way to the foot of the table, where there was an empty chair. Warren York sat at the head.

"Good morning, everyone," I said.

Warren's eyes darted to the doorway and back to me. "What...?"

I held up a hand. "I found it unnecessary to wait for permission from the receptionist. Sorry to startle you." After a quick glance around the table, I realized Ellison wasn't there. The good news was the rest of the C-level executives seemed to be in attendance. "I'm here to talk about the restructuring. As of thirty minutes ago, I own the majority of stock in the company."

Warren's eyes crinkled with amusement while several of the other executives began firing questions at me and each other. A few younger people I assumed were assistants began tapping frantically on cell phones. Little did they know Marcel's magic messenger bag held a signal jammer.

We'd learned some lessons the hard way early on.

Warren clasped his hands together and leaned forward on the table. "Sir, I'm not sure exactly what kind of prank you're attempting here, but York is privately held. It's a family-owned business and has been for over a hundred and fifty years."

"I understand," I said, leaning forward and resting my hands on the table. The fact Warren didn't recognize me needled at me, but I ignored it and carried on. "It doesn't surprise me that your brother failed to notify you of the details of the transaction. Mark was understandably upset when he realized he'd transferred his shares to the same person who'd also recently acquired your uncle's portion." Upon the uncle's death, his shares had gone to a very young society widow who'd been more than happy to allow me to swap those pesky business shares out with cold, hard cash. Knowing I'd managed to get both his uncle's and his brother's shares would be a blow to Warren York.

As I spoke, Warren's smarmy grin died, and his face lost its ruddy hue. "That's impossible."

I wanted to turn to Marcel and lift an eyebrow before asking if it was possible, just so I could hear his dry, professional "Yes, sir, I assure you it is." But I refrained. Instead, I let Marcel hand out the individual packets to the executives. Some held resignation requests, along with generous severance packages, and some held new contract offers, depending on my team's assessment of each player on the corporate roster.

Marcel held Warren's folder back since we would need to discuss the details of his immediate departure in private.

"Take a moment to look over the information in your packets," I continued. "My team will be arriving shortly to answer any questions you have. Feel free to return to your office if you need some time to formulate your questions and, in some cases, gather your belongings."

My attorneys and Human Resources consultants were most likely already set up in their temporary offices on the floor below, and it was only a matter of time before they came in to help oversee the expected chaos. Between the cell jammer and the temporary internet and phone outage on this floor, there wasn't much risk of the news getting out before tempers had simmered down.

In most cases, anyway. Warren York was the exception.

"This is ridiculous. Get out of my office this instant. *Nikki*! Call building security."

Marcel winced. He hated when people yelled at their underlings. I'd done it one time—*once*—and he'd spent half an hour lecturing me on respect. If he hadn't already proven himself to be so invaluable, I would have tossed him out on his ear.

"Michael Pruitt has already confirmed my ownership," I said calmly.

"Who the hell is Michael Pruitt?" Warren asked.

This was a prime example of what I hated about people like Warren York.

"The head of building security," Marcel responded before I had a chance to. He had a way of saying it that heavily implied Warren was both an idiot and an unfeeling jackass for not knowing who Mike was. "I assure you if he comes up here, Mr. Blackwood is not the man he'll be escorting out of the building."

One slender, waxed eyebrow lifted on Marcel's face, and Warren's own face reddened even more. The older man reached for the phone on the conference table and tried making a call. His assistant continued tapping furiously on his cell. "This is preposterous. Why won't any of these damned phones get a call through? *Nikki*!"

The harried receptionist hustled in. "Yes, sir?"

"Find out why we can't get a call out. None of these phones are working. If building security won't respond, call the police, for god's sake."

I took a breath and tried not to laugh. Several of the executives glanced nervously at me as they tried to determine the truth of the matter and choose the correct side. Others opened the packets Marcel had handed them and began to look through the paperwork. Warren's eyes bounced from person to person, trying to determine how best to get me out of the room.

I walked to Marcel and took the final small packet out of his arms. After placing it in front of Warren, I opened the folder. "Here are copies of the share transfer instruments for my shares as well as a current summary of all shares and their ownership. As you can see, the transfer paperwork was approved by—"

His gaze landed on the name before I had a chance to say it, and his eyes darted for a middle-aged woman sitting halfway down the far side of the table. "Lillian, what's the meaning of this?"

I'd never met the CFO in person before, but Lillian Moffit's reputation preceded her. She was one of the executives I was most interested in retaining. The woman sat up straight but appeared relaxed. "It was a straightforward transaction approved by three members of the board in addition to yourself," she said.

"It says here, Mark sold those shares to Milton Vernor, a member of my club and a longtime family friend."

I saw the barest edge of Lillian's mouth turn up. "No, sir. He sold them to Milton Vernor *LLC*, a company owned by a holding company under the name of BWH, I believe. Judging by what's happened here this morning, I would imagine BWH stands for Blackwood Holdings, one of the world's best capital investment firms according to the most recent Forbes Midas List."

I gave her a small nod while Warren's face lost a little bit of its flush. "You tricked us? You pretended to be someone you're not? That's fraud."

"I didn't pretend to be anyone. I own Milton Vernor LLC. I've owned it for at least eight years. Your brother sold York shares to Milton Vernor LLC. He did not sell them to Milton Vernor, the mediocre golfer with a preference for expensive scotch. And believe me, your brother was well aware he wasn't selling to Milton Vernor. I approached him personally and made him an offer he couldn't refuse. The fact you chose not to do your due diligence before board approval on the transaction is on you."

Warren grabbed his assistant's arm. "Go find a phone that works and get a hold of Ellison. We have a lawsuit on our hands. This can't be legal."

The assistant nodded and took off for the door. Marcel looked over at me, but I shook my head. My heart hammered at the mention of Warren's son, but I ignored it.

"No attorney in the city will take that case when they discover your brother and I met personally to negotiate this transfer. I have a very clear-cut paper trail proving he knew who he was dealing with."

"My son is one of the most successful corporate attorneys in the city, and he works for me," he said with flared nostrils. "He'll sue you into bankruptcy for perpetrating this fraud on our company. There is no one more fiercely loyal to me and this company than Ellison."

Like father, like son. The image of Ellison York doing his father's bidding made me sick. Before everything that had happened in that closet in the club, I'd noticed Ellison. I'd paid attention to him.

I'd thought he was different.

He'd seemed like a scared child playing dress-up in his father's clothing. The kid had gone through his first three years at Yale like someone living two lives. I'd catch him studying his ass off alone in the library, the cafeteria, or under a shade tree on campus during the week, but on the weekend and over the summers at the country club, he was every party boy acting like an entitled asshole with his friends. It wasn't all that rare for students to live these two lives, but with Ellison, it had seemed the party part of his personality had been all for show or maybe to fit in and be considered one of the cool kids.

I'd mistakenly thought the "real" Ellison was the guy grinning to himself while reading Don Quixote while chowing down on a burrito between classes at a table by himself in the corner. The guy who'd run in every charity race held near campus and who'd volunteered one rainy weekend at a fundraiser for homeless youth. I'd only noticed because the charity had reached out to me once to offer me help when my mom and I were close to needing it. I would rather have died than had him discover I knew who they were.

But then he and his fucking friends had set me up. I'd lost every promising opportunity I'd worked so hard for. The men in that room had made sure my name had been smeared all over the industry before I'd even graduated from school.

I'd heard, of course, that Ellison had followed his father's plan for him. He'd dutifully gone to Columbia Law School and then jumped right into working for the family business. Instead of fighting for any of the worthy causes I'd thought he'd believed in, he'd gone to work making more money for his already obscenely wealthy family.

But now his family was going to lose everything, because Warren York was a selfish bastard who'd tried to avoid taxes by hiding his personal assets in the company.

And now I owned the company. And I owned Warren York.

Whether he'd begun to understand the full scope of his loss yet, Warren York had just lost their home, their cars, their vacation properties, their private jet, the charity foundation that they used to hide payments to their daughter, an extensive and extremely valuable art collection, and even some of Mrs. York's jewelry.

"You may tell your son to have at it," I said as coolly as I could. I'd be damned if I would allow Warren to see a speck of emotion from me besides extreme satisfaction. "But I would suggest he start with my one-time-only offer."

Warren's teeth clenched, and his jaw tightened. "And what is that?"

"Tell him if he agrees to be my personal errand boy throughout the transition, I'd be happy to consider letting you and the missus keep your house in Greenwich."

Seeing the whites of his eyes was more satisfying than it should have been. The last time I'd seen such shock and horror on the man's face had been fifteen years ago when he'd witnessed his precious baby boy and heir to the capital investments throne on his knees for another man.

The only thing better would have been seeing the look on Ellison's face when he discovered who he now worked for. The man who'd taken everything from his family.

2

ELLISON

"The supreme art of war is to subdue the enemy without fighting."

~ Sun Tzu, *The Art of War*

The teacher's lounge at the academy always smelled like microwaved feet. I opened my reusable lunch bag and peered inside, trying to remember what I'd thrown in there before dawn that morning.

Protein bar, small bag of almonds, two fresh apples sliced up in a baggie, an overripe banana, and bag of generic cheese curls.

I reached for one of the apple slices and took a big bite.

"Are those from that cute orchard we passed the other day?" Gigi asked, reaching over me to take a slice. "Sunday Brothers?"

"Pfft. Too rich for my blood. These are from Price Chopper." I glanced over at her with a raised eyebrow. "And they're not organic."

Instead of gasping and tossing it back, she just laughed and popped it in her mouth. "Welcome to the way the other half lives, brother. I stopped eating organic five years ago. I might die young, but at least I'll go to heaven."

I didn't need to wonder what had happened five years ago. That was when she'd finally made the decision to leave her consulting job in the city to come work for Warrington Academy full-time. After spending both of our trusts to purchase a private boarding school in financial trouble just after I'd graduated college, we'd hoped we'd be able to take hands-on roles at the school right away. In reality, though, it had taken us ten years to get the academy funded well enough through charitable donations to sustain the financial hit of losing even one of our big-city salaries. Since Dad had manipulated me into an employment contract with York Capital as a condition of allowing the company's charitable foundation to support the academy programs, I'd been the one to stay in the city while Gigi had moved to the academy's campus in southern Vermont.

But now here I was. Finally. With only two weeks left on my employment contract at York, I'd put in for a two-week vacation, put my apartment on the market, and cleaned out my desk three days earlier.

When I'd left York, my father had made it very clear that I would no longer be able to "sweet-talk" my "girlfriend" into giving "all of our money away" to the academy. Never mind that I hadn't dated Nessa in fifteen years, or that the money she managed for the York Foundation wasn't endowed by my dad's personal wealth but his company's, or that the foundation donated to lots of nonprofits besides Warrington Academy.

He was right that it wasn't going to be easy keeping the fundraising up from Vermont, but I was determined. This school was my heart, and seeing our first high school graduates were already finding spots and scholarships at some of the highest graduate programs in the country in addition to coveted internships and post-graduate jobs made me proud in a way that corporate law never could. Like I'd finally done something good with my wealth and connections.

"You look significantly happier than most teachers on the first day back," Gigi said with a laugh. "Maybe it's because the kids won't be here for another week."

"Maybe it's because I'm not a teacher," I said, tossing an apple slice at her.

"Yet," she corrected, tossing the slice into the nearby trash can. "Just wait till our first callout emergency. You'll be conscripted in no time. It's one of the hazards of our rural location. Substitutes are thin on the ground."

My phone buzzed for the third time in as many minutes, but I ignored it. My father and others from the office had been trying to get in touch with me all morning, and I was having to practice tough love. The number of interruptions to my weekend for stupid questions anyone in the legal department should have been able to handle had been enough to make me consider getting a new number. If it hadn't been for the valuable fundraising contacts who had my current number, I might have actually done it.

"As long as I don't have to teach Calculus, I'll be fine," I assured her.

"I thought you were good at math," she asked before taking a bite of her own sandwich. "You were in high school anyway."

I shook my head. "I didn't pay enough attention in class. Barely passed it at Yale." I felt the telling heat on my face. "I had a crush on someone in my class. Couldn't pay attention to the professor to save my life."

The memory of Grey Blackwood was old and soft from use. Pulling it out was familiar and comfortable like a worn pair of jeans. That moment in the supply closet with him, the soft brush of lips and the harsh command to get on my knees, had changed something in me irrevocably.

And watching him lose everything while I'd stood there and done nothing had ultimately changed the course of my life. That night, my mind had been wrenched open, leaving me faced with some harsh new realities. As a result, I'd chosen new goals for myself, new directions.

And one of those directions had led me here, to the academy.

Gigi took a sip of water. "Was that when you met Mallory? I never told you this, but she wasn't my favorite."

I pictured Grey's wide shoulders and square jaw next to Mallory Derringer's petite, curvy frame.

"Not Mallory. We didn't start dating until I started law school. She was an undergrad at Columbia." I didn't tell my sister that I'd only dated Mallory to make her parents happy. In reality, she'd made it clear she had no desire for a serious relationship because she wanted to backpack around the world after graduation. Since I hadn't been able to stop obsessing with the memory of my time in the closet with Grey Blackwood, it had worked out just fine for me. My parents hadn't tried setting me up and Mallory had been able to get through graduation without her own family pestering her to get serious and settle down. Ironically, the first week she'd spent in the Swiss Alps, she'd met her soul mate and had married him the following Christmas.

"Crystal?" Gigi asked.

"I never dated anyone named Crystal," I said absently, pulling my buzzing phone out of my pocket. "Maybe you're thinking of Kristen."

"There've been so many, it's hard to keep them all straight," she teased.

"Mpfh." I was well versed in putting off curious questions about my love life. As far as I was concerned, my family could ask as many questions as they wanted about the women I brought to family functions, but who I slept with—who I actually got close to—was off-limits. I'd started that practice years ago with the expectation that eventually I'd sleep with a man and wouldn't want to tell my parents about it. But then I... simply never had. It hadn't taken me long to realize I didn't want to sleep with men.

I wanted to sleep with Grey Blackwood.

Period.

So I'd entered into this weird kind of dating situation where I became the perfect fake boyfriend. Not fake exactly—I definitely slept with most of the women I dated. But I made it clear from the beginning I didn't want anything serious. There were a million reasons why, but the most important one was knowing I would be selling them a fake bill of goods. While I was the heir of a large venture capital firm and a corporate attorney in my own right, with all the accompanying accoutrements such as multiple club memberships, an impressive Central Park address, wealthy and influential friends, and access to extravagant vacation properties, I wasn't going to be that man forever. There was always an end date on the Ellison York they knew.

And now it was here. I could finally be the Ellison York *I* knew, and I was relieved and excited to be starting my more genuine life. I couldn't wait to finally have time and room to breathe. Now that I could be myself, I could find someone to date for real, someone who might like me for who I actually was, not who they thought I was based on my name and corporate title.

"Want to go for a run tonight on that trail by the river?" I asked. "I'm dying to stretch my legs after all that time in the car the other day, and some of the leaves are already starting to turn out that way."

She nodded. "I have to stay to help organize the theater inventory this afternoon, but I can go after that."

I grabbed a handful of almonds and threw them in my mouth before glancing down at my phone. Six missed calls and several texts. One of them was from Skyla Palmer, who'd been my assistant for the past three years. She wouldn't be messaging me if it wasn't important. She was the only one at York who knew how permanent my move was.

Skyla: *Code red. Shit hitting fan. Call ASAP.*

Skyla: *Not fucking around, Ells. Call me.*

I glanced up at Gigi, who noticed the frown on my face. As soon as Skyla answered, I didn't even have a chance to say hello. "Some hot-ass dude just took over the company. Your dad's about to lose his shit. Everyone's running around like it's the apocalypse. You need to find out what the fuck is happening. They won't tell me anything, and every story I hear is different."

"What?" I asked. "The company can't just be taken over, Skyla. It's privately held."

"Well, tell that to the grumpy underwear model in the Carlisle conference room because he seems to think he's in charge, and I'm pretty sure he's about to make your dad cry. People have been coming in here for the past few hours asking me to find you and get you back here, but I pretended not to know your 'new number.'"

I took a deep breath and calmed down when I realized what was happening. "Whoever came up with this prank idea needs to be a little more creative. Maybe they should have said my dad got arrested for tax fraud or something. That, I might have actually believed."

"No, really, Ells," she said, suddenly being serious. "The man's name is Grey Blackwood, and he bought your uncle Mark's shares yesterday. Apparently, he already had your great-uncle Leon's shares too. So that gave him majority ownership."

I didn't hear much after the words "Grey Blackwood." My heart thundered wildly in my chest, and spots poked around idly in my vision. "Who? What?" I could barely breathe. Something was wrong with my chest.

Everyone in the venture capital space knew who Grey Blackwood was. He'd come screaming out of nowhere almost ten years ago when he'd provided the seed money for a small start-up company called Lumeniar that had turned into one of the most lucrative venture capital investments of the past decade. Once he had the money from Lumeniar's acquisition by Zillin Biotech, he'd invested in seemingly every damned thing that was slated to pay him back a thousandfold. The man had become a titan in the VC world.

And my father had been incensed.

I remembered the breakfast meeting at work that day when Dad had gotten the news. The grin on my face had been obscene. Grey Blackwood had made good in the industry after all, and people like Warren York could suck it.

But there was no way he could have taken over York. Was there?

"Skyla, tell me what you know. How did you find out?"

"Apparently he came in and breezed past Nikki's desk to help himself to the conference room, where your dad and the company leadership were doing whatever it is they do. Probably crying about losing you. Mr. Blackwood's assistant began handing out severance packages while he calmly told your father to kiss his ass. Well, that last part might have been wishful thinking on my part, but I did hear he was cool as a cucumber while he was in there. No one's phones would work for a while, and then a whole team came in to help manage the transition. They sent out a company-wide email about the takeover and advised everyone to consult their individual packets from Human Resources. I got a contract, thank god, but Nate and Rory got a severance."

I was having trouble concentrating on the details, but I'd heard enough to know she was being serious. "I've gotta go. My dad's been trying to get in touch with me."

She snorted. "No shit. Call me back and tell me everything."

I hung up and told Gigi that York Capital had been the victim of a hostile takeover this morning because of our uncle's inability to remain solvent. "Instead of him owning up to it and asking the rest of the family to buy him out, he apparently took a better offer from a stranger," I explained, not telling her the new majority shareholder wasn't exactly a stranger to *me*. Gigi pulled me through the door to her office and sat me on the sofa before taking the seat next to me. I noticed her hands were shaking.

"I'm sure it's fine," I said, lying through my teeth. "We'll figure it out. Maybe it's all a big misunderstanding."

Gigi's lifted eyebrow called me on my bullshit. Mark went through cash like water. If anyone would sell out the family firm, it was him. It was bad enough that my father had asked me to look into ways to safeguard the company from doing just that several years ago. I'd drafted documents to include new rules requiring three board members to sign off on any significant stock transfers. If this had actually happened, more people had known about it than Uncle Mark.

"Ellison, if we lose the pledged donations from the York Foundation... we could be in major trouble."

She was right, but there was no use worrying about it based on a rumor. I dialed my father.

He answered with his familiar booming voice. "Why the hell did it take you so long to answer?" Before I could respond, he kept talking. "I need you here right away. Charter a plane if you have to. Mark has really screwed the pooch, and you're going to need to find a way to get us out of this mess."

I was tempted. The fact Grey Blackwood was involved meant part of me wanted nothing more than to fly back to the city and get right in the middle of my father's drama. But I'd sworn, *sworn*, I was no longer going to bow to his commands. I no longer worked for York, and I needed to make a clean break. If it was true, and my father's company had actually been taken over legally, there was nothing I could do to help him anyway.

On top of that, I didn't trust myself in the same room with Grey Blackwood.

"I can't," I said. "I have commitments here. I'm sorry."

The moment of silence before he blustered his disapproval felt like a vacuum sucking all the air out of the space between us. "You what? You're *sorry*? Sorry doesn't begin to cut it. Was it or was it not you who I tasked with making sure something like this never happened? Get your ass down here and fix this now. This is your mistake. You're going to clean up the mess you made, and you're going to do it right now."

"I don't work for you anymore, *Dad*. So no, I'm not coming back to New York. You have brilliant attorneys on staff. Ask them for help."

His voice lowered dangerously as if he was speaking through clenched teeth. "Technically, *legally*, you still work for me. According to the terms of our agreement, the foundation will not send the final payment to your little charity project until you've completed your contract with York."

My stomach dropped. He was right. The academy was counting on the final contribution the York Foundation had committed to, and the only reason the York Foundation had agreed to such a large donation was because of my contract. If we could get the company back, or if Grey was the kind of man to honor the foundation's pledges, it would matter.

"I did complete my contract," I said. "I am entitled to two weeks of vacation."

"Vacation is at the discretion of the manager, and this manager says it's an inconvenient time for you to be out of the office. We will pay you the value of the missed vacation days, of course. That is, unless you can provide written proof your vacation was approved by your manager?"

His smarmy tone made my skin crawl. Warren York was well versed in manipulation, and he wasn't stupid. He would have made sure he could back his threat up before insisting I return. Of course I hadn't gotten my vacation approval in writing. No one ever did. And my manager had been my father.

"Ellison, I need your help," he said, suddenly lowering his voice and sounding sincere for once. "He's going to take the house."

I glanced up at Gigi, whose smooth skin was marred with wrinkles of concern. How the hell was I supposed to tell her the money we'd counted on wasn't coming? And how would she take the news that my parents were now homeless because of a revenge scheme I'd inadvertently triggered all those years before?

Because suddenly my brain was kicking into gear with a vengeance, and I knew without a shadow of a doubt Grey Blackwood had planned this. He'd deliberately targeted York to get back at us for screwing him over in college.

And it was all my fault.

After ending the call, I stared into space, trying to process everything he'd said.

"Ellison, what the hell? Say something." Gigi's face had lost some of its color. "Is it true? Did Mark sell his shares to someone else?"

I nodded. "Grey Blackwood." The name said it all. Gigi may not have known my true feelings for Grey, but she damned well knew the name.

"Wait. The kid from the country club? The one who—"

"Yeah. That one."

"But he's..." She frowned. "Wasn't he a scholarship kid? Who does he work for? How could he afford to buy a majority share of York?"

I let out a humorless laugh. "He was a scholarship kid to *Yale*, Gigi. And he works for himself. He built a career around investing in high-risk venture capital projects until he had enough money to begin taking over other companies. He's a billionaire now."

"That kid who tried seducing you—"

"He didn't seduce me," I hissed. The last thing I needed was for fellow staff members to overhear me. "I've told you guys this a million times. It was my idea. That closet thing started out as a dare—I'm the one who lured him into the closet. It wasn't his fault. Also? I wanted it. I had a crush on the guy. Okay?"

Her eyes were wide. "I know you said that, but... we all just thought you were trying to save face. Especially when you didn't end up dating any guys or coming out or anything." She looked understandably confused.

"He's getting me back," I said, almost to myself. I ran my hands through my hair, which was getting way too long since I hadn't had time to get it cut. Finishing up my job at York had been a whirlwind this summer. Now that I'd finally broken free of the place, here I was again. All because of a mistake I made when I was twenty-one.

"What do you mean?" Gigi asked. "Getting you back for what?"

"For not standing up for him! For not speaking up at the time and telling everyone it was my fault. He lost everything because of me. His job at the club, the internship at a VC firm after graduation, the respect of his coworkers. Jesus. My friends humiliated him. They told everyone he'd been the victim of a killer prank that night. It was awful. I don't blame him for wanting revenge."

Her face turned soft and sad. "I'm sorry."

"It's all my fault."

"No it isn't. You're not responsible for what someone else does, but I'll tell you this: you're a brilliant attorney. If someone can find our family a way out of this, you can."

I ran a hand through my hair and stood up. I hadn't imagined going toe-to-toe with Grey Blackwood ever again, but if he wanted to come at my family, I'd have no choice but to stand up and fight him.

3

GREY

"Stir opponents up, making them respond to you; then you can observe their forms of behavior, and whether they are orderly or confused."

~ Sun Tzu, *The Art of War*

I was combing through a stack of commercial real estate contracts when I heard a commotion in the hallway outside the open conference room door. Warren had been talking at me all day, but I'd long since stopped listening. The only reason he hadn't been kicked out of the building yet was because he'd promised to produce his precious baby boy.

"There you are. What took you so long?" Warren griped, standing from his seat at the foot of the table. As petty as it may have sounded, I'd taken his spot at the head of the table the minute he'd taken his first visit to the men's room earlier in the day. From that position, it had been easier to see people coming and going, which was why I was surprised that Ellison York had managed to slip into the conference room without me noticing.

"I only got your call four hours ago, and I was in *Vermont*," Ellison said.

I refused to stand or pay him any kind of special attention. In fact, I refused to acknowledge him as anyone special at all. No one could possibly know that my breathing had shallowed and my skin prickled uncomfortably in his presence. All of this—the York takeover—was because of him, because of his cowardice and entitlement. Because he'd been a spoiled rich kid who hadn't thought anything of ruining my life for a few minutes of fun with his friends.

At least now I was on top. I controlled his family's life, their wealth, their privilege. Ellison York was going to have to come begging if he expected any mercy for his family.

And the image of Ellison on his knees again was something I'd spent a long, long time imagining. This time maybe someone else would get fucked besides me.

Warren waved off Ellison's excuse and pointed an accusing finger at me. "This is the man who did this. Grey Blackwood."

I could see Ellison's eyes bounce between his father and me, realizing with surprise Warren had absolutely no idea I was the same man who'd supposedly ruined his son's life in the club storage room years ago.

"Yes, I... I know Grey," Ellison said hesitantly, eyes flicking to me again. The tension in the room was suffocating. Ellison was no longer a slight twenty-year-old. He'd filled out in his shoulders and chest. His dark hair had grown out of its conservative short style and was now slightly overgrown, revealing a sexy wave that threatened to turn into curls near his collar and over his ears. His brown eyes were still as warm as ever, and I knew from memory they had flecks of green around the edges. Those summers at the club when he'd spent time on the golf course, he'd had freckles on his nose and cheeks, but they were gone now.

Instead of risking my voice breaking with nerves and anger, I simply nodded in his direction.

Ellison cleared his throat. "Dad, can I talk to Gr—Mr. Blackwood alone, please?"

"Anything you say to this... *thief* can be said to me as well. I'm the CEO of this firm."

Ellison met my eye and tried to communicate something to me before turning on his heel and walking out. Warren blustered and followed him, lecturing Ellison about respect and commitment. When they got about as far as the receptionist's desk, Ellison turned back and raced past his father into the conference room and slammed the door, pressing the lock before his father could reach for the handle.

I felt my mouth open in surprise, and I quickly snapped it closed. "That was... something," I said dryly.

"I'm sorry, but I don't have time for this. I need to get back to my job."

"I thought you worked here," I said, not enjoying the feeling of being misinformed.

"No. I quit. I work... somewhere else now." He obviously didn't want me to know where he worked, but I had news for him.

"According to an employment contract I have in one of these stacks here, you're obligated to work for York another two weeks. Is that correct?"

He let out a frustrated sigh. "Can we skip past all this bullshit and get to the point? What do you want?"

"I want to see your father begging for money with a little cardboard sign in Times Square. I want to see your mother reduced to having to wear clothes from thrift stores. And I want to see you go to hell." I growled that last part, losing some of the cool I'd promised I'd retain throughout this process.

Ellison's eyes met mine. I expected to find in them a worthy opponent, anger and resentment at lowly Grey Blackwood, who'd somehow ended up making good. But that's not what I found at all.

He looked at me with pity.

I clenched my hands into fists. "And since you're legally obligated to give me the next two weeks of your life, I believe we can make all three of those things happen quite easily. Your father said you'd be more than willing to act as my personal assistant during the first two weeks of transition in exchange for allowing them to keep their home in Greenwich. You may start by ordering me dinner. I sent my *real* assistant home an hour ago."

I went back to the stack of documents in front of me and tried not to listen to the silence between us.

"I'm sorry," he said softly.

His words were gentle and kind. I heard the truth in them, and it made me want to scream and claw at anyone within reach.

Ellison York was the only one within reach, though, and I wouldn't give him the satisfaction.

"For what?" I asked without looking away from the document in my hand.

I heard him move closer until he took the seat closest to mine. "I'm sorry I didn't say anything that night. I'm sorry I was such a coward. I tried apologizing to you afterward... the week after... but you wouldn't listen."

My teeth ached from grinding them together. Of course I hadn't listened to him. I'd been in the process of trying to fight my mother's eviction. Despite his fancy words, I noticed he hadn't apologized for setting me up in the first place.

"I do not accept," I said carefully so he wouldn't mishear me. While his apology might have been sincere, it was also too little too late.

"I understand," he said. "But please don't hold your anger at me against my parents. They don't deserve it."

I glanced up at him. "Your father had me fired. He blackballed me from working in my chosen field. He tried to get me expelled from Yale."

Ellison blinked in surprise. "He did?"

I made a production of checking my watch, the Rolex Cosmograph Daytona I'd bought myself upon the sale of my first batch of Lumeniar stock.

"I'm thinking Italian for dinner," I said, looking back at the document I held, even though I couldn't focus on it. "I'll take the lasagne.

Feel free to get yourself something too. Nikki can give you the new company credit card. The old ones have been deactivated."

I was trying to piss him off, provoke him into reacting like an asshole. Anything to get him to stop being sweet. I didn't want some strange kind of sweet version of the man who'd fucked me over. I didn't want to have any doubts that he was selfish and entitled the way he'd proven himself to be.

So when he stormed out, I could at least fall back on the knowledge I'd been right.

Sure enough, Ellison left in a huff. I couldn't help but feel a little satisfied, even though I'd been enjoying his apologies and pleas.

His father came back in after a little while and took his seat again. "Where's my son?"

I shrugged and continued reading the report for the millionth time. When Warren began making his idle threats to me again, I ignored him. I really was hungry, though, and I wondered how long I was going to stay here in this pissing contest with Warren York. I generally extended deposed CEOs the courtesy of not getting evicted from the premises immediately after the takeover—Marcel called it "playing with my food"—but Warren York tested my patience like no one else ever had.

Harris Dinsmore of Carmont Holdings had given me a grudging handshake before he'd left the building. Even Bob Kelty of Heath and Kelty—the venture capital company that had revoked my offer of employment in what was ultimately their single worst corporate decision —had given me an almost respectful nod on his way out the door and told me to call him if I was ever in Palm Beach. But Warren York? He took a seat in *my* conference room and repaid my courtesy by needling me.

"I've heard about you, you know," he began. "You have a reputation for stealing companies right out from underneath hardworking, dedicated professionals. Does that make you feel like a big man? Like a success story of some kind?"

I didn't bother looking up from my computer, so he continued. "My son told me who you are. Who you were. You were nobody.

Trash under our feet. A hanger-on who would have done anything to be someone you weren't."

I felt my blood pressure climb, and it took all my self-control to keep from snapping back at him.

"Hell, you even thought tricking my son into some kind of sexual perversion would somehow get you what you wanted. Well, it didn't work, did it? You ended up with exactly what you deserved."

I smiled grimly. "Ownership of York Capital? Thank you. I agree."

Warren made a wordless squawk of outrage that was music to my ears, and I glanced up at him with one eyebrow raised. "What would you say if I told you that it was your son who approached me in that closet? It was your son who initiated the 'sexual perversion.'"

He scoffed. "My son would never be with a man. He had a girl-friend at the time, if you recall. And he's dated several women since then. No. Whatever game you were playing backfired on you, and now you're here to seek revenge. Well, it isn't going to happen. Ellison graduated near the top of his class at Columbia Law, and he's going to find a loophole in this deal. Then we're going to come after you and take everything you have."

I knew beyond a shadow of a doubt the takeover was not only legal but airtight. And I knew Ellison knew it too. I would never have risked moving forward with it until I was sure it couldn't be reversed on a technicality. But now I was pissed.

If Warren thought he could come in here and disrespect me to my face while trying desperately to get his company back, he was mistaken.

"I wonder what it would take to convince you that closet *blow job* was Ellison's idea," I mused, tapping my chin.

Warren's wince was like candy, and I wanted more of it.

The door to the outer office opened, and a moment later, Ellison showed up with an armload of takeout bags. I tried to keep a neutral face instead of gawking in surprise. He'd actually done as I'd asked. The man was clearly desperate enough to go along with my plan.

He was willing to debase himself for a chance to help his asshole father out. Well, maybe we needed to see just how far he was willing to go.

"Your dinner, sir," he said, setting the bags down on the conference table. I couldn't decide if he was mocking me or being serious, but it didn't matter.

"You may serve me," I said, looking back at my laptop as if asset reports were that compelling.

Ellison stood there a minute before slowly pulling the food containers out of the bag. I glanced up at him. "I prefer to eat from a plate with a place mat and linen napkin."

"I don't care what you—" he began.

I cut him off. "Do you ever eat on plates at your *parents' home in Greenwich*?" I asked innocently. "With place mats and linen napkins?"

The reminder of our deal—his work as my assistant in exchange for his parents' greatest personal asset—was enough to make him clench his jaw and stop arguing.

"Yes, sir. And it's quite nice. In fact, why don't I find you those accoutrements so you can enjoy the same level of dining here at the office? I'll just be a moment."

He walked out, leaving an enraged Warren York. "What the fuck do you think you're doing?"

"It turns out, how high you graduated in your class at Columbia Law is inversely proportional to how good you are at setting a nice plate. It shouldn't surprise me, really." I went back to perusing my reports.

"He's not your beck-and-call boy," he gritted out.

I met his eye. "Want to bet?"

Somehow, Ellison found a cloth hand towel that he made a big production out of shaking out and draping on the table in front of me. He stood so close to me, I could smell a familiar combination of coffee, airplane, and male sweat on him, but there was something else in it too... something my nose and lungs wanted more of.

He laid a second towel down in a neatly folded rectangle. "Your cloth napkin, sir."

I looked up at him. "Place it in my lap."

The air shimmered between us as he swallowed and tried to act like none of this mattered. He was a shit actor.

He draped the small towel in my lap and then snapped a metal cutlery set into place on the makeshift placemat. Once that was ready, he produced a small porcelain serving tray of some kind. It must have had something decorative on it at some time, but he clearly intended to use it as a plate for my meal.

"Did you take that out of the ladies' room?" I drawled. "Did it have perfumes and lotions on it when you found it?"

He began to transfer my lasagne to the tray. "Close. It's actually an antique piece from my dear great-grandmother's vanity. There was a matching hairbrush and mirror set at one point, but she had to sell those, along with her long, lustrous hair, in order to get enough money to begin the company."

It took me a second to realize he was pulling my leg. Maybe I needed to rethink his acting talent after all.

"Sad tale," I said, wiping an invisible tear off my cheek. "How can you bear the memory?"

He shrugged and sighed. "They were this close to naming it Golden Capital, after her blond tresses, but... it brought back too many memories."

I bit my tongue and tried to maintain a dignified scowl. "The service at this place is awfully mouthy," I muttered.

When he set the food in front of me with a flourish, I remembered how hungry I was. Instead of shoveling the food in without taking a breath, I sat back and looked up at him.

"Feed it to me."

Ellison's eyes widened. We stared at each other for a beat before his father's angry voice broke the silence. "What did you just say?" he growled

"I told your precious boy to hand-feed me my dinner. My hands are stiff from signing all of those legal documents with your brother Mark's attorneys. I would like my assistant to... *assist*."

As I spoke, I kept my eyes on Ellison to see how he would react. I kept waiting for him to balk, to storm out in an angry tirade.

But he didn't.

His father did. He pushed his chair back so hard it smacked the wall and left the conference room while threatening all manner of retaliation.

I didn't watch him leave. I only had eyes for his son.

I raised a finger to halt Ellison, then made a very brief phone call, holding his gaze all the while. "Marcel? Yes, I know you're at home. Yes, tell Luca I'm extremely sorry. Please have security remove Warren York from the premises immediately and permanently. His time here is done."

I threw my phone on the table with a clatter and quirked a brow at Ellison. "Proceed."

Ellison leaned over me, much closer than necessary, and cut a small bite of lasagne before squatting next to me and bringing the fork to my mouth. "Open up, *sir*." His voice held the barest hint of breathiness, and it made my mouth dry up completely.

My dick roared to life against my leg. Every other muscle in my body stiffened. He was so close, I felt the warmth of his body, saw the individual curls against his collar, noticed two eyelashes crossed in a tangle over one eye.

Fucking Christ.

I opened my mouth for him. The warm, savory pasta slid onto my tongue as the fork pulled out. My stomach flipped wildly, torn between hunger and excitement. I forced the excitement down and focused on the hunger. The *food* hunger.

What the fuck was I thinking? What was I doing? This was a waste of my time. It was beneath me.

"That will be all," I said after swallowing. "You may eat. Hopefully you picked up your own food as well."

Ellison's gaze was all too knowing. I hated him even more than before, if such a thing were possible. So I did my best to ignore him.

I hadn't eaten much in several days. Convincing Mark York to sell me his shares hadn't been easy, but it had been worth it.

As I ate, I watched Ellison out of the corner of my eye as he unpacked his food. The rounded fall of his trousers over his ass, the narrow waist accentuated by a close-fit button-down shirt tucked into his pants and nipped with a belt. His shirt was rolled up at the arms, and the veins leading down to the back of his hands caught my eye. He had slender wrists and long fingers, even though his arms had muscle definition.

Hands that had been born holding a silver spoon.

His fingertips ended in neatly trimmed nails. I wondered if he'd ever done even an hour's worth of physical labor with those hands, changed the oil on a car or tried to fix a busted garbage disposal. Of course, I already knew the answer to this. He had the soft, perfect hands of a businessman who didn't even need to change the toner on his own printer or write his own checks.

"Are you still hungry? Do you want some of mine?" Ellison's question had a note of false innocence.

I glanced up to see him smirking at me. He'd caught me staring at his dinner. Hopefully he didn't realize it hadn't been his food I'd been salivating over.

"No, I'm fine. Uh... thank you." I took a moment to calm myself. "Now, let's talk about the deal."

Ellison paused with his fork halfway to his lips. "Alright."

"As I mentioned, your father has assured me that you will act as my personal assistant for the next two weeks during the transition."

Ellison blinked at me. "You were serious about that."

I smiled evilly. "Dead serious. For a man as self-important as your father, he owns surprisingly little in his own right. All of his real estate, for example, is now owned by York Capital, and since I am now in charge of York Capital, I am now the owner of the property in Greenwich and the apartment on Fifth Avenue. The Greenwich house is quite a valuable asset. I can't imagine it would be fair to take it out of the company without proper remuneration."

The shock on Ellison's face made me downright giddy inside. He knew his father banked on his reputation as one of the wealthiest investors in the city, and his luxury home in the burbs was part of that reputation.

"As I told your father, I will be happy to give him lifetime rights to reside in the home if you'll simply assist me during the final two weeks of your employment contract."

"Rights to reside?" Ellison repeated. "He agreed to that?"

I hesitated. Technically, negotiations hadn't gotten that far. "He will. I hold all the cards."

Ellison's eyes never left mine. He seemed to see right through me.

"You'll sign it over to him in full," Ellison said calmly. "And in exchange, I'll give you what you want."

A bead of sweat made itself known between my shoulder blades and slid lazily down my spine. Images of Ellison York on his knees for me, bent over the conference room table for me, and tied up and begging me for mercy flashed erratically through my mind's eye.

How could he possibly know what I wanted? Because despite my baser tendencies to want Ellison naked and writhing beneath me, I wanted something greater than that, bigger than this one acquisition.

I wanted for once in my life to no longer be the poor kid from White Plains begging for a seat at the table and pretending to know which fork to use when I finally got that seat.

I wanted acceptance.

I wanted to belong.

But I would never let on to this entitled prick that I gave a shit about any of it.

4

ELLISON

"Appear weak when you are strong, and strong when you are weak."

~ Sun Tzu, *The Art of War*

Grey was colder than I remembered, and why wouldn't he be? He'd been through hell and had to fight ten times harder to get where he was today.

The man was an angry shell, full of bitterness and resentment. He'd always had some of it. I'd seen the looks he'd flashed the rich country club members behind their backs when he was caddying, the judgment and impatience, but this was different. I hated seeing the jaded adult where the idealistic and eager kid had been before.

Despite the hard edge to him—or maybe because of it—he was sexier than ever before. Grey Blackwood was blistering hot, the kind of person I both couldn't look at directly and couldn't look away from. My heart skittered around wildly in my chest as if begging to bust out and fling itself pell-mell at the corporate raider in front of me.

But my heart didn't know jack shit. The man at the head of the table was clearly here on a mission of hateful revenge. He'd be happiest when my father and I had been thoroughly ruined, dragged through any available mud, and buried beneath whatever rubble might remain. His eyes were glinty with steel, and his lips were tight with thinly veiled annoyance.

He was fucking magnificent. And I wanted him with every fiber of my being.

Whatever spike of attraction I'd had fifteen years ago on the night of the tournament celebration had been child's play compared to how I felt sitting across from Grey Blackwood, the billionaire venture capitalist and infamous hostile-takeover expert, with only a conference table between us.

Little did Grey know, I was at his mercy. And I had been for fifteen long years. I'd fantasized about him more times than I could possibly count. Sure, most of those fantasies had involved naked body parts and grasping fingers, lips swollen with beard burn and breathy gasps filling the silence around us. For sure a big one had been about finally being able to reciprocate by taking his dick in my mouth and trying my best to swallow it. But some of the fantasies had been different. Some had included heartfelt apologies and long-winded explanations of what a coward I'd been. Some had simply been dreams of coming home from a particularly horrible day at work and walking silently into his comforting arms.

Over the years, I'd turned my memory of this one man into the representation of everything I wanted in a partner. I was well aware of how unreasonable and unrealistic it was. I knew the real Grey Blackwood was most likely nothing like the dreamy version of him in my head, but it gave me comfort to imagine someone like him in my life. Someone who'd clearly trusted me. Who'd intrigued me. Who'd offered to help and who'd given a shit about me even for one moment despite who I was.

"Do you agree?" I asked Grey after declaring I would, in fact, act as his personal assistant for two weeks if he'd let my parents keep their house.

He tilted his head as he assessed me.

"You will be at my beck and call at all hours and do as I say." It wasn't a question, and the way he stated it as a fact made my lower belly tighten.

"Within reason," I said, just to try and keep some semblance of cool. I'd already determined the best way to get close enough to figure out how to tackle the problem of Grey Blackwood was to go along with whatever he said. "I will not shave your face or scramble your eggs, for instance."

The image of Grey Blackwood dripping wet and wrapped in only a low towel around his waist waved happily to me like a flag in the stands of a major sporting event. It wanted my attention, desperately.

I ignored it. For the moment.

"But you will stay in the guest room at my penthouse. We'll need to work late every evening to make the most of these two weeks." He looked back down at his paperwork, so I couldn't interpret his expression.

My throat dried up like a raisin. "Uh. Huh?"

I'd meant it as a clarifying question, but my grunt must have come out as a sound of agreement because he nodded. "Very well, then. They can keep the house in Greenwich." He waved the back of his hand through the air as if the twenty-million-dollar property was child's play.

As though two weeks of my time was adequate compensation for it.

I didn't know what to say. I had no idea how to feel. Except...

"Excuse me for just a moment."

I pushed my salad away and stood abruptly, nearly stumbling from the room in my haste to get to the executive washroom down the hall. Once inside, I locked the door behind me and took my aching cock in my hand. Christ, when was the last time I'd been this hard?

Maybe fifteen years ago, my brain helpfully reminded me.

Grey Blackwood had pushed every one of my buttons even before I'd heard him order my father removed from York Capital as easily as he'd ordered lasagne for dinner, but now? After witnessing that?

Fuck. I was so turned on I couldn't possibly sit in the room with him without embarrassing myself.

I can't believe I'm doing this.

I felt embarrassed and out of control, hot and dirty. I'd never jacked off at work before. But Grey Blackwood was here and bossing me around like he owned the place, and oh, by the way... *he owned the place.*

"*Agh.*" I sucked in a breath of cool, climate-controlled, air-freshened oxygen. The dim lighting in the washroom glinted off black granite countertop and nickel faucet. The hard throb of blood in my cock made my legs tingle and shake.

This was happening. I was going to jack off to the image of my new boss, the man who'd gone down on me and rocked my fucking world. I fumbled for a few pumps of hand lotion from the tray of toiletries on the counter.

I grunted, grabbing my dick again and wondering if I wanted to come fast or draw it out. "*Fucking fuck.*"

At this rate, I wouldn't have a choice.

I'd noticed every sexy inch of Grey in that conference room. While he told me I'd have to be at his beck and call, my dick had started chubbing up, and my brain had gone on a porny fantasy spree. Then he'd mentioned me staying in his penthouse and...

"*Oh god.*"

I thought of seeing him broad-shouldered and shirtless as we accidentally met in the kitchen in the middle of the night, running into him dripping with sweat coming out of his home gym, or seeing him unshaven and tired after a long day.

My balls tightened. This was awful. It was like an odd kind of invasion of privacy, wasn't it? I was using thoughts of him to get off while he was busy working like a responsible adult.

He was a hot fucking adult. Bossy and confident and powerful as hell.

I felt my orgasm approaching quickly, and I let my head fall back against the door with a *thud*. Behind my closed eyelids, I replayed the memory of Grey on his knees for me in that storage closet, of Grey saying...

"Ellison?"

Oh, fuck. Grey was outside the bathroom. Literally inches away from my naked dick.

My eyes popped open, and I saw my own reflection in the mirror over the sink. Red-faced. Glassy-eyed. Totally lost.

"Y-yeah?" I said a little breathlessly.

"Are you okay?"

My suit pants hung around my spread thighs. My Brooks Brothers oxford was rucked up over my chest. The head of my dick was slick and shiny with precum and lotion. I was a fucking mess.

"Never better," I assured him in a strangled voice, my hand still working my cock slowly and—I really hoped—noiselessly. "Be done in five minutes or less."

Less. Definitely less.

I could sense his hesitation through the door.

"If you... if you need anything," he began almost reluctantly. "I could—"

Oh, god, I needed so many things. For him to touch me. For him to want me. For him to go the fuck away so I could finish this without mortifying myself further.

"*Fuck it,*" he muttered under his breath. In a louder voice, he commanded, "Hurry it up, York. I need your ass in the conference room. Come *now.*" Then he stomped off down the hall.

I stifled a little whimper and throttled the base of my cock quickly, unable to reply without giving myself away. His words echoed in my head, in my ears, in my throat, and in my balls.

Come now.

Come now.

Come now.

As soon as I let go and drew my fingers up my shaft one more time, it was all over. I bit down on the fist of my free hand while I stroked myself through my release with the other.

It had been a while since I'd come at all, but I couldn't remember how long it had been since I'd come this hard.

What the fuck was wrong with me?

I washed my hands in the sink and tried to calm my flushed cheeks with cold water, hiding the evidence of my activities as much as possible, but the unvarnished truth I'd revealed to myself was impossible to hide.

Grey Blackwood was willing to give up a twenty-million-dollar property in exchange for two weeks of my company, but the joke was on him because I would have gone home with him for free.

"What time should I arrive tomorrow?" I asked. It had to be close to eight o'clock at night now, and I'd woken up before six this morning to get ready for work at the school. I'd also spent the entire weekend moving into the converted barn I'd rented near the school in Vermont, which meant my muscles were sore and needed a good stretch before bed. Not to mention, I'd just orgasmed my spleen in the washroom, which also took it out of a man.

Grey didn't look up from his laptop. "You're coming home with me, or did you forget already? To be honest, that doesn't bode well for your skills as a personal assistant, not to mention a contract attorney."

He sounded bored, which was the exact opposite of how I felt. Despite my fatigue, I felt jangly and weird, like I'd been injected with adrenaline and a sedative at the same time. Jerking off hadn't helped. There was no way I'd be able to spend the rest of the evening with Grey Blackwood without saying something pathetic and ridiculous, like asking him to make all those washroom fantasies a reality. I needed time to wrap my head around this.

I cleared my throat. "I think it makes more sense for me to stay at my old apartment tonight and start fresh in the morning. I can be here as early as you'd like."

He carefully closed the computer and looked up at me with that icy glare. "I would ask you if you always back-talked your employer, except I happen to know you've never truly had an employer, and you certainly wouldn't second-guess your precious father. So let me make myself clear. Not half an hour ago, you agreed to stay at my place for my convenience. I noticed you arrived with a suitcase, which means you shouldn't need to stop anywhere for your belongings. That suits me even better. Seeing as how you don't have the car service number yet, I have already summoned my driver, and he awaits us out front. Let's go."

He didn't wait for a response from me. He gathered his belongings into a buttery leather messenger bag and slid the strap over his shoulder as he stood up.

Grey was even taller than I remembered. He dominated the room, even though we were the only two people in it.

As he stepped closer, he looked me up and down, leaving prickles along my skin everywhere his eyes touched. "I seem to remember your ability to walk. Is that still the case, or do you need some help?"

"Don't be an ass," I blurted, going against my secret promise to be cordial and remain calm.

For a split -second, his eyes flared with emotion, but he quickly shuttered them. "Then don't act like a virginal maiden who's afraid of the big bad wolf. I can promise you, Ellison, I wouldn't touch you again for all the money in the world."

He stepped past me and out of the conference room, leaving a vacuum that nearly pulled me out the door after him. But his words had landed hard and fast like a kick to the gut, leaving me breathless. This time the breathlessness wasn't caused by his proximity or my sexual fantasies, but embarrassment and the sharp sting of rejection. I'd been so fucking stupid. Of course he wouldn't want me. Maybe I was the naive idiot who *needed* to be more afraid of the big bad wolf.

After gathering my wits and trying my best to pull a protective shell of nonchalance around me, I followed him out the door and down to the lobby.

This was going to be a long two weeks.

5

GREY

"In the midst of chaos, there is also opportunity."

~ Sun Tzu, *The Art of War*

Putting one's opponent off-balance was a known battle tactic. It was also delicious to watch. Ellison sat stiffly in the town car that carried us uptown.

"What's in Vermont?" I asked conversationally as if we were two friends taking a drive.

He did a little double take. "Beg your pardon?"

"You said you'd come from Vermont. Were you on vacation there? Berry picking, perhaps? What else is there to do in Vermont in the summer?"

"No, I... no. I wasn't vacationing. I live there now."

How had I not known this? I'd had researchers combing every inch of intel on all the major players involved in York Capital. "You live in Vermont?"

"I moved there this past weekend."

He didn't elaborate. I hated his silence. I'd much rather hear him talk, even if he was an entitled asshole.

"For work? I was surprised to hear you were leaving the family business."

He glanced at me from the corner of his eye. "Why do you care?"

"I hate to lose a promising young lawyer on staff."

He turned to face me. It was clear I'd pushed his button successfully because his nostrils flared slightly. "Thirty-five is hardly young. Besides, we're the same age. Would you consider yourself a promising young corporate raider?"

I couldn't hold back a soft snort at the phrase. "You make it sound dashing and dangerous. Like I strap on a ninja mask and sneak through the city at night to see what kind of companies I can steal away before morning."

Ellison lifted one eyebrow as if to say, "Am I wrong?"

"But yes," I continued. "I am quite young to be in the position I'm in. According to the magazines, I'm the youngest self-made billionaire in the venture capital space." Something I took great pride in when Marcel had informed me of it. There were fewer than a thousand billionaires in the country, and I was one of them. The knowledge of my wealth still blew my mind.

"Congratulations," he said, and he actually sounded like he meant it. "Are you happy?"

His words jolted me out of my self-congratulatory indulgence. "Happy that I'm a billionaire?"

Ellison turned to look out the window. "Never mind. Silly question, I guess."

He sounded disappointed, like being obscenely wealthy wasn't reason enough to be happy. If he'd ever been poor, he might have felt differently. It was yet another reminder of how different we were and how entitled *he* was.

"Yes, I am happy I'm financially secure. I'm also proud of how hard I worked to get here, especially since I did it all myself." I felt the anger from fifteen years ago bubbling under my tongue. Since Ellison was finally here in front of me, it was hard to hold it in. "I can only imagine where I would be if I'd actually had help, if I'd had a leg up in the industry and had been able to learn from other VCs."

I could tell from the tension in Ellison's shoulders I'd scored a direct hit with my sarcasm. Good.

"Maybe you'd still be under their thumb," he said. "Maybe you wouldn't have gone out on your own to amass your own wealth. You never know how that would have changed the trajectory of your success."

My hands itched to punch him. "Yes, I'm so *grateful* I started off flipping fast-food burgers while trying to save money to start my own business. It must have been those three jobs I struggled to balance that shot me right into the rarefied air of the ultra-wealthy."

Ellison sighed. "Well, clearly something worked."

Me, I thought. *I worked. I worked my fucking ass off every hour of every day of every month and year. And I'm still doing it.*

Silence fell between us again. While the car made its way slowly through the shadowed city streets, I studied Ellison York. He was broader than before but still elegant, as if being born with money somehow gave you birdlike qualities. The drape of his pants gave a hint of muscled thigh that shifted under the fabric when he moved. His clothes were the highest quality, even though they looked wrinkled and worn after the long day he'd had. He wore an Apple Watch on his left wrist with a brown leather band that looked old and soft from use.

His shirt carried a hint of male sweat, a musky scent I easily could have leaned over and snuffled for under his arm if he was anyone other than who he was. But it also carried a hint of something expensive, something a high-end shop would no doubt describe as masculine and virile. I didn't recognize it, but I'd be damned if I didn't want to memorize it and search it out at the perfume counter, if only so I could be reminded later of Ellison York's signature scent.

I hated my reaction to him, but I wasn't surprised by it. Physically, he was damned near perfection. Tall, sexy, elegant. Educated, well-spoken, polite. Calm.

He should have raged at me when he realized who'd taken over his family's business. But he hadn't. Instead, he'd agreed to my demands and calmly made some of his own.

Why? Why not first try to finagle a legal challenge to the acquisition? He hadn't even asked to investigate the stock transactions or interview the board members who'd approved it.

And who the hell agreed to live with their boss? Even if it was only temporary, his fairly easy agreement to stay at my penthouse had shocked me. I'd only thrown the command out there to insult him. One of the cornerstones of negotiation is to ask for way more than you expect so you seem the hero by accepting less than you'd asked for. I hadn't expected him to agree.

But as soon as he'd said he'd stay with me, as soon as I'd pictured his sexy ass sleeping between the soft sheets of my guest bed... I'd known I wasn't going to back down. It was too good. While he was there, I was sure I could come up with hundreds of other ways to humiliate and embarrass him.

I'd make him fetch my coffee and book my appointments. I'd take the opportunity to get his legal advice on several issues so he never knew whether I was calling him into my office for a coffee run or a contract consultation. I would keep him guessing and on his toes until he was frustrated enough to break and tell me how he really felt about the takeover.

And then I'd laugh all the way to the damned bank.

He shifted again, and I felt his thigh brush mine just barely.

"I heard about the Heath and Kelty Investments acquisition last spring," he said without turning to look at me. "Kirby said his father has barely left the golf course all summer. Mr. Heath is telling everyone how much he's enjoying early retirement."

I thought of the man I'd looked up to in college, the man I'd wanted to learn from. I'd felt like a million bucks when I'd landed the first-year associate job at Norm Heath's firm. And then I'd felt like scum when he'd yanked it away from me.

"He's lying," I said coolly. "The man cried like a baby when I took over the firm. Bob Kelty, on the other hand, sold me his shares with no qualms and never looked back. He moved to Florida and bought a fishing boat."

"Does it bring you joy to do what you do?" Ellison asked. He finally turned to meet my eyes. I met his gaze straight on.

"Without a doubt, yes."

And it did. The more resources I had to help me assess and invest in new opportunities, the faster I could grow my empire. Contrary to popular belief, I didn't acquire companies simply for revenge. I took them over because it was the most efficient way to harness the talent and experience of the country's best investment specialists. I craved the opportunity to help great ideas get off the ground, but I was only one person. I couldn't attend every promising presentation or listen to every great idea out there. But I wanted to be involved in them from the ground up regardless.

"One day you might learn that money doesn't buy happiness," Ellison muttered under his breath.

I bit back a laugh. "Spoken like someone who's always had it."

He nodded. "True. Can't argue with that. And I'm grateful for it."

His platitude was nothing more than empty words. I wasn't even sure someone who'd grown up like Ellison York could have enough perspective to comprehend gratitude in that way, but I didn't say anything.

The town car pulled up to the door of my building. "Here we are. Home sweet home."

"You live a block away from my parents' place in the city," he said in surprise when he realized I lived on the Park too.

"I realize that now. Funny I haven't noticed them at the local market."

Ellison let out a soft laugh. "You wouldn't have. I'm not sure my mother could even find such a thing as a market without Evelina leading the way."

It hadn't taken me long to change my mind about opening up a normal conversation with Ellison. I didn't want to hear him joke about his parents or express his own vulnerabilities. I didn't want to care about whether the stress of the day had made him sick in the washroom earlier. I wanted to keep my ice-cold anger for him bottled up tight where nothing could defrost it by accident.

That anger had driven me for years, and the last thing I needed was to be duped and drawn in again by his deceptively easy company. I'd been down that road before. He'd initiated a conversation with me in a math class at school, and I'd mistakenly thought he was a good guy. I'd thought we could be friends, even though I'd known he was a member at the club where I'd worked.

I'd been wrong. And from here on out, I'd remember that.

"Mr. Abbot," I said, nodding to the doorman who held the door open for us. "This is my temporary PA, Ellison York. He'll be staying with me for a couple of weeks."

"Very good, sir," he said with a nod. "You had a courier delivery earlier. I gave it to Jenny."

I thanked him and continued to the elevators without waiting for Ellison to sort out his misbehaving suitcase. When he finally caught up to me with a curse, I stepped into the elevator and punched in the code for my floor.

He was annoyed. "Thanks for waiting. You know, if you're only a block away from my parents' place, I could have stayed there. You could have called me if you needed me. I could still—"

I held up a hand. "Stop arguing with me."

"But I—"

I turned and speared him with a glare before stepping into his personal space. "Did you or did you not make a deal with me?"

He was tall, but not as tall as I was. His eyes narrowed almost imperceptibly. "I don't think it's necessary for me to stay at your place like some kind of houseboy."

I stepped closer until he leaned back against the wood-paneled wall. "You *are* some kind of houseboy," I said in a low voice. "Remember? You said you'd do anything within reason. What I want from you right now is respect and obedience. Is that so hard for you to comprehend? Do you not think I deserve respect, Ellison? Is that too much to ask in exchange for your parents' home?"

I felt the air move between us as his chest heaved with his

breaths. His scent swirled between us, making me feel light-headed. Against all my better judgment, I wanted Ellison York.

Desperately.

I wanted him to follow through on the interrupted promise he made when he dropped to his knees in that closet. I wanted another taste of his sweet mouth and hot dick. I wanted to run my hands into his slightly overgrown hair and yank it until he glanced up at me with lust-glazed eyes, begging to suck me off.

"Yes, *sir*," he said through his teeth.

My dick roared to life, and I shoved him back so I could get some distance between us. "Then stop arguing with me, and do your damned job."

"And what *is* my job, exactly? What does being your personal assistant mean?"

"It means whatever I want it to mean."

His lips parted, probably in shock and outrage, but for just a second, I let myself imagine he felt something different. Something *yearning*.

Thankfully, the elevator doors opened seconds later, spilling us out into my foyer. The air was cool and silent. Jenny had left on the lamp on the entry table, and the area glowed with a soft light. Through the arched doorway ahead, the city lights were visible. The living room's wall of windows was like a magnet to anyone who visited. Not that many people did.

"Christ," Ellison muttered, leaving his suitcase behind and following the view until he stood silhouetted against the evening sky. "You can see Jersey from here."

"My housekeeper, Jenny, will be in at six. She can make whatever you want for breakfast. We'll leave here at seven to make a seven-thirty meeting at the Plaza. Just a reminder, you have a nondisclosure agreement on file, and that now covers our discussions as well."

"Only to the extent they're relevant to York Capital work product," he corrected without looking away from the city lights.

"The meeting is relevant to York Capital. I'm interviewing someone we may choose to invest in."

I found the package that had been delivered and ripped the large envelope open to read the documents inside. They were the signed real estate agreement for one of the properties I was acquiring for a special project. I smiled to myself. Only one property remained before I owned the entire city block and could move to the next phase of the project.

"Who?" Ellison asked.

I shoved the papers back into the envelope. "Ben Aldeen. He's—"

"The inventor of Smart Resin." Ellison turned to face me. "Does he know you're working for us? I mean, for York? He turned us down a couple of months ago."

"Because your father insulted him and went to the initial meeting underprepared. But no, and he doesn't need to know yet. If he doesn't want York to invest, he can choose from any branch of Blackwood. He won't be accepting seed money from York Capital. He'll be choosing to partner with *me*, regardless of where the money comes from."

I could see Ellison was impressed. Ben Aldeen wasn't an easy man to get a meeting with. He'd been burned pretty badly with his first venture capital experience and was understandably antsy about working with another.

"What if he meets me and gets scared off?"

"Have you met him before?" I asked. "Were you in the meeting your father had with him?"

"No. But he'll obviously recognize my last name."

I gestured for him to grab his bag and follow me. "Why would he know the last name of my personal assistant?" I asked, leading Ellison down the hall toward the guest bedroom. His silence was delicious.

"Okay," he said slowly when we reached the bedroom. "What exactly do you need me to do during the meeting, then?"

"Just sit there and look pretty. Take notes if I ask you to. That sort of thing."

I expected him to balk, but he just grinned. "I can do that. It's been a long time since I've had so little expected of me. Might be a nice change."

Cocky bastard.

"Bed, bathroom, television," I said, gesturing around the room and trying not to picture his naked ass in my home. What the hell had I been thinking? The temptation of having him so close was going to ruin me. "The kitchen is on the far side of the living room. Help yourself to anything." I cleared my throat and walked out before he had a chance to say anything stupid.

And before I had a chance to grab him and toss him face-first into the bed.

As I made my way down the hall, I called Marcel.

"When you didn't call back after the Emperor of Evil was escorted out of the building, I thought Ellison York might be your new favorite assistant," he said with mock sadness.

"No you didn't. Listen, I'm having Ellison attend the Aldeen meeting with me tomorrow morning, so I won't need you there. Don't worry, you're still my favorite," I said dryly. "I'll brief you on everything after the fact."

Marcel was uncharacteristically hesitant. "Grey, you know I make a point not to interfere in your business decisions—"

I snorted. "Since when?"

"—but have you really thought this through? What is this thing with Ellison York going to accomplish? It's not like you."

"I've got it under control," I assured him, though I wasn't sure at all. "Can you get Ricky or Ted over here? If I don't get rid of this tension, I won't be able to sleep."

"No problem. I'll text you after I get a hold of someone."

"Thanks." I ended the call and let out a breath. I put the real estate paperwork in my office before sitting to wait for the masseuse to show up. It had taken months of doctor visits before I'd learned the headaches I was having were from tight muscles in my neck and shoulders. In the run-up to the York takeover, I'd missed several massage appointments, and I was feeling the results.

My hands shook with a strange combination of nerves and excitement. Ellison York was here under my roof, willing to do just about anything to help dear old dad out of trouble. Instead of being surly and argumentative, he was downright agreeable and personable.

I began to wonder who was doing a better job of keeping the other off-balance.

Because I was the one who felt unsure of what was going to happen next and which Ellison York was going to appear at breakfast.

And I hated feeling out of control.

6

ELLISON

"So in war, the way is to avoid what is strong, and strike at what is weak."

~ Sun Tzu, *The Art of War*

Even though I thought I'd have trouble falling asleep under the same roof of the man who'd haunted my dreams for fifteen years, as soon as I finished studying the acquisition paperwork I'd snuck a copy of, I was out. I slept hard until my alarm pinged at five thirty. There was a missed text from my sister the night before asking for an update, and I kicked myself for forgetting to contact her.

Me: *I'm handling it, but I have to work my two weeks' notice. Sorry.*

I knew she wouldn't mind my absence since my role at the academy was fundraising and development, but it still rankled. I'd waited so long to finally be free of my father and York Capital, and now here I was again.

After showering in the expansive guest bathroom, I perused a basket of complimentary bath products. It was clear Grey cared about money and luxury brand names. No generic cheese curls at the Price Chopper for him.

I didn't blame him, but everything about this place screamed expensive and soulless. The view, the modern furnishings, the art, the plush silky bedding, and little details like the little flower-shaped bar of soap by the sink. All of it was calculated to impress. None of it showed his personality or his individual taste. Every stitch of clothing he'd worn the day before was bespoke, but he wore them like he didn't care about them. The contrast between this man and the kid who'd taken care to treat a stain on his uniform shirt at the club when he'd accidentally brushed up against some grease on a golf cart was night and day.

It was a stark reminder that this Grey Blackwood wasn't the kid I'd kind of known in college. He'd changed. Of course he had. We all had. But I wondered how long it had taken him to get used to having wealth and whether or not he worried about losing it all as quickly as he'd gained it.

I had to admit to myself I'd never really known the real Grey Blackwood. Yes, I'd had an enormous crush on him back in the day— something it had taken me a long time afterward to put the right words to—and yes, I had fantasies aplenty, but we had never shared a meal or gotten to know each other. I'd spent time with him on the golf course, but again, it hadn't led to any kind of groundbreaking intimacies about hopes and dreams.

What I knew about Grey could fit in a tiny storage closet, literally and figuratively, but I was anxious to learn more. He'd always intrigued me. His ambition and drive had been legendary. But how had his rise to fame played out? I'd read as many articles about him as I could find in recent years, but he never really let any of the interviewers in. He talked of acquisitions and opportunities, exciting breakthroughs and upcoming tech. But he never talked about his past or told the story of his humble beginnings.

They would have loved it. The media would have eaten it up. But the real Grey was carefully hidden away.

Grey Blackwood was a mystery I wanted to solve. Maybe that was why I'd agreed so easily to working closely with him for two weeks. Well, that and the overwhelming lust I felt whenever he was in the vicinity.

Regardless, I planned to be agreeable and friendly. I knew I could never make up to him for not standing up all those years ago and telling the truth about how we'd been found in that position, but I vowed I wouldn't cause him another moment of doubt or distress.

I owed him that much at least.

I shaved and dressed quickly, silently cursing having to wear a suit again so soon after I'd thought I was done with them for a while. When I finally made my way out to the kitchen, I was surprised to hear laughing.

Grey's deep chuckle stopped me in my tracks.

"He threatened to book me onto a yacht and instruct the captain to sail anywhere without satellite reception," he said. "As if Marcel would ever survive a vacation without internet himself. He thinks I'm bad, but he's worse."

A woman's voice joined him in laughter. "Tell him we know the truth. He can't be away from his Pornhub that long."

"Do they have a Pornhub for designer shoes? I wasn't aware." Both of them laughed some more. I entered the room, hoping to get in on the fun, but the minute I stepped onto the hardwood floor with a soft thunk, Grey's laughter stopped.

"Good morning," I said with a cheery smile. "You two are awfully awake this early."

Grey's scowl had returned. "Ellison, this is my housekeeper, Jenny Mays. Jenny, Ellison York."

Her eyes flared wide at my name, but she hid it quickly. "Nice to meet you. Coffee?"

I agreed and took a seat next to Grey at the high counter on the island, ignoring the way his body stiffened as I sat beside him. The kitchen was a gourmet playground with all the bells and whistles. I wondered if he ever entertained.

When Jenny handed me a mug with a set of cream and sugar containers, she asked what I'd like to eat.

"What is Grey having?"

"Egg white omelet with veggies and cheese."

"That sounds good. Thanks."

When she turned to continue chopping the vegetables on a cutting board, I glanced over and found Grey scrolling through his phone.

"Is there anything special you need me to know before this meeting?" I asked, trying like hell to focus on business, even though Grey looked deliciously half-asleep.

A pillowcase crease still ran up the side of his face, though it was clear from his damp hair and soapy smell he'd already showered and dressed for the day. His crisp white button-down was pristinely starched, but he hadn't fastened the top button or put on his tie yet.

I'd wanted to know the real Grey Blackwood, but this much intimacy felt heady. Dangerous.

"Keep quiet unless asked a direct question," he said without looking away from his phone. "Note any topics that make him especially reactive, but don't be obvious about it."

"What do you mean, reactive?"

He put down his phone and reached for his coffee to take a deep gulp before responding. "As much as we may wish otherwise, negotiations hinge on emotions. Everyone has weaknesses that can be exploited. The way to find them is to watch what topics make someone react emotionally. What does he care most about? What's his greatest fear? What would cause him the most joy? Anything that elicits a strong reaction is most likely something we can figure out how to take advantage of when convincing him to go with us." He glanced away. "I mean, *me*."

I couldn't decide if that sounded awful or smart. He wasn't wrong. Of course we all had emotional buttons that could be pushed to elicit strong reactions. And taking advantage of people's weaknesses was a well-known tactic in business. But it still rankled.

Grey, annoyingly perceptive as always, smirked a little. "Don't make that face. Your father uses the exact same techniques, and you know it."

"Actually, I don't know," I said honestly. "My father never had me involved in negotiations. My bleeding-heart tendencies were a liability."

He grunted in disbelief, but I wasn't sure which part he didn't believe. "Well, none of that will matter today since you won't be saying a word."

I nodded. "Okay. Sounds good. Is there anything else you need me to arrange for you today before we get going?" I asked, pulling out my phone to take notes.

Grey eyed me suspiciously. I kind of loved that I'd surprised him with my offer. He clearly hadn't been expecting my easy compliance. I grinned at him.

"Mpfh" was all he said before taking another sip of coffee.

Jenny spoke over his shoulder. "Beauty and the Beast. He's a beast before the second cup. Then he's a beauty."

To my delight, a pink flush crept up Grey's neck. "Silence, woman," he grumbled. Jenny only laughed.

"Is that right?" I asked. "I didn't know he had beauty in there at all. I assumed it was all beast."

He grunted again and busied himself with his phone. "We have a meeting with Ian Duckworth at two. He's the lone holdout on a real estate deal I'm trying to put together."

I opened my mouth to mention that I knew Ian very well, but then I decided Grey wouldn't appreciate my name-dropping. Besides, if Grey knew how close I was to the Duckworths, he might try to ask me what Ian's weaknesses were so he could "take advantage" of them in the negotiation. Better to keep my damned mouth shut and behave like the submissive servant he obviously wanted me to be.

After tapping the appointment into my phone, I looked up in anticipation of anything else I needed to add to the schedule.

"I'd like to sit down with Lillian Moffit and Desi Martinez to touch base with them about staying on at York. Right now, we're scheduled to meet with Lillian over lunch and Desi at four. I'd like you to make us a lunch reservation somewhere nice but close to the office."

He'd obviously done his homework. Both executives were worth their weight in gold.

"Lillian loves Indian food," I said, searching for the number of the place I had in mind. "That okay with you?"

"I'm not picky. For the meeting with Desi, get Nikki to arrange coffee."

"I'll have her get a tray of cheesecake brownies from the bakery down the street. Desi says he avoids sweets, but he'll do anything for those things."

I could tell Grey was surprised I was being so helpful, and I was very happy to keep him on his toes.

"How do you know so much about everyone there? Didn't you spend any time actually working?"

I ignored the jab. "I talk to people. Don't you know your coworkers' idiosyncrasies?"

"I don't have coworkers." He kept his eyes on his phone and took a bite of the large omelet Jenny slid in front of him.

Jenny turned back for my plate and placed it in front of me. "The elevator was broken in my building today," she said, seemingly apropos of nothing.

Grey looked up with a frown. "Your building doesn't have an elevator. It's a walk-up. I remember every step of carrying that damned mattress when your neighbor had the flood."

Jenny met my eyes with a wink. "Exactly."

Grey didn't seem to understand the point she'd just made, but I appreciated her gently correcting him in my eyes.

If he thought he was going to try and convince me he was the heartless corporate raider he wanted the world to think he was, he was in for some hard work. I tended to think well of people regardless, but I sure as hell wanted to think well of him. He'd been dealt many shitty hands in his life, and he'd worked his ass off to overcome them. Surely that kind of person couldn't be a heartless asshole. At least I hoped he couldn't. I was more likely to think the entitled pricks I'd grown up with were the heartless assholes.

I swallowed another bite of breakfast before getting up the nerve to ask the question I needed to bring up. "Can we schedule some time to talk about the takeover?"

"Why?"

I wanted to snap back, "*Why do you think?*" But I held my tongue and stayed calm. "I'd like to determine what you'd like to gain out of the transaction and what options we may have to lessen the... negative impact on my family."

Grey's body tightened on the stool next to mine. I was incredibly aware of him in a way that made me edgy and tentative. I hated that feeling.

"And I give a shit about lessening the negative impact on your family, why?" He stopped eating to glare at me.

Why indeed. I swallowed.

"I like to think if your ancestors had started a business in the late 1800s that had survived this long, you might want to hang on to it at all costs," I said carefully. "Even if you were willing to..." I searched around for the right words. "Sacrifice other things for it."

He lifted a dirty-blond eyebrow at me. "Like what?"

There was a very slight tremor in my hands, so I quickly banished them to my lap and clamped them around the linen napkin there.

Dignity. Pride. Heterosexuality.

That last one didn't really have anything to do with the company takeover, but it was hard to avoid thinking about my sexuality when I was finally faced with the one man who'd ever tempted me to forsake my interest in women.

"Assets," I said, clearing my throat when my voice cracked a little. "We could determine a fair—"

He cut me off with a smirk. I hated that he looked even sexier when he was being smug. "Pretty sure I already have all the assets. And who said I'm interested in fair?"

"I'm just asking you to give me a chance to come to you with a proposition to help my family save face."

He huffed out a soft laugh. "Not interested in helping your family save shit."

I could hardly blame him. I turned back to my omelet to take another bite.

"But by all means," he said, surprising me. "Give it your best shot. I always reward creativity in business. When you have your magical argument ready, I'll hear it."

He went back to reading something on his phone while he ate the rest of his breakfast. Even though I knew the chances of me saving York from his clutches were slim to none, it was at least something.

Now I simply needed to find a loophole and put my damned legal experience and education to good use.

While I left Grey's apartment feeling positive and hopeful, it didn't take long for all the warm fuzzies to be burned clear away.

"Be a dear and fetch Mr. Aldeen another latte," Grey said at the early morning meeting.

I gritted my teeth and did as he asked. I wouldn't have minded getting the potential client a coffee, but it was the condescending tone that made me want to punch him.

"Yes, sir," I said instead, with a wide, easy smile for both of them. When I returned to the table, I also brought a blueberry muffin on a china plate, a place mat, and a full place setting of silverware. I placed the latte in front of Mr. Aldeen before setting a formal place in front of Grey.

He ignored me until I cut into his muffin and tried to feed him a bite of it on the end of the fork.

"What... what the... what are you doing?" he gritted out in a low voice.

"Feeding you, sir. I know your hands are valuable assets that—"

The look he shot me went straight to my lower belly. It promised revenge. I wondered if he'd be angry enough to shove me up against the back wall of an elevator when we returned to the office. His strong hand would latch around my throat as he got in my face to warn me about respect.

My heart rate fluttered like a drunk bird knocking against its cage. An angry Grey Blackwood was way more enticing than I would have imagined.

"I am not hungry at the moment," he said, pulling the fork out of my hand and setting it down carefully. "But thank you for your attentive devotion to my comfort. You may wait for me outside."

I walked out of the meeting with an unexpected boon. Apparently, upsetting Mr. Angry-Britches got me out of being his PA for a little while. Score.

It didn't last long.

"Ellison here will arrange a car for you when we're done," he said to Lillian at lunch a little while later, even though I'd worked hand in hand with the woman for years on complex legal contracts. Her eyebrows lifted at me in question, and I couldn't help but respond cheekily.

"Mr. Blackwood doesn't know how to work a phone. He apparently has 'people' for that. You don't want to know what else he has people for." I'd heard him task his real assistant with finding him some "tension relief" last night. The overheard phone call had made me grumpy as fuck—not because I begrudged him the sex he needed but because I was there and willing if he needed someone to use for that purpose.

Just the thought of it made me flush red-hot. I hadn't hooked up with a man ever, present company excluded, but it wasn't for lack of interest. The problem was, the only man I'd wanted to hook up with all those years was Grey. And he was the last man on earth who'd want to get with me.

Grey's mouth opened in surprise, and a little firework of warm satisfaction went off in my gut. *Yes, I know about your little dalliance last night.*

His eyes narrowed at me, but I didn't allow myself to look away. The air thickened between us.

"Cooking him breakfast," I added, turning back to Lillian. "His housekeeper makes a mean omelet."

While I'd intended to soften the blow of my initial words, it didn't occur to me until after these were out of my mouth that I'd pretty much confessed to being at Grey's place for breakfast. My face burned, and I suddenly had trouble drawing in enough air.

Grey cleared his throat and remained his usual calm, cool self. "Ellison helped me prepare for the Aldeen meeting early this morning. It went well. I expect to get legal involved in a formal offer this afternoon."

I blinked to cover my surprise. I'd thought part of his purpose in having me as his gopher was the opportunity to smear my reputation. To let the whole world know that Warren York's heir was staying at Grey's apartment, debasing himself at Grey's whim.

When would I stop underestimating this man?

Grey was right. The meeting with the creator of Smart Resin had gone very well. Ben Aldeen had taken one look at Grey Blackwood and practically purred through his drool. Clearly, the man was gay or bi, and when Grey had shot a full smile his way, Grey could have asked him to sign away his own mother and Ben probably would have done it.

But Grey had remained professional and respectful. He'd acted like nothing uncomfortable was happening at all, like Ben wasn't fawning all over him and blushing wildly in his presence. I had to admit to having been impressed with how Grey had handled the man. He hadn't taken advantage of Ben's attraction. He'd been fair and honest with his offer of what York Capital could do to help Ben succeed.

And I'd gotten my first glimpse of how Grey had gotten to this level of wealth and success so rapidly. Nothing seemed to ruffle him. It was irksome, really. I wanted to see what he would look like ruffled, but I sure as hell didn't plan on being the man to ruffle him.

We finished up the lunch with Lillian. She, too, had been

impressed with Grey and had agreed to give him six more months at York to see if they worked well together. I wondered at his ability to schmooze everyone since he had a reputation in the industry as cold and heartless. Watching him subtly praise Lillian's accomplishments without seeming to be deliberately flattering was like taking a master course in manipulation. That didn't mean I thought he was trying to be deliberately manipulative, but the results were the same. Everything he did and said with her led to her decision to trust him and give him a chance.

I wouldn't have expected it from a woman who'd been loyal to my father for twenty years.

When we left the restaurant, I asked why we weren't sharing Lillian's car back to the office.

"We're going to visit with my attorneys."

He didn't explain further, leaving me to wonder if this was related to the takeover or about something else altogether. I walked beside him without saying anything and took the opportunity to enjoy the early September weather. The sun shone brightly on the streets while the shadowed sidewalks were noticeably cooler.

I was surprised when we didn't enter one of the shiny corporate towers but instead made our way through a nondescript door almost hidden between a hotel and a café. A little brass plaque indicated this was the law office of Cage and Grant. I'd never heard of them.

We walked up a flight of stairs to a surprisingly clean and bright office space on the second floor. I realized the office was located above the cafe, and the faint smell of coffee permeated the room. The woman behind the reception desk lit up when she spotted Grey.

"How'd it go yesterday?" When I stepped out from behind Grey, the woman looked taken aback. "Oh, uh, hi."

"It went smoothly, thank you. This is Ellison. He's assisting me today. I was hoping to pick up a report Gabe put together for me on the Hell's Kitchen property."

"Of course. Let me tell him you're here."

Grey checked his watch and then slid his hands into his pockets. Within moments, a man around our age came out from a hallway behind the woman's desk and greeted Grey with a big smile. "Hey, man, how'd it go yesterday?"

I couldn't decide whether to be annoyed at the congratulatory tone of these people on the ruination of my family's legacy or be secretly pleased to know how much the takeover had clearly mattered to the otherwise stoic man beside me.

"Shitty," I said with a big smile before things could get even more awkward. "Thanks for asking."

The man's smile faltered. Before he had a chance to ask who I was, Grey intervened.

"Gabriel Grant, meet Ellison York of York Capital. Ellison, Gabe and his partner manage my legal work."

The man studied me for a beat before tentatively reaching out a hand to shake. "Nice to meet you."

I nodded and shook his hand. When Gabe turned to lead us back to his office, I turned to Grey. "*All* of your legal work? You don't have your own team?"

"They are my team."

"But..." I stopped talking to think about what I wanted to say. "I just assumed Blackwood had a legal department of its own."

"This is Blackwood's legal department," he said, clearly trying not to lose his patience with me. "They have twelve attorneys and at least a hundred support staff. All of them serve Blackwood full-time."

I glanced back at the understated decor in the tiny lobby. "Why don't they work at your corporate office?"

"I don't have a corporate office," he said casually. "And stop asking questions. Remember we talked about you not speaking until spoken to? Let's get back to that."

It didn't make any sense. Running an investment firm as large as Blackwood would require office space. An acquisitions department, Human Resources, legal specialists, investment analysts, and business development teams. He would need massive accounting support as well as tax experts. His holdings were significantly larger than my father's, and York had hundreds of employees.

I stayed quiet while the man gave Grey what we'd come for. When we stepped back out onto the sidewalk, the crowd was just as thick as before. We hung a right and continued walking when Grey took a call from his assistant, Marcel. A block later, Grey stopped and pointed to a Starbucks. "Grab me a coffee."

He went right back to talking to his "real" PA on the phone as if he hadn't just bitten out a rude command. I wanted so badly to snap, "Make me, asshole." But I refrained.

"What kind?"

His nostrils flared. Perhaps he wasn't used to having to inform his underlings of his preferences. This was going to be fun.

"Brewed coffee. Sugar and cream." He went back to talking to Marcel. This time he was asking about something involving market reports.

For a split second, I bristled at the dismissive way he was treating me, but then I realized he was trying to break me down, upset me, make me feel like trash. I didn't have to let him. Moreover, my only commitment to him was to be a PA for two weeks. No one said I had to be a good one. And I was bound and determined to get this man to stop being such a stoic asshole.

I put a fingertip to my chin. "You know they make a crème brûlée latte that's to die for."

A little wrinkle appeared between his eyes. "Just the coffee."

I frowned. "Or what about the Very Berry Hibiscus Refresher? I hear that's very... refreshing."

His forehead lines deepened. "Just. The. Coffee."

I looked at the Starbucks for a minute before turning back. "What about a snack? I can recommend the pumpkin bread. It's super moist. Has like... pumpkin seeds on the top edge. They kind of taste like pistachios. Wait... maybe they are pistachios. Do you think—"

"We just had lunch. I'm not hungry. Get me the goddamned coffee."

I put a hand to my chest. "You don't have to yell. I'm trying to make sure your needs are met. *Sir.*"

"My needs will be met when you put a fucking coffee in my hand like I asked."

I wriggled. "Oooh! Coffee. That sounds amazing. I'll take a salted caramel mocha, please."

He opened his mouth in surprise.

"With whip," I added with a big smile. "Thanks, dollface." I wanted so badly to boop his nose, but I refrained.

Grey kept laser eyes on me. "Marcel, let me call you back. And if you don't hear back from me in five minutes, meet me at the Midtown North precinct with bail money," he growled.

As soon as he ended the call, I blew him a kiss. "Just kidding, boss. One boring-ass old man coffee coming right up." Then I turned on my heel and bolted out of his reach toward the shop.

Thanks to my little coffee fun, Grey decided to send me back to the office instead of taking me along to the meeting with Ian. His exact words were "Get the fuck out of my face and hope I calm the hell down before I get back to the office."

I couldn't decide if I was relieved or disappointed, but I dutifully did as he asked. On my way back to the office, my mother called to pressure me into a social event I'd already turned down a million times.

"I can't leave town right now, Mom," I said. "I'm being forced to stay on at York, and I'll probably be working through the weekend." *Oh darn.*

"But it's their fiftieth anniversary, and I know how much Binnie would love to have you there. She's been begging me, absolutely begging me, to convince you to come. I think there's a young lady there she has her eye on for you."

Even more reason not to go to the annual house party. My parents' friends took great pleasure in trying to matchmake me. At least this year I had an excuse not to go.

She continued when I didn't answer. "Unless, of course, there's someone you'd like to bring as your plus-one? That would be delightful also."

"Sorry. I wish I could, but I can't," I lied. "Dad's counting on me to try and find a way out of this mess we're in."

She sighed. "Speaking of that... do you think there's any way to get my jewelry out of the safe deposit box? I want to take my diamond and emerald set for the formal night event."

I opened my mouth to ask why she didn't just go get them herself when I realized the safe deposit box was most likely paid for and owned by York Capital.

"Can't dad's secretary get them for you?" I asked.

"They've taken her off the account and frozen access to the box."

I was going to kill Grey Blackwood. Did he honestly think he was going to take my mother's jewelry too?

Mom continued. "What's going on over there? Your father won't tell me anything, but someone from the club said the man who's stealing the company was that same boy who... who caddied for us that summer."

We didn't talk much about "that summer." We never had. As far as my parents were concerned, a lowly club employee—a kid from the wrong side of the tracks, no less—had taken advantage of me by luring me into a situation I was wholly unprepared for. Even when I'd finally sobered up and tried telling them the truth, they hadn't listened. They'd assumed I was downplaying it to keep the truth of the matter from causing a scandal.

"His name is Grey, and he's not stealing the company. His acquisition was completely legal. Uncle Mark sold him his shares." Although that didn't mean I wasn't still hell-bent on finding us a way out of the transaction. "I'll take care of it," I promised.

As soon as I got back to the office, I called my father.

My father wasn't trustworthy in business. I'd learned that early on, so I didn't take any chances by mentioning Grey's business to him. But I did want to spend my time alone finding out if there was any way to save York from being lost to us forever. I may not have had much respect for my father, but I loved my mother and sister, my aunts and cousins. York was our legacy. Even if Grey stripped it of most of the best investment assets, it would be worth trying to retain the name and history for my family.

"Where the hell have you been?" my father asked as soon as he answered the call. "I've been trying to reach you all day."

"I was attending to my new daddy," I said before dropping into a chair in the empty conference room.

"Don't be flip. What have you learned?"

Unfortunately, I didn't have good news. "I stayed up last night studying the relevant contracts, stock transactions, and legal issues, and it seems pretty airtight. Did you talk to Uncle Mark?"

He sighed. "He's ducking my calls. I'm going to have to drive out there and confront him."

Mark lived out in Danbury, and my father hated battling traffic to visit him. "Unless he was impaired somehow when he signed the paperwork, and I'd find that hard to believe considering the firm he used as witness and notary, then it's legitimate."

We already knew the other transaction had been fully above-board since my great-uncle Leon had left his shares to his third wife, who'd only married him in the first place for his money. It had been a relief to approve her share sale to a reputable investment firm. At the time, we hadn't known that firm was in the process of being taken over by Grey Blackwood. He'd used their name and reputation to hide the transaction.

Devious and underhanded but completely legal.

After ending the call with my father, the phone buzzed.

Grey: *I need you to pick up my new suit from Brooks Brothers on 6th. Jenny had something come up.*

Me: *New phone, who dis?*

Grey: *Do you get beat up a lot?*

Me: *Sometimes. But I like it.*

Grey: *Just pick up the damned suit.*

Me: *You know... if you paid a little extra they'd deliver it to your building. Want me to loan you some money?*

Grey: *Yes, please. I'll take twenty million. Feel free to pay it in the form of a nice estate in Connecticut.*

I sighed. Playtime was clearly over.

Me: *Sir, yes, sir.*

Grey: *Be back at the office before the 4pm meeting. I need to ask you about Desi.*

I reread the text, wondering what he wanted to know about Desi Martinez, York's CFO. More than that, I was taken off guard by the fact he might actually want my opinion on something having to do with the business.

Maybe we were finally getting somewhere. And maybe he'd be willing to trade my help for access to my mother's jewelry.

7

GREY

"If you know yourself but not the enemy, for every victory gained you will also suffer a defeat."
~ Sun Tzu, *The Art of War*

Ian Duckworth was as ornery and combative as the first two times I'd met with him, if not more so. I wasn't sure what his problem was with me, but I could safely assume it had something to do with my takeover of his buddy's company.

It turned out Ian Duckworth and Warren York were close family friends, or at least their wives were. *Great.* It wasn't often that I missed a crucial piece of intel, but then again, I didn't usually need to investigate the spouses' friends of the people I targeted.

I wondered if Ellison had known about the connection, and I figured he probably had but had let me go in blind anyway. No doubt he'd tell me this was what came of instructing him to speak only when spoken to.

It turned out compliant, dutiful Ellison York had a sassy streak.

Even more surprising was the fact that it made me hot as fuck.

I came back into the office in a horrible mood. Even though I knew better than to get emotionally involved in a business endeavor, it seemed like that was all I'd been doing lately. This Blackwood Center project was the effort of my fucking heart, and I wasn't going to let one stodgy old man keep me from success.

I needed to retrench and reassess.

Someone shoved a cold water bottle into my hand. "Drink this," Ellison said, meeting me in the hallway.

"Why? Are you trying to poison me?"

"No. That's scheduled for this evening. Right now, I'm trying to perk you up. You're going to need your wits about you when you meet with Desi."

I followed him to the large conference room. "Isn't it usually coffee that perks a person up?" I cracked open the water and took a grateful gulp.

"Yes, but you've already had enough of that for now. If you down the water, I'll let you have another cup of coffee during the meeting."

I glanced over at him to see if he was trolling me. He seemed to be serious. "I think you're taking this personal assistant thing too seriously," I muttered before taking another grateful sip of the cold water. "Next, you'll be monitoring my fiber intake. I already have one know-it-all PA."

"As a matter of fact, I've asked Nikki to include some apples in the snack tray for the meeting. Be sure to eat one." He grinned at me, and it made something in my chest flip. "Kidding. I'm kidding. Well, I'm not. But only because I like apples."

Ellison York was ten times more charming and engaging than I remembered, and I remembered him being charming and engaging as hell. I didn't want to like the guy. Maybe this PA idea had been a mistake. It wasn't the first time I'd had the thought.

"Okay, but seriously," he said once we were closed off in the conference room. "What did you want to know about Desi?"

I thought of the York CFO and his longtime loyalty to Warren York. "I want to know how trustworthy he is."

"He's always seemed completely aboveboard to me," he said with

a wrinkle of confusion on his forehead. "Are you asking for a particular reason?"

I nodded. "He has some questionable personal investments."

Ellison seemed taken aback. "What do you mean by questionable?"

I tried ignoring the way Ellison's shoulders and chest filled out his
shirt or the way his unruly hair flicked out above one ear. The spot
under his chin that he must have missed while shaving this morning
was a magnet for my eyes, so I forced myself to concentrate on his
mouth instead.

Mistake.

I swallowed and refocused on the topic at hand. During my
massage last night, I'd thought long and hard about how much of this
to trust Ellison with. "Outside of the scope of his job here, he has
invested in three of York's clients' companies as well as two Heath
and Kelty client companies."

"Personally?" he asked, frowning. "That's against company policy
because of the obvious conflict of interest. Are you sure?"

I nodded and told him how I'd accidentally discovered it in a few
conversations with clients.

"Could it be a miscommunication of some kind?"

"I wondered the same. But I learned he owns an interest in a
company that's listed in the investor rolls for the companies. I saw a
name I didn't recognize repeated several times and looked into it. It's
an LLC Desi has partial ownership in."

I could tell this was the first he'd heard of it. "Maybe he doesn't
manage the holdings and didn't know about the investments?"

"Maybe. That's what I'd like to find out. I didn't have time to
research it more thoroughly. I'd like to discover I'm in the wrong here.
Desi is a valuable asset to this company, but not if I can't trust him."

Ellison nodded. "I think you should ask him about it."

"I agree. Let's ask him, but what's the best approach? I don't know
him like you do."

A slight flush crept up Ellison's neck, and his eyes flitted away
from me. His response coiled tightly in my gut.

"Well, if you truly want to get him to confide, I'd probably suggest having me talk to him alone casually before you come in. Maybe you can show up late to the meeting, and I can chat him up in the meantime."

I studied him, wondering if he would tip the man off instead of actually questioning him for my own purposes. How would I know which he chose?

My idea was unethical, but I didn't trust either man enough to care. I surreptitiously set my phone to record and slid it into the seat next to mine under the table, where it was hidden from view under the edge of my computer bag.

"Okay," I said, standing up.

"How did it go with Duckworth?" Ellison asked.

The memory of that belligerent man set my teeth on edge. "He is immovable."

Ellison studied me for a minute. "I may have some insight for you on that front, but we can talk about it after the meeting."

I nodded and headed out, murmuring that I needed to consult with my transition team downstairs for a few minutes. When I made my way down to the temporary office, Marcel's face lit up. "There he is. The man who no longer needs me. I can't tell you what an absolute joyous vacation I've had today. Oh wait, I seem to have forgotten the stacks and stacks of tedious monotony you left for me to handle in your absence. Silly me."

I sighed and flopped into the chair in front of his desk. "I would have rather had you with me all day. I'm an idiot."

Marcel always seemed to see right through me. "How so?"

"York Junior is taking all the bullshit treatment I dish out, or worse, turning it back on me. It's not as much fun as I'd hoped."

Marcel bit his tongue and tried not to smile but failed. I glared at him.

"Grey, perhaps the incident in the past doesn't carry as much weight for him as it still does for you. And maybe he doesn't care as much about his reputation at the office as you think he does. I did the research you asked. It looks like he's moved to Vermont to work for a small private boarding school. Warrington Academy."

The news surprised me. I might have expected him to teach at a small law school or even teach law at a community college. But high schoolers? "Never heard of it. What's he teaching?"

"He's the head of development, which usually means corralling the alumni and pressuring them into donating money."

That didn't make any sense. "He went to a boarding school in Connecticut. I could understand him returning there out of some kind of... sentimentality. But why Vermont?"

"I'm not sure yet. His sister works at the school too. Maybe that was the draw."

I thought back to the young woman I'd seen with the York family at the country club during those summers. Gigi York had been a stunning woman, tall with long, wavy blond hair. She'd always been kind to the people around her, and I'd wondered if she'd taken after her mother while Ellison had taken after their father. Mrs. York had also never had a cruel word to say to any of the servers at the club, but that didn't mean she was a good person. Plenty of those club members had the ability to act one way in public and quite another in private.

"I wonder why he no longer wants to practice law," I thought out loud. It was curious. An ambitious, very well-educated attorney with over ten years of experience in New York could earn obscene money on a partner track at almost any firm in town. With degrees from Yale and Columbia, he could probably write his own ticket. I couldn't imagine a development director salary even broke six figures. I knew from the company reports he'd been making over half a million a year at York before any profit sharing. "Could there have been a falling-out with his father?"

Marcel shook his head. "I did a few discreet inquiries with some of the junior staff members here. Supposedly, Ellison and his dad aren't close. He's much closer to his sister and mother. And according to the head of Human Resources, Warren offered Ellison a huge promotion and raise to renew his employment commitment to York. He turned it down."

I didn't want to like Ellison, but I couldn't help thinking of the ancient proverb: the enemy of my enemy is my friend.

Screw that.

Ellison York would never be my friend.

I stood up and glanced back at Marcel. "See if you can find out why. Is there a woman in Vermont? Maybe he met her through his sister. If he didn't move for money, he had to have moved for love. It's one or the other."

The thought of Ellison and a faceless but attractive high school teacher who wanted to play house with him made my skin crawl. He was about the right age to find a wife and settle down. Surely his mother would be thrilled for him to find a nice, upscale suburb to raise a family in.

I could just picture him with a house and yard, a family SUV with bumper stickers on it bragging about their lacrosse stars and honor students. The nausea I felt at the image was my own abhorrence of anything so conforming and domestic. I would have loved for my mother to have had the opportunity to become one of those moms, but life wasn't fair to most of us. At least now she got to live a life of comfort and ease, but it would never take away the things she'd sacrificed first.

After leaving Marcel, I made my way back upstairs and entered the conference room again, quickly taking my seat and murmuring an apology to Desi for being late.

I glanced at Ellison, who looked uncomfortable and anxious. That was unexpected.

I got right down to business. "I wanted to take the opportunity to check in with you about your thoughts and feelings regarding the transition of majority ownership and find out what your own goals are. As you know, I wanted to meet personally with several of the top executives before coming to a decision about your future with the company."

Desi seemed completely at ease. He proceeded to flatter me and try to impress me with several humble brags. When I asked him about specific plans and goals for the next several years of asset management at York, he answered in generalities and made ridiculous comments like "I see York continuing to grow and flourish over time. We have an excellent team and will stay focused on our mission to create wealth and support successful investment endeavors."

When I encouraged him to speak more specifically about how he'd like to see York change and/or grow, he repeated the same generalities. I even asked targeted questions about what industry sectors he felt the company should focus on and what rounds of seed or series funding he felt were best for York's portfolio.

"All of them," he responded with a grand wave of his arm. "The more, the better if you ask me."

I glanced over at Ellison and saw the same look on his face I probably had on mine. Surprise mixed with serious concern. This was the CFO of an incredibly large venture capital firm, and he was speaking like a first-year marketing intern. The man was playing me.

"That sounds excellent, Desi," I said, standing up to indicate the end of the meeting. Whatever reason Desi Martinez had for answering my questions so vaguely, it was clear he was not going to continue in his role as CFO any longer. "Why don't I think over your outlook and come back to you with any questions I have? I appreciate your time."

We shook hands before Desi turned to thank Ellison too. "Ellison, son, I hope to see you back with us now that we're under exciting new management," he said with a smile. "I'm sure your dad would be happy to have a York on the team regardless of who's in charge."

"Yes, sir. Thank you," Ellison said politely.

As soon as Desi left, Ellison moved to close the door behind him. "That was a disaster," he muttered.

"Where the hell did he come from? Is he that uninformed, or was he trolling me?"

"Does it matter? If he's uninformed, he needs to go. If he's disrespecting you by acting uninformed, he needs to go. It's the latter, by the way. Besides, when I asked him about the investments, he claimed ignorance. That didn't surprise me. What did surprise me was the look on his face. Like we both knew he was lying about it. He had a kind of... I don't know. Twinkle in his eye, like I was supposed to know the truth of it somehow. Regardless, if he did this knowingly, he deliberately violated company policy. That could have legal ramifications. If York was ever tied up in litigation over questionable business practices and it came to light that the executives—"

I held up a hand to stop him since he seemed fairly upset about it. "You're right. The truth doesn't matter if we're going to let him go anyway. I appreciate your honesty about it." And it was true. I was pleasantly surprised, not only at his candor with me, but by the obvious disappointment he felt at the disloyalty by the York CFO. It implied Ellison himself had an ethical standard. And that he chose the side of right rather than the side of family loyalty.

I wasn't sure I could trust it, but it was at least a promising start.

He let out a shaky breath. "I'm fucking pissed. Makes me wonder if my dad knew about it."

I had no doubt Warren knew about it. The man was shady as hell. Marcel had already found plenty of instances of Warren's nefarious business practices, which was one of the reasons I felt zero guilt at taking over his business. He was a snake who lied, cheated, and would steal if he could get away with it.

York Capital's investment partners were in much better hands without Warren York and people like Desi Martinez at the helm.

"Tell me about Duckworth," I said, changing the subject.

"First, tell me what you're trying to do that requires his help."

I almost snapped at him that I was the one who gave the commands, not him. But I reminded myself of what I knew about negotiations—that I would get further if I gave a little. If I let him think he was winning.

"I have purchased the real estate covering almost a city block in Hell's Kitchen. The only remaining building I need to acquire is owned by Duckworth and houses his law firm. He refuses to consider any purchase offer. The man won't even take a meeting."

Ellison looked interested. "What do you want to build? Housing? Retail?"

I didn't want to disclose all the details of the project to him, so I simply said, "Mostly office space with retail on the ground level and a few residential spaces. The problem is, Ian Duckworth's building is in the center of the block. The project can't move forward until he agrees to sell, and so far, he's not even coming to the table to negotiate."

"He's not easy to do business with, especially real estate business," Ellison agreed. "There's a reason for that."

When it looked like he wasn't going to elaborate, I almost made a snide comment to encourage him to spill the beans. Thankfully, he finally continued.

"He's been burned before. Badly." Ellison studied me as if trying to decide how much he should say. "None of this is public information, so I'd appreciate you keeping it to yourself."

His words surprised me. Why the hell would he trust me of all people with anything? He shouldn't have. I was no more loyal to retaining his secrets than a stranger off the street.

He proceeded to tell me a story of Ian Duckworth's brother, best friend, and law partner cheating him through a series of complicated real estate investment deals.

Ellison leaned forward, his passion on the topic obvious. "Imagine being swindled by someone you trusted. Imagine finding out you were used in such a way."

"I know what it feels like to be used," I reminded him in a low voice.

His eyes snapped to meet mine, and the air grew thick between us the way it had done several times since meeting each other again yesterday.

"You're wrong," he said breathlessly. I could almost see the pulse fluttering in his neck. This subject seemed to make him nervous, which I found entirely too tantalizing. "I... I truly am sorry for what happened to you, Grey. But I wasn't—"

I shook my head to stop him. "So, Duckworth," I said, clearing my throat. "What did he do?"

Ellison grabbed a shiny red apple from the bowl on the conference table and sat back. "He swore off doing that kind of business investment anymore. I guess he realized his wealth was already large enough he didn't need to risk it that way. He doesn't even take investment tips from my dad. He eventually married a wonderful woman named Binnie McArthur, who's helped him relax a little." He grinned. "She's fiercely protective of him and would rather give up all their money than see him upset again."

"How do you know all of this?" I asked.

"Ian and Binnie are my godparents," he said before taking a bite of the apple with a big audible crunch.

I stared at him. The lone holdout on the most important project of my career was Ellison York's godfather. Of course he was. The room around me wavered in my vision. Suddenly, I felt like I was right back in that storage closet, discovering yet again that Ellison York held all the power.

And once again, he was going to do his best to ruin my future happiness. And why wouldn't he? I'd treated him like shit. I'd made him feed me, for fuck's sake.

I blew out a breath and tried to come to terms with the loss of my Hell's Kitchen project. I fully expected Ellison to encourage Duckworth to continue holding out on me. It would be sweet revenge for what I did to his family.

"And if you want," he continued, shocking the hell out of me. "I can put in a good word for you."

8

ELLISON

"Begin by seizing something which your opponent holds dear; then he will be amenable to your will."

~ Sun Tzu, *The Art of War*

I could tell, as I told the story of Ian's hesitations, that Grey didn't trust me. It was a blow to my confidence in dealing with him, but not an unexpected one.

"I'd have to talk to him before they leave town, though. They're going to the Hamptons for at least a week."

"When are they leaving?"

"Any day now, probably. They host a house party there every September for their wedding anniversary," I explained. "It's like... like if your grandmother wanted to try recreating a mashup between *The Great Gatsby* and a family reunion at the Kennedy compound on Cape Cod. Or maybe a *Downton Abbey* house party... oh, who cares. It sounds like a total bore, but it's actually really fun. I've only been a few times since college. I usually have to work. But I went a lot growing up and remember loving it. I learned how to play croquet and backgammon."

I could tell by the look on his face, Grey wasn't impressed.

"How nice for you," he drawled. "I had similar summer fun growing up. It involved hanging our neighbors' clothes out on the line on washing day when brownouts left the dryers inoperable. A penny a shirt added up when you hung out laundry for most of the people in the building."

I was an idiot. Our upbringings had been horribly different to the point I would never be able to truly understand how he'd grown up.

"We should go," I blurted without thinking. "To the house party. It'd be the best way to get to know Ian personally. You can try to build trust with him or at least get to know him a little. It might help."

Okay, now I was an even bigger idiot. What the hell was I thinking? And why was I offering this gift to the man who was trying to steal my family's business?

Grey lifted an eyebrow at me. "Go? To the Hamptons?"

"Never mind," I said quickly. "That's a terrible idea. Forget I said anything."

I shoved the apple in my mouth to give myself time to think. Grey wasn't the type to let an opportunity like this go.

"I don't think it's a terrible idea," he said slowly. "I think it's an excellent idea. How do I get an invitation to the house party?"

"You don't," I said after swallowing the apple. "Only their closest friends and family are invited."

"And friends of friends," he prompted.

"No," I said, shaking my head. "Only spouses and partners."

His eyes lit up. My stomach dropped as soon as I realized the direction of his thoughts.

"No," I said again.

"You and I are partners. Of a kind."

"We're not."

"I've had my tongue in your mouth," he said silkily. Those eyes pinned me in place until I felt like I couldn't breathe, couldn't move. "And other things of yours. It could be said that you owe me."

Oh god.

"No, but—"

"We're going," he said in his low, commanding voice, the one that had a history of literally bringing me to my knees.

I needed to get some power back. I needed to remember my goal.

"If I do this for you, introduce you to them as a stand-up guy and reputable businessman, you have to agree to give me back York Capital."

Grey almost laughed. "Not happening."

"I don't mean the full value of the company. I just mean the name, history, and any investment holdings that predate my father's tenure. You can transfer the remaining investment assets to another holding company." I thought this was excessively fair.

"I can succeed with Duckworth on my own," Grey said, exposing the newly annoying ego he had.

"No, you can't. Not if I warn him off you."

Grey eyed me with suspicion. "You can't work against me while under contract at York."

"That's correct. But I'm only under contract for two more weeks, and I happen to know Ian won't be signing any legal paperwork on a deal that big before he returns from vacation in a few weeks. I will have time to stop him."

"You would risk your parents' home?"

"Our agreement was my working as your PA for the remainder of my term. I am doing an excellent job of it. Unless you truly are a dishonorable businessman, I don't believe you'll renege on our deal."

I could tell he'd *like* to, but I also knew he didn't want to be known as a thief or a liar. There was one thing he held tightly to since that night at the club, and it was the fact he'd been honest and true. Unlike with my father, honor meant something to Grey. It wasn't easy to accuse my father and me of being dishonorable if he was as well.

He took a moment to think about it, and damn if the man didn't always look so calm and steady. Finally, he met my eyes again. "If Duckworth agrees to sell to me at a fair price, I will agree to your terms."

"That's ridiculous. I don't have any control over whether or not he'll sell."

The very edge of Grey's lip curled up. "Then you'd better help me find a way to convince him."

"If I do this, and he doesn't sell, we still get the company back, but you strip all the assets, including the historical ones," I counteroffered.

"Ellison, you're not in a position of strength in this negotiation."

My name spoken in Grey Blackwood's deep voice made my stomach tighten. I was beginning to think he was right. Part of me wanted to do whatever he said.

"It's my personal reputation on the line. The only way this works is if I actually take you as my boyfriend. Do you have any idea how that's going to look?"

The more I thought about it, the more my stomach revolted, but I didn't miss the flare of... *something*... in his eyes when I said he'd have to be my boyfriend.

"It's going to look like you're gay," he said in that annoying-as-fuck calm voice.

"I'm not gay."

We stared at each other. I didn't bother adding that I was obviously at least bi. Surely that had been obvious when I'd been willing to suck him off in the closet.

"Sure you're not. You just like dick." He muttered something else that sounded like "Typical."

I hated him thinking I was homophobic. "I don't like dick," I snapped. Grey's eyes narrowed in anger, so I did my best to press on. "I just like... uh..." I couldn't exactly say *your dick* since I'd never actually seen it. "I was attracted to *you*, not to men in general. So, yes, it would be quite a surprise to my family if I brought a man along as my plus-one."

I'd deliberately used past tense when mentioning my attraction to him. His ego was big enough without me letting on that I still wanted him, still craved him to the point of embarrassing, emergency-jerk-in-the-washroom levels of need.

"But you'd do it," he said.

"If the price was right." I sat up straight.

"Gay for pay?" he asked slowly, as if tasting the words. "How very mercenary."

"No. I don't mind them seeing me with a man. I mind them seeing me with the man who betrayed my family."

Grey shifted in his seat. His long legs moved under the thin drape of his suit pants. I noticed a flash of bright yellow on his socks, but his pants quickly lowered again to hide it before I could see what the design was.

Lucky fucking socks.

"But you would do it?"

"To save York? I can't say I'm immune to some pride in my family legacy. York Capital has been in my family for a very long time. I'd hate to see it lost because of my uncle's stupidity."

"Can't you tell them I'm just a friend?" Grey asked.

I shook my head. "Me being friends with the man who took over York Capital would be nearly as bad. Besides, he's paranoid. I told you. As it is, Ian will suspect us because you're trying to purchase his building."

Grey cocked his head at me as if trying to figure me out. "Suspect? Won't he see right through you?"

My face heated. How was I supposed to admit that Ian was the only person I'd ever told about my attraction to Grey? "He, ah... he..." I swallowed. "Let's just say, he knows the truth about that night in the closet. He knows I went willingly."

Again, Grey's eyes flashed with an intensity that unsettled me. "Is that right? And he believes you?"

I nodded. "I told him I'd been watching you in Calculus class that semester. He knew it wasn't... wasn't really about the dare."

A barely perceptible change in Grey's chest rising and falling clued me in to the changes in his breathing. He went instantly silent. Watchful. Predatory. "Is that so?"

I wasn't sure if he believed me, and I could hardly blame him for not trusting me. But it was the truth. I'd confessed to Ian Duckworth that I'd had a crush on a kid in my class and had fucked it up. Terribly.

Ian had been the one to lead me through my feelings and everything that came after.

"Anyway," I said, quickly, before things could get even more awkward between us. "Ian is the one person who might actually believe me if I tell him something's going on between us." I swallowed. "And, um, he's not super close to my father. It's my mom who's close to Binnie and Ian. They were her parents' good friends for years and became like an aunt and uncle to her. Ian thinks my father is... not great."

"We have that in common, then," Grey said. He leaned forward and rested one forearm on the table. "Would they believe we got together when I was in the process of taking over York? I find that hard to believe."

He was right. It was implausible. Besides, getting together and being serious enough to bring him to a family event less than a week later was hardly believable either.

"You're right," I said. "He'll think I'm a terrible person for dating the man who acquired York against my father's wishes, and he'll blame you for corrupting me."

"Surely we can come up with a plausible explanation. We'll think on it. In the meantime, I need you to make us dinner reservations. It seems Ben Aldeen enjoyed our meeting this morning and would like to discuss the offer in more detail."

"Really? He wants to discuss the *offer*?" I asked, unable to hold back a snicker.

Grey frowned. "You seem surprised."

"Not at all. I saw the way he looked at you. But you have to admit it was an awfully fast turnaround, especially if he was already set on declining you."

The haughty businessman returned. "He was never set on declining me. He was set on declining York."

I rolled my eyes and reached for my phone to find a restaurant.

"He mentioned being vegetarian, so I'll try Avant Garden. I think he'd like it."

I felt Grey's eyes on me as I searched up the reservation app. It was unnerving to feel that stare on me all the time. I couldn't figure out if he was looking at me with active dislike or if he was simply trying to figure me out. Either way, it left me itchy and restless.

Being in the room with Grey made every hair follicle on my skin tighten. I was aware of him in a way I'd never felt about anyone else before. I tried to suppress my reaction to his presence, even though my brain had been spinning nonstop since coming into contact with him yesterday after a long, fifteen-year absence.

How many times had I thought of him—dreamed of him—in those intervening years? Hundreds? Thousands? Millions?

As cornball as it was, Grey Blackwood was the one who got away. No, I didn't know him well enough to claim he was my perfect match or any kind of soul mate. That would be absurd. But he was the one I'd wanted with a desperation at the time and the one I wanted still, for good or bad.

I made the reservation with heat crawling up my neck, and when I was done, I discovered Grey had begun talking on the phone to someone about technical performance reports related to one of his investments. Assuming I wasn't needed for the moment, I took the opportunity to slip out and make my way to the men's room.

The dim, cool space was quiet and peaceful. Quite a change from the night before. The faint scent of cleanser filled the air, and light sparkled off the clean fixtures. I leaned my hands on the counter and glanced at myself in the mirror, wondering how Grey saw me now compared to all those years ago.

I had little wrinkles next to my eyes I hadn't had back then. My hair was longer, but only because I'd been so busy over the summer wrapping up my work at York. I'd worked nights and weekends transitioning my projects over to other members of the legal team. When I hadn't been at work, I'd been preparing my apartment to sell and packing my things for the move to Vermont.

My phone rang, and I answered it without thinking. "Ellison."

"Finally. You haven't answered my calls," my father whined. "That asshole has you running around like crazy."

"How do you know that?" I wondered out loud. Grey had banned him from the building, but clearly he still had spies. "I would have thought you'd be busy meeting with your attorneys."

He let out a humorless chuckle. "You are my attorney. Or have you forgotten?"

I rolled my eyes. I was his attorney first and his son only when he wanted something. "I can't see a way out of this, Dad. You might want to consider early retirement. What does Mom think?"

"I'm not about to let that pissant force me into early retirement, and your mother is too busy planning her trip to the Hamptons to pay much attention to what's going on. I assured her you would find a way to reverse Mark's stock sale."

"That's not possible," I said baldly, leaning against the counter. "The only thing we can hope for now is to convince Grey to leave us the company and just take the assets."

"He's not taking my life's work from me. If you can't find us a way out of this mess, I have some other people who will."

"What does that mean?" I asked impatiently.

"I have people looking into Blackwood's business practices. He can't have gotten to where he is as quickly as he did without cutting some legal corners. I'm going to find them and threaten to turn him in if he doesn't give us back the company."

"I'm going to pretend like you didn't just confess intent to blackmail," I said with a sigh. "You're angry, and I get that. But this isn't the way to go about it."

"Then find me another way," he growled before disconnecting.

I sighed and looked back at the mirror. I'd been this close to freedom, this close to a cozy life in Vermont away from the unethical and aggressive business practices here in the city. I didn't love this industry, but I'd stayed in it for the purpose of funding the academy.

Since finding out about the takeover yesterday, I hadn't let myself think about how this change in ownership and management would affect the York Foundation and its charitable efforts. What would

Grey do to the future of it? I'd worked so fucking hard to grow that part of York Capital, and after bringing Nessa on, the two of us had made sure a healthy portion of York's profits had gone to good causes.

And now this.

I hadn't even thought to check in with Nessa since this happened. After quickly finishing up in the men's room, I made my way down the hall to Nessa's office. "Hey, you free?" I asked after knocking on her open door.

She turned around and shot me a wide smile. "For you? Always. How was Vermont? I heard you got called back early."

I sat in her guest chair and slumped down. "That's putting it mildly. What's the word down here about the takeover?"

Her office was part of the Human Resources and support staff office block, which meant she usually had the best gossip around.

She glanced past me to make sure no one was in earshot. "Honestly? Most people are happy about it. Blackwood has a good reputation. And you know how people feel about your dad."

It was true. My dad treated non-executive-level employees like furniture. To him, they were a line item on an expense list. His goal was to keep profits high by keeping expenses down, so he was not known for treating employees particularly well.

"How does Grey have a good reputation? I haven't heard anything about him besides his acquisitions."

She rested her chin on her hand. "Did you know Grey Blackwood is one of the largest donors to Robin Hood here in the city? Supposedly, poverty and homelessness are two of his biggest charitable causes. Miranda says she thinks he's an even bigger donor under anonymous donations."

Miranda Cho was the director of HR. Her husband was the director of a youth arts foundation and sat on the board of a couple of other charity organizations in the city as well. If anyone would know about Grey's involvement in good causes, it was Martin Cho.

"Besides," she said with a grin, "anyone that hot has to be a better boss than Warren. Don't tell my husband I said this, but I wouldn't mind a visit in the storage closet with him. I'm a little jealous of you if you want to know the truth."

I groaned and willed my face not to heat up. "I'm sorry."

"What for?" she asked, sitting back in surprise. "We were broken up."

I shrugged. "I know, but still. I didn't want you to think..." I shrugged again. "I don't know."

Nessa laughed. "I knew it was just pranks and dares. You guys were always doing that stuff. Remember when Porter Kingsley showed up in a bikini at Caroline Moser's sweet sixteen?"

She must have realized I hadn't joined in her laughter. "Ellison? It was a dare, wasn't it?"

I nodded. "There was a dare involved, yes."

"So why do you look like you just swallowed a lemon? You're not still embarrassed, are you? You've been paying penance on that situation for a long time now."

I nodded again. "I'm embarrassed for not sticking up for him. I'm embarrassed for not... admitting that I wanted to be in that closet with him regardless of the dare."

There, I'd said it. I'd admitted my attraction to someone other than Ian. I watched Nessa for her reaction.

Her smile was soft and understanding. "That explains a lot. I've often wondered based on everything you've done since. Did Grey know it was more than a dare?"

I opened my mouth to tell her yes, of course he had. But I stopped and reassessed. "He does now. I thought he did at the time, but now I wonder if I was wrong. It doesn't matter, really. Too much water under that bridge by far."

"There's no such thing," she said. "At least, I don't think so. It's never too late to apologize to someone for being wrong."

"I'm trying."

"And do you still wish you were in the closet with him?" She flushed pink. "The literal closet, not the metaphorical one."

"God yes," I blurted. "So freaking much. But that makes me a horrible person. Doesn't it?"

"Why? Because of your father? Because of York?"

"Yes."

"Do you want to be in that closet for love or lust?"

The question stopped me in my tracks. It could only be lust since I didn't know Grey Blackwood well enough for love. But if I'd only wanted to get with a guy physically, there'd been many other men since then I could have experimented with. It wasn't just about the physical. There was something about *him* that attracted me. Like a kind of magnetism.

"I don't know," I said, because it was easy.

Nessa shrugged. "We can't help who we like. Don't forget how I met Jaxon."

I chuckled. Her now husband was an investigative journalist who'd uncovered corruption at the charity where Nessa had worked after college. The exposé he'd written had led to the charity's closure and Nessa's sudden joblessness. She'd hated him for it, right up until the moment she'd started loving him instead. Their subsequent relationship had falsely convinced her work friends she'd been his source for the article, and she'd lost all of her friends.

"True," I said with a laugh. "So, everyone around here basically thinks the Blackwood acquisition is a good thing?"

She shook her head. "Not everyone. I worry about his plans for the foundation."

That surprised me. "You said he was a large corporate giver. Surely, you don't think he'd close down the foundation?"

She shrugged. "He might simply consolidate it into the Blackwood Giving Program, which would put me out of a job."

"Unless he brought you over to their program," I suggested, even knowing it was unlikely. Finding a good job in corporate giving wasn't easy.

"True. But at least he's charity-minded, unlike your father. You and I both know once you left, Warren would have found a way to make the foundation smaller and smaller until it didn't need an actual director any longer. I've been on borrowed time for a while now."

She was right. My father had already threatened to dismantle the foundation once before to get me to bend to his will, and I'd caved to his demands for Nessa's sake. Now that I was gone, he'd have no incentive to protect her job. This was the updated version of him taking away Gigi's allowance when I disappointed him.

"I'm sorry."

"None of this is on you, Ellison." Nessa crossed her arms in front of her chest. A small photo of her daughter and son caught my attention on the shelf behind her. One looked like her, and one looked like her husband. Mini-me's. "Your father's never cared about corporate giving—*you* have. All he wanted was a tax write-off. You know this."

She was right. About all of it.

"Well, hopefully Grey isn't the selfish jackass many people think he is," I added with a weak smile.

"He's definitely not. And I think you already know that."

I stood up, trying to hide my hot cheeks. "I'd better go. He'll be looking for me. He probably has a toilet that needs scrubbing."

Nessa got up and walked around her desk to give me a tight hug. "He doesn't know what he's missing," she whispered as she held me. The familiar embrace was a comfort. I appreciated the friendship we'd managed to have all these years since reconnecting.

"Oh yeah?" I asked, teasing. "Am I that good in bed?"

She pulled back and winked at me. "Second-best, maybe."

I laughed and turned around, almost colliding with a solid, broad chest. Grey's hands shot out to keep me from running into him, and I caught a quick whiff of his apple scent. It didn't smell like any of the fancy scents offered in his guest bathroom at the apartment, and it made me wonder idly what it was.

"Sorry," I grunted, fighting the heat of embarrassment.

"I need you," he said gruffly before clearing his throat. "There's been a change in the dinner arrangements."

He had his stoic mask on, but I also sensed he was a little bit ruffled beneath his put-together veneer. I nodded and agreed to follow him back to the conference room, throwing a quick wave back to Nessa before leaving.

When we got back to the conference room that was serving as Grey's office, I asked what change was needed to the reservation.

"I didn't realize Vanessa Roberts worked here. *Your* Vanessa." Grey looked frustrated for some reason. The fact he thought of her as mine, that he knew my history with her, made me feel a strange kind of satisfaction.

"Her name is Vanessa Worden now," I corrected.

His eyes blinked over at me. "She's married?" Was that relief I saw on his face? Surely not.

"Yes, for at least eight years. They have two kids."

"Ah, well. Glad to know she's... settled, then. We need to add a few extra people to our dinner reservation," Grey said, changing the subject.

He explained Ben Aldeen's request to bring along a couple of additional people, and I proceeded to change the reservation. When I was done, I noticed Grey frowning.

"Do you ever smile?" I asked without thinking.

His eyebrows lifted. "Of course I smile."

"When?"

"When I inform pompous assholes they no longer own their family business."

I let out a breath. "Touché."

"Why do you ask? Are you disappointed in my professional demeanor?"

My eyes couldn't help but travel up and down Grey's whole body. It was true he came across as very professional. His tailored suits were perfection; his haircut was pristine. His height and commanding presence screamed corporate commander. Everything about the man did it for me, even when he looked annoyed or angry.

"Not disappointed," I managed to say, swallowing thickly. "I just wonder if you've ever heard of the concept of catching more flies with honey than vinegar."

Suddenly, his face split into a wide grin, dimples popped out on his cheeks, and white teeth sparkled like a damned toothpaste ad. It was startling and absolutely stunning. My heart leapt off the high dive and went flying through the air.

"Better?" he asked.

I realized the giant smile didn't reach his eyes.

"No," I said, looking away in disappointment. "I was hoping you'd smile for real."

Uncomfortable silence stretched between us before Grey cleared his throat. "Well, it's a good thing I don't work for you, isn't it?"

A few minutes later, his phone rang, and he stayed busy with work calls the rest of the afternoon.

It wasn't until late that night, after an endless boring dinner with Ben Aldeen and his aggressive personal attorneys, that I finally realized Nessa had inadvertently given me the solution to the Duckworth house party problem.

9

GREY

"The opportunity of defeating the enemy is provided by the enemy himself."

~ Sun Tzu, *The Art of War*

Ellison didn't say much on the way home from the restaurant. He looked exhausted, and I couldn't blame him. Aldeen had brought his attorneys with him, and they'd spent hours hammering Ellison with questions about every possible topic from York Capital, to contract language in investment agreements, to obscure cases in which venture capital companies had taken advantage of small businesses via legal shenanigans, to his legal education, and more.

"You handled that very well," I said in a low voice as we entered the elevator of my building. Ellison's eyes blinked up at me. When he stood this close, I was reminded of our slight height difference. "With the attorneys, I mean."

"Thank you. That was... unexpected."

"Agreed. I thought he was bringing business partners or even family members."

Ellison let out a soft laugh. "Two of those lawyers were cousins of his. And they both work for one of the big-name firms in town. I should have known. I should have done my due diligence."

"You weren't going there as an attorney. There was no need for you to prepare in that way."

He looked up at me. "Even more reason I should have been prepared. I'll bet Marcel wouldn't have let you go in there blind."

I was surprised he'd picked up on enough of my real PA's competence over the past day and a half, even though Marcel had stayed primarily in the temporary offices on the floor below the main ones.

"No, probably not," I admitted. "But then again, he wouldn't have been able to correct the jackass who tried insisting a clause disclaiming future work product was standard practice in VC contracts."

Ellison's smug grin made my stomach tighten. "Scheming prick," he said with a laugh. "Does he really think you'd hire any attorney who'd let that shit through? Christ. What an idiot."

When the elevator door opened to reveal my familiar entry hall, I let out a breath and felt my shoulders fall in relief. I didn't realize how obvious I was until Ellison commented on it.

"Looks like maybe you need more 'stress relief' tonight," he muttered before turning toward the guest room. He sounded envious, like he resented me having a massage while he hadn't had the luxury.

"I didn't think to offer you the same," I said, surprising myself. Since when did I offer to hire a massage therapist for my temporary assistant, the same assistant I was supposed to be humiliating? Still, if he needed it and it was in my power to offer... "I'm happy to have him come back tonight and work you over if you'd like."

Ellison turned back to me almost in slow motion. The open-mouthed shock on his face was comical. "You *what*? You'd bring him back here to *work me over*?" His voice ended up high enough to be almost squeaky by the end. I was confused by his shock.

"He's very good. Well, Ricky is better than Ted, but it depends on how hard you like it."

"I... I... I don't know how hard I like it, to be honest. But I know I don't want it from Ricky or Ted. Jesus." He turned back toward the bedroom as my brain finally put two and two together.

"Massage," I called after him. I tried to bite back a laugh. "They're professional massage therapists, not rent boys. Naughty, naughty, Ellison. What a one-track mind you have."

I very carefully did not mention that my own mind had been rolling down the same track since he'd stepped into the York Capital conference room.

Ellison froze with his back to me. His ass looked downright edible in those suit pants, and the wrinkles in the back of his shirt made him look human and vulnerable. I wanted to run my hand down the back of his shirt and feel the warmth of his body underneath, lean forward and inhale the scent of a workday on the back of his neck.

I forced myself to look away and stop teasing him. "Anyway, let me know if you need a massage. I'm happy to arrange it."

Before I could turn around to head back to my own room, he faced me again. His cheeks were dark pink with embarrassment. "Oh. Ah... no. I mean... that's okay. I don't... I don't need to be... worked over."

I could see a hint of a quirky smile at the edge of his lips and in his eyes. I lifted a brow. "You sure?"

The air crackled between us. My brain helpfully supplied me with a speed reel of images of me shoving Ellison down on my bed and working him over myself while he writhed beneath me and groaned in pleasure.

He bit his lip and nodded. I wanted to lunge for him, chase him down the hall and slam him up against the wall, tear his clothes off and force him to submit to me. I'd grumble all of my complaints about him being way too sexy, too annoyingly irresistible, into his ear while I fucked him breathless. I could almost feel the tight clench of him around my cock, and it made me borderline resentful I couldn't have what I wanted.

To keep from saying or doing something inappropriate, I turned to make my escape.

"Grey?" he asked, sounding unsure.

I didn't dare turn back around. "What is it?"

"I have an idea for the house party."

I closed my eyes and swallowed. The pretentious weekend in the Hamptons where I would have to pretend to be in a relationship with the man I both hated and wanted.

After taking a slow, deep breath, I turned back around, ensuring my face hid all of my conflicting emotions. "What's your idea?"

Ellison's jaw moved back and forth as if he was second-guessing himself. I decided to loosen his tongue.

"Why don't we have a drink?" I offered, tilting my head in the direction of the living room. "Glass of wine or a beer?"

He nodded and followed me. "I'll take a beer. Honestly, I wish I'd thought to pack my running shoes. A jog in the park would relax me more than anything."

I thought about asking what size he wore so I could offer him the use of a pair of mine, but I clamped my lips closed. We weren't best buds. If he wanted running shoes, he could buy some.

Instead of waiting in the living room, he followed me into the kitchen and took a seat at the island. I grabbed two bottles of beer and opened them before handing him one and taking the stool next to his.

It was hard to believe that we'd been in these same seats just that morning, and his proximity had made me tense and irritable. Now it felt almost... comfortable.

I didn't like it.

Ellison took a long gulp of the cold brew before spilling his thoughts. "The only way Ian and Binnie would believe a relationship between us was serious enough for me to bring you to their party is if we've been together longer than this week."

I nodded and sipped my own beer. That was the problem. It would mean I was the worst of boyfriends for taking over the father's company while dating the son. Ian might easily believe that, since he had plenty of reason to dislike me, but it would hardly make him more amenable to doing business with me.

Ellison continued. "So we'd need a reason for you taking over the company with my blessing."

Not a bad idea.

"Maybe you'd lost trust in your father's leadership," I suggested. "Or maybe there was a legal reason someone else needed to be in charge? Maybe it's the opposite. Maybe you were trying to save your father from some... negative consequence."

He blew out a breath. "I know you don't trust me, and I completely understand why. But what I'm going to share with you... it means I would like to think I can trust you." His eyes met mine with hope and questioning.

Could he trust me? *Should* he? Probably not. Did I care about betraying his trust? Absolutely not.

Liar.

I ignored the devil on my shoulder. "I appreciate your trust," I said, because it was the truth. "Go on."

"My father and I don't get along. Ever since... well, for a long time we haven't exactly been on good terms. I went to work for York Capital under a very specific set of conditions, conditions that were enumerated in a legal contract between us."

His confession surprised me. I had wondered why Warren York had a binding employment contract with his son, but I hadn't imagined it was because Warren had forced his son into some upper-class version of indentured servitude. He was an even bigger ass than I'd thought.

"What kind of conditions?"

His long fingers idly drew lines through the condensation on the side of his beer bottle. "My sister and I started an education program for... it doesn't matter. Suffice to say, it is a charity project that needed, and continues to need, significant funding. My father agreed to create the York Foundation in order to fund our school but only if I agreed to get my law degree the way he'd always planned and join the company for a twenty-year term."

"You didn't want to go to law school?" I asked, completely abandoning the point of the conversation.

"Definitely not. I don't enjoy the law. That's not to say I didn't enjoy law school itself. I studied under some of the best legal minds of our time, and I love to learn. But practicing corporate law is... not at all what I wanted to do with my life."

It was on the tip of my tongue to ask him what he did want to do with his life, but I held back. It was none of my business.

"So why did you leave after... what, twelve years?"

"A little over eleven. I negotiated him successfully down to a ten-year commitment. He most likely assumed I'd be entrenched by that time and unwilling to give up my lifestyle in the city for a no-name school in rural Vermont. He was wrong. I counted down the days, weeks, months, and years until it was finally time for me to leave. According to our agreement, he would continue to fund the school for five more years after my departure. That would hopefully give me enough time to find alternate funding sources for the charitable arm of the program."

He took another sip of beer. Finally, I learned the reason for his move to Vermont.

Ellison let out a bitter laugh. "At the ten-year mark, he threatened to fire Nessa and dismantle the foundation. He claimed he'd continue the donations for the five years to honor the letter of our agreement, but that would be the extent of York's corporate giving. All of our other charity recipients would be screwed, and Nessa would be out of a job. She was four months pregnant with her second child. I agreed to one more year to give her time to find another job—which of course was impossible while she was pregnant and then on maternity leave—and notify the charities that York's donations would only be single donations from here on out rather than repeating commitments."

"That was awfully generous of you," I said. "You must still have strong feelings for her."

Ellison shot me a look. "Strong feelings of friendship and respect. And on the practical side, I didn't want York to be hit with a lawsuit—which I would have secretly encouraged her to pursue—accusing York of firing her for her pregnancy status."

"Your dad is a horrible person," I said dryly.

"Oh, yeah. And the worst part is? I don't know if he actually would have fired her. I have no idea whether he was bluffing, because he lies and threatens and manipulates so much, I swear he convinces himself. But he also has no sense of decency, especially regarding people he thinks are beneath him—which is to say, pretty much everyone—so I wouldn't put anything past him."

"You really dislike him."

He snorted. "What gave it away? My point is, Ian and Binnie know all of these details. So here's my idea. I tell them that you and I have been dating in secret for years. Once you and I were dating long enough, I confided my fears in you, and you decided to take over the company to secure my pet project, the York Foundation."

"Why would I do that?" I asked.

Ellison frowned at me. "Because you love me. And you want to make me happy."

He was so fucking beautiful, even when frowning. My fingers itched to touch his late-day stubble, run through his messy, over-grown locks. Kiss his soft lips and tell him... yes. There was a part of me—as horribly ill-informed and stupid as it may have been—that wanted nothing more than his happiness.

But that was stuff better left in my dream world. In my dream world, Ellison York wasn't the selfish prick who'd set me up in that closet.

"I meant," I said carefully, "why wouldn't I simply take over York's commitment to your charity with the Blackwood Giving Program?"

Pink suffused Ellison's cheeks, and I marveled at how his fair skin was so good at betraying his emotions.

"Good point," he admitted in a defeated tone.

I hated seeing him disappointed, so I racked my brain for another solution. And I didn't pay too close attention to why I felt the way I did. I was in search of a solution to my Duckworth problem. That was all.

"What if... what if I bought your uncle Mark's shares to keep them in the family?" I suggested, thinking out loud.

Ellison's eyebrows shot up. "Like... like we're serious enough in this fake relationship, you wanted to make sure Mark didn't sell his shares to a random stranger? You did it to save us from being taken over by someone with hostile intent."

The irony wasn't lost on either of us.

"It would make sense," I said as the thought began to settle in and flesh itself out in my mind. "And then my leadership changes could be explained by my disapproval for how your dad has been running the company. If you and your dad aren't close, and if *Ian* and your father aren't close, then it wouldn't be seen as such a bad thing, right?"

"And since they know I don't want a future at York Capital, it would be like forcing Dad to pass the company down to *you*, his future son-in-law."

This was ridiculous. Surely, no one in their right mind would believe any of this.

"It's an awfully big lie to tell your godparents," I warned. "Why would you risk your relationship with them in that way?"

Ellison hesitated. "To get my family business back. Obviously."

I felt my back teeth grind together. For some reason, I hated the fact he was still fighting for his father even though he'd tried telling me he had no loyalty to him anymore.

"And how will you explain things afterward? Once we're no longer in our fake relationship and you're left with the shell of a family business?"

Ellison's eyes met mine. "Maybe I will tell them I was deceived by a corporate raider. You used me all along to get your hands on our family business."

If he expected me to be affronted, he was going to be disappointed. I let out a huff of laughter. "Somehow I feel like that was your intent in this fake boyfriend scheme all along. Leave me looking like an ass."

He eventually grinned at me. "If the Gucci brogue fits..."

I looked down at my dress shoes. "They're Tom Ford, actually."

His laugh came free and easy, bubbly enough to make me almost join in, and I rarely laughed. For some reason, I'd been closer than usual since spending time with this confounding man.

"Do you think it will work?" Ellison asked when he pulled himself together. "We'd have to really sell it. Ian knows me better than most people. He also knows... about... what happened at the club. I told you that already. So he knows..." He seemed to be stumbling over his words.

"What?" I asked with some frustration. "Just say it. You already told me there was more to it than the dare. Are you saying he knows you're attracted to men?"

"He knows I'm attracted to *you*," he blurted. His face flushed again, which made me sit up taller with a little pride.

"I believe you meant that in the past tense," I said as if I didn't care at all.

I cared.

"Well, that too," he muttered, focusing intently on his beer bottle. The kitchen sparkled cleanly around us in the warm light from only the hanging fixtures over the island. A faint smell of lemons and bleach lingered from Jenny's attentions earlier in the day. It took a minute for his implication to hit me.

I opened my mouth to quiz him on it before I shut it with a snap. I wasn't going there. His attraction to me was irrelevant. It wasn't like I was going to act on it anyway.

"Won't that work in our favor?" I asked. "Make a relationship between us more believable?"

Ellison kept his eyes on the bottle. "Well, yes. But... it's possible he could ask you about it. Maybe ask you if you forgave me or how we got past the misunderstanding all those years ago."

"*Misunderstanding*?" I asked. "Is that what it was?" My voice came out way more biting than I'd intended, exposing how much this still bothered me. I tried to rein it in. "Never mind. We would have to... let it go. Pretend to let it go, anyway."

Ellison studied me, looking noticeably less confident than before. "And could you do that? Pretend to let it go?"

It was a good question. It certainly wouldn't be easy for me to lie about it if asked directly. As for pretending to be Ellison's boyfriend, though? That would probably be all too easy.

Dangerously easy.

"I would have to, wouldn't I?" I asked, standing up and taking my unfinished bottle to the sink.

"You want that building pretty badly, don't you?" He didn't ask in a snide way, but more in the tone of dawning realization.

He'd been candid with me, so I was candid with him. "I do. Yes. This project is incredibly important. More important to me than York, as you can see." I turned back around to see his reaction. He nodded.

"And York Capital's legacy is more important to me than the incredible betrayal my father will feel when he sees us together."

Fuck.

"Your father will be at the house party?"

"He wasn't planning on going, but as soon as he finds out you and I will be there together, he'll change his plans. I have no doubt."

The party would be excruciating with Warren York there. "And you don't trust him enough with the truth."

Ellison nodded. "No way. He would tell me it wasn't worth it. He'd rather lose the company, lose everything, than imagine the two of us happily together, even if it's fake. Appearances are everything to him."

I ground my teeth together again. "He hates me that much?"

Ellison brushed past me to set his bottle next to mine by the sink. On his way out of the kitchen, he looked back over his shoulder. "No. He hates *me* that much."

And then he disappeared down the hall.

After rinsing the bottles and dropping them into the recycling container, I poured a glass of water and made my way to my bedroom. I'd spent years studying strategy, and I used the next hour thinking through how I would tackle the challenge of a high-society house party.

Google got a workout on my laptop, considering I barely even knew what an event like this would even look like.

Hamptons house party.

The results were horrifying. There were hundreds of drunk yuppies half-dressed standing by a large swimming pool. I changed my search terms to "old people Hamptons house party" and saw a man in a douchey suit holding the reins to a fancy horse, also standing by a large swimming pool.

I groaned and shut my laptop.

I knew what it was like to be a fish out of water, but this would be taking it to the extreme. According to the internet, there would be long, lavish dinner parties and possible *lawn bowling*. I'd need to know what the fuck *shuttlecock* was and how to play it. No.

No.

This was impossible. It had been hard enough hiring someone to teach me etiquette several years ago after I'd embarrassed myself at a business dinner. This would be a hundred times worse.

I almost threw myself on Marcel's mercy, except I knew if I asked him how to *jack balls* in lawn bowling, he'd never let me live it down.

I marched down the hall to the guest room, where I knocked on Ellison's door, fully intending to back out of his proposed scheme.

"What is it?" he called through the door.

I was so disturbed by my own anxiety, it didn't occur to me he hadn't actually invited me in. I opened the door to find Ellison York completely naked. His back was to me as he reached for a pair of pajama pants on the bed.

His body was city-pale, but god... there were miles and miles of damp, creamy skin, slightly pink from a recent shower. The tight globes of his ass bunched as he leaned a little to one side, and the slender curves of his leg muscles shifted under his skin. I only had a split second to drink it all in before he processed my entrance and scrambled to get the pants on.

"Shit, fuck, sorry," he said quickly.

I turned my back to him, ostensibly to give him time to dress, but in reality to give my dick time to stand down. Upon catching him like this, all the blood in my body had shot south with alarming speed. I couldn't remember the last time I'd had such a strong reaction to someone.

"No, I'm sorry. I didn't realize you hadn't invited me in." I cleared my throat. "I, uh..."

What had I come in here for? My head was busy and loud with images and thoughts that were no help in remembering my purpose.

"You can turn around," he said a little breathlessly.

I turned around and saw him pulling on a soft T-shirt. The wash-worn shirt was inside out, hiding the print from view. I couldn't help but take in this casual version of him, even though I probably looked like a greedy voyeur.

"Did you need something?" he asked.

I opened my mouth to say yes, finally remembering my purpose. I'd come in here to tell him the plan for the Duckworth house party was untenable. It would be impossible for me to pass as his... *anything*. I wasn't one of them. I wasn't elite or from an old-money family. I would make a fool of myself and embarrass him in the process.

But he looked so sexy and sweet standing there in his old pajamas with his bare feet and wet, curly hair. I thought of what it would be like to hold his hand, to lean over and whisper in his ear, to... *hell*. To share a room with him.

I swallowed. He was too tempting, and this was too dangerous. I opened my mouth to tell him that this would never work and we would simply need to find a different way of introducing me to Duckworth. Besides, I wasn't about to risk losing York Capital when all I'd ever wanted was to screw Warren and Ellison York over.

"I wanted to make sure you remembered to make the necessary arrangements with a helicopter charter," I said instead. "I don't want to spend hours in traffic trying to get out there on Labor Day weekend."

Ellison's face split into a wide grin.

And I was well and truly fucked.

10

ELLISON

"Appear where you are not expected."

~ Sun Tzu, *The Art of War*

I was unexpectedly happy about the plan despite my giant dumpster full of misgivings. Maybe I was secretly excited to screw my father over, or maybe I was subconsciously relieved to get away from the city and the York Capital offices. Regardless, I spent the next couple of days with a spring in my step. But on Thursday morning, it came crashing down.

The unexpected blow came from my mother.

"Why does Binnie Duckworth think you are bringing a young *man* to the Hamptons party?" she asked.

I hadn't told my godmother the identity of my boyfriend, but I'd obviously had to inform her I was bringing a plus-one to her home for the week. She hadn't been nearly as surprised as I'd expected, but I'd chalked it up to her distraction this close to hosting so many people. I was sure she was slammed with arrangements that still needed to be made.

"Because I am bringing a man to the party," I said, trying to stay calm. It wasn't every day you outed yourself to a parent, especially when you were thirty-five. "Although I might argue with the term 'young.' He's in his midthirties like me."

A soft snort on the other side of the kitchen reminded me I wasn't alone. Grey was pouring his second cup of coffee for the morning while Jenny had run downstairs to sign for a delivery of some kind.

I shot Grey a middle finger when he made a judgy face at me about the age crack.

My mother's voice came back over the phone. "A man? But... Ian and Binnie only allow spouses and serious partners, Ellison."

My heart rate spiked, and my palms started to sweat. "I know. He, uh... he is. A serious... partner, I mean. My, um... boy—" My voice broke on the word and squeaked loudly enough to jerk Grey's head up. He frowned at me, and I gave him a weak smile. "He's my boyfriend," I said, as if it wasn't a monumental announcement.

Grey Blackwood is my boyfriend.

My stomach somersaulted.

"So, yeah," I said, "That's... that's the situation."

The repetition of the soft snort made me want to kick my *boyfriend* in the nuts. I narrowed my eyes at him, and he held up his hands in defense.

"When were you going to tell me? I didn't even know you were gay!" She whispered the last word as if it was an embarrassing plague like leprosy or hemorrhoids.

"I'm not gay," I corrected. Grey's opinions made themselves known again with a dramatic eye roll. I gritted my teeth. "I'm bi. There. That. That's what I am. I'm bi. Bisexual, that is."

"Christ," Grey muttered, turning back to his coffee.

I muted the call and hissed, "Do you want to do this? Be my guest, asshole. It isn't as easy as you think!"

"But," my mother continued, now sounding a little hurt, "why wouldn't you tell me before now? I thought you told me everything."

"Definitely not," I said before realizing now wasn't the time for harsh truths. Other than the whole bi thing anyway. "I mean, I tell you lots of things, but this... this was a first. I didn't want to tell you until... until I knew it was serious."

I was a total asshole. Lying to my mother wasn't easy. She hadn't done anything to deserve the deception.

"Well," she said with a sniff. "Not exactly a first. There was that boy you, erm... kissed... at the clubhouse that one time..."

My face flooded with heat. "Yes, well. Maybe I should have... Listen, it's not important. The bottom line is, I'm bringing Gr... *him* to Ian and Binnie's, and I hope you'll treat him with kindness and respect regardless of... of what you think of him. That's important to me, Mom. Okay?"

"What? Of course I will. Don't be ridiculous. Since when do I not show proper respect and kindness to your dates?"

I sighed. "Okay, good. Thank you."

"But I do have another reason for my call today. I wanted to find out if you've had any luck getting access to my jewelry?"

I glanced up at Grey, who was scrolling through his phone and taking a bite out of a piece of toast with strawberry jam on it. He had a tiny blob of red jam at the corner of his lips, and my tongue twitched to lick it off him.

I closed my eyes and breathed. "Not yet. But I'll try to do that today. I promise."

"I'm worried about my jewelry, Ellison. Some of those pieces mean a lot to me."

"I understand. I'll do my best."

"Thank you."

When I ended the call, I took a sip of my own coffee to buy myself some time to strategize.

"Well done," Grey said after a few moments. "I know that wasn't easy."

I looked up to see if I could determine whether he was pulling my leg or not. He seemed to be genuine. "It wasn't. You're right. But it probably would have been much harder had it all been true."

His eyes cut right through me. "It isn't?"

The moisture disappeared from my mouth and throat. "That we're dating? No."

That wasn't what he'd meant, and we both knew it. He was asking about my sexuality. Thankfully, he let it stand without pressing me.

"What did she ask you for at the end?" he asked, pretending not to care much as he reached for his toast again. I'd been around him enough this week to recognize this tactic of his.

"It's something I need your help with, actually. She wants some of her jewelry out of the safe deposit box at the bank."

Grey paused for a split second before continuing to eat his toast casually. Once again, I knew this tactic. I waited him out.

"I believe you mean *my* jewelry."

I rolled my eyes and set my phone down before wrapping both hands around my warm mug. "I mean York Capital's jewelry, and my family still actually owns forty-five percent of York Capital."

The edge of one of his lips lifted. "But not the part that controls the jewelry."

"Stop being an ass. What do I have to trade you for my mother's jewelry? Surely you want something."

We'd already done this a few times this week, trading my degradation in some manner for additional rights or assets. It had become a kind of game between us.

He pursed his lips in thought. "I want you to spend some time debriefing me on this week's events at the house party. Sports we might be expected to participate in, lingo these people use in various situations, who's who of the guest list, the layout of the property and house, the length and courses of the meals, the type of food, the expected socializing methods, Ian and Binnie Duckworth's preferred topics of conversation, how to treat the 'help,' how to handle anything I'm unfamiliar with, and anything else you think might be relevant to my success as a guest at this... thing." He paused. "And, more specifically, what a shuttlecock is."

Grey turned his back to me again as if to wipe the counter down of his toast crumbs.

He's nervous.

The realization hit me swift and hard. This kid from low-income housing and a single mom in White Plains was worried about being the black sheep during a gathering of old money families.

"I would do that anyway," I admitted softly. "If you simply asked me."

"Not necessary," he said stiffly. "We shall stop at the bank on the way to our lunch meeting and pick up what you need. I will also need to know what kind of clothing to bring, and I assume we will have to procure some items for you as well since you hardly expected to be traveling to such an event when you were summoned here from Vermont."

He was right. "Yes. I guess that's true. I'll need some time off this afternoon if we're leaving tomorrow."

Jenny came into the room with a box and set it down in front of me. "It's for you. Now, what can I make you for breakfast? How about waffles?"

I nodded my thanks and opened the box, wondering who the hell knew where I was staying. As soon as the brown paper came off, I saw the Nike logo on the box. I glanced up at Grey, who had his same old stoic face on, revealing nothing.

I opened the box to find a pair of sleek running shoes in my size.

"We'll get the rest of what we need this afternoon," he said roughly. "My personal shopper will be waiting for us at Neiman's after our meeting."

For a poor kid from White Plains, the man sure knew how to impress.

"Thank you," I said as sincerely as I could. The gesture had been incredibly thoughtful. I wanted to hug the shoes to my chest. My legs vibrated with the need to stretch and run. "Maybe I can find some time tonight to go for a run."

He glanced up at me for a second before looking away again. "There's a treadmill in the gym down the hall past your room."

My chest felt fluttery and light. Was the man actually making an effort to lighten up and connect with me? Well, maybe "lighten up" was a stretch, but I definitely got the sense he was making some kind of effort. That boded well for our upcoming acting challenge.

I didn't have any worries for my part. In fact, my worries went the other way. It was entirely possible I would enjoy being Grey's boyfriend too much. It wasn't the house party week that concerned me, but the following one. After returning to Vermont to start my new life at the academy, how the hell would I shake off the memory of having Grey Blackwood by my side?

Jenny slid a plate of waffles in front of me, and my stomach balked. Suddenly, I was nervous. Was my potential disappointment worth it to get some piece of York Capital back? Of course it was. I needed to stop being emotional about this and keep my eye on the prize.

"Aren't you hungry?" Grey asked, glancing at my untouched plate. I looked up at him and saw a tiny crinkle of concern between his eyebrows.

I wanted him. I wanted him so badly it hurt. Maybe... maybe York Capital wasn't all I could get out of the week at the Duckworth's house party. Maybe there was a chance I could try and win Grey over, convince him to date me for real.

Execute my own kind of hostile takeover, on *him*.

"I am hungry," I said, meeting his eyes.

"Then eat." He resumed his usual commanding tone, which reached right into my gut and grabbed me with its tight fist.

"Yes, sir," I said. And then I dared a wink at him. His eyes flared wide for a moment before narrowing at me.

"Cheeky bastard," he muttered.

He had no idea.

Later that afternoon, after an interminable meeting with the most douchey blowhards I'd ever met, Grey and I made our way to Neiman Marcus for our clothes shopping. I'd deliberately moved our lunch meeting to a restaurant close to the store so we wouldn't waste time trying to cross the city during the Friday lunch crush.

"Thank god that's over," I said. "I thought that one guy was going to ask to lick your face."

"I beg your pardon?" Sometimes Grey sounded like he was from Greenwich instead of White Plains. It usually made me snicker, but this time I was too annoyed from the meeting to laugh.

"I've never met three more sniveling suck-ups in my life. They acted like you were Jesus." If there'd been a rock on the sidewalk, I would have kicked it.

"Who says I'm not?"

Okay, fine. That got a snort out of me.

"Do people act like that around you often?" I asked.

"Nowadays they do," he admitted. "Not sure you can be a billionaire without people bowing and scraping for a piece of your pie."

I was too miffed to make a joke about wanting a piece of his pie. "But they didn't even try to get to know you. All they wanted was your approval."

"And my money," he said dryly, reaching for the door of the department store.

"Are you going to give them the seed money?" I really hoped he didn't. Those men had given me a bad feeling, and I didn't trust the data behind their software testing.

"Of course not," he said with a huff. "They're selling vaporware. The product doesn't even exist. They're full of shit."

"Then why take the meeting in the first place?"

He led me through the clean, open displays. He obviously knew where the men's department was.

"One of my companies invests in ClutchSoft."

I turned to stare at him as realization dawned. "You were investigating the competition! You devious genius."

He shrugged and pointed down a side aisle. His hand rested briefly on my lower back as he gestured for me to turn. I felt the strong warmth through my suit coat only for a beat before it was gone.

"I didn't become a billionaire by winning a lottery," he murmured.

I thought about how smart he had to be to have earned a full-ride scholarship to Yale. And then he'd gone on to build mind-blowing wealth in only fifteen years.

"How did you do it?" I asked. I wanted to know the real story, not the watered-down version he alluded to in interviews.

"Mr. Blackwood," a young woman said with a wide smile and clear affection in her expression. "So good to see you again. Welcome back."

"Roni, it's good to see you again. Thank you for agreeing to help us on short notice. This is my... partner, Ellison York." Grey's hand returned to the small of my back, only this time it was possessive and not at all fleeting.

I swallowed and nodded at the woman. Apparently, we were doing this. "It's nice to meet you," I managed to say.

She had obviously been notified of my sizes somehow. Maybe Jenny had snuck into my room and done some investigating the same way she'd admitted after breakfast to discovering my shoe size for Grey. Roni led us to a private room where two racks stood packed with various articles of clothing. I felt like I was in a movie montage where the ugly duckling was being made over by a wealthy sugar daddy.

It should have grated on me a little, but it didn't. I was too busy ogling Grey in every outfit I spotted him in. While one of Roni's assistants marked and measured me in some of the clothes that needed adjusting, I craned my neck to check out my "partner" in his.

The man filled out designer clothes like nobody's business.

He was tall and broad, trim and fit. My eyes hungered for him. They took every chance to skim across the angles and planes of his body regardless of what he wore. Several times he caught me staring and lifted that imperious brow of his. It was like a cattle prod to my heart rate. Every time he caught me staring, I felt like my heart was going to skitter out of my chest. By the time he tried on a pair of light beige linen pants that draped over his ass and thighs like a slinky lover... well, I was having a hard time fitting into my own pants.

"Done," I squeaked, turning around quickly and accidentally pricking myself with one of the tailor's pins. "Sorry. Done. I'm done. This looks good."

I shuffled back to the semiprivacy of my dressing room before letting out a breath, stripping off my shirt, and opening my damned pants. I looked down at the misbehaving bulge in my boxer briefs.

"If wishes were horses," I muttered at it, "beggars would ride. It's me. I'm the beggar in this scenario."

"Mr. York, are you feeling okay, sir?" the prim tailor's assistant asked. I could see the tips of his dress shoes under the door.

"Yes, sorry. I just need a little fresh air. Please tell Mr. Bl—"

I jumped back as the door opened. Grey stood in the narrow opening and looked me up and down. "Are you sick? What's wrong? Do you need to sit down? Do you need..." He turned to speak over his shoulder. "A bottle of cold water, please."

I clutched at my tight chest, which had only gotten tighter since Grey's large frame had entered my personal space. I could smell his familiar apple scent. I'd finally identified it as the shampoo he used. The nerves I'd been shoving down—about the trip, the loss of our family's wealth and control of the foundation, the lies about our relationship, the close contact with the man I'd wanted for so long—sprung up with a vengeance, stealing the air out of my lungs.

For some reason, I shook my head frantically. I couldn't catch my breath. Grey reached for my face with both of his large hands. "Shh. Take a breath. You're okay." His voice was low and calm, the way it was most of the time. He was always so put together. How was that possible? "Sit down. There's a bench right behind you."

He helped me sit and then pressed his hand on my upper back to bend me over until my head was between my knees.

"Sorry," I gasped, wishing the floor would open up and swallow me whole. I'd tried so hard to be agreeable, nonchalant, act like none of this was affecting me very much. But the truth was—it was terrifying. Losing the family business, possibly losing the necessary funding to keep the academy running, all of the children and their families counting on me—on us—to keep things running smoothly, to provide a future for those kids.

"No apologies," he murmured. "Thanks," he said to someone else. I felt him shift as he reached for something. "Leave us, please."

I heard the snick of a door closing and then blessed silence. Even the softly piping music turned off. Grey knelt in front of me on the floor and cracked a water bottle open before sitting me up and urging me to take a sip. One of his hands stayed on my shoulder as the other held the bottle to my lips.

"Take it slow."

His voice was soothing. I tried to regulate my breathing and drink the water. His hand on my shoulder moved a little until I noticed him gently rubbing the muscles of my shoulder and neck. His fingers brushed against the hair on my neck, bringing up goose bumps everywhere. I closed my eyes and allowed myself a few moments of comforting touch.

When I finally got my breathing under control and took a few more sips of water, I felt the flush of embarrassment wash over me. I sat up straight and put my shoulders back.

"Sorry," I said again, looking for the shirt I'd worn into the store. "Apparently, I'm a lightweight when it comes to shopping. Who knew?"

Grey's hand moved around to grab my chin and force me to look at him. "What really happened? I know it's not low blood sugar, considering you ate your entire panini and then finished my salmon. Are you sick? Do we need to postpone the flight?"

I needed him to be an asshole right now. Badly.

I shook my head. "No, I just... I just thought of everything that's happened this week and... it's a lot. I don't... I don't want..." What the hell was I even trying to say?

Grey's hand moved from my chin to my head. His fingers brushed through my hair gently for just a second before he realized what he was doing. He yanked his hand away like it had been burned. "It is a lot," he agreed. "And I've barely given you time to breathe. Why don't we head home... ah, back to my place and order in. You can relax and do whatever you want."

"No, it's okay. We have that client dinner. You've been looking forward to it all week."

He looked surprised I'd picked up on his excitement over the client visit. "It's not a problem to reschedule," he said. "They come to town once a month."

"Why don't you go and I'll stay back? You'd have more fun without me there anyway."

Grey looked like he wanted to argue with me, but he held his tongue for a beat. Finally, he said, "Why don't you let me worry about the client, and you worry about getting your clothes back on while I finish up with Roni. She needs to get these things to the tailor if we want them delivered before our trip."

I couldn't even imagine how much they charged for Friday night alterations on designer clothes, but then again, I couldn't imagine being a billionaire either. While I'd grown up in a very wealthy family, my family's spending had remained in my father's control. Still, it was easy to let that money stress go. If Grey wanted to pay for last-minute tailoring, let him.

He stood up and handed me the half-empty bottle of water. "Drink the rest of this before you get up."

"You're very bossy," I said to his back. I could have sworn I heard a huff of laughter.

When I finally dressed, all the clothes and racks were gone, and Grey was back to his buttoned-up businessman persona. He led me out of the store with thanks from both of us to Roni and her team. Throughout the week, I'd noticed the way Grey treated service personnel. He was incredibly kind and gracious. It was clear the man hadn't forgotten where he came from, and he did his best to make sure everyone who helped him in some way was personally thanked and fairly compensated.

I loved that about him. It didn't surprise me at all, of course, but it was a refreshing change from my father and some of the other people I'd grown up around. I'd come dangerously close to becoming just like them, and I was still terrified of acting with the same kind of entitlement I'd been raised into.

As soon as we walked out of the building, I noticed Grey's car and driver waiting at the curb. We quickly took our places in the back seat and let ourselves be rolled through the city traffic at a snail's pace.

Grey spent the time alternately tapping on his phone and talking to Marcel. I let the sounds fade into the background while I looked out at the people heading home from work for the weekend.

I loved the city. Gigi worried how I would assimilate to Vermont in the long term since I'd always loved living in New York. She was right to worry; I worried too. But I wanted the academy to succeed more than I wanted anything else, and I couldn't afford a life in the city while supporting the school, so it wasn't much of a sacrifice when I looked at it that way.

"You like pizza?" Grey asked. I glanced over at him.

"Is there anyone who doesn't?" I asked, noticing the driver smile at my response.

"Emery, what do you think?" Grey asked the driver. "You know anyone who doesn't like pizza?"

"My neighbor Ms. Petra. She says pizza is a no, but *pica*, pica is a yes." He smiled in the rearview mirror.

"Ahh," Grey said with one of his rare smiles. "Is she Croatian by any chance?"

"Just so, Mr. Blackwood. Just so. Pretty sure they're the same damned thing, but who am I to judge?"

I wanted to know how Grey had known a Croatian term, but I didn't ask. Instead, I let the light conversation between them fill the car. Hearing Grey talk to Emery without his businessman mask on or any of the corporate posturing was relaxing. It made me realize how little of his real self he'd allowed me to see all week. Usually, I only got these glimpses when he wasn't aware of my presence.

They chatted most of the drive back uptown. Grey inquired about a nephew who he'd helped place in a job, and Emery chattered on about seemingly his entire family. At some point I must have dozed off because I awoke to Grey's warm hand pressing against my forehead as if he was taking my temperature.

He quickly pulled his hand back when I moved. "You still with us?" he asked gently.

Emery stood holding the door open, so I scrambled out of the car. "Yeah, yeah, I'm good."

When Grey stepped out behind me and dismissed Emery for the night, he put his hand on my lower back again. This time I allowed myself to relax into it by telling myself we might as well go ahead and pretend to be boyfriends. What was the harm?

"I arranged for you to be worked over," he said as we entered the building. There was a noticeable smirk in his voice that nearly made me bark out a laugh in the quiet lobby. Instead, I closed my eyes for a second to enjoy the hush of the cool, quiet space after the noise of the street.

"Thank god. I could use a good working over," I said back as seriously as I could.

"Mm. That's what everyone at the office has been saying."

I looked over at him in slack-jawed shock. "Mr. Blackwood, *sir*, did you just crack a joke? Is the world coming to an end?"

Even though he kept his eyes ahead on the elevator door, his smile was everything.

When we got to the apartment, Jenny was there with a beer bottle in each hand. "Ricky is set up in the office, and Ted is set up in the gym. I suggest you down these first and get the relaxation started. I'm going to order the pizza. Ellison, you seem like a supreme kind of guy. Am I right?"

"I'll eat anything except Hawaiian. Thank you."

Grey's hand resumed its spot on my lower back as he urged me down the hallway to the left. I'd never been down this way. When we came to a dark, wood-paneled room, I realized he was giving me the preferred masseuse.

"Ricky, thanks for fitting us in this evening. This is Ellison." After the introductions, he left us alone. Ricky proceeded to turn me into a thick puddle of goo over the next hour, and the best part was when he left and informed me I could stay in my melted-down state as long as I wanted to since the massage table belonged to Grey.

I fell asleep for a little while and woke up to the low tones of Grey's voice as he walked past the door. After stretching and putting my clothes back on, I made my way to my room to shower and changed into sweats and a T-shirt.

When I got to the kitchen, Grey was there dressed in similarly comfortable clothes, pecking away at his laptop. Clearly he'd decided to cancel his client dinner, and he didn't seem overly upset by it. I apologized anyway.

"Sorry about your dinner plans."

"Don't be. We have a long day tomorrow. That reminds me, I had your mother's jewelry couriered to their apartment. You should check with her to make sure she got it."

I'd completely forgotten he'd offered to carry it in his messenger bag for me after our visit to the bank. "Thank you. You didn't need to do that."

He waved a hand through the air. "One less thing for you to pack. There's pizza in the oven keeping warm."

I helped myself to a plate from the cabinet and another beer from the fridge before sliding some pizza slices onto the plate and taking my usual spot at the island. A television that had been previously hidden behind a cabinet door played the news at a low volume.

After downing my first slice of pizza and half the beer, I decided to broach one of the topics that had low-key been stressing me out. "Do you think we should get to know each other a little bit? For the boyfriend thing?"

Grey didn't look away from his laptop. "I already studied everything there is to know about you."

I let out a laugh before taking another sip of beer. "No, really. I mean we should share some basics in case anyone asks questions."

He turned to face me. "I know what you mean, and I was serious. I already did my share of research. Ask me anything pertaining to Ellison Gareth York, date of birth—"

I stopped him. "I already know my birthday, and so does anyone who's ever seen my driver's license. How do I take my coffee?"

"You claim to prefer a salted caramel mocha, but you never order one. You actually drink regular coffee with plenty of cream and too much sugar. Next."

Okay, that had been an easy one since we'd been together in the office all week. "What did I want to be when I grew up?"

He clearly didn't know the answer, but he took a moment to study me. "When? Before or after college?"

"Before," I said, since the last thing I wanted to do was talk about why my dreams had changed after college.

"Before college, you were still daddy's boy. You would probably have assumed you'd go to law school like daddy wanted, but your little act of defiance would have been legal aid or public defender of some kind."

"Wrong," I said, lying through my teeth. "Ballerina. Next."

He laughed, and I wanted to throw myself a party to celebrate the gorgeous look on his face.

"What's the question?" he asked.

"Who's my best friend?"

"Your sister."

I swallowed. "Lucky guess. What's my favorite kind of music?"

"You don't really have one, and if you do, it's instrumental. You prefer silence."

I stared at him. "How the hell would you know that?"

"I'm not telling you all of my secrets. Why do you think I had them turn off the music at Neiman's?"

Fucking hell, I was going to fall in love with the man if he didn't shut his face.

"Okay, you know everything," I said, desperate to change the subject. "But I don't know shit."

"I like my coffee black," he said before turning back to his computer.

"No you don't. You like plain coffee, but you get cranky if it doesn't have at least some cream and sugar. You aren't picky about how much of either one."

He grunted. "I wanted to be a fireman when I graduated high school."

"Bullshit. You wanted to be a venture capitalist or at the very least, an investment banker."

He tapped a few keys on the keyboard. "I grew up the poor son of a sharecropper."

"Be serious."

He glanced over at me and sighed. "I never knew my father. My mother told me she didn't know who it was, but I found out later she knew exactly who it was, but he'd gone to prison before she discovered she was pregnant. He got out three years ago. I hope to god he never finds out she had his baby and that baby grew up to earn more money in a day than he'll probably ever see or steal in his lifetime."

I stared at him. "Okay... I didn't know that, but I'm hoping that subject doesn't come up at the croquet match," I teased gently.

The quirk of his lip settled me a little. "Let's hope. What kind of topics might come up at the croquet match?"

"Do you lean more toward momentum trading or fundamental trading? Where is your primary vacation property located? Which clubs do you belong to? Where do you hold your money offshore?"

"When you have as much money as I do, you do momentum, fundamental, swing, scalping, and technical trading," he said with a wink. "My primary vacation property is the chair in front of the next potential client. I belong to the Yale Club here in the city, Augusta National Golf Club in Georgia, Baltustrol Golf Club in New Jersey, and I might still be a member of Sam's Club, but only because I mistook it for a gay nightclub on a business trip once and accidentally signed up for bulk discounts on paper products. And, finally, I hold no money offshore. As far as you know."

He lifted that damned eyebrow at me, only this time it was sassy instead of judgy. I bit my lip against a laugh.

"I once went into the army on a drunken dare," I admitted. "Thankfully it was the Salvation Army, and I got an incredible deal on a Calphalon frying pan while I was in there. I couldn't believe someone had let that bad boy go. I still have it."

"And what's the official story of how we met?" Grey asked, lowering my giddy scale into the negative.

I stared down at my remaining half slice of pizza. "I saw you in Calculus class. Couldn't keep my eyes off you. You had this..." I glanced down out of the corner of my eye to his bare ankle. "Little starfish-shaped scar on your calf. At first, I thought I was just bored in class and fascinated by how someone would get a scar in that shape. But then I realized I wasn't focusing on the scar so much as the shape of your leg... the shifting of your muscles... the way the hair covered your skin. I followed your leg up to the edge of your shorts and wished I could see higher." I swallowed. "I never would have gotten up the nerve to talk to you, but then one day, you asked to borrow my calculator."

"I didn't have one," he admitted in a rough voice. "Those fuckers were like eighty bucks."

I still couldn't look at him. "And then... I guess... let's say we ran into each other on the golf course at Baltusrol back in the spring. You were golfing with clients, and I was at my cousin's wedding. Our conversation was fucking awkward as hell, but you graciously allowed me to apologize for everything that had happened back... you know. That night."

"You looked damned good in that paisley bow tie and douchey seersucker suit," Grey added with a slight grin.

"Hey, it was a linen suit, asshole. And it was an ascot, not a bow tie."

His mouth dropped open until he realized I'd pulled his leg. "Fuck you," he said.

"We talked longer than we realized, and when your client came looking for you, you gave me your business card and mumbled something about..."

"Wanting to touch base with you back in the city to ask you a legal question about a VC contract," Grey added helpfully.

I nodded. "So we arranged a business lunch, but we spent more time talking about..."

"Yankees versus Mets."

"Yes. Than the legal issue. You agreed the Mets were the devilspawn, and we talked about various players and random other topics until we realized several hours had passed."

I watched Grey think through the next part. "You were relaxed and easy to talk to," he said. "I was surprised. I decided I wanted to see you again, but I convinced myself it was only to get legal advice."

My heart thunked. "I couldn't stop remembering what it was like to kiss you in that closet," I said softly. "I wanted to do it again."

Grey coughed and moved to stand up. His voice returned to the all-business tone, and his mask fell back into place. "So, that was that. We started dating, and here we are. You should get some sleep."

Within moments, he was gone.

And I was left wanting him more than ever before.

11

GREY

"All warfare is based on deception."

~ Sun Tzu, *The Art of War*

The next morning went by much faster than I'd anticipated. Ellison debriefed me about the house party week with the same competent efficiency he'd used to explain an investment contract to a potential client earlier in the week. I was happily surprised not to feel embarrassment or shame, and part of the reason was because Ellison treated it like a game the same way he had our conversation the night before.

While we were walking out to the helipad in Hudson Yards, Ellison wrapped up his thoughts. "The best piece of advice I can think of is to act like all of this is beneath you, and/or you've been so busy making your billions that you hadn't even had time to *think* about croquet, much less play it."

He was obviously at home on a helicopter and climbed in it as if it was nothing special. I'd only taken my first ride in one a few years before, and it still felt like an incredible indulgence every time I flew in a helicopter or the private jet I now owned. It was a stark reminder of how differently we'd grown up.

"Also, it might help if we act like disgustingly attached lovebirds so I'm always with you when you run into something you're unfamiliar with," he added. "You know the type of couples I mean. My sister and her fiancé are like that."

"Will they be here this week?" I asked, having forgotten about Gigi altogether.

"No. Gigi—that's my sister—can't leave work since school just started."

"I know who Gigi is," I said. "I remember her from the club."

Ellison looked surprised. "You have a really good memory for details and names. It must come in handy for what you do."

He was right, and it did. One of the reasons I'd gotten such a strong start had been my ability to remember people and take advantage of claiming a connection with a few well-placed classmates and even a former coworker of my mother's. Before I'd had my own money to invest, I'd built a reputation for connecting people in need of investment money with others who had money to invest. It helped me get invitations into business opportunities and social circles I wouldn't have had before. Once there, I was able to keep my ears open for other opportunities until I found a few small and risky enough to afford. It wasn't easy. Those first five years were full of long hours and late nights, pushing myself way out of my comfort zone and trying to be someone I wasn't.

But eventually, it worked. And when I finally had serious capital, I knew the right people to turn it into bigger money quickly.

This week was going to be very different. While some of these old-money families had welcomed me into business opportunities, they'd never welcomed me into personal ones. It rankled. Over time I'd convinced myself it didn't matter, but the truth was, it still bothered me.

And I hated that it bothered me.

"Networking is everything in business," I said, reaching for the seat belt.

"Here and I thought it was money," Ellison said with a teasing tone of voice.

"That too."

When the helicopter landed, I was happy to climb down and stretch my legs on the tarmac. The afternoon sun was shining, and I could see how tiny the airport was. The pace was going to be hellishly slow compared to the hectic schedule I usually kept in the city.

"By the way," Ellison said, walking past me to grab his suitcase from the attendant, "while you were watching the tutorial video on how to play backgammon last night, I found a dangerous loophole in one of your contracts with Quicksilver Studios. I'd be happy to point it out to you... for a small fee."

"Ells, the driver will get those," I said, shortening his name without thinking. My teeth clacked together with irritation. "And what could you possibly want in exchange for that tidbit of legal advice?"

"That tidbit could cost you future profits of all licensed material they produce. If you don't think their future work product will be worth very much money, why did you invest in them in the first place?" He was toying with me, and I had to admit—at least to myself —that it was kind of hot. In an annoying way.

"Your demand for payment, please," I growled. "Perhaps you'd like the little wooden airplane that used to live on your father's desk at the office?"

He glared at me. "That was my great-grandfather's. He got it as a christening gift from Wilbur Wright himself."

I laughed loudly enough to startle the driver, who'd rushed up to help us with our bags.

"You're a terrible liar. What do you want?"

"Okay, fine. That plane was a gift from Gigi for his birthday one year. She got it at FAO Schwarz."

I refused to ask him again. Instead, I greeted our driver and began making small talk. Ellison followed me to the car. When we finally slid into the back seat, he turned to face me. "I want you to relax. It's going to be fine. And you work yourself to the bone. I'm worried you're going to have a heart attack out here and all of your money will be reclaimed by the state. I can't let that happen before you draw up a new will, leaving all your wealth to your new and very handsome boyfriend." He batted his eyes at me.

"My mother is still alive, you know. Not sure she'd take kindly to some random dude taking her inheritance."

"How is she?" he asked, dropping the teasing manner. "Where does she live these days? Is she retired?"

Talking about my mom to Ellison York was unexpected. I reminded myself he wasn't quite the selfish asshole I'd thought he was, and it wasn't as if my mom's life was a state secret.

I cleared my throat. "She's really good. Right now, she's on a cruise in Europe with two of her best friends. They go everywhere as long as they can get there on some kind of boat."

I thought of the Instagram account she'd set up to share her travel photos. The last shot she'd uploaded had shown her red-faced and happy from a day spent touring fields of tulips.

"She must be very proud of you," Ellison said.

I nodded. "She is, but she worries too. The amount of money I handle makes her nervous. It took a long time before she'd allow me to spend any of it on her. She was always afraid it would disappear one day. She didn't calm down about it until I locked a portion of it away in cash investments and promised her it would be our 'just in case' fund."

"How much is in that fund?" Ellison asked with a knowing twinkle in his eye.

I huffed out a laugh. "An obscene amount. It makes my investment manager twitch to have that much money sitting in cash."

"I'll bet."

The drive wasn't long. Before I was ready, the car turned into a driveway marked by large, open gates and a stone planter overflowing with colorful flowers. A small, hand-painted wooden sign on the gate read "McArthur."

"Binnie's maiden name," Ellison explained. "Her parents built the house." He shifted in his seat. "It's not going to be as bad as you think, Grey. Most of these people are very nice."

"So nice they abhor outsiders?"

Ellison sighed. "They don't abhor outsiders. They're simply... cautious."

"Forgive me if being a close friend of your father's gives me the wrong impression of Ian Duckworth," I muttered.

"I told you, Ian and Binnie are closer to my mother. They put up with my father for her sake. I still haven't heard that he's coming. Maybe he's been too busy scrambling to get York back to hear about my new boyfriend. That would have made this a real shitshow."

He was right, and I would have been grateful for that small pleasure if it hadn't meant having to staff several people in the York office whose sole job it was to make sure Warren didn't turn up and cause trouble while I was gone. His company login credentials and key cards had been deactivated, but I still assumed he would make a nuisance of himself there and try to convince his former employees to give him access.

The driveway meandered through a large expanse of pristinely clipped grass lawn toward an incredibly large building that would be more appropriately referred to as a chateau than a beach house. It was beautiful, especially with the golden light of the late sun slanting across from behind us, illuminating the stone house and the ocean beyond it. Maybe Ellison was right. Maybe I needed to relax. This place wasn't a resort on a private island with pretty men in small swimsuits, but it was definitely slower-paced and idyllic.

"How will you know if I've sufficiently relaxed to meet your negotiation requirements?" I asked.

Ellison reached out a hand and ran a fingertip between my eyebrows. "This line might go away." He moved his finger to the outer edges of my eyelid. "And one might appear here." He moved it down to the side of my lips. "Or here."

I didn't move a muscle. The gentle caress of the pad of his finger reminded me that for an entire week this man would have the freedom to touch me like this in front of others. It was a kind of intimacy I hadn't shared with someone in a long time. I'd dated a few men in my midtwenties, but when my business had finally taken off, I'd run out of time for dating. My love life had turned solidly into a sex life, at least when I had the time for it.

I moved out of his reach by pretending to look out the window. "It's more rural than I imagined."

He made that little sound of soft laughter I was coming to recognize so well. "Yes. People who are used to the city are usually surprised by how different it is in the rest of the country."

"I golfed at St. Andrews once," I told him. "Out in the middle of nowhere. It was awful. Worst day I've ever spent trying to get that damned ball in a hole. I wouldn't have gone if it hadn't been for the opportunity to meet Richard Branson."

The car pulled closer to the large home. I tried to quell my nerves. Was Duckworth going to be angry at me for going to such extremes to meet with him? If he agreed to sell the building to me, there had to come a time in the future he would realize what had happened.

"I thought you hated golf," Ellison said.

The sight of the house getting bigger as we drove closer distracted me from the conversation. "I do."

"Then why do you play? Why belong to multiple golf clubs?"

I glanced at him out of the corner of my eye. "Business deals are won or lost on the golf course. Surely your father taught you that."

He was quiet for a beat. "That explains a lot," Ellison eventually said. The car finally pulled up to the front of the home, in a circular drive of pea gravel. A large fountain filled the center of the circle, and bright sprays of water shot out of copper bugles held by nymph sculptures. A besuited man stood on the stone steps, ready to greet us.

An honest-to-god butler.

"Stop scowling," Ellison murmured. "That's Henry. He likes Zabar's cinnamon babka and chocolate chip cookies. Once you give him those, he'll love you forever."

"I don't—" I started to say I didn't have either of those items, but then I remembered Ellison had asked the driver to stop at the

Broadway deli on the way to Hudson Yards. He'd come out with a bag of treats I'd assumed was for Ian and Binnie. "Sneaky little shit," I murmured at his back as he climbed out to greet his old friend.

"Henry! So good to see you. How's Catherine?"

The butler's eyes lit up, but he tried his best to keep a professional expression on his face. I could tell he had a soft spot for Ellison, though, as he took particular care to direct another man to grab our bags.

"I've put you and Mr. Blackwood in the Magnolia Room because we had word a few hours ago that your father is coming."

I glanced at Ellison. The surprise and disappointment on his face were genuine, and the butler noticed it right away.

"Which means you'll be on opposite ends of the house," Henry said with a small cough.

Ellison lowered his voice. "How did you know who I was bringing?"

Henry's eyes blinked over to me for a moment before focusing on Ellison again. "Your godmother said to tell you—and I quote—she knows everything all the time and for you to stop thinking you're so smart." He glanced at me again and lowered his voice. "But if you want to know the truth, someone from town told her they'd seen you two together at Neiman's."

Ellison sighed and rolled his eyes. "Devious. Did you see her reaction when she found out?"

Henry stood up straighter. "If I did, it wouldn't have been any business of mine, sir."

Ellison quickly introduced me to the butler before unzipping his backpack and pulling out the Zabar's bag. "For you."

Henry took them with a formal nod. "Thank you. For what it's worth, Mrs. Duckworth loves you very much. She only wants what's best for you."

Ellison's face lit with an affectionate smile, the kind that made my stomach tighten and something inside of me *want*. What would it be like to have that expression turned my way?

Another car's tires crunched on the driveway. Henry turned to see who it was. "I'll have someone show you to your room," he said when he turned back to us.

"No need," Ellison said. "I remember where it is. Thanks."

He leaned in and kissed Henry on the cheek. The older man blushed and waved him off with a huff. I followed Ellison into the house and tried not to look like a gawking tourist. The fittings were old but pristine. The wooden panels and staircase were waxed to a healthy lustre, and the antique rug under the heavy marble-topped table in the center of the entry hall gave the space warmth and elegance. There were framed seascape paintings on a few walls and brass light fixtures here and there that looked like they'd come from the captain's cabin in an old wooden sailing ship.

I could hear muffled conversation from deeper in the house, but Ellison gestured me away from it and toward the grand staircase.

Once we were safely on the second level and wandering down a long hallway, I asked Ellison if he was worried about Binnie's reaction to my presence.

"No," he said, offering me a reassuring smile. "Henry's reference to her wanting me to be happy is his way of informing me she will support my bringing you as long as you make me happy." He came to a room with an open door and movement inside. Before entering the room, he looked at me over his shoulder and added, "And you do."

I stood there staring after him. What the hell did that mean? Was he being a cheeky boyfriend right now because people were listening? I glanced around but didn't see anyone who could be paying attention to us.

As I entered the room, I saw an attendant setting our bags on matching luggage stands under the windows. The room wasn't overly large but had the same elegant comfort the rest of the house seemed to have. I didn't feel as intimidated in this space as I'd anticipated.

At least, I didn't feel intimidated until I saw the queen-sized bed. The only bed in the room. The bed we were going to have to share since there didn't seem to be any other furniture to sleep on in the room besides a small desk and velvet-upholstered desk chair.

I swallowed back the images of the two of us trying to share that bed. When I reached into my pocket for some cash to tip the man who'd brought up our bags, Ellison gave me a subtle head shake. I lifted an eyebrow in question, and he repeated the head shake.

"Thank you," Ellison said to the man instead. "We really appreciate it."

The man smiled and nodded, murmuring an offer to help us with anything else we may need, before leaving and snapping the door closed behind him.

Ellison let out a breath and tilted his head back and forth before shaking out his arms. "Okay, let's strategize, because if my father is coming, that changes everything."

I was relieved he didn't say anything about me getting the tipping thing wrong. When he had the opportunity to cut me down, Ellison never seemed to take it. He moved on instead. Maybe he'd matured more than I gave him credit for.

He was right about his dad. "The shitshow is in town," I remarked calmly. I'd noticed this past week that Ellison tended to stay calmer if I did. He was like the Queen Anne's lace flowers my grandmother used to pick on the side of the road, sucking up the colors of whatever was around him.

Ellison turned to look at me, and that's when I noticed the fear in his eyes. I reached out and clasped the side of his neck. "Look at me. You're going to do fine. *We* are going to do fine. Your dad is a selfish prick. Want to know how I know?"

Ellison took half a step closer to me. "There are too many answers to that question."

"Because your godmother has the right of this. If you are happy— regardless of the family business or anything else—if you're truly happy, your father should be happy for you."

I felt the warm thrum of Ellison's heartbeat under my thumb. His hair brushed the tips of my fingers and made them itch to run through his thick curls.

He ran his teeth over his bottom lip. His chest rose and fell more rapidly as his breathing shallowed. "I don't think many people could be happy finding out their son is dating the man who took over their company and basically fired their ass."

Ellison was right. This was going to be a disaster. But it was too late. We were here. And we had a deal. "He doesn't know you're trying to save his ass," I corrected. "Maybe he needs to trust you."

Ellison threw up his hands. "He's had thirty-five years to trust me, and he hasn't. He's unlikely to start now that he thinks I betrayed him! The better question is why I care. I shouldn't. He's an asshole who ruined your life. Who ruined your life, thanks to *me*."

Okay, we'd skipped past Nervousville and were entering Panic Town. "Slow down and breathe," I cautioned.

He paced back and forth, ignoring me completely. "This is never going to work. You hate me. Everyone is going to see that. It's not like you can hide it, especially from the people who will already be suspicious of you. Oh god. Oh god."

I stood up and grabbed him by both arms, stopping his pacing and forcing him to look at me. "I don't hate you."

"Of course you do. And you *should*." He was losing his composure. His eyes were wide with fear, and he was audibly gasping for breath. Did he always have panic attacks when he got overwhelmed? Somehow I doubted it. This weekend was an unusual challenge. His reaction was very understandable.

I leaned in and pressed my lips to his before he could say anything else. If my words wouldn't convince him I could do a convincing job of being his boyfriend, then maybe my actions would.

He made a soft sound of surprise that quickly turned to a low moan as his entire body relaxed into mine. I quickly moved my arms around him to hold him upright.

The kiss was shockingly good. Easy and natural. Our lips fell into rhythm together like they'd always been meant for this, always been meant to be together, lazily stroking each other and searching for more.

I couldn't stop. My arms tightened around him as I explored his lips and mouth with my tongue. The little noises of pleasure he made went straight to my groin. I could get used to this. I could do this for a very, very long time and be perfectly happy. More than happy.

Ellison was a damned good kisser, maybe the best I'd ever had. He kissed me like he did most things, with enthusiasm and joy, a little bit of mischief. His hands fisted the front of my shirt where he'd grabbed me in surprise. I ran my hands up and down his back, wishing desperately I could run them down to the rounded muscles of his ass and pull him tightly against me in a hot grind.

I hadn't thought this through. Maybe if I had, I wouldn't have risked something so intense. Because it was earth-shaking, life-changing, difference-making.

Panic inducing.

I forced myself to pull away, setting him back from me by grabbing his upper arms again.

I cleared my throat. "See? I can fake it. No problem."

He stared at me with glassy eyes and wet lips. The tip of his nose was red from my late-day stubble. "Uh... yeah. Uh..."

I turned around and busied myself with my computer bag while I thought about Warren York's response to my assault of his son's person. That wasn't as boner-deflating as I'd hoped. I quickly imagined my mother picking out a tulip-shaped key chain for me at a cheesy tourist shop in Europe.

Boner problem solved.

Ellison's voice was deliciously breathless. "That... um... yeah. So... yeah. Faking. Good faking. It was definitely... believable." The last word came out a little squeaky. I looked back at him and noticed his flushed face and nervous eyelash movement.

Before I could say anything, the bedroom door burst open and Ian Duckworth stormed in. His rage was palpable, and it was completely focused on me.

"What the hell are you doing here?"

12

"Opportunistic relationships can hardly be kept constant."
~ Sun Tzu, *The Art of War*

"Ian! Ian, wait," I said, rushing over and stepping between him and Grey. The heat of Grey's body against my back was hard to ignore, especially after the kissing encounter that had just knocked me on my figurative ass and left me frantically trying to find a way to finagle a repeat. "He didn't want to come. I had to beg him. Grey didn't want you to think he was using our relationship to get an in with you. But he came because it was important to me. And I'm important to him." The lies came off my tongue easily now that we were here, now that I was bolstered by Grey's commitment to being convincing.

"Why didn't either of you tell me about this supposed relationship sooner? Why did I have to find out about it from the help?"

I felt Grey shift behind me. He wasn't the type of man to appreciate someone else handling his shit. Too bad.

"Because I was afraid of you acting just like this," I snapped. "I wanted to tell you in person so I could explain."

"So you could explain why you'd date someone who wanted to destroy your family business?"

"So I could explain why I would date someone who wanted to *save* my family business," I corrected. "You don't know the whole story here, so stop acting like an ass to my... to my b-boyfriend."

Fine, saying that word after thirty-five years of fairly comfortable heterosexuality wasn't as easy as it might have been, but I'd said it.

Grey's hand landed on my hip and startled me. "Why don't we go somewhere to talk?" he suggested in his irritatingly mature manner.

Ian's eyes narrowed at Grey over my shoulder before turning to me. "Bring him to my study. I'll have Henry pour us a drink. I know I could sure use one."

As soon as he was gone, I let out a breath. Grey squeezed my hip for a beat before pulling away. "That was pleasant," he muttered. "Should we go ahead and dress for dinner before meeting with him?"

The attendant who'd brought our bags to the room had mentioned a casual family dinner tonight. I told Grey we were probably fine dressed as we were. It was even cooler here than in the city. Grey wore a slim-fit pair of chinos with a casual button-up shirt in a dark blue pattern. I'd mostly noticed it because the sleeves of his shirt were rolled up and I'd spent plenty of time on the helicopter staring at his forearms.

"You're wearing jeans," he said with the same amount of disdain he might have used had I been wearing bloody medical scrubs.

"They're designer jeans, and I'm wearing a cashmere sweater with them. I look like I could be on the cover of a 'smart-casual looks for fall' mash-up thanks to your peeps at Neiman's. Besides, it's just family tonight."

"Great," he said with heavy sarcasm.

"Family in this case is at least twenty people. You'll be fine."

"At least wear the boots instead of sneakers."

I looked down at my canvas sneaks. He had a point. After opening my suitcase to find the soft leather Chelsea boots that had shown up with all the Neiman's stuff, I sat on the desk chair to slip them on. They felt like they'd been made for my feet.

"Thank you for these," I said, standing back up. "I hope you can find someone who wears a size eleven to appreciate them when I'm done with them."

Grey's forehead wrinkled in confusion. "They're yours. Why would I find someone else to give them to?"

"I'm not taking the stuff you bought. You had to have spent at least ten grand yesterday. Have Marcel or Jenny figure out a way to sell them to a designer resale shop or something."

He huffed out that little laugh. "I spent more on aviation gas last month flying Marcel to California to surprise his husband for their anniversary. And that wasn't even business related. This is."

I didn't respond. He must have realized I was annoyed at the thought of accepting all of these designer clothes because he gentled his voice.

"Ells, you work at a private boarding school. Surely you can wear your new clothes there and fit right in."

It was the second time he'd shortened my name, and I kind of liked it, even though I didn't think he realized he was doing it.

We walked out of the bedroom and closed the door. I suddenly realized Grey thought I worked at the kind of school I'd attended myself, an elite boarding school for the rich and famous.

"My school's not like that," I corrected. "Half the kids there are on full scholarship."

Before he could say anything else, we ran into my good friend Cate coming out of the bedroom next to ours.

"*Ellison*," she said with a squeal, bouncing forward to hug me tightly. "You're here. Thank god. I missed you. Jesus. I don't think I can handle you moving to the sticks."

Her familiar perfume reminded me of summers in the Hamptons and the times I'd escorted her to various social events in the city. She was a welcome sight.

When her eyes flicked over my shoulder, I remembered my manners. What in the world would Cate think about me dating a man?

"Grey, this is Cate McArthur. She's Ian and Binnie's niece. Cate, this is Grey Blackwood." I couldn't bring myself to call him my boyfriend again this soon. I sounded like a teenager when I said it that way.

After he greeted her, Grey slipped his hand into mine, and my heart took a little wobbly swan dive. I glanced over at him, but his face was as stoic and controlled as ever.

I was holding hands with him. Holding hands with a man in semipublic. It was different and weird, but something about it felt good too, like reminding me I had a partner in crime. For the first time since planning this scheme, I realized it might actually be nice to have someone to talk to late at night in the privacy of my bedroom, to debrief with about the day and gossip with about the odd characters I'd encountered.

I'd never had that before. My sister and I had gone away to boarding school and been placed in separate dorms. Having teenage boys as roommates didn't make for a safe place to confide any secrets or deep thoughts.

Even when I'd had girlfriends, I'd been more of a listener than a participant in the gossip. My father had warned me against giving too much away to anyone, even in a relationship, so I'd been reserved with the people I'd dated.

Knowing Grey would never actually want a real relationship with me meant I didn't need to worry about giving too much of myself to him. I could give him all I wanted, and he'd drop it like a rock as soon as we were done.

That realization didn't feel great, but it was the reality of our situation. I'd known what I was getting myself into when I signed on for this plan.

In the meantime, I enjoyed the solid warmth of his hand in mine. Cate's eyes widened a little when she noticed it, and my face heated in response. But I held on tight to him anyway.

"Nice to meet you," Cate said with a friendly and open smile. Her long blond hair was pulled back in a loose braid, and the sundress she wore showed off her curvy figure. She was as gorgeous as ever.

"Has Ellison warned you about all of the riveting adventures we're going to get up to this weekend?"

Grey felt stiff next to me. What would it take to get him to relax? Hard-core Valium, most likely.

"He promised me there would at least be plenty of alcohol," Grey replied with the barest hint of a polite smile.

Cate laughed. "True. And they don't skimp on the good stuff either. Be sure to ask Uncle Ian for a taste of his thirty-year-old McCallan. He won't share his fifty-year-old Bowmore, but he'll gladly pour you a glass of the McCallan."

Grey seemed surprised Cate knew her whisky. He thanked her for the tip but then added, "Any tips on impressing him enough to encourage such generosity?"

Cate looked between the two of us with a twinkle in her eye. "Tell him what you love about his favorite godson. He'll be putty in your hands."

My face felt like it was on fire, and I tried tugging my hand out of Grey's grip. He held on tight.

"Not sure Ian is ready for *that* conversation," he murmured low enough only I could hear. Little hairs stood up all over my body.

When we got downstairs, Cate left us to find Binnie, and I pulled Grey in the direction of Ian's study. The following meeting was awkward, but I explained things to my godfather the way Grey and I had planned. I told him about running into Grey in the spring and developing serious feelings for him. I explained my fears about the foundation as well as "other concerns" to do with the way my father was running York Capital. Even though Ian understood my fears about the future of York, he still seemed suspicious of Grey.

"What exactly are you hoping to accomplish here this week?" Ian asked Grey directly.

"While, of course, I'd like nothing more than to convince you to listen to my proposal about the property in Hell's Kitchen, I'm here at Ellison's request. He seems to think I lack the ability to relax and take time away from work. I'd like to prove to him I can enjoy our time together here away from the office and away from the never-ending list of responsibilities in the city."

"So, am I to understand you will refrain from discussing work matters this week?" Ian asked.

"No, sir. It's unrealistic to ask a workaholic to change overnight. I can't possibly promise not to talk about the things that matter most..." He glanced at me with an unusual intensity. "*Almost* most to me."

God, he was good at this fake boyfriend thing. I swallowed and tried to look convincingly at Ian. "He's a good man, Ian. Give him a break."

Grey continued as if I hadn't said anything. "My dedication to work is part of my identity, as I'm sure you understand. I wouldn't be the man Ellison... deserves if it weren't for my rabid attention to my career. I would still be salting french fries in White Plains if I didn't work this hard and want success enough to work my ass off for it."

Ian studied the man for a few moments before nodding. "You're probably right about that. You certainly wouldn't have attracted his notice all the way out there. Ellison is a city boy through and through. My wife and I have bets placed on how long he'll last out there in the wilds of Vermont." He ended this little jab with a soft laugh. It might have actually been funny if it wasn't a real fear of mine as well.

"Thank you for understanding," Grey said. "I look forward to meeting your wife. Ells has had nothing but great things to say about her. He also tells me she's the love of your life."

Woah. No wonder this guy had people eating out of the palm of his hand in business. He knew exactly where to strike to get someone on his side. Ian's eyes went soft, and his entire body relaxed.

"That she is. I don't want anything to upset her this week. She looks forward to this event every year, and this year is no exception." He gave Grey a reluctant smile. "You are welcome here, Grey. I expect to see you enjoying time away from work. There comes a point in every man's life where he needs to take stock of *why* he works so hard. What's it all for if not enjoying time off with friends and family?"

Even though Grey nodded, I wasn't sure he actually understood or agreed. He didn't seem like he was anywhere near that point in a man's life. And that was fine. Maybe when he met the right man for him, someone who hadn't accidentally fucked his plans up during college and who didn't give him a hard time as often as possible simply because it was so much fun, he'd be ready to reassess what was important. In the meantime, both of us *were* actually here for work reasons.

I stood up and stretched, trying to put an end to this awkward meeting. "You said something about offering us drinks. Maybe we could take them and find your lovely bride?"

Thankfully, Ian agreed. We left the study and followed him to a glassed-in room at the side of the house, perfectly situated to watch the sunset over the edge of the large formal gardens. There was a bar set up with a uniformed bartender, and another uniformed server meandered through the room with canapés.

"You sure we shouldn't have dressed up?" Grey murmured against the back of my ear.

I shuddered at the feel of his warm breath as my eyes took in familiar and unfamiliar faces in the room. "Very sure. One of the McArthur cousins is in ripped jeans and a graphic tee. We're fine."

Grey's hand slid along my side to rest on my lower back again, asserting his claim by keeping me by his side. I didn't mind it one bit.

We made our way to the bar to get a drink while Ian crossed the room to greet some newcomers.

"What would you like to drink... darling?" Grey said in his serious voice. I wanted to laugh out loud at his forced endearment, but I bit my tongue against the urge.

"Gin and tonic, please."

He kept his arm around my waist as he ordered the same for both of us and waited for the bartender to make the drinks. I knew from the couple of business dinners I'd attended with him this past week, he would only allow himself one drink to avoid the risk of losing mental sharpness. He'd never admit such a thing to me, but I sensed he lived in fear of saying the wrong thing sometimes, and staying mostly sober was part of the way he held tightly to his control.

When a server walked by with some food, I grabbed a few pieces onto a napkin and offered one of them to Grey. Since the bartender had just handed him two lowball glasses, his hands were too full to take the little toast point covered in brie and jam.

"Open up," I said softly before placing the snack on his tongue and feeding myself one immediately after. "God, that's good. I was starving."

"You're always starving. Here." He handed me one of the glasses, and we made our way over to a nearby group of people.

I recognized a few of the people in the group and greeted them with a smile. After introducing everyone to Grey, we had a rousing round of "where are you from and how do you know Ian and Binnie" that was thankfully supplemented by several passes of the cheese tray.

Grey was very quiet, but his reticence didn't surprise me. He tended to listen more than he spoke anyway, especially when he was sizing up a prospective investment client or potential adversary. It didn't take long, however, for Binnie to notice we'd joined the gathering.

"Get your ass over here and give me a proper hug hello." I turned to see her sparkling eyes and catch a whiff of her familiar hairspray. She wore a sheer floral top over a spaghetti-strap tank and white capri pants. Gold bracelets jangled on her wrist, and the giant rock on her ring finger caught the warm light in the room.

I gave her a tight hug. "Hey. It's good to see you. Sorry it's been so long."

She pulled back and grasped my arms, giving me that loving look the way moms in cornball movies sometimes did. "It shouldn't surprise me that we have to travel out here to see each other when we live in the same damned city, but it does."

I turned and reached for Grey's hand to pull him closer. "Binnie, this is Grey. Grey, Binnie Duckworth."

She put out her hand for him to shake, but he pulled it to his lips and kissed it. "Ma'am. Thank you for hosting us at your beautiful home. I've never seen anything like it. It's both elegant and comfortable. I can't imagine the memories you've made here over the years."

I stared at him. Where the hell had this guy come from? Grey stage-whispered at me out of the corner of his mouth. "Stop staring at me. I can be polite when I choose to be."

Binnie's laughter filled the space around us, and I could tell she was instantly charmed. "I love it. And thank you for your kind words. This place is special to us, and we always enjoy sharing it with family and friends. Make yourself at home, dear."

Grey slid his arm around me and pulled me close. "This one has told me all of his favorite parts with special attention paid to the fresh scones at breakfast and the lobster at dinner. I worry a little about what else we might do besides eating. It seems that's the only activity he recalls with any clarity."

I smacked his chest with the back of my hand and muttered, "*Ass.*"

Binnie laughed again and told him I was right. The chef was worth his weight in gold. She told us a few of the special meals and dishes they'd planned for the week, and Grey expressed his anticipation. At one point, while he spoke of a particularly memorable seafood dinner he'd had on a business trip to Maine, Binnie glanced at me and winked.

She liked him. She approved.

My gut soured at the thought of disappointing her someday soon by telling her there would be no future between me and this charming man. Something in my body language must have changed because Grey glanced down at me with a frown.

"You okay?"

I smiled. "'Course."

Grey lifted his free hand to run his thumb along my cheekbone. I watched his face and wondered what he was doing.

"Eyelash," he murmured before turning back to Binnie and continuing the conversation. My eyes stayed glued to him as my stomach somersaulted from his gentle caress. His touch made me hungry for more.

Throughout the evening, I began to feel like a child at a parade. Grey Blackwood was the celebrity on the float, throwing out handfuls of candy. I desperately wanted him to look at me, notice me, give me just a taste of something sweet. A tiny piece would do.

While he calmly moved from person to person, charming everyone with interesting stories or by asking people to share their favorite travel destinations or a recent book or movie recommendation, I slowly but decisively lost my ever-loving shit.

I wanted to sleep with him. Like... actually fuck him. Kiss him, suck his dick, run my hands over every inch of his naked body. All of it. I wanted him with a kind of desperate hunger that almost scared me, or would have if he wasn't so freaking comforting and reassuring. He stood or sat by my side all night with either a relaxed arm around my waist or his hand in mine. Even when we were separated and talking to different people, every time I searched for him, I found him glancing over to make sure he knew where I was.

And it wasn't because he was nervous. At least, I didn't think it was. He seemed to handle himself just fine. I thought maybe it was because he had the same need I did to know where the other was at all times. Somehow we'd become a team, two halves of a whole who gravitated toward each other as a default.

I'd expected him to spend the first evening out of sorts. He'd supposedly been nervous about not knowing how to handle himself, but then he'd come in and wooed everyone. And once he'd told me about golfing with Richard Branson? I should have known this wouldn't have been the first time he'd be in company with some of society's elites. The man golfed at exclusive clubs, had been to a Yankees game as a personal guest of Hal Steinbrenner, and had dined with Ariana Rockefeller. He was no stranger to manners, and yet, I could see as the night went on the encounters seemed to wear on him.

By the time the old grandfather clock in the corner of the large drawing room struck midnight, I had begun to feel a very faint tremor in the hand I held.

I cleared my throat and spoke to the group of Duckworth cousins we'd been talking to about current investment opportunities in personal space travel, a topic I couldn't have possibly cared less about. "Sorry to duck out for the night, but it's been a long day. Binnie said there's a tennis round-robin tomorrow, and I need to get plenty of sleep if I plan to wipe the courts with all of you." I stood and shot them a cheeky grin, pulling Grey up beside me.

We said our good-nights, making sure to stop by the seating area where Binnie and Ian were holding court to thank them for dinner. Once we left the room, I dropped my smile but held on to Grey's hand. I planned to enjoy it as much as I could before we were alone in the room and he went back to treating me like a business partner, or worse, his mortal enemy.

"If I'd known you were tired, I would have made our excuses earlier," he said softly as we headed up the grand staircase.

"No, it's fine. I'm not too tired. I've just had enough small talk for the night." I didn't mention my assumption that *he* was the tired one.

"Did you determine when we're to expect your parents' arrival?"

We turned down the hallway toward the wing that held our bedroom. "Tomorrow afternoon, I think. I'm glad we were able to have tonight without that added stress."

When we entered the room, I noticed the bed had been turned down. Fresh flowers were in a vase on the desk, and a little tray sat next to it with bottled water, a small bottle of wine, two crystal glasses, and a ceramic dish of individually wrapped chocolates. It reminded me of something that might have been in a honeymoon suite, even though I knew it was a standard evening treat with the turndown service provided by the stewards who tended the rooms during the house party.

Suddenly, the bed seemed huge. I hadn't let myself think much of it before now, but if I was going to insist it was time for bed, someone was going to have to face the elephant in the room.

"Oh," I said without thinking.

Grey's small huff of laughter filled the quiet room. "Oh, indeed. Don't tell me you faced all of those people, one of whom was literally British royalty, and now you're afraid of a bed."

"Pfft, me? Pfft. Afraid of a bed? Pfft." How many times was I going to *pfft*? I glanced around as if looking for the hidden Murphy bed in one of the walls. Maybe if I tilted a particular decorative sculpture forward, the panel would slide open, revealing a second bedroom...

"Change out of your clothes and get in bed, Ells. You can make a little Hadrian's Wall down the center if it will make you feel more comfortable."

I noticed Grey wasn't paying much attention to me despite the teasing. He'd found his phone and began scrolling through the messages Marcel had no doubt sent him while we'd been away from the room.

"Yeah, fine," I said, moving to the large armoire in the corner of the room. I'd noticed the suitcases were no longer on their stands, which meant the attendant had unpacked our things for us. Sure enough, our clothes hung neatly in the armoire or sat primly folded in the nearby chest of drawers. It was oddly endearing to see Grey's boxer briefs stacked next to mine.

I pulled out pajama pants and a T-shirt before going to the bathroom and closing the door. It was cool in the mostly marble room. The sweet scent of gardenia filled the small space from the complimentary bath products in a dish by the sink. Maybe if I took a shower, I could buy myself a little time.

Once the water was warm enough, I stripped down and stepped into the glass enclosure and closed the door. I let the hot water beat down on the skin of my neck and shoulders for a long time. I thought about all of the times Grey had reached for me tonight and all of the times I'd felt the warm solid presence of his body against mine.

I thought about the kiss.

How the hell was I going to share a bed with the man without humping him in my sleep? Impossible.

When the sound of the bathroom door opening hit my ears, my eyes shot open.

"Sorry," Grey said, averting his eyes. "I couldn't wait any longer. I'll just..." He stepped past the shower to the tiny toilet room and closed the door.

I stared after him. My dick was rock hard from imagining the two of us in bed together. Had he seen it? Would he care if he had? Should I have been embarrassed?

Just in case, I turned my back to the glass door so the most he'd see on his return trip was my bare ass. Hell, he'd already seen that before when he'd walked in on me by accident at his apartment.

Wait. Had it been an accident?

Yes, of course it had. Grey Blackwood might have been warming up to me as a human being, but he sure as hell didn't want me as a *man*. And why would he? Not only was I inexperienced with men, thus unable to bring anything good to the sexual table, but I was also the bane of his existence. Hell, he'd probably want to lecture me the entire time he fucked me about various things I'd done wrong or ways I'd annoyed him.

Stop imagining angry sex. Fuck.

Now I was harder than before. Why didn't the embarrassment negate the inappropriate wood? Maybe because getting hard in the shower was a completely normal occurrence. Barging in on someone while they're showering wasn't. He could have gone to any number of bathrooms in this place. Hell, this place had bathrooms in the double digits. Why did he insist on using this one?

"Sorry," he mumbled again before shutting the bathroom door with a snick.

"Fuck," I said under my breath. "Fucking fuck."

My soapy hand went immediately to my dick, and I stroked it fast and rough. I just needed this over with. If I was going to sleep with the man without the nighttime humping, I needed to nut right the hell now.

While Grey Blackwood was just outside the door.

For the second time this week.

This was kind of becoming a habit.

"*Argh,*" I groaned when my release finally came. I spilled hot and hard against the shower wall and into my hand. As soon as I caught my breath, I finished washing myself and turned off the shower.

Thank fuck. Now maybe I could sleep with the sexiest man on the planet without performing the sex version of sleepwalking.

I made my way into the room and pulled back the thick duvet before I noticed he'd turned off most of the lights and changed into his own pajama bottoms. Only, his were sleep shorts made out of the softest-looking cotton on earth.

And it was obvious he wasn't wearing anything under them.

I stared at the front of his shorts without realizing I was doing it. How big was his dick? What did it look like? Was he seriously unaffected by seeing a naked man in the shower? I wasn't the hottest man in the world, but I wasn't bad.

Was I?

Grey cleared his throat. I looked up at his face and caught him smirking at me. "Have a nice shower?"

And just like that, I was chubbing up again.

At this rate, I was going to sleepfuck him for sure.

13

GREY

"Being ruled by your emotions... can only lead to catastrophe."
~ Sun Tzu, *The Art of War*

I wanted to fuck him. It was as simple as that. Apparently nothing had changed in fifteen years despite many, many, *many* hours of self-lecture about how, if given the chance, I would never, ever let Ellison York get close to me again.

Now, here we were.

"Get in the damned bed, Ellison," I said before making my way to the steamy bathroom and searching for my toothbrush. I didn't take kindly to strangers going through my things, and I was on edge from discovering the room stewards had unpacked my bags.

I could hear Ellison scrambling between the sheets while I opened a drawer in the vanity to discover my toiletries. I took plenty of time brushing my teeth and washing my face so Wild-Nerves McGee could settle down in there. You'd have thought being gay was somehow contagious the way he was trying to avoid even the idea of us sharing a bed.

While I didn't for a minute imagine his intent was purposeful, Ellison had been tempting me all night. The way the thin cashmere sweater draped over his broad shoulders and toned chest, the way his slender fingers twitched between mine as he held my hand, and the way his eyes always searched me out regardless of how far away from me he was in the room. The way he smelled like all of the bath products in my guest room at home. He was seriously knocking me off-kilter.

I'd enjoyed holding his hand so much tonight that I'd finally used the excuse of drinking several glasses of water to keep from reaching for him yet again.

And then I'd had to pee while he was buck naked and *wet* in the shower.

This night, this weekend, was going to be impossible. If I wasn't worried about being discovered and offending our hosts, I might have tried to arrange a clandestine hookup with the attractive red-haired man we'd met from San Francisco. From the looks he'd given me at dinner, I gathered one positive word from him might have taken care of my little pent-up problem.

But I wouldn't do that to Ellison, no matter how fake our relationship was. Also? I didn't want the redhead. I wanted the New Yorker who'd eaten half my salad and then finished my dessert.

I stared at myself in the mirror. "Welp, here we are. So much for fifteen years of being over Ellison fucking York."

It hadn't helped that several people had mistakenly assumed Ellison was dating Binnie's niece instead of me. I'd gotten the feeling their relationship was one the guests at this house party had speculated about for years since Ellison and Cate were of similar age and both wealthy, successful, and attractive.

And it hadn't helped that they appeared to be great friends with plenty of things in common. They'd spent part of the evening discussing risk-based capital requirements for merchant banking investments as it related to the law. Instead of falling asleep midsentence, they'd chatted excitedly about the various challenges to areas of legal practices surrounding the regulations.

While I was incredibly turned on by Ellison's demonstration of intelligence and legal education, I was selfishly annoyed that he'd chosen to speak to someone else about such a thing when I'd been the one in the room with the most financial exposure to the risks inherent in the issue at hand.

When I finally turned out the bathroom light and returned to the bedroom, Ellison was dead asleep with his mouth wide open and his arms and legs starfished across the bed. There was absolutely no sight of a Hadrian's Wall of pillows.

His hair was wild with messy curls still half-damp from his shower. I reached over and gently shoved his arms and legs over to his side of the bed before sliding in beside him and lying on my side to face him. He was beautiful. More attractive today than he'd ever been in college. He was noticeably more comfortable in his skin, and his face now bore traces of his life experience. He looked like an adult, a man, someone who knew there was more to life than frat-boy dares and drunken pranks.

There hadn't been a single moment in the past week that had proven any of my assumptions about Ellison York from that night at the country club.

He wasn't a user. He wasn't uncaring or unkind. He wasn't a pompous asshole. In fact, he was the opposite of everything I'd ever tried to tell myself he was.

I reached out and pushed a wayward curl off his forehead. Despite being tired, I felt like I could stay up for hours simply watching him sleep. It was the only time he truly shut up, but it was also the only time I knew for sure he wasn't worrying about me.

At first, I'd thought he was worried I'd fuck up—either in manners or in our fake boyfriend story—but at some point during dinner, I'd realized he hadn't been worried about my actions. He'd been worried about my *feelings*. I wasn't used to people looking out for my feelings, but when one of Ian's friends—who I vaguely knew through a friend at Goldman Sachs—had begun pressing me aggressively about acquiring Heath and Kelty earlier this year, Ellison had butted his nose into the conversation and defended me like a rabid Yorkie.

"Did you know the net asset value of Heath and Kelty has gone up nineteen percent since the date of acquisition?" Ellison had asked, leaning around me to make a nuisance of himself. "And because of the transition, Stitch Trend reversed course and gave Heath and Kelty a healthy ownership stake after turning Bob Kelty down only three months earlier."

He was like my own little public relations firm. I wasn't even sure when he'd had time to gather the information he'd shared, but I wasn't complaining. It was nice to have a champion after all these years.

I ran my fingers through his hair one more time just to make sure it didn't dry in a big bird's nest, but then I forced my hands to myself and closed my eyes to sleep.

It shouldn't have surprised me to wake up with an armful of Ellison York, but it did. He was plastered sweatily against my side with his cheek mashed against my neck and his hair in my face. One of his legs was thrown over one of mine, and his morning wood pressed against my hip.

Both of my arms were around him, and I took a few moments to inhale the warm, masculine scent of him.

I could get used to this. But even thinking about something like that was dangerous. I sighed and nudged him away from me. Today was the first full day of activities Binnie had planned for everyone. This was the part of the week I'd most been dreading since I would have done just about anything to spend the day researching potential new investments instead of making a fool of myself in unfamiliar sporting situations.

Thankfully, I'd taken tennis lessons a few years ago at the country club after one of the members had invited me to play with him. I wasn't exactly championship material, but I at least understood the rules of the game and could hold my own for a casual day of social tennis.

I made my way into the bathroom to shower and shave. Last night had gone better than I'd expected. After reconnecting with Ellison York, I'd gone right back to that headspace of thinking I was the poor kid from White Plains who didn't know shit about anything, so it had taken me a little while to realize that I was as well educated and well traveled as anyone at this party now.

I'd carried the mantle of my poor upbringing for so long, I hadn't noticed when I'd begun to feel more comfortable around people with money and culture. Somehow, though, I still felt like I didn't belong.

I didn't know if that feeling was simply a holdover from my years caddying at the Crosbie club job or as a scholarship kid at Yale, but I was tired of feeling like an outsider. It had been my biggest hesitation in agreeing to this plan and was one of the many reasons I dreaded the arrival of Ellison's parents.

When I came back out of the bathroom to look for clothes to wear, Ellison was just waking up. "I'm going to get dressed and go in search of coffee," I told him. "Take your time. I don't think we have anything scheduled for a couple of hours."

His hair was hilariously messy, and his eyes were only half-open. "I fell asleep fast. How'd you sleep?"

"Good. Yeah, you were out before I even finished brushing my teeth." I pulled clothes out of the drawer and returned to the bathroom to change. I hadn't missed Ellison's furtive glance at the towel around my waist. Good. Let him be the one disconcerted for once. I'd spent plenty of time lusting after his ass; it was about time the tables were turned.

Not that he was lusting after me. It was most likely simple curiosity. Regardless, it gave me inappropriate thoughts that needed tamping down.

I dressed quickly and left the room. The butler who'd greeted us the day before was on hand to direct me to the breakfast room, where a few of the guests were already gathered at one of several round tables. "Good morning," I said before making a beeline for the coffee station set up on a table against the wall.

The redhead from San Francisco, whose name suddenly came to me after my first sip of coffee, invited me to sit at his table. "I've decided to stop doing the time-difference math to justify my jet lag," he said with a sleepy grin. "Instead, I'm going to try to remember my Stanford days when staying up all night wasn't a big deal."

I took a seat next to him and reached for one of the scones from the porcelain tray in the center of the table before placing it on the little plate in front of me. "Are you normally an early riser?" I asked politely.

The woman on the other side of him leaned over to answer for him. "Jake hates mornings. When we were growing up, he slept past noon as often as he could."

The redhead nudged her with his shoulder. "Ignore my sister. She thinks I'm still the sleepy teen from a decade ago."

I sipped my coffee and devoured the scone while the sibling pair teased each other. The sun was shining on another clear day outside, and I looked forward to getting some exercise later.

"Do you both play tennis?" I asked. I hated this kind of small talk, but I was very familiar with it. It was an integral part of networking and making connections with people.

"Jake played singles in college," the sister said. "Which means he's a terrible doubles partner if you actually want a chance to hit the ball yourself."

I eyed the attractive man with a smile. "But it probably means you win."

Jake laughed and nodded. "And isn't that the most important part anyway?"

We were still laughing when Ellison walked in. He had an odd look on his face that I couldn't interpret. I pulled back the chair next to mine and gestured for him to join me. I could tell he was still half-asleep, so I stood up to fix him some coffee.

When I returned to the table, I noticed Ellison had moved to my seat, which meant I was relegated to the seat farthest from the conversation. That was fine by me. I grabbed the plate with my scone crumbs on it and helped myself to another one.

I wasn't paying attention to the conversation, so when Ellison's hand reached for mine under the table, I blinked over at him in surprise. He was in the middle of talking to Jake, who was asking Ellison questions about how we'd met. Jake's sister had wandered off to talk to someone at another table.

Jake's eyes met mine. They carried the same heat and promise he'd looked at me with last night. I kept my face as neutral as possible.

Ellison responded to the man's question. "It took me a while to stop thinking of him as that kid I'd kind of known at Yale," he admitted. "I realized people can change a lot in fifteen years. Grey certainly has."

"How so?" Jake asked, keeping his hungry eyes on me.

Ellison's hand tightened in mine. "Unfortunately, he's harder to impress. He doesn't trust as easily. But he's also incredibly kind and generous. He's charity-minded, which he may have been back then and I just didn't realize it. He's also..." He glanced at me before looking back at Jake with a pointed stare. "Rabidly monogamous."

It took my brain a beat to process what he'd said, and then I had to fight not to laugh. I leaned in and whispered in his ear. "If there's going to be a catfight here, save me a seat in the front row."

His eyes were angry slits when he turned his glare on me. God, he was sexy as fuck, especially when annoyed. I loved that he was pretending to be jealous over a fictional relationship.

"Message received," Jake said with dancing eyes. "But if you know your house party history, you'll admit sometimes the rules were meant to be broken in the pursuit of entertainment."

I ran the tip of my nose down the thin skin behind Ellison's ear to his neck, where I nuzzled him and pressed kisses. "Mm. Not me," I said. "Not sure I could handle more *entertainment* than what Ellison provides."

Ellison's skin flushed dark pink, and I noticed the growing bulge between his legs under the edge of the table.

Well, shit.

Was that for me? Either Ells was one hell of a Method actor, or he was a lot more interested in me than I'd allowed myself to believe, and that knowledge made my throat go dry.

I desperately wished I could take it further, secret him back upstairs and continue this ruse behind closed doors. But I knew that wasn't possible.

Eyes on the prize, Blackwood. I was at this party to acquire a building, not to get laid.

Not that I believed for a minute that getting laid was actually on the table, whether Ellison was attracted to me or not.

Jake laughed and made a teasing comment about Ellison's red-faced discomfort. Instead of ignoring the pompous ass, Ellison said, "I'm just remembering some *entertainment* we got up to last night when Grey walked into the bathroom while I was in the shower and — Sorry, that's too much information."

I noticed Ellison's palm had turned damp in mine. I let go of it to put my arm around him instead. "Jake doesn't want to hear about our shenanigans, sweetie," I said before pressing a kiss to Ells's cheek.

Jake must have thought all of this was a kind of flirting. "Not true. I'd like to hear about it or join it. Just let me know what room you're in, and I'll be happy to *add* to the entertainment."

Thankfully, Binnie's niece Cate joined us before I could growl out a warning for Jake to stay the fuck away from Ellison.

"I love this place so much," she exclaimed. "I wish I could come more often. Remember when Aunt Binnie let us paint the boardwalk for Fourth of July that one year?"

The conversation turned to childhood memories of previous visits here. Jake eventually wandered off to find more interesting people to talk to, and I felt Ellison's body lose some tension at his departure. I wondered if he only cared out of concern for our reputations here or if it was possible there was another reason. For all I knew, it was his habit to be jealous of someone flirting with his partner regardless of who it was and how serious he was about them.

Against my best interest, I enjoyed the fictional jealousy. It was nice to have someone claim possession of me, even if it was all for show.

I removed my arm from around his shoulder so I could finish my scone and coffee. After a few minutes of listening to Cate and Ellison talk about their favorite memories, I realized Ellison had taken my hand again. I wasn't even sure he realized he'd done it. It felt natural to sit there like that with him, and when I needed to use my hand again, I pulled his hand over and rested it on my thigh while I reached for the pot of strawberry preserves in the center of the table. It was awfully domestic for someone like me, but I liked it.

Until I tuned back into the conversation between Ellison and Cate.

"Fair warning, Mom wants you to escort me to the Ballard's charity ball in November, and she's hoping you'll come to Thanksgiving at the house in Connecticut since your parents have plans to do some traveling in the Mediterranean that week."

"Sounds good," Ellison said before taking a big bite of scone.

I cleared my throat and returned my hand to his with a squeeze, reminding him of my existence. If we were truly dating, I wouldn't be able to let this conversation go without participating. Also, I wouldn't exactly be thrilled hearing about all of the damned dating events they'd been to together. "Actually, sweetheart, my mother is expecting us for Thanksgiving. Let me talk to her and see if we can change our plans."

Ellison nearly choked on the scone. "Shit, er, crap. I mean, sorry. Of course. Sorry." His stammering was actually kind of adorable. I loved it when he was thrown off-balance. "Yes, we'll check with... with your mom before making any solid plans. I'd, uh, hate to disappoint her."

I smiled serenely at Cate. "Thanks for the invitation." *Not that you invited me.*

She was obviously embarrassed by the oversight, but I wasn't quite that quick to forgive. It was a common experience the gay men I knew in relationships had mentioned before, having the relationship completely ignored when making social plans, but experiencing it here now was still startling.

"I'm so sorry," she said. "Of course you're welcome. And feel free to bring your mother too!"

"That's not necessary," Ellison assured her before looking at me with an apology in his eyes. "I assumed your mom would be on one of her cruises. We'll have to ask her what she has planned for the holidays."

I smiled at Cate with my most polite mask on. "It's true. My mother can't get enough of cruises. She's on one right now on the Danube. Says it's beautiful this time of year."

She seemed relieved at my change of subject and proceeded to ask questions about other cruises my mom and her friends had been on. Her parents had been on some of the same trips, so we were able to speak comfortably enough until a uniformed server invited us to help ourselves to the breakfast buffet they'd laid out on the sideboard. I quickly offered to make Ellison a plate so I could stand up and make a temporary escape.

An older woman next to me at the sideboard shot me a smile. "Aren't they adorable together? Ellison and Cate have been thick as thieves for years. They make such a lovely couple. I keep asking Binnie when that young man is going to get to the point, but she tells me he's not quite ready yet." Her gold bracelets, similar to the ones Binnie wore, clacked as she reached for some eggs with the long serving spoon. "You two seem like good friends. Maybe you can put a little bug in his ear, hm? They would make lovely children. Just imagine, the heir of York Capital and the future general counsel of the Securities and Exchange Commission. It's a match made in heaven. Maybe when Marianne gets here, she'll talk some sense into him. Just look at them. So beautiful and kind. And both charity-minded." She sighed and returned to her food selection.

I glowered at her before turning to look at the "happy couple." Sure enough, their heads were bent together, and they were whispering furtively. Both of them had big grins on their faces. It was one thing for this old lady to misunderstand the situation, but yet another for those two to act like the couple everyone thought they were.

I turned back to the chafing dishes and piled a giant blob of stewed prunes on Ellison's plate next to a pot of sugar-free, fat-free yogurt and a single walnut from the waffle toppings caddy. After returning to the table, I plonked the plate in front of him and set my own down before going to refill my coffee. When I finally sat down to eat, I noticed my plate was the one with the prunes and walnut while Ellison munched happily on my bacon and eggs.

Asshole.

I stood back up and made another plate. My body needed plenty of fuel if I was going to beat Jake's ass on the tennis court and win a popularity contest against the brilliant legal mind of Cate fucking McArthur.

14

ELLISON

"Do not swallow bait offered by the enemy."
~ Sun Tzu, *The Art of War*

Grey had been acting weird since breakfast.

"Are you sure you slept okay?" I asked him for the second time. We were in our room changing for the upcoming tennis round-robin, and I was desperate to distract myself from the sight of his bare, muscular legs.

"Yes. Why do you ask?" He grabbed something from the chest of drawers that looked like a bright orange elastic waistband with nothing attached.

"Are you... are you putting on a jock?" I squeaked.

Grey looked up at me slowly and held out the item in his hands. "It's the strap that goes around my suitcase. Whoever unpacked my suitcase must have stashed it here by mistake. No, I'm not wearing a jock to play tennis. Why? Did you have plans to aim the ball at my junk?"

"Pfft. Me? Pfft." *Oh god, not this again.* I bit my tongue and clamped my lips together tightly. Someone needed to change the subject. "So, that guy Jake wanted to sleep with you. With me. I mean, with us?"

Excellent choice.

Grey's eyes looked thunderous. "Stay away from him."

"You jealous?" I was teasing out of nervousness, but he didn't seem to pick up on it.

"No. But that man will chew you up and spit you out, Ellison. Stay away from him."

"You don't think I can hold my own with a guy like that?"

His eyes were so intense, my stomach tightened in response. "Can you hold your own with a guy, period?"

"Pfft. Me? Pfft."

Mother of Christ.

Grey snorted out a soft laugh. "Get your clothes on, Stonewall. I don't want to be late."

As I changed my clothes, I muttered under my breath about how I could handle sex, I wasn't a virgin, and just because sex with a man was a little different than sex with a woman, I was smart enough to figure it out even if I didn't have experience with it yet. He seemed to be ignoring me, which was fine, but when I was finally ready to leave the room, Grey stopped me before I could open the door.

He grabbed my arm and stepped closer until he'd backed me up against the door of our room. My heart pounded at his nearness, his scent, the inexplicably thunderous look on his face. I wanted him to kiss me again. For... practice. "W-what're you doing?" I asked.

His chest bumped mine, and one of his legs nudged mine apart until his hip was against my dick. "You can hold your own with a man?"

Grey brought a hand up to clasp the front of my throat, gently at first and then firmly enough for me to feel all five fingers pressing into my neck. His grip pinned me in place, and his strong body was immovable against mine.

With a man? Sure. With *this* man? I was probably going to have a heart attack.

I stared at him. He moved closer until we were almost nose-to-nose. His voice was low and fierce. "Being with a man is not the same as being with a woman." He moved quickly to grab my wrists and pin them above my head. I struggled against him out of habit of not wanting any man to get one over on me, but it was clear he was stronger than I was. We grappled for a moment until he had me pinned again. "Don't fuck around with men like that guy downstairs. You want to experiment with a man? Find someone else."

I hadn't really thought he was jealous, but now I wasn't so sure. I decided to test him.

"Maybe I like being dominated by a stronger man," I suggested as calmly as I could. The slight tremor in my voice betrayed me, but it wasn't fear. It was excitement. Hopefully Grey couldn't tell the difference. "Maybe I like a little fight in bed."

Grey struck quickly, flipping me around until my front was mashed against the door and his body was pressed hard along the length of my back. His stiff cock jabbed one of my ass cheeks, and I sucked in a breath and closed my eyes.

"Fuck," I breathed, noticing my own dick was hard against the unforgiving surface of the door.

Grey's lips brushed my ear. "If you won't listen to my warning about that guy, then listen to this one: you are mine this week. Got me? You don't fuck around with anyone else while these people think you belong to me. I don't fucking share."

The blood in my body danced a staccato beat in my brain. *I want you. I want you. I want you.*

"Yeah, okay," I said, sounding a little squeaky. "Only sex with you this week. Got it."

I felt the moment he processed my words. His entire body tensed. I would have laughed if I hadn't been out of my mind with lust.

He stepped away from me with a grunt. "Stop fucking around, and let's go."

I stayed against the door for a long minute to suck in a fresh breath of oxygen that wasn't overloaded with pheromones. When I finally had as much brainpower as I was going to find in this small shared room, I opened the door and stepped out.

Cate was coming out of her room at the same time. "Oh good. Can I walk with you guys to the courts?"

I opened my mouth to say yes when Grey's soft rumble came from behind me. "Her either."

For some reason, this made me want to laugh and dance, skip around the upstairs hallway like a fool. But I kept my composure. "Of course," I said to Cate. "Who can resist the company of a lovely lady on such a beautiful day? Not me, that's for sure."

She was wearing a short, ruffly tennis skirt with a matching tank top. Her hair was up in a ponytail, and a tennis bag hung from her shoulder. Cate took her game seriously. She'd been competing in club tournaments back in Connecticut since she was about as tall as her current racquet.

The courts were located down a crushed-shell footpath through a thick stand of trees. Several other guests joined us on our walk to the courts, and I enjoyed catching up with Cate's mom on our walk. She asked me how the job change was going, and I learned not everyone had heard the news about the takeover at York.

It had only been a week, so it made sense word hadn't spread outside of the venture capital community, but it still surprised me. She asked all about Gigi and her wedding plans. When we arrived at the courts, she and Cate headed out to warm up.

"I didn't bring my racquet," Grey said, looking uncomfortable. "Hopefully they have some here to use?"

I nodded and led him into the small tennis house located between the two courts. Inside, there were racks with various racquets on them as well as cooler bins with bottled water and trays with granola bars and bananas.

Binnie was greeting everyone with a smile and happy conversation. She was dressed in her tennis outfit also and looked as fit as ever. Grey and I selected racquets and answered the coordinator's questions about our skill level. I was surprised to hear Grey describe himself as anything other than a beginner, but then again, I was quickly learning he'd spent time at country clubs making sure he knew how to fit in with the membership. If a prospective client wanted to bond with him over tennis at the club, Grey would most likely find a way to learn how to play tennis in order to close the deal.

Despite claiming to be an experienced player, Grey looked uncomfortable in this environment. When we returned outside to socialize with the other players while the coordinator created the round-robin playing order, Grey was even quieter than usual.

At one point, I caught his eye and lifted my eyebrow. He gritted out his version of a reassuring smile that was anything but reassuring.

I finally pulled him off to the side. "What's going on? If you don't want to play, that's—"

"I want to play."

"But you seem—"

"I'm fine."

I stared at him. His jaw was tight, and he was white-knuckling the grip of his racquet. "You're not fine. Tell me what's going on."

Grey glanced over at a man I didn't recognize. "Nothing is going on. Stop looking for drama around every corner."

His words stung. Clearly something had happened, and his inadvertent glance had clued me in to who it had happened with. I didn't let his pissy attitude stop me from pestering him for information. "Who is that man?"

"What man?"

I threw up my hands, nearly knocking him with my racquet. "Fine. Be this way, but don't get mad at me if I start refusing to talk to you the way you're refusing to talk to me. You're such a fucking hypocrite."

His stoic mask came down, shuttering himself against the world. "You've forgotten who's in charge here," he said softly. "And it's not you."

I wanted to knock him off-balance the way he kept doing to me.

Those fucking walls of his were impossible to breech, and when he stepped back into his protective shell, I wanted to punch something. What would it take to make him feel half as much whiplash as he was giving me?

Now wasn't the time to confront him about being a buttoned-up prick, so I forced my anger down and reached for his hand to return us to happy goddamned couple status before we returned to the group. Grey yanked his hand out of mine like it had burned him, and I caught him glancing at that stranger again.

Fuck this.

I grabbed the back of his head and slammed my lips on his right there in front of everyone. He tried pulling back, but I had a strong enough grip on his hair to stop him. Within seconds, he stopped struggling and kissed me back. His arms came around me, and his broad hand splayed across my lower back.

He tasted like toothpaste. He must have brushed his teeth after breakfast. Who did that? It was sweet and unexpected.

"Mm." The low rumble of satisfaction in his chest made me light-headed, but I needed to stop this ridiculous power play.

I tried to pull back, but Grey's arms tightened like steel bands around me. His tongue teased me as the fervent kiss turned into tiny nibbles of my bottom lip.

He could win kissing trophies. *All* of the kissing trophies.

I needed to explain to him why this was wrong, why we needed to stop. "But…" I kissed him again. "We…" One more tiny taste. "I just…" *Oh, god.* I needed to stop making a fool of myself, but it was too good. Kissing him was like taking a deep draw on the laughing gas at the dentist. Suddenly everything was pleasantly buzzy, and life made complete sense.

When Grey finally stopped kissing me, he continued to hold me tightly against his body. His eyes met mine with their typical intensity. "That was unexpected." His usual calm demeanor made me crazy. How could he possibly be so damned poised after that? I felt like a sweaty, slutty, drooling mess with a public erection and what I had to assume was the most transparent fuck-me face I'd ever worn in my life.

"I hate you," I said. It came out in a tender, affectionate tone for some reason. I cleared my throat and tried again. "I hate you," I hissed. But I was pretty sure it was a loving hiss, if such a thing was possible.

"I know." He ran his hand along my forehead and into my hair. I wanted to preen under his touch. "The feeling is mutual."

We stood together like that for a few more moments, acting like lovers but in reality letting hate-boners deflate before facing the tennis party.

I turned to walk back to the court, but Grey stopped me.

"He's someone I have a date with in a few weeks."

"What?" I squawked. "Who?"

He tilted his head toward the handsome older man. "That guy over there. Marcel and his husband have been trying to set us up for a while. I finally agreed to take him to a Giants game later this month. I've never met him, but I recognize him from photos. Now it's awkward because I'm here with you."

Obviously, I hated the stranger already. "Oh."

"Right. I'll have to tell him things have changed." Grey watched me for my reaction, so I did my best to act like I didn't care one bit.

"I'd hate for you to miss out on a date because of me."

He leaned in and pressed a lingering kiss to the skin in front of my ear. As he pulled away, I could have sworn he whispered, "Liar."

When we finally did return to the group, I noticed Jake's heated expression licking up and down Grey's entire body. Great. Was everyone here after my fake boyfriend? I wanted to punch the redhead in the face, but instead, I busied myself returning to the scene of the crime to pick up the tennis racquet that I must have dropped while I was busy playing stupid kissing games with sexy assholes.

The tennis was invigorating. It took me a few games to remember my years of lessons, but when I did, I enjoyed myself without too many unforced errors. Cate and I were paired up a couple of times, and I also enjoyed partnering with Binnie once. When I was part-nered with Jake, he surprised me with his skill. The two of us were unstoppable, but so was his mouth. He asked me a million questions about my "hot boyfriend," venture capital investing, and the gay scene in New York. Since I only really had impressive knowledge in one of those areas, I tried keeping the conversation focused on VC funding when I couldn't change the subject back to tennis itself.

Finally, the competition winnowed the field down to some play-off games to determine winners. The final pairing was Grey and Jake against Cate and me. Part of me wanted to forfeit and declare it past time for lunch, but I couldn't do that without looking like a jerk.

Grey's eyes met mine across the net. "I should have figured you could hold your own," he said. His face didn't break into a smile, but I could tell he was teasing me. "All those summers at the club with those sexy pros."

"I don't remember the pros being sexy," I said.

"Don't you remember Sam Dodd?" he asked with a laugh.

"I do," Cate said with an exaggerated dreamy sigh. "All the ladies tripped over themselves trying to get his attention."

"While all the men slept with him in the back of the pro shop," Grey said under his breath. I wanted to ask if that had included him. Just the thought of it pissed me off.

"That sounds like my kind of pro," Jake said, slapping Grey on the back. His slap turned to a caressing shoulder massage before I glared at him to cut that shit out.

He walked away with a chuckle. "Let's have some fun," he said over his shoulder. "Grey, babe, would you like to serve, or do you want me to?"

Babe?

I expected Grey to bristle at the cheesy endearment, but he didn't. He smiled and gestured politely. "You're the better server by far. Lead us out."

Cate touched my elbow. "You want to stay on the ad side like we've been doing? I don't mind mixing it up."

"Ad's good," I said, hoping I'd get a chance to accidentally aim an overhead at Jake's solar plexus. "You kick ass at deuce."

The game started friendly enough until Jake served an ace at me that spun wildly off to the side. I nearly fell on my face lunging for it.

Grey turned a big grin on his partner as he walked back to high-five him. "Great serve, man. You'll have to show me how you do that sometime. That was gorgeous."

I stared at him. Was he for real? This pompous show-off wanted nothing more than Grey's fawning approval, and Grey had just given it to him. I clamped my teeth closed against a sarcastic comment.

During the next point, Cate got into a fierce rally with Jake. She had unending patience and waited for him to get frustrated and try a high-risk shot. It was a tactic I'd seen many women use against men in mixed doubles. Jake finally sent a topspin forehand slamming into the net.

I let out a soft snort before glancing back at Cate with a wink.

Grey's friendly voice surprised me. "Bad luck, Jake. We'll get 'em next time."

I turned to see him pass Jake on the court with another high five. Jake followed it up with a casual slap to Grey's ass. Motherfucker. Was this some kind of flirt fest, or were we playing tennis?

The next point's loss was my fault. Jake had tried the nasty spin serve again, and I'd been so proud of returning it, I hadn't been ready for the next shot.

"Sorry," I muttered to Cate. "Stupid mistake."

She walked up and patted me on the shoulder. "Happens to all of us. That was a killer return, though!"

I glanced over at Grey, but he was talking to his partner.

Jake put his arm around my hot, sweaty boyfriend and turned their backs on me so I couldn't overhear or, apparently, lip-read their strategy. I took the opportunity to stare at Grey's muscular back and ass. Fuck, he was sexy. But I sure as shit didn't want to see Jake touching him as possessively as that. Or at all.

Jake's next serve to Cate ended in another baseline rally until I found a shot to pick off. I angled it shallowly on Jake's side since he was too deep to get there in time.

Cate squealed and ran over to hug me. Since she'd been bouncing up and down at the time, I ended up with a face full of boobs. Not a bad way to celebrate a point, to be honest. "We're at deuce! Great job!"

When I moved back to the baseline to get ready for the serve, I noticed Grey shooting daggers at Cate. Was he fucking jealous? Seriously? After all the "great shot, Jake" bullshit?

Game on.

I played as hard as I could after that, trying to balance brutal competitive play with the facade of a man who was simply out enjoying a nice social round-robin on a pretty day.

The harder I played, the harder Jake flirted with Grey until all I wanted to do was smash the ball in the redhead's face and end the game. The score went to deuce at least twenty times. Other guests started wandering back to the house when it went on so long, but the most competitive of them stayed riveted on the back-and-forth.

At one point, I managed to volley a ball right at Grey's feet, and he got me back the next point by sending it down my alley. Jake hooted with glee every time Grey took a point off me, and he took every opportunity to touch Grey's butt. Grey reciprocated, which made absolutely no fucking sense to me considering the lecture I'd gotten about "men like Jake."

So maybe I hugged Cate in celebration a little too often after that.

"Your man seems to be out for blood," Jake teased after one particularly stressful point. Then he lowered his voice so only Grey and I could hear. Cate was back behind the baseline. "But don't worry, babe, you can always drown your sorrows in my room if he stays angry long." He shot me a wink.

I suddenly realized I was a sucker. I'd allowed this asshole to bait me so successfully, I'd forgotten one of the lessons I'd learned in team tennis in high school. Figure out how to win without your ego.

I stepped back to the baseline and whispered my new strategy idea to Cate, who laughed. "I was waiting for you to remember that winning doesn't have to be pretty."

I grabbed her shoulders and mock shook her. "Dammit, stop being so smart, woman!" She laughed and slapped my butt with her racquet.

"Let's do this. Come on."

On the next serve, I barely managed to return it, but when Jake sent it back to me, I was ready. I began a loopy lob game up and over Grey's head deep into the far corner of the court. Jake raced to return it on the defensive, which meant I was able to send another loopy lob up and over Grey's head again to the opposite corner of the court. After six of these lobs, Jake was out of breath from racing back and forth, and Grey was losing his patience at the net. We won the point easily.

Thankfully, we were able to do it again on the very next point since apparently Cate had been trying and perfecting the strategy all along without talking to me about it. We jumped up and down and hugged in celebration for the win before walking to the net to shake hands with our opponents.

Jake grinned and congratulated us, but he made a point of slapping Grey on the ass again when he thanked him for the game. Grey swatted him back with a grin. I was seriously tempted to swat Cate's ass the same way just to point out how ridiculous it was. But I wasn't that guy.

I took my time downing cold water from the bottle on the bench while several of the guests gave us kudos for such an entertaining match. Grey smiled and thanked the people congratulating him and even approached Cate again to compliment her on her playing. Eventually, everyone wandered back to the house except Grey and me.

I had a mouthful of words that needed spewing. I bit my tongue against them because I knew it wasn't going to be pretty, and there was no point to my vitriol. If I could avoid looking at Grey, maybe I could avoid shouting at him.

"You seriously have the balls to be mad at me right now after that show you just put on?" Grey's voice held that same calm patience it always did which made me even madder.

"Fuck you, Grey," I said between tight teeth.

He barked out a humorless laugh. "You sure you don't mean 'fuck Cate'? Because the two of you looked pretty happy out there."

I glanced up at him. "Me? Are you fucking kidding? You practically let that fucker hump your leg!"

"Get your things. We're going back to the house," he growled.

"You're not the boss of me, asshole. You don't get to—"

Grey slammed his hand over my mouth and leaned his face into mine. His voice was so low and commanding, I felt it in my balls. "There are people listening. Get your ass in that little tennis house right this fucking minute."

I stormed into the tennis building and spun to give him a piece of my mind. As soon as he entered, he closed the door and flipped the lock.

"There's no one out there," I snapped. "Everyone went back to the house."

"You're wrong. Jake was deliberately lingering on the path to hear us fight, and you were giving him exactly what he wanted. You let him bait you like a damned child. Anyone with eyes could have seen what he was doing, so why didn't you see it?"

His voice got louder as he spoke until he was shouting at me.

"If you knew he was baiting me, why did you go along with it?" I countered. It was cooler in the shade of the house, and the sweat on my skin suddenly chilled enough to make me shiver.

"Because I was trying to figure out what you were actually reacting to," he admitted. "And why it was making you angry."

"I was angry because you were flirting with the same man you told me to stay away from! Apparently what's good for the gander isn't good for the other gander."

Grey's jaw tightened. "I didn't realize you wanted him."

"I didn't," I shouted. "I don't! Not one single bit. I didn't want... I didn't want..." After realizing what I was going to say next, I stopped myself.

"You didn't want what?"

"Never mind. None of your fucking business. Let's just go." I wanted to get out of here, go back to the house where polite manners were the norm and I could remind myself none of this mattered.

Grey crossed his arms in front of his chest, which of course emphasized his biceps and muscular shoulders. "We're not leaving until you tell me."

"I didn't want you to want him either," I admitted. "There. You happy now? You can go crow about my actual jealousy to your little redheaded fr—*gnfh!*"

Grey's mouth crashed into mine as he lunged forward. His hands grabbed the sides of my face, and within seconds, his body had crowded mine up against the clapboard wall behind me.

Grey's kiss was rabid, all energy and teeth and claws. I scrambled to grab hold of him to keep from falling over from the sheer loss of blood to my brain. I was light-headed and desperate, a combination that left me feeling jacked up and melty all at once.

The scent of our sweat, of sunshine and fresh air, filled the space around us, and the only sound was stuttered breathing and the light smacking and sucking sounds coming from our frenzied kisses.

"Please," I managed to croak. "Please, Grey. Please." It was the only word I could get out, but it said everything I needed to say.

"You'd rather be here with Cate," he bit out against my jaw.

"No."

"You'd rather be here with Jake," he said before nipping my chin.

"No, god. *No.*"

"Tell me, then." Grey's dick pressed hard into my lower belly. "Tell me or it stops."

"You," I breathed. "You. Always you. Only you. You. Please. *You.*"

His hands were everywhere. My shirt hit the floor before I realized he'd yanked it off, my shorts were yanked halfway down my legs, pulling my hard dick with them until it slapped back up against my stomach. I groaned and reached for it, but Grey's growl stopped me.

"Mine."

I closed my eyes and leaned my head back against the wall, trying my hardest to slow down so I didn't nut on the floor before he even touched me. So when the warm wet cavern of his mouth encased my dick, I squeaked and blinked in surprise. "Oh fuck. Oh fuck yes. Please."

He was on his knees, looking up at me with an angry expression. "Close your eyes. You don't get to look at me."

"Why?" It came out as a whine. I would have paid every cent I had to watch him suck me off.

"Do it or I stop."

There was no time or brainpower to wonder why. I closed my eyes and leaned back, focusing on the intense feeling of his mouth on me. His big hands roamed over my thighs and up my stomach to my chest as his tongue swirled around my cock.

"Oh fuck." I didn't have better words than that. This was heaven, and in heaven, my vocabulary took a hike. I wanted to thrust into his mouth, but I didn't dare. When one of his hands moved down to cup my sac, I sucked in a breath and prayed for more. More touching, more sucking, more any kind of sexual interaction with the hottest human I knew.

"You smell so fucking good," he mumbled. "Taste even better."

I made mewling and begging sounds, the kind of thing I would have been embarrassed about if I had the capacity to think clearly.

I didn't.

"Thank you," I said, trying to remember my manners. I didn't want him to stop. I was terrified something I did or said, or failed to do or say, would make him stop, make him regret me. "Thank you so much oh god, fuck. God."

"Come in my mouth," he grunted between sucks.

I opened my eyes in surprise. The view I saw was all it took to make me come. He was debauched. His face was red, and his damp hair was sticking up everywhere because apparently my hand was in it, even though I hadn't even realized I was holding his head. Grey's eyes were glassy, and his lips were stretched and wet.

"*Fuck*," I shouted, throwing my head back again and coming hard. Grey kept his mouth on me until I had to pull away to keep my sanity.

I slid down the wall until I landed my bare ass on the cold stone floor. "Fuck," I said again.

Grey stood back up and loomed over me, reaching into his shorts and pulling out a giant dick. Here was my chance.

I'd owed him a blow job for fifteen years. For fifteen years, I'd fantasized about finally being able to pay him back.

I reached for him, but he didn't let me. He stroked his dick fast just above my face. I looked past it to meet his eyes. They carried heat and intensity that made my chest tighten.

"Come on my face," I whispered without looking away. Even if he wouldn't let me suck him, I needed him to know I was willing to do anything for his pleasure. "Come all over me."

He roared and came a couple of strokes later. Some of his release landed on my cheek, but he caught most of it in his fist.

When he was done, he pulled his shorts back up, found a tennis towel on the nearby counter, and cleaned off his hand before squatting down and carefully wiping my face off. I watched him, wondering what he was going to say, whether he was going to kiss me, confide in me, ask me about my feelings.

But none of that happened. He grabbed my hand and yanked me up before turning without a word and walking out of the tennis house. By the time I put my clothes back on, gathered my wits, and followed him out, there was no sign of him.

I lowered myself onto one of the court benches and leaned over to put my face in my hands. I'd just had the hottest sexual encounter of my life.

With a man who clearly still hated me.

I lifted up my head and turned in the direction of the path back to the house. I was sick and tired of feeling sorry for myself. I'd apologized to Grey a million times. Why in the world would he agree to suck me off if he hated me so much? And how rude was it to walk away from someone without a word after nutting on their fucking face?

Grey Blackwood was an asshole. And if he thought I was going to help him get his precious building sale from Ian while treating me like shit, he could think again.

I stopped silently ranting and took a breath. Was I falling for Grey's bait the way I had fallen for Jake's? Was Grey simply fucking with me to keep me in a state of confusion and hostility?

I needed to keep my eye on the prize and make sure I didn't let my ego get in the way of achieving it.

And, especially after what had just happened between us in the tennis house, I was very clear on the prize I wanted.

Grey Blackwood. Whether he liked it or not.

15

GREY

"Startled beasts indicate that a sudden attack is coming."
~ Sun Tzu, *The Art of War*

My long legs ate up the gravel path as I strode back to the house. My balls were singing a happy tune of thanksgiving while my brain was busy lecturing me on the epic fuckup to beat all fuckups.

It was one thing to touch Ellison, to kiss him even, when we were in front of others trying to pretend to be something we weren't, but there'd been absolutely no excuse to pretend to be boyfriends behind closed doors.

None of that was pretend.

I gritted my teeth. It wasn't pretend from my side, but from his?

No, even as pissed off as I was, I knew it couldn't have been fake on his side either. I'd seen the naked desire in his eyes, heard the pleading sound of his voice. He hadn't faked anything.

After all this time, he'd finally gotten round two of the little gay experiment he'd been looking for in that closet at the club. And I'd happily handed it to him on a silver platter.

Fool me twice, shame on *me.*

"Fucking fuck," I muttered. I knew this had been a mistake. Why hadn't I just stayed in the city and taken my chances with Duckworth? It was clear he wasn't going to soften toward me here any more than he did back home.

Ellison was too tempting, too enticing. All he had to do was look at me and I wanted him with an urgency that scattered my wits. When Ellison was around, my rational brain was nowhere to be found.

And I was nothing without my rational brain.

God, he'd tasted good.

Ellison had received that blow job the way he did most things: with enthusiasm and utter openness. I envied him that freedom of spirit. He had a casual confidence I would never have. It was one of the reasons I was drawn to him against my better judgment.

When I stepped into the house through the open glass doors of one of the sunrooms, Ian Duckworth was the first person I saw. *Great.*

His face lit up with a genuine smile. "Great game out there. I didn't realize you were so talented."

I nodded and tried to drop the residual anger from my self-imposed lecture. "Thank you. It's not talent so much as dogged determination to hold my own," I admitted with a tentative smile. I took a deep breath and tried to let it out slowly.

"Well, I was impressed by your sportsmanship. It's not easy to lose when everyone's watching, but you handled it well. I've seen plenty of people lose their cool even during a social match, and I appreciated how gracious you were both on the court and off. It speaks well of your temperament in general."

His compliment surprised me. "Thank you, sir. I'm grateful to be here, and I enjoy getting a chance to spend time outside moving around, especially when the weather is this nice. I have to admit, your facility made me envious. Sometimes I wish I could just walk outside and start up a game without heading out of the city."

Ian nodded and gestured me toward a table with a selection of cold drinks. I grabbed a flavored sparkling water and cracked the bottle open before downing several gulps.

Ian looked back toward the open doors. "Where's Ellison? Didn't he come back with you?"

"He's a bit behind me. I went ahead so I could beat him to the shower." I smiled through the lie. "I should probably head upstairs before he catches up."

He laughed and squeezed my shoulder. "Alright. Be sure to make it quick. I believe Binnie will be announcing lunch on the patio in a few minutes."

I thanked him and headed up to the room, intent on showering and dressing as quickly as I could in hopes of avoiding Ellison.

No such luck. When Ells entered the room, he looked even hotter than before. Damp, dark wisps of hair were plastered to his forehead and neck, and his eyes shone with anger.

"Coward," he bit out angrily. "Is that what you do, big man? Run away from your mistakes? I wouldn't have thought you'd be such a fucking baby. Not to mention wishy-washy. One minute you're hot and then, boom, cold. Make up your fucking mind."

"Shut your mouth," I warned.

"Whatever," he muttered, moving past me to the bathroom. I grabbed his arm and held him still.

"Not whatever. You're calling me a baby? Stop acting like a child. Wasn't it enough that I got on my knees for you again? That you got to relive your big gay experiment? Did you expect me to cuddle you too?"

The words were out before I saw what was really written in Ellison's eyes. Behind the anger, there were true hurt feelings. I opened my mouth to apologize, but he shoved me before I could get the words out.

"Fuck you," he spat. "And get out of my fucking face. I don't need shit from you."

It wasn't true, and we both knew it. He needed his father's company. He needed his pride. And he needed control back over his life. It had only been a few days, but I'd already seen enough of Ellison's life to notice he did what everyone else asked of or expected from him but rarely had the chance to do what *he* wanted.

What had I been telling him just the other day about how the key to any business negotiation was understanding your opponent's emotions and motivations?

Too bad I couldn't take my own damn advice.

"Ells," I began.

"No," he snapped over his shoulder as he went into the bathroom. I followed him in before he could lock me out. He stripped off his clothes anyway and yanked the shower controls on. "Get away from me."

"I'm sorry I walked away from you in the tennis house. I shouldn't have."

"Not listening to you," he said under his breath before stepping his fine naked ass into the shower and putting his head under the spray. I kicked off my shoes and stripped off my clothes before following him in and closing the glass door. "What are you doing?" he asked in surprise. His eyes betrayed him. They skated all over my body as if memorizing details for an exam later.

"We need to talk."

"Like this?" he squeaked. I loved it when he did that.

I stepped closer. "Yes, like this. Without anything between us. I want the truth from you."

"About what? I've been nothing but honest with you from the start! You're the one who keeps all your shit buttoned up so tight."

I moved even closer until my dick brushed against his, and then our thighs, stomachs, chests came together. Finally, I leaned in until our noses almost brushed against each other. "Besides what happened between us back in Connecticut, was that the first time you had sex with a man?"

Ellison's face was already red from anger, so I couldn't see whether or not he blushed, but his eyes blinked rapidly, and he didn't seem to know where to look. "Yes."

"Will it be your last?"

"What do you mean?"

I tried to ignore the wiry scratch of his leg hair, the hard, warm roll of his cock next to mine. "After all these years, did you finally satisfy your curiosity? Prove to yourself you're not gay after all?"

"I'm not gay," he said defiantly. I shook my head and stepped back, but Ells grabbed my arms to keep me from leaving his personal space. "I'm bi. And to answer your question, no. It didn't come anywhere near satisfying my curiosity."

I searched his face. "You need more?" I asked with a laugh.

His eyes stayed riveted on mine. "Much, much more." His voice was soft but sure. Like an invitation. Like temptation itself.

I considered it. And for a few moments, I almost, *almost*, took him up on it. The lure of pressing into his tight heat while the shower spray pounded down on us was irresistible, but it was also a path of no return. If I dared to slip inside Ellison's body physically, I would never be able to pull back from him mentally. There was no way I could give Ellison York that kind of power over me ever again.

I leaned in close until my lips brushed against his jaw to land against his ear. "Too bad," I whispered before reaching behind him for the soap and stepping away to wash my body with forced calm.

He stared at me wide-eyed. I tried not to see the hurt in his eyes or the anger in his tense muscles. I told myself it wasn't any more than he deserved. I was not here to fulfill Ellison York's needs.

We were at this party for a reason, and that reason had nothing to do with his dick or mine. After washing, I rinsed and stepped out of the shower. Lunch was going to be served any minute.

And I had a real estate deal to close.

I forced myself to calm down when I stepped out onto the patio for lunch. Colorful flowers tumbled out of planters, and the sound of clinking silver and glassware accompanied the clusters of conversation at several large round tables set under shade umbrellas. In the distance, white triangle-shaped sails dotted the deep blue of the ocean. It wouldn't be long before the colder weather would blow in and slow down even the most weather-hardened sailors.

"Beautiful, isn't it?" Binnie asked, approaching me with a drink in each hand. I'd wandered to the edge of the patio to wait for Ellison to arrive in case he wasn't too mad to sit with me. "I can't get enough of this view. Here, I brought you a fruity cocktail. Give it a try. It might relax you a little."

"I'm plenty relaxed," I said stiffly.

She laughed softly. "Sure you are. Drink it."

I took a sip of the fruity drink. "Mm. Thank you. That's really good."

"Bahama Mama. Can't beat a classic."

I almost snorted the drink when I laughed. Binnie began laughing at me, too, and then chastised me for being a snob.

"What makes you think I'm a snob?" I asked with a grin.

"When you thought you were drinking something exotic and fancy like a... a Pixie Moonblossom."

I took another sip and smacked my lips as if assessing it. "Nah, too hippie. I thought maybe it was more of a... Persnickity High-Hat. You know, on account of the citrus."

She laughed even more and waved Cate and two other young women over to join us. "Girls, come here. You have to ask Joe to make you one of these drinks. You simply must try it."

I looked down at the ground to keep from laughing.

"Ask him to make you a Persnickity High-Hat with extra..."

"Zazzle," I said under a cough.

She nodded solemnly. "Yes. That's it. Ask for extra zazzle. Or else it just tastes like something from a cruise ship."

As soon as they walked away, the two of us started snickering again. "God forbid you drink something they might serve on a cruise ship," I said, clutching the front of my throat.

"Hey, don't knock cruise ships, young man. I came this close to putting in a soft-serve frozen yogurt machine by the pool out here."

Tears streamed out of my eyes as I remembered my mom raving

about the free soft-serve on her cruise to Mexico one time. Binnie's hand clutched my arm as we tried to catch our breath.

"I like you," she said after we stared out at the sailboats a little longer. I turned to return the compliment when I realized she wasn't finished. "But if you hurt my sweet Ellie, I will tear your fucking heart out."

She turned and wandered back toward the tables, offering a cheerful hello here and there as she passed her friends. I stared at her in shock until I noticed Ellison walking down the steps from the house. He was showered and dressed in a pair of light gray shorts with a pink golf shirt. His hair was still damp from the shower, and it made me feel a strange kind of intimacy to remember I'd been with him in that shower.

When he noticed me, his eyes turned thunderous for a split second before he saw someone he recognized. Then it was all cheery smiles and polite chatter as he made his way to an empty spot at a table. The table with Cate and all of her attractive lady friends, including Jake's sister.

I hated this feeling. Like I'd let someone important down. I hadn't. He was the one who'd...

I stopped short.

Done what? Had an honest curiosity about what it was like to be with a man? Waited fifteen damned years for another chance to try it? Why? He could have had a million anonymous hookups with men by now in the city.

Why me? Why now?

I watched him join the women. They all flirted with him, even the two women who'd brought a husband or boyfriend. He was charming and sweet, attentive and sexy. Of course they flirted with him. Why wouldn't they want him? Why wouldn't everyone want him? He was the most attractive, engaging, intelligent man out here.

"You're Grey Blackwood," a man said, approaching me from a nearby cluster of people. He looked to be in his early forties with a little bit of gray mixed in with his short, dark hair. The laugh lines next to his eyes put me at ease right away. "Binnie pointed you out. I'm Adrian Mahoney."

The name rang a bell. I reached out to shake his hand. "The architect?" I asked in surprise.

He nodded and smiled. "Ian mentioned you were working on a commercial real estate project, so I thought I'd introduce myself and ask if you needed any help or had any questions. I designed the Ventura building in Chelsea."

"I'm familiar with it. You also did the Lockett project in Midtown. It's incredible. John Sloane speaks very highly of you." One of the companies I'd invested in had gotten the interior design contract on the project. Being awarded such a large contract had helped the company's burgeoning reputation skyrocket.

"Likewise. He has told me how much he credits his company's success to your support."

We talked shop for several minutes while the small line at the buffet table thinned out, and then we proceeded through the line and took seats together at a nearby table. I quickly discovered Adrian and I knew many of the same people. We talked about mutual friends and projects before I inquired what his schedule was like.

"I'm actually surprised Ian mentioned my project," I admitted. "He's the lone holdout on the property I need to acquire in order to make the project work."

Adrian nodded and grinned. "He told me that too, but I have some ideas. That is, if you're okay with me butting my nose in where it doesn't belong."

I laughed. "Are you kidding? I'd love it."

We talked through lunch and were still exchanging ideas when I noticed the crowd had thinned and the servers were cleaning up the tables. I'd kept my eye on Ellison the entire time and had progressively lost my appetite as every woman at the table had flirted and tried touching him.

I could no longer kid myself into thinking my annoyance was because of the reputation of our fake relationship. No. It was pure, gut-snarling jealousy. I didn't want any of those ladies to even consider they could take what was mine. And Ellison York was mine regardless of how conflicted that knowledge made me feel.

At one point, he caught me staring at him, and his eyes immediately scanned the area to see who I was sitting with. When he saw Adrian's hand on my shoulder, Ells's eyes narrowed.

Good. Now he knew how I felt.

Even after that had happened, I was surprised when Ellison walked over and took the now empty seat next to me on the other side and reached out to run his fingers lovingly through my hair. "I missed you at lunch. You were sitting so far away."

He wasn't a good actor, but Adrian didn't seem to notice. He wouldn't have any reason to, considering the man was married to one of Binnie's friends.

I took his hand down from my hair and pressed a soft kiss to his knuckles before holding his hand on the table. "You seemed to be having fun. I didn't want to interrupt you." I lifted an eyebrow at him.

"True. It was nice to catch up with Cate. We have so much shared history, and she was desperate to spend time together." Ellison took a sip out of my water glass.

I wanted to laugh at this game. It was completely different now than when we'd played it on the tennis courts because now I knew the truth. He didn't want Cate. He wanted me.

And he had to know my truth too.

Adrian made a soft throat-clearing noise. I turned back to him and apologized. "Adrian Mahoney, this is Ellison York... my fiancé."

Ellison choked on the water and nearly upended the glass as he tried to set it down on the table. I took it from him before reaching over to smack him hard on the back. "Baby? You okay?"

The look he shot me was full of the heated promise of retaliation, and I couldn't wait. How long had it been since I'd felt so alive, so engaged with another person I cared this much about?

"Totes fine, *darling*," he sputtered. "You just reminded me of something I forgot to tell you, and I was so excited to get it out, I inhaled my water. Silly me."

I deliberately didn't ask him what he wanted to tell me because I knew it would be over-the-top. Instead, I patted him again and told him to take it easy and maybe not speak for a little while.

His eyes flashed at me. "No, no. If I don't tell you now, I'll forget again. I was able to get you in with Madame Desdemona for the day we get back to town. She knows how important her sessions are in helping you make your business decisions. But she did warn me she won't have the crystal ball that week, so you'll have to make do with a tarot reading. I said that was fine. You mentioned the other day feeling more spiritually connected to tarot these days anyway." He looked over at Adrian with a sweet but serious smile. "Who knew crystal balls needed their own mystical regeneration periods? I sure didn't. Apparently she has to send it off to this place in Arizona where they're... re... Honey, what's the name of that process again?" He blinked at me with complete innocence.

I wanted to grab him by the throat and kiss his fucking face off. He was magnificent, and I wanted him more than ever before.

"Reconfigure and rejuvenate the refractivity," I said with a nod. "I believe it takes around ten days unless, of course, there's a full moon. You know how testy balls can be."

Adrian looked back and forth between the two of us as if trying to deduce how much of our bullshit was real.

I leaned over and whispered to Adrian even though we all knew Ells could still hear me. "He enjoys trying to embarrass me with crazy stories, but he doesn't realize that I love hearing them too much to be embarrassed. And as long as this sexy man is on my arm, how could I regret a single moment?"

Adrian smiled wide and let out a laugh. Ellison's face turned a deep shade of pink, and I reached over to grasp the side of his neck before leaning in and pressing a kiss to the edge of his mouth. "I'm sorry," I whispered in his ear.

He shook his head slightly, disengaging my hold on him without making it obvious. "He's right," he said, leaning around me to speak to Adrian. "I made up part of the story. Her name is actually Madame Hollyhock, but that's too ridiculous to say out loud."

Adrian let out another laugh and told Ellison he might need to consult with the woman himself. "I have high hopes of landing a new project soon, but I wonder if she could give me advice on how to find out if I stand a chance." He glanced at me with a cheeky grin.

"No fortune-teller visit needed," I said. "I'd love to connect when we get back to town and discuss things further. I'll find you later and give you one of my cards."

Ellison reached into his pocket and pulled a card out of his wallet. "Here's his card."

I stared at him in surprise. Ellison shrugged and grinned. "I'm part fiancé, part PA. I try to be indispensable." He added a laugh, but I could see some truth to it. He was a people-pleaser.

After saying our goodbyes, Ellison and I got up and walked out toward the boardwalk that led over the dunes to the beach. We didn't speak, but when we got to the end, we both took off our shoes before proceeding down the stairs to the sand.

"You may continue your apology," Ellison said with a sniff.

I reached for his hand and held it as we walked. Thankfully, he let me.

It took me a little while to organize my thoughts. "I don't trust people easily."

Ellison snorted. "You don't say."

"And I've spent a lot of years blaming you for things." Thankfully, he stayed quiet. "Which isn't really fair considering you were a drunk twenty-one-year-old."

"I tried apologizing back then. I tried making it right. I've apologized again to you this week. I don't know how else to tell you how sorry I am." The anguish in Ellison's voice squeezed my chest.

"I know. I didn't want to hear it back then. I needed to think of you as a villain. And I can't be sorry for that now because that anger was part of what fueled me and eventually led to my success." We walked through the sand to the edge of the surf, being careful to avoid the sharp spikes of broken shells underfoot. Seagulls squawking and the regular soft crash of the waves reminded me how long it had been since I'd visited the ocean.

"I don't need those fifteen years back," Ellison said. "They're gone.

But I want... I want this time back. Now. Here. I want you to give me a break and acknowledge that I never intended for you to get hurt. I want you to believe me when I tell you that the biggest regret of my life is that I didn't speak up for you right away but that I'm not that scared, immature kid anymore. That what happened that night changed me, too, and made me a better person."

"I know," I said softly. And I really did know... when I wasn't fighting my growing feelings for him.

"I don't need you to like me. I just want you to stop hating me."

I huffed. "I don't hate you." Before he could argue with me, I squeezed his hand and continued. "I thought I did, but it's not hate. It's fear. I'm attracted to you, Ells. A lot. And I know you're not looking for what I would want from you. So I resent this attraction because it's going to lead to more disappointment. And I've already had too much of that from you."

Ellison surprised me by stopping our progress on the beach and turning his body into mine. He hugged me tightly with his arms around my sides and his nose pressed into my neck. After a beat of hesitation, I wrapped my arms around him and held tight.

"I'm attracted to you too." His voice was muffled against my skin and soft with insecurity. "And being rejected over and over again is killing me. But I can't... I can't stop wanting you. It's not an experiment, Grey. If it was, I would have found someone else long before now. It's not *men* I want to try it on with. It's you. Just you. Only you."

I felt the slight tremble of his body. He was nervous. I pulled back to cup his face. His eyes were open, and his heart was right there for the taking. "What happens if you walk away from me again?" I asked. My voice was rough, and I felt the tension in every muscle.

Ellison pinned me with his glare. "Need I remind you that so far this past week, it's been you who's walked away from me over and over again? I've laid myself at your fucking feet, begged you for more, introduced you to people who matter to me. Do you want promises? You know I can't make them, and you also know you yourself wouldn't make them this early on. But I'm here. I'm not walking away from you. This is me fighting, dammit. And I want to break through this infernal fucking wall you have built up and see the real Grey Blackwood. I hate when you get that stoic look on your face and act like you don't have a heart. You do. I know you do, so fucking show it to me!"

His hands gripped my shirt tighter as his voice got louder. I could see his frustration clear as day. I bent forward and kissed him softly, sipping from his lips gently until he made a sound of surrender. Our lips explored each other tentatively at first, sweet and lazy like we had all the time in the world. His fists smoothed out and held me tightly pressed to him before one of his hands moved up into the back of my hair.

I lowered my own hands down from his face to his hips and then around to his ass. He had a nice fucking ass, and I didn't want to ever take my hands off it.

"I like the way you argue," Ellison murmured against the skin of my cheek. "Remind me to yell at you more."

I chuckled. "Pretty sure you don't need any reminders for that."

We kissed and caressed for a long time, murmuring a few teasing comments to each other here and there until the sound of someone calling to us carried on the wind.

I felt Ellison's entire body stiffen up before I noticed who was at the top of the boardwalk stairs with Binnie.

His parents.

And they didn't look happy.

Ellison's voice was low, but I could hear the smile in it. "Maybe we don't mention the engagement just yet."

16

ELLISON

"Therefore, the skillful commander imposes his will on the enemy by making the enemy come to him instead of being brought to the enemy."

~ Sun Tzu, *The Art of War*

My parents had impeccable timing. Just when I finally got a taste of what I'd wanted for so long, they turned up to spoil it.

"This is going to be a treat," I murmured under my breath. Even the sand seemed to be against me as I struggled to slog through the too-soft surface to get to the boardwalk stairs.

Grey's hand reached for mine with a confidence I didn't feel but that he always seemed to have in abundance. "It's going to be okay," he said in his same calm manner.

"You never get ruffled. It's annoying as fuck," I grumbled. He let out the familiar little huff of laughter that seemed to have a magical ability of melting the tension out of my shoulders. I took a deep breath and glanced at him. "I apologize in advance for how horrible this is going to be."

"I didn't get to where I am today by being easily intimidated by men like your father."

He was right. But that didn't mean *I* wasn't still easily intimidated by them. We climbed the stairs to greet them. My father looked Grey up and down like he was trash. I tried to stop trembling.

"Ellison, explain yourself."

At my father's brusque command, Grey's hand tightened possessively around mine. He spoke before I could. "Hello, Warren. And you must be Marianne. I'm Grey Blackwood. It's nice to see you."

He was all politeness as he exchanged greetings with my mother and complimented her on her necklace. "It reminds me of the sundial in Binnie's rose garden," he said.

My mother's and Binnie's faces both lit up. "That's exactly what it is," my mom said in surprise, reaching up for the simple gold pendant on her chest. "I gave Binnie and Ian the sundial on their twenty-fifth anniversary, and then Binnie gave me this on my birthday the following year."

Binnie cut in. "Marianne's gift card had included a lovely quote about the steadfast nature of the sun on its course and how like our friendship it was. It touched me so much, I had the necklace made so she knew I felt the same way."

Damn that man. He was so charming, the two ladies hadn't stood a chance. They tutted over him and his keen observational skills until Binnie side-eyed Grey. "Wait a minute. Did Ellison tell you that story about the necklace already?"

Grey laughed and said no while I sputtered. "I didn't even *know* that story," I said. "It's so sweet, my teeth would have rotted had I heard about it before now."

My mom laughed and gave me a big hug, enveloping me in her familiar scent. "I haven't seen you since Easter weekend. It's like we don't even live in the same city anymore."

"We don't live in the same city," I said. "I live in Vermont now."

"Pfft," Mom said, dismissing the truth.

Grey barked out a laugh. "Now I see where Ells gets the *pfft* from," he said.

My dad continued scowling. "Are you going to explain yourself?"

"Wasn't planning on it," I said, trying to project the same calm Grey always did.

Dad looked at Grey. "Taking my life's work wasn't enough. Now you're going to take my son too? What kind of sick fuck are you?"

Binnie's face turned to thunder. "Warren, you will not attack one of my guests. Either keep a civil tone or leave."

He turned his outrage on her. "You can't seriously condone this ridiculous farce!"

"It's not for me to judge. Nor is it for you to. I trust Ellison knows what he's doing. He's not a child, Warren. He's a grown man."

My mom tried smoothing everyone's ruffled feathers. "Why don't we go back up to the patio and get a drink? I want to ask Ellison about Gigi and the wedding plans."

We followed Binnie back up the boardwalk to where the tables had been cleared and the buffet spread had been replaced by a bar attended by one of the bartenders on staff this weekend. I made a beeline to it and started ordering drinks for everyone. Grey and my mother made polite small talk while my father stewed and Binnie smirked. Once I'd brought everyone their favorite drinks, I took a seat next to Grey.

Considering our conversation right before my parents' arrival, I was jumpy and untethered, unsure of where exactly we stood. Were we fake boyfriends? Real boyfriends? Horny acquaintances? The confusion infuriated me. I'd hoped for clarity and had come away more confused than before.

My father shot me a narrow-eyed glare. He was clearly waiting for an explanation, and despite all of our careful planning about our story, I was at a loss for what to say. After a few more words of useless chatter, Grey finally took charge.

"Warren, I understand your anger and frustration at learning I am here as Ellison's personal guest. While I do not apologize for any action I took to acquire York Capital, I *am* sorry you had to find out about Ellison's and my relationship secondhand. I'd like to assure you that my personal relationship with your son is just that: personal. It doesn't have anything to do with my interest in York Capital, and it has everything to do with my interest in a man who is intelligent, kind, funny, energetic, adventurous, curious, engaging, and sexy enough to stop people in the street. I promise my interest in your son has nothing to do with trying to take anything from you or do you any kind of wrong."

I stared at him. He looked relaxed and sure of himself, but since that was his default, it was nearly impossible to tell if he'd meant what he'd said.

Until his pinky finger moved the slightest bit over to curl around mine under the table. And then I pretty much wanted to fling myself on him bodily and promise to bear his children.

"Aww," my mom said, clasping her fingers together under her chin. "That's so sweet!"

My father sighed. "He's a master manipulator, dear. Don't believe a word he says."

Coming from my father, the criticism was particularly ironic.

"What could he possibly be doing this for otherwise, right?" I snapped, forgetting for a moment the truckload of reasons he was actually doing this for otherwise, namely to get close to Ian Duckworth.

"I don't know yet, but he's been using you to get to me for years now, and I won't stand for it."

Finally, Grey's calm facade began to weaken. His body tensed, and he took a deep breath. I knew if he opened his mouth, he would flatten my father, so I jumped in first.

"I was the one who started everything back in college. I told you that already. I had a crush on him. I wanted to... kiss him. I found him in the hallway. It wasn't his fault. None of it was. Yet all of you ruined his life. I ruined his life." Saying the words out loud was worse than all the times I'd thought them. Emotion filled my throat, and helpless anger made me shake. "I'm so sick and tired of you treating me like a victim. I was an adult! And I was the club member while Grey was the employee. Even if it had been his idea, which it wasn't, I would have been thrilled, but it still would have been my fault!

Please. Please stop blaming this man for something I did. Me. I did it."

My voice broke, and Grey shot up out of his chair, grabbing my hand and pulling me up into his embrace. "Hush, baby. Hush."

He muttered polite excuses to my mother and Binnie and ushered me away from the party. Within moments, we were inside the house. I followed Grey blindly up the stairs and into the cool quiet of our bedroom. Once the door closed behind us, Grey pulled me into his arms.

"I'm so sorry," I said, trying to pull back from feeling so emotional. I was sick to death of this. Sick of the guilt, sick of being deliberately misunderstood, sick of explaining myself.

Instead of responding with words, Grey kissed me. And kissed me. And kissed me some more. I grunted and moaned against his kiss but fisted his shirt to make sure he didn't stop. This was all I wanted: him, me, us. Here together without anyone else around getting in the middle of things.

I refused to beg again. I'd done that enough earlier. But I felt it all the same. The words were there between us, even if they were left unsaid.

Please. More. I'll do anything you want.

His hands took charge of my body, stripping my clothes off until I was completely bare to him. Grey's growling sounds vibrated through his chest, and the heat in his eyes when he looked at me almost turned my legs to jelly.

As soon as I realized I was letting him take the lead, I changed things up. I wanted to be the one growling in pleasure at seeing his body bared to me.

I yanked at his clothes awkwardly, nearly strangling him with his own shirt. The rumble of his laughter made me smile, and I ducked my face into his chest to hide my embarrassment.

"You're fucking beautiful," he murmured, tipping my chin up with a finger. "Don't hide from me."

My heart felt like a drunken bumblebee knocking around happily in my chest. I reached for the button and zipper on his shorts and opened them to see the bulge in the front of his underwear. "Oh hell yes," I whispered to myself. I ran my hand over it, reaching down into the front of his shorts to tease his balls with my fingertips. He was hot and hard. Even though I hadn't done this before, hadn't deliberately felt up another man's junk, I didn't hesitate for a second. I'd wanted this, *him*, for so long, it was more relief than anything else.

Thank fucking god.

Grey groaned and arched into my hand. "Don't stop."

I pulled his shorts all the way down and then knelt in front of him with my face level with his dick. It was intimidating, big enough to give me pause, but gorgeous enough to make my mouth water. I leaned in and brushed my face against him, relishing in the intimacy of the moment, the gentle feel of his fingers in my hair, the private peek of the starfish-shaped scar on his leg I'd noticed all those years ago.

I ran a fingertip over it and felt Grey's fingers tighten in my hair. "Don't tease me." His voice was stern, commanding.

I grinned up at him. "You don't scare me."

His mouth frowned, but his eyes twinkled with amusement. "Then I'm doing something wrong."

Grey leaned over and grabbed me under the arms, hoisting me onto the bed behind us and crawling on top of me. The heavy weight of him was hot as fuck. I wrapped my legs around his and arched up into his body. I wanted him to touch my dick. Suck it, stroke it, hump it. I didn't care.

"Make me come," I said.

He laughed against my collarbone, where he was sucking up marks. "We're nowhere close to that point. Lie there and be patient."

"No." I arched into him again. "Not possible."

Grey moved down my chest to suck one of my nipples. I drew in a breath as his tongue flicked over the sensitive spot. "Fucking fuck."

"Mm."

He explored with fingers and lips and eyes. I felt like the only thing in his world, and that thought made me even dizzier than I already felt.

I ran my fingers through his hair and tested the thick strands with a gentle yank. The resulting noise out of Grey's throat made me laugh. "You like that."

"I like you," he corrected before moving his tongue and teeth farther down my chest.

It was too good to be true. The physical experience, the words he was saying, all of it. I wanted to drink it in and hold it forever. Somehow, despite our arguments and tense history, I felt completely comfortable with Grey. I was able to let go, be open, simply experience the joys of this encounter without second-guessing.

Why? How was it possible the person I felt most comfortable with in bed was the man who'd always despised me?

Right now, it didn't matter. All that mattered was getting his mouth on my dick again. As soon as I had the thought, I remembered I owed him. I'd waited fifteen years to reciprocate, and now I finally had my chance. In the tennis house, I'd been so intoxicated with desire, I hadn't thought about what was happening. I'd simply given myself over to pleasure.

"Turn over," I said, sitting up and pushing his shoulder. "My turn."

Grey didn't argue. He simply climbed off me and turned onto his back, crossing his hands behind his head and grinning in anticipation.

"Cocky bastard," I muttered, even though he was a very sexy one. I moved between his legs and pressed a kiss to his inner thigh. The muscle curved inward, and the dark blond leg hair turned to darker blond hair trimmed neatly around his dick. His huge, hard dick.

He was fucking gorgeous. Big, broad, fit. His chest, shoulders, and arms were sculpted, and I knew from living with him a few days he prioritized his time in his personal gym. Suddenly, I was intimidated by him. I had zero experience in sucking a guy off, and presumably Grey had been serviced by some of the best over the years.

I glanced up at him and was startled by the soft expression on his face. "I'm going to suck at this."

He grinned. "Hope so."

"No, but like... I don't know what I'm doing." I settled in and reached for his cock, stroking it with my hand while I tried gathering my nerves to suck it. I wanted to taste it, feel the thick girth of him on my tongue, but I didn't want to look like some inexperienced virgin who was clearly out of his depth.

Grey ran his fingers through my messy hair. "You do. Do what you know feels good to you. It's not rocket science."

"No, I know. I just..." I swallowed. "I can't tell you how many times I've imagined doing this. To you. And now I'm here. *We're* here. And I don't want to fuck it up." The last part was confessed in a whisper. I was embarrassed.

"When you imagined it, what did you do? Lick my shaft? Suck on the tip? Tell me."

Those words out of his mouth were making me harder and ruining any chance I had at rational thought. "All of that. I imagined sucking it, trying to swallow it and gagging. I dreamed of making you scream, of feeling your balls draw up in my hand while I drove you crazy with my mouth."

Grey groaned and closed his eyes, arching his cock up toward my face. "Do it. Do something. Anything."

The scent of his cock and balls made me hungry as fuck. I took one long draw of it into my lungs before putting my mouth on him. I started by running my tongue up and down his shaft and watching his dick jump in response. Then I ran the tip of my tongue just under the edge of his cockhead where I knew it would feel the best. Sure enough, he groaned again and stretched his legs and feet out on the bed.

Every sound he made encouraged me until I was licking and sucking his cock with abandon. Saliva coated my mouth and chin, his cock, and his balls. His fist held my hair without yanking too hard, and his stomach muscles tightened with each strong pull on his cock.

"Fuck, Ells. Like that. Like that. Fuck."

I moved up so I could get a better angle to try taking more. His dick was big and thick, but I wanted to impress him by taking as much of it as I could. I gagged and tried again until tears were streaming down my face.

Sucking Grey's dick was the hottest thing I'd ever done, even hotter than getting sucked off by him in the tennis house. Hotter than him shoving me against the door and putting his hand on my throat or crowding me naked in the shower.

I felt debauched, used. At his mercy, but also, strangely, in control. Making him feel this good was intoxicating. His eyes rolled back in his head, and guttural noises escaped his throat.

"Fuck my face," I croaked.

His eyes were hazy with lust. "Want to fuck your ass."

I wanted that too, but I was scared. What if it hurt too much? What if I chickened out? What if I disappointed him?

But I wanted nothing more than his utmost pleasure, and if that meant changing things up and taking him that way, then I wanted to try.

I swallowed. "Okay. Yeah. You, ah, have stuff?"

He palmed the back of my head and bent to kiss me even though my mouth was a mess. "Yes. Stay here."

After he moved off the bed to get supplies from his bag in the bathroom, I turned over and lay on my back, wiping my messy mouth on the closest discarded shirt I could find.

When he came back into the room, he pinned me with his intense gaze. "You sure?"

"Not one single bit," I admitted with a smile. "But I know I want to make you feel good."

Grey climbed onto the bed and propped himself over me, dropping the condom and lube bottle next to us on the bed. "You already make me feel good." He leaned down and kissed me gently before pulling away and meeting my eyes again. "I don't want you to do something you don't want to."

"I want to," I admitted breathlessly. "Really fucking badly. I'm just a little nervous." I swallowed. "Or a lot nervous."

"What if we go slow and you can tell me if we need to stop?" He brushed the hair back from my face, and that simple gesture made me begin to relax. This wasn't Grey Blackwood, the angry venture capitalist bent on revenge. This was Grey Blackwood, the sweet, kind man who'd helped his housekeeper move a mattress in the middle of the night when the apartment above hers flooded. The man who asked about his driver's nephew who he'd helped find a job. The man who'd had Neiman Marcus turn off the music in the dressing room after I had a panic attack because he'd noticed I preferred the quiet. The sweet college kid who'd found me, drunk and nervous and babbling, in the hallway of the Crosbie country club and brought me into a closet for the hottest sexual encounter I'd ever had... at least until today.

That was the man I wanted to please, and that was the man I trusted to take care of me.

I nodded. "I want you," I said softly, just to make sure he knew.

His face broke into a genuine smile. His smiles were rare enough to still make my stomach clench when I saw one. "Try to relax, okay? Let me take care of you."

Why was he the one always taking care of me? Shouldn't it have been the other way around? Every time I found myself on the receiving end of his sexual attentions, I lost my fucking mind with pleasure and had almost no brain cells left to realize how one-sided it was.

"What do you want? What will make you feel good?" I asked, even if the answer was obvious. I didn't want to assume he was happy topping, even though it seemed like we'd naturally gravitated toward the idea. "I want to take care of you too."

"Ells," he said with a laugh. "Fucking you will definitely make me feel good. I've wanted to sink into this ass for a long, long time. Let me do this and stop worrying."

I was embarrassed by his laughter because I already felt so vulnerable and unsure of myself, but I trusted him. He was forthright enough to stand up for what he wanted, and he'd never shied away from commanding me when he felt like it.

Grey thrust his cock against mine before reaching down to stroke us together. We kissed again, searching each other's mouths and dueling tongues until he moved his fingers down along my balls to the tender skin behind them. I spread my legs even more and made a sound of invitation. I craved his touch. The aggressive way his hands took charge of me was so different from any of the women I'd been with. Even the most confident woman I'd slept with had never gone there. Grey's fingers finally brushed across my hole. I instinctively clenched and felt my face ignite.

"Shh," he said with another chuckle, this time against my throat. "It's okay. It's all okay. Stop thinking you're going to do something wrong. It's just us here. No one will know if you do something weird."

"You'll know," I said, moving my arm to hide my face.

"Mm, but everything you do turns me on." He reached for the little bottle of lube and poured some onto his hand. I peeked past my arm to watch him. I was fascinated by his familiarity with the process when it was all so new for me, and incredibly excited by it.

His eyes met mine again before his slick fingers landed on my hole. I sucked in a breath and tensed, which made him laugh again.

"You're awfully giggly," I said, covering my face again.

"I'm in bed with the sexiest man I know. Sue me for being giddy about it."

I moved my arm. "You don't have to make shit up. I'm sure you've slept with hotter guys." I wasn't fishing for compliments as much as stating facts. Hell, I'd even seen photos of him online with other men, guys who looked like fashion models.

"I've slept with hot guys, yes. But never anyone as hot as you, as engaging as you, as tempting as you." As he spoke, he moved his fingers gently between my ass cheeks until the sensation finally hit the pleasure center of my brain.

I threw my head back and let out a long, broken sound. "Oh, god. Oh fucking Christ. Grey, fuck."

The rumbled chuckle filled the room again. "This is going to be fun."

"Fun" might not have been the word I would have chosen. It was filthy, dizzying, and life-changing. Grey's fingers erased any remaining doubts I might have had about my sexuality. When he began fingering me for real, inserting one, then two, then three of his thick digits inside me, I writhed with unrestrained greed beneath him, begging and hissing for more. He'd introduced me to the joy of prostate stimulation, and I was a convert. I wanted his thick dick to press against it as he fucked me.

My head swam with the fog of need as my body built up to its release. Grey murmured words of encouragement and praise in my ear as he worked me loose enough to take him. By the time he donned the condom, I was a puddle of sweat and precum.

"Sexy as fuck," Grey murmured, gazing at me like I wasn't a flushed, damp mess. "Never wanted anything more."

His words made my heart throw itself against the cage of my ribs like a teenaged fan who's just spotted her favorite rock star, but I knew it was just sex talk. He wasn't declaring feelings. He was talking about fucking.

Which was fine with me. I wanted the fucking just as much, if not more. I was beyond ready for him.

"Please," I said for the millionth time.

He reached for one of the pillows beside my head, exposing the sexy armpit hair I'd already snuck several sniffs of. For some reason, I was completely drawn to his pits, so much so that I'd moved stealthily across the bed the night before to stick my nose in his while he slept.

It wasn't weird if no one saw. At least, that was my motto.

Grey shoved the pillow under my ass until it was propped in the air like a car on jacks. Before I could squeak out a complaint, he shot me a look. "You'll be more comfortable this way."

I bit my tongue and trusted him. Sure enough, when he lined his cock up with my hole, it was the perfect angle. I hated the reminder he'd done this many times before, but at the same time, his competence was a total turn-on. After several tense moments of him taking it slow and reminding me to relax, he finally pushed inside and began to thrust slowly. My entire body was strung tight as a bow, expecting pain, expecting a burn, but it didn't come. It took me a minute to realize I was okay. Then I grinned up at him.

He laughed again. "You're killing me."

I squeezed around him in reflex, and he groaned, dropping his face down until his forehead was against my neck. His hips pulsed in and out, trying to get deeper inside me. When he finally thrust harder, I felt that same intense wave of sensation as I had when he'd fingered my gland. My fingers clutched his arms and then scrambled to wrap around his back as if pulling him closer would repeat that incredible sensation.

"More," I choked.

Grey kissed me again, savagely, before picking up the pace of his thrusts. I heard the squelch of lube and the soft grunts coming from Grey, the slap of our skin together and my ragged breathing. The room was full of the smell of us, sweat and sex, and I was drunk on it all.

"Grey," I said on a gasp, reaching for my dick. I needed to come, I needed to crest the building wave.

"That's it, sweetheart. Want you to come. Just like that. You feel so fucking good. Come for me."

I stroked and squeezed as I focused all my attention on the incredible release building inside me. Sensations hit me from so many places, I felt overwhelmed in the best way. Just as Grey began to roar, I felt the climax hit me hard. My muscles contracted for a split second before letting go in a delicious flood of mind-numbing surrender.

Grey's body pushed tightly into me, and the warm liquid of my own release landed on my chest and belly. Aftershocks hit me one after the other until I lay there, still and brainless.

After a few moments, I looked down at Grey, whose head rested on my chest. I ran my fingers through his damp hair and down over his shoulders to the arm he had stretched across me. "Holy fuck," I breathed.

"Mm."

We didn't need to say more. In fact, I didn't want us to say more. I was too afraid any more words between us would fuck everything up.

Grey must have felt the same way because he got up without a word and returned with a warm, wet cloth to help clean me up.

Then he climbed back into bed and gathered me in his arms. I chose not to make a snarky comment about snuggles and aftercare. Instead, I lay there enjoying every minute of postcoital bliss.

Until my parents knocked on the door a little while later, reminding us both there was a real world out there intent on tearing us apart.

17

GREY

"The captured soldiers should be kindly treated and kept."
~ Sun Tzu, *The Art of War*

Instead of feeling blissfully fucked out after the incredibly satisfying sex with Ellison, I felt restless and awkward. I was caught up in the crossfire of two parts of myself: the half that had loved every minute of being that close to Ellison, and the half that insisted on protecting myself from future disappointment at his hands.

Maybe it was a good thing his parents interrupted us. At least it got me out of a potentially disastrous conversation about our feelings, something I had no doubt Ellison would bring up at some point. I wasn't quite ready for that level of intimacy. Give me someone's body and I could enjoy intimacy all day long, but sharing actual vulnerabilities with another person? No, thanks.

"What do they want?" Ells whined, turning his face into my side and hiding under my arm. "How embarrassing."

I turned onto my side and kissed the top of his head. "It's early afternoon. We can't exactly hide in bed all day."

"Says who?"

His father's stern voice cut through the door. "I know what you're doing, bringing that man here, and you can forget about it right now. Just ask Ian. He knows Grey Blackwood is just using you to get to him. If you think Ian is stupid enough to agree to that scheme, you're off your rocker."

I felt Ellison tense.

"Need I remind you, this scheme was your idea?" I asked softly, trying to keep my calm.

"I know."

"You don't believe his bullshit, do you?"

Ellison sat up and stared at the door before turning to me. "What? No. Of course not. It's just..."

I sat up against the headboard and ran my hands into my hair with a sigh. "It's just what?"

"It doesn't matter if it's true or not. If Ian *thinks* you're using me to get the building, Dad's right. He won't agree to sell."

Ells had a point. That could become a problem.

"Maybe you should talk to Ian," I said, moving off the bed to take a quick shower. "See what he's thinking. I can't quite get a read on the man myself."

Ellison moved over to the bedroom door and told his parents he'd meet them on the patio in a few minutes. Then he joined me in the shower.

"Don't do that," he said, flaring his nostrils in annoyance.

"Wash my hair?"

He pulled the shampoo bottle out of my hand and poured some of the liquid into his own palm before setting the bottle down. Then he reached up to wash my hair for me. "No, don't put on your asshole mask," he said softly. "Pisses me the fuck off. I can't tell what you're thinking when you do that."

"Maybe I don't want you to know what I'm thinking." I closed my eyes to keep the soap out but reached for his hips to keep from losing my balance. His wet, warm skin felt just as good in my hands now as it had a half hour ago. I wanted him again.

He *tsk*'d. "Too bad. I don't want things to get awkward between us, especially because of my parents."

Ellison's fingers felt amazing in my hair. I took a moment to enjoy the scalp massage before he leaned my head back to rinse off the shampoo. While he ministered to my hair, I moved my hands around to squeeze his ass. "I think we should ignore your parents and have more sex."

Ellison's lips pressed into the side of my neck before he took my earlobe between his teeth. "Me too. Maybe this time I top you?"

"I don't think so," I said, trying to sound casual. The truth was, I'd thought about it plenty. I'd let the Ellison from my dreams fuck me all day long. But the real Ellison? The one I wasn't quite sure I completely trusted? No.

I was a hypocrite. I knew that. But there was still too much water under our bridge for me to let myself be that vulnerable to him.

"Maybe later," I added, opening my eyes to judge his thoughts. He didn't look bothered. "But the next time we fuck, I want inside you again. Unless you didn't like it?"

His eyelashes flitted together rapidly. "No, no. I liked it. I definitely liked it."

I grabbed his chin and kissed him hard. "Good."

We washed each other slowly and thoroughly, taking the opportunity to learn each other's bodies. I kissed his slick shoulders, his spine, the indentions over his ass cheeks. By the time I was considering rimming him, he was hard as a rock and ready again.

"No," he said with a breathless laugh. "If anyone's sucking anything, it's me."

He dropped to his knees and began sucking me off again, just like he had before. I was plenty hard for him, and seeing him on the tile floor looking up at me with spiky wet eyelashes drove me even closer to the brink. I thrust into his mouth without thinking. Ellison's eyes widened in surprise, but his hands tightened on my hips and pulled me closer.

I gripped his head and kept thrusting until finally shooting in his mouth with a muffled grunt. It was quick and dirty, but something about it seemed to please Ellison even more than the sex we'd had before the shower.

I helped him to his feet. "You okay?"

He grabbed my face and kissed me so hard, our teeth clacked and my lip almost got pinched. The taste of my cum coated his tongue, and the sweet smell of gardenia soap surrounded us in the shower steam. I wondered if gardenias would always remind me of tasting my release on Ellison's tongue.

If so, I'd need to buy several plants for my condo.

I reached down to jack him off but felt his dick hanging flaccid against his leg. He sucked in a breath and pulled back with a laugh. "Already came. Shower floor."

I looked down just as the last of his release swirled in the water and got washed away.

Knowing he got that much enjoyment out of sucking me off made me feel ten feet tall. We finished washing and dressed for the second time in a matter of hours. When Ellison left to meet up with his parents, I stayed behind to call and check in with my actual assistant.

"God almighty, I feel like I haven't heard from you in twenty years," Marcel said when he answered the call. "I'm not used to going this long between summons."

I let out a deep breath. "No shit. And I'm not used to going this long without working. Give me some updates on where we are with everything."

Marcel went right into business mode, summarizing our current issues and giving me several important items of new information I needed, including the latest communications from Ben Aldeen's pack of sharky lawyers. He asked for clarification on some things and corrected me on others. I sat down at the desk and pulled out my laptop so I could digitally sign a few important documents and respond to several emails he wasn't able to take care of himself.

"Now give me the scoop," he said. I could hear the grin in his voice. "You're actually at the shore and actually taking time out for relaxation. It's like a miracle, even though you're probably not taking advantage of it the way normal people would."

He didn't know the details about Ellison's and my need to pretend to be together in a relationship, but Marcel knew I'd come to this event as Ellison's guest in the hopes of meeting Ian Duckworth.

"I'll have you know I had actual sand between my toes a couple of hours ago," I said. "And that was after drinking a fruity drink with alcohol in it."

Marcel made a big dramatic sighing sound. "No way. Tell me more. How does Ellison York look in a tiny swimsuit? Better yet, send pics so I can get the full effect."

"No one has worn any tiny swimsuits, and even if he had, I wouldn't be creeping on him with my phone camera." At least, I wouldn't have been sharing the photos if I had.

"Party pooper. Then what can you tell me? Did you talk to Duckworth yet?"

"I haven't even been here twenty-four hours yet. I've talked to Duckworth but not about the deal. He's not receptive to discussing business here, but I hope to develop a little more of a friendship so he'll accept a lunch or dinner invitation when we get back to town."

"Good plan. Meanwhile, tell me what you're not telling me."

He was always like this. Meddling asshole.

"I'm not *not* telling you anything," I insisted.

He knew I was lying, but he didn't call me on it. "I heard Adrian Mahoney is there. He's that architect John Sloane wants you to use. I wouldn't mind, if only because that man is hot as shit."

"I met him earlier today. He's definitely hot. I'd get his number for you so you could ask Luca for a threesome for your birthday, except Adrian is married to a woman. Probably not interested in a gay throuple situation."

Marcel's familiar laughter was successful in relaxing me. I let out another sigh.

"Grey, tell me what's going on with Ellison York. You've been tied up in knots all week. Is he really that bad?"

He's really that good.

"No. He's not bad. That's the problem. I..." Well, here went nothing. "I like him."

"You like him," he repeated. "As in, the way you *like* a healthy egg white omelet? Or as in the way you *like* taking over multimillion-dollar companies and making rich old white men cry into their high-thread-count handkerchiefs?"

I swallowed hard and admitted in a rough voice, "I like him... the way I like seeing all those zeroes at the end of my net worth."

Like something necessary to my happiness.

Like something I very much didn't want to be without anymore.

Like something I still thought would slip through my fingers anyway when I least expected it.

"Oh. Ohhhh. Oh fuck." Marcel had a way with words.

"Yep." I walked over to the bedroom window and looked out on the long driveway. Thankfully, our room didn't have a view of the ocean because then I'd be able to look down and see Ellison talking to his parents on the patio. And I would want to race down there and protect him from his asshole of a father.

"Well, good!" Marcel turned chipper, and his voice took a tone I was very familiar with, the one where he was energizing himself to tackle a challenge and overcome it come hell or high water. "We can work with this. It's a good thing. When was the last time you liked a guy? Never? That sounds about right. So what we're going to do is..." His voice trailed off.

"He lives in Vermont," I reminded him glumly. "And he's Ellison fucking York, son of Warren 'Emperor of Evil' York, remember?"

"Yes," he said happily. "And we rock at vanquishing evil villains! We eat villains for breakfast. Hell, we've already overcome York bullshit once, we can do it again. Now, tell me everything. Let's formulate a plan."

"No plan. I don't need a plan," I said tersely. "And even if I did, I wouldn't need your help with it."

"Okay, you stop this right now, mister. Don't push him away, Grey," Marcel warned. "You're going to do something stupid, I just know it."

He was probably right. "No, I'm not. But I'm also not going to seriously consider an actual future with the man who's..." I lost my train of thought.

"Gorgeous? Smart? Well educated? Funny? Nice to strangers? Yes, of course. Why would you want a future with that *nonsense*?"

"You're not as funny as you think," I grumbled.

"You're more transparent than *you* think. And I have no doubt Ellison is smart enough to see through your tough-guy bullshit."

"Mpfh."

Silence landed between us while I thought about what I really wanted out of a fling with Ellison.

After a few moments, Marcel interrupted my tangled thoughts. "Please give this a chance, Grey. I can tell by the sound of your voice that you've already accepted defeat like it's a foregone conclusion, and that's bullshit. The Grey Blackwood I live to torture thrives on challenge! The underdog-ier he is, the better! And more than that," he added more softly, "you deserve to find someone to build a life with. This wealth and success you've been working so hard to build isn't going to love you back. It isn't going to make you chicken soup when you're sick."

"I have Jenny for that," I said. "And food delivery apps on my phone."

The judgmental silence fell again, and it rankled.

"Ask yourself this, Grey: What comes next?"

"Well, I was thinking I might nap if my personal assistant would ever shut—"

Marcel ignored me. "You've taken down Warren York, the biggest evil of them all. You're *this close* to getting Duckworth to sign. Then what? When all the wrongs have been righted and the vengeance is done, what's left?"

"I have to go," I said eventually.

Marcel sighed. "Okay, but let me say one more thing."

"Could I stop you if I wanted to?" I closed my eyes and braced for the lecture, but he surprised me.

"He likes apples."

I opened my eyes as if it would help me understand better. "Who does?"

"Ellison. I was in the elevator with someone yesterday who had a big basket of apples, like from an orchard. I asked about it, and she said they were a gift for Ellison because he has a thing about apples and she'd been apple picking with some friends."

"Yes, I know he likes apples. I prefer oranges. What does that have to do with anything? Are we making fruit salad? Why are you telling me this?"

I heard Marcel mutter something under his breath that sounded suspiciously like "Beyond me how a brilliant businessman can have the emotional intelligence of a fucking rock," but I couldn't be sure.

Then his voice rang clear again. "Never mind, Romeo. Enjoy your nap. Good luck with everything."

I could have sworn he muttered a "You're going to need it" at the end, but I couldn't be sure about that either.

18

ELLISON

"He who wishes to fight must first count the cost."
~ Sun Tzu, *The Art of War*

On my way outside to find my parents on the patio, I ran into Ian, who insisted I meet with him in his office for a few minutes first.

"I didn't want to approach the subject with Grey until I'd had a chance to speak to you and your father," Ian began once we were seated together by the empty fireplace in the cozy paneled room with the door closed.

"What subject?"

"It's about the building Grey Blackwood wants to buy."

My heart took a little leap of excitement until I realized he'd mentioned my father. If he was taking my dad's advice, Ian would never sign over the property to Grey.

"What about it? Do you want me to go get Grey so he can answer any questions you have?"

"No, that's just it. I wanted to talk to you alone because the issue is... complicated." He took a breath. "You see, one of my tenants in the building has a right of first refusal clause in their contract. If I intend to sell the building, they would get the right to offer for it before anyone else. Based on knowing who they are and what their situation is, I think they would exercise the right and buy it."

"So then Grey would have to buy it from them?" I asked.

"Theoretically, yes, except in this case, they would never agree to sell it to him. The tenant is a company your father has partial ownership of."

"It is? What company?" I asked. "If it's one of York Capital's investments, then Dad doesn't own it anymore. Grey does."

Ian shook his head, looking noticeably disturbed about all of this. "No, this is a personal thing. Your father and a few of his friends co-own a company called Marlette Venture Partners. Marlette leases three of the five floors of my building. Part of the reason they have a right of first refusal is because one of the companies they're invested in is a specialty science lab that needed to invest quite a bit of money in retrofitting their own space on the top floor. If I were to sell the building, they wouldn't be able to recoup their losses on the specialty outfitting."

None of this made any sense. Marlette was my mother's maiden name, so if that was the name of the company, my father had to be involved. "My father co-owns another VC company? Since when?"

The fact he'd never told me about it all these years felt like a betrayal. Who the hell had done his legal work?

Even worse, my father had let me believe that everything he owned was tied up in York Capital—that my parents would have ended up homeless if I hadn't agreed to be Grey's assistant and save the Greenwich house—when all the while, he'd owned another company. A company with enough assets to buy Ian's building outright.

Ian shifted uncomfortably. "That's not the point, and honestly, that's between the two of you. It's not my place to tell you any of this, but the reason I'm doing so anyway is because I can see how much you care about Grey. I can see he cares for you as well. I'm sorry you're in this predicament with your father."

"Maybe Grey can make an offer to the lab to cover the expense and inconvenience of fitting out a new space?"

Ian sat back in his chair. "I'm afraid you'd still have the issue of your father to deal with. He's not going to agree to sell to Grey Blackwood. Ever."

My head spun with this new information. I finally looked back up at Ian. He'd always been more like a father to me than my own dad in some ways. I'd looked to him for advice many times. "What do I do?"

Ian tapped his fingers on the arm of the antique, upholstered chair while he thought about it. "Think about something your father wants. Negotiate with him for it. His currency is power. Find a way to give him some. Help him save face and you might have a chance."

He was right, and I suddenly felt more hopeful. If Ian agreed to sell to Grey, Grey would return York Capital to my father. That was already the deal we'd struck. I could offer my father York Capital in exchange for him agreeing to let Ian sell the building to Grey. Surely he'd go along with it if it meant getting his company back and restoring all those years of our family's legacy.

I thanked Ian and made my way out to the patio to meet up with my parents. It wasn't a sure thing, but at least I now had a plan. Everything was going to work out fine. Dad would get York Capital back, Grey would get the final property he needed for his development, and I would be able to return to Vermont to get to work at the academy. With Dad back in charge of York, the foundation's financial commitments to the academy would stand.

And I could just... not think about living so far away from Grey.

He had money. Maybe he wouldn't mind spending some of it to come see me in Vermont.

I blew out a breath and stepped outside into the afternoon sunshine. My parents were already settled at a table by the edge of the boardwalk which would give us plenty of privacy for the discussion I wanted to have. Unfortunately, as soon as I sat down to talk to them about everything, Cate and her parents joined us.

My mom's face lit up. "Well, hi. It's so good to see you all. Cate, you look just as beautiful as always." Mom glanced my way. "Ellison, doesn't Cate look beautiful?"

Christ.

"Yes, of course," I murmured, shooting Cate a wink.

My dad sat up straighter. "And I hear she's doing amazing work at the SEC counsel's office."

Cate's dad puffed up. "We're very proud of her."

The three of them took seats around the table and began the usual small talk with my parents about what everyone had been up to lately and wondering why they hadn't seen each other at the club in a while. At one point, Cate leaned over and whispered, "Sorry about this. They insisted on coming over to say hello."

"It's fine. I enjoy your parents."

She kept a polite smile on her face. "They still have high hopes for us despite knowing I started seeing someone."

She'd already told me about her new-ish relationship, and I was happy for her. "Don't they like Drake?"

I'd hardly had any dealings with Drake Lou since that night at the club fifteen years ago, and it was hard to imagine what someone like Cate saw in him. But then, here I was trying to convince Grey that I was a different man than I'd been back then. The least I could do was believe the same could be true for Drake.

Cate let out a soft mock gasp. "But, darling, he's..." She made a show of looking around as if to make sure no one was listening. "*Asian.*"

"You're kidding. I've never noticed your parents being prejudiced before."

"They try not to be, but it's still there." She picked at the edge of a cocktail napkin on the table. "Maybe they just need time to get to know him better. I think they'll be impressed with him once they realize he's even smarter than I am."

"Not possible," I teased.

"Enough about me and my new man. Tell me about yours! He's beautiful, but sometimes he looks like he wants to murder everyone around him. I can't deny he's intimidating."

I laughed. "No kidding. He gets this stoic face. Sometimes it reminds me of a dragon who makes the villagers scream and run in every direction."

We spent the next several minutes dishing about Grey Blackwood. And if I ended up blushing and nervous giggling, at least Grey wasn't nearby to see it.

19

GREY

"If the enemy leaves a door open, you must rush in."
~ Sun Tzu, *The Art of War*

After the call with Marcel ended, I sat back at the computer to finish a few more critical tasks before making my way back downstairs to look for Ellison. When I walked out onto the patio, I saw Adrian Mahoney first.

"There he is," Adrian said with a big smile.

While I'd enjoyed my conversation with him earlier, he wasn't the person I'd been looking for. No, the man I wanted was sitting farther out at a table by the boardwalk, sipping a glass of wine and laughing at something Cate McArthur was saying. After another older couple wandered away from their table, it was just the four of them: Ellison, Cate, and Ellison's parents. What a happy little family.

"Hi," I said, trying to avoid being rude to Adrian. "Let's get together back in the city and talk about the real estate project."

"That sounds great. Would you like to get a drink and tell me more about it right now? We have some time before the formal dinner party tonight. Unless, of course, you were hoping to join the backgammon tournament happening in the library."

His eyes twinkled with humor. I smiled back and shook my head. "I'm afraid this morning's tennis wiped out my daily ration of fierce competition. But I'll take a rain check on the drink if you don't mind. Ellison's expecting me to join them." I gestured to the table of Yorks. The Yorks were definitely not expecting me, but I also didn't want to sit and talk to Adrian when the man I really wanted to sit and talk to was within a stone's throw.

And I didn't really give a shit what Warren York wanted.

"Absolutely, but now I'll have to face my wife across the backgammon board. The resulting carnage will be on your head." He shot me a wink and turned away. I felt bad for dismissing his offer and not inviting him to join me with Ellison, but I also didn't want to invite a total stranger into the tense family situation between the Yorks and myself.

I ordered two Bahama Mamas from the bartender and walked over to Ellison's table. "I got you a Persnickity High-Hat," I murmured, setting one down in front of Ellison. I offered the other one to Cate. "Would you like one too?"

A slight frown wrinkled her forehead as she turned to look at the bartender. "Yes, if you don't mind. They wouldn't make one for me earlier. Said they didn't know what it was."

"Hm," I said. I glanced at Mr. and Mrs. York. "Can I get you a drink?"

Ellison's body was strung tight while he waited for their response. His mother opened her mouth to say something, but Warren stood up abruptly and excused them both to get ready for dinner.

It was four in the afternoon.

Once they were gone, I raised a brow at Ellison.

"Sorry," he muttered, looking dejected. I leaned down and pressed a lingering kiss to his cheek.

"'S'okay." I turned and made my way back to the bartender to get myself a gin and tonic.

When I got back, Ellison and Cate were laughing again. I hated the feeling of jealousy that slithered in my gut, but Cate said something that cut it off at the source.

"I was talking to Ellison about one of the guys he went to boarding school with," she said with a blush. "He and I have been dating for a few weeks, and I really like him."

Ellison turned to me and grabbed my arm. "You know him, actually. Remember Drake Lou from the club? Short guy with dark hair? He was always laughing. Great sense of humor."

"The one who couldn't golf worth a damn but could sink any putt?"

Ellison laughed. "Exactly. What the fuck? I never understood it. He had plenty of muscle too, just couldn't hit a drive to save his life."

I shifted until Ellison was holding my hand instead of my forearm. Once our fingers were tangled together, I let out a breath and tried to relax my shoulders. "Yeah. I remember him. Didn't he go to college in DC?"

Cate nodded. "He went to Georgetown and got into politics. He's a political consultant in the financial field."

"I didn't stay in touch with him after college," Ellison said. "What's he been up to besides work?"

That was the only opening she needed to talk our ears off about the perfect specimen of man that was Drake Lou. At one point, Ellison moved his hand down to my thigh under the table and began stroking it higher and higher until I was hard as fuck and couldn't even pretend to pay attention to the conversation any longer.

I slid my arm around his shoulders and began playing with the little waves of hair resting on his collar. Every once in a while, when my fingers grazed the warm skin of his neck, he would shudder.

We drank and talked for a couple of hours as the sun lowered behind the house. Other guests came and went, and eventually our conversation turned to other topics.

"Wait," Ellison said, interrupting Cate's explanation of a project she was involved in at work. "I thought you wanted me to take you to the Ballard's charity ball. What about Drake?"

"He's going with his parents to Hong Kong to visit family. He won't be here, and if I go alone, I'll have every society mom in the city trying to fix me up." She suddenly frowned and turned to me. "Unless, of course, that would bother you, Grey. I'm sorry I didn't even think of that. I'm just used to asking Ellison to fill in when I need a friend to take me."

How different the situation was than I'd expected. Even though I knew Ellison was more interested in me than Cate, it still took away some of my stress to hear the same lack of interest on her part.

"I don't mind at all," I said. "Ellison is his own man. I don't begrudge him his friendships."

Ellison rolled his eyes. "What he means is, he'll enjoy the chance to work late without being lectured. The man is a workaholic."

I stared at him. "Aren't you? You're a corporate attorney. By definition you must be a workaholic."

"Wrong. *As you know*, I work in development and fundraising for a private school in Vermont now. With all that clean living and fresh air, I'm bound to be frolicking in nature in the evening before turning in by nine o'clock." He shot me a cheeky grin.

Cate laughed and shook her head. "Finally. I know how much you hated practicing law."

"*Hated* it," Ellison agreed with a laugh. "Good riddance. I counted down the fucking hours till I was done. I'm not sure how I'm going to do living in the country, but I'm really excited to get into the work and feel like my time is being spent helping people for once."

I wanted to ask him more about his work at the academy, but Cate got to him first. "Why don't you stay in the city and work from there? It seems like most of the money is there anyway. You could take potential donors out to lunch and see and be seen. Might help raise more money if you're still active in the social world. And then you and Grey wouldn't have to be long-distance."

Ellison looked down at his empty drink glass and shook his head. "I can't afford it. I took a huge pay cut and need to sell my apartment in the city to even be able to afford to buy a car," he said with an embarrassed huff of laughter. "Until then, I'm using Gigi's bike to get to and from work."

That shocked me, but I tried not to show my surprise. If we were actually dating seriously, I'd know all of this already. And it wouldn't be happening in the first place since his finances would be tied to mine and I'd never let him want for anything.

The subject changed again to the kind of car he was going to get, and before we knew it, the bartender came by to let us know the formal dinner party would be starting in a half hour.

Cate yelped and raced off to get ready while Ellison and I took our time making our way up to the room and dressing. Ellison was in a talkative mood and told me all of his thoughts about Cate and her rocky relationship history.

"I kind of feel sorry for Drake, honestly. Cate is married to her career. In fact, that's probably why she's dating Drake in the first place. She's a financial attorney on Wall Street. She works for the SEC. I'd bet a hundred bucks she's only into him because of his in-depth knowledge of financial policy." He held up a hand to stop the comment I wasn't going to make. "Now, I know what you're going to say. That's pessimistic and unfair of me, and maybe it is. Maybe this time is different. But consider this. The last guy she dated was a hedge fund manager. The guy before that was a futures trader. And the guy before that was her boss at the SEC. Don't ask. Anyway, you tell me how it looks."

As Ells talked my ears off, I watched him strip down to his boxer briefs and rifle through the armoire for his suit. His body was tight and fit. Just watching his slim waist nip in before swelling to a fantastic ass made me hot for him again. I sat down on the foot of the bed and enjoyed the show. When he finally turned around and caught me staring at him, he froze. A pink flush started on his chest and climbed up his neck.

"Why are you just sitting there?"

I leaned back on my hands. "Because most men would pay big money for this strip show, and I get it completely free."

He walked over and climbed onto my lap, straddling me until he could push me down onto the bed by my shoulders. "Want more than a strip show?" he asked before leaning in to kiss me. He still had the casual, easy smile on his face, and I was taken aback by how relaxed he was around me and how comfortable he seemed to be with this shift in his sexuality.

"You're not nervous about being with a guy anymore?"

His forehead crinkled. "I wasn't ever nervous about being with a guy as much as I was nervous about being with you. I don't care what a random guy thinks of me."

It was implied he *did* care what *I* thought about him, and that made me stop and think through his behavior to see if it lined up with what he was saying. It seemed to.

I ran my hands down his back to his ass and squeezed. He smiled again and thrust his covered dick against mine. "I think we should be late to dinner," he said with mischief clear in his face.

"No way," I said, gently nudging him back so I could sit back up. "We need to stay focused on our goal. I need to make a good impression on Ian tonight."

Ellison let out a breath of frustration but climbed off and returned to the armoire. I didn't miss the little butt jiggle he did as he adjusted himself.

I rubbed my face and stood up. *Eye on the prize, Blackwood. You're here for Duckworth, not a romance.*

I forced myself to focus on getting dressed and making a good show at dinner. When we entered a wing of the house I hadn't seen yet, I couldn't hide my shock.

"Why do they have a room made up to look like the dining car on a luxury train?" I whispered to Ellison.

His eyes brightened. "Binnie is obsessed with the Orient Express. This is amazing!"

"So, it's not usually like this?"

"No way. It's actually a ballroom. They've hosted weddings and charity galas here before with dancing and an orchestra. Ian must have done this as a surprise for their anniversary. He loves indulging her."

I looked down at Ellison's bright smile and realized I understood for the first time how that might work. How seeing pure delight on the face of the person you cared about would bring you more joy than any amount of money ever could.

Sure enough, the surprise of the night was Ian's indulgence of his wife's love affair with all things Orient Express. He made a heartfelt toast to her at the beginning of the evening and thanked her for fifty years of happiness. Even though I didn't know them well, the love between Ian and Binnie was obvious.

I was glad Marcel wasn't there to point out the stark contrast between the Duckworths' happiness and my own.

I stayed quiet most of the night, choosing instead to listen. I learned more about Ellison and gradually began to realize how unfair I'd been to expect him to be the same spoiled kid I'd known back at the country club. He wasn't that guy anymore, if he ever was.

I'd made many assumptions about him, I realized now, based on the lifestyle he'd been born into and my opinions about the country club kids in general. I also made assumptions based on who Ellison's father was.

It hadn't made any sense that a selfish, conceited prick like Warren York would be able to raise a warm, caring man, but he had. I was ashamed to think I'd judged Ellison as harshly as all those country club men had judged me based on things he couldn't control.

Ellison stayed close to me all evening. When he'd done it the night before, I'd assumed he'd wanted to keep an eye on me, but now I wondered if it wasn't something less nefarious.

"He likes you a lot," Binnie said, nodding her head toward Ellison where I'd left him talking to a group of other attorneys about corporate contracts. I stood at the bar waiting for two glasses of ice water. We were expected to get up early for croquet followed by a sailing excursion, and I didn't want either one of us to run the risk of being hungover.

"The feeling is mutual," I murmured, moving so she could access the bar ahead of me. She shook her head.

"I don't need a drink. I came over to talk to you. I can see you really care about him."

I felt my back teeth tighten. I wasn't used to talking to people about my feelings, and I didn't intend to start now. "Ellison York is a good man," I said instead. It was the truth.

She nodded and gave me a knowing smile. "So you know all about Warrington Academy? That project has been close to his heart for so long. Thank god he's finally getting a chance to pursue it full-time."

I felt like an idiot. Of course I didn't know much about the academy, other than the fact he worked there and it was a private high school in rural Vermont. I'd done a little research on it last week, but it seemed fairly standard as private boarding schools went. But he'd mentioned recently half the kids were there on scholarships.

"I know he's been waiting a long time to focus on it," I said.

"How are you two going to manage the distance? Even if you have a plane at Teterboro, it'll take you at least a couple of hours to get out to his place for a visit."

It was none of her business, but since Ian was watching us from a nearby table, I certainly didn't want to be rude to her. "We'll manage."

"Warren is convinced you're only dating him to get to him through his son."

I turned to look at her. "Warren is an ass."

She barked out a laugh. Several heads swiveled toward us, including Ellison's, and I forced myself to plaster on an easy, relaxed smile.

"That is true. I know you're not *only* dating him to get to Warren, but I'm not sure if you're *also* dating him to get to Warren."

"I can assure you I'm not dating Ellison to upset Warren in any way." At least that was the truth. "I hope that you trust your godson to be smart enough to stay away from someone who would use him like that."

She studied me until I felt like a specimen on a slide. "I'm trying to figure you out, Grey. I don't believe for one minute that you took over York Capital to help Ellison protect the foundation. You have a history of hostile takeovers. But at the same time, I can see you both care about each other very much. You can't fake the softness I see there when the two of you look at each other."

She was wrong. Very wrong. We didn't look at each other with anything other than sexual hunger.

Suddenly, she laughed again and patted my arm as if to reassure me. "You're fighting it, though. That much is clear. Well, we'll see, I guess. Just remember what I told you earlier."

I recalled the threat clearly. "I couldn't forget it if I tried," I said with a forced smile.

She walked away laughing.

Thankfully, the night didn't last too much longer, and when Ellison and I finally made our way back up to the room, I let go of the fake pleasantness I'd been putting on for the final hour or so. I wasn't great at socializing to begin with, and when I felt as far out of my comfort zone as I did here among old-money families, it was even more exhausting.

I ripped off my tie and shucked off my coat, expecting to be the only annoyed person in the room.

"I'd be happy never to have to talk to those fuckers ever again," Ellison spat, kicking his shoes into the corner of the room. I blinked at him.

"Who? What are you talking about?"

He flapped his arms in the air. "That asshole who always tries to one-up me on legal shit. He was the year ahead of me at Columbia, and he thinks that one year made him my permanent superior in all things legal. Well, he can fuck right off because I don't give a shit. I'll be happy to never assess another corporate contract as long as I live."

I wanted to laugh at his discontent. But he continued before I could make a noise. "And the two guys with him. They all work at the same firm. Pompous jerks, all of them. They acted like I'd single-handedly lost my father's company because of my legal ineptitude. Which is what my father thinks, too, so that's extra awesome."

"Wait. What? York Capital's vulnerability didn't have anything to do with you or your legal work."

"I know that," he said, flapping his arms again before unbuttoning his shirt cuffs. "But they don't know it, and my father isn't about to correct them either. Why do I even care? I shouldn't."

"You care because you have a strong work ethic," I said. "Of course you care about your reputation in your field."

"It's not my field anymore, thank god. I can't wait to be done with this bullshit. Sorry. No offense. I know you love it."

"Love it? Love what?"

Ellison looked up at me while unbuttoning his shirt. I tried to ignore the temptation he was revealing between his nimble fingers. "Aggressive corporate maneuvers and posturing. One-upping opponents. Winning. Making more money. Conquering more challenges. Whatever. Being the big man on campus. It's just not for me."

His words stopped me in my tracks. "Is that what you think of me? I'm out to win?"

He sighed and leaned his forehead against the armoire door. "I'm sorry. Ignore me. I'm just annoyed, and I took it out on you. That wasn't fair."

"I get that, and thank you, but I want to know how you really feel."

He finished stripping his clothes off until he was in boxer briefs, and then he slipped into the crisply made bed and flopped his head back on the pillows. Thankfully, a room attendant had hooked us up with fresh bedding during dinner.

I continued undressing as he sighed. "I think you let your anger fuel you. You want to prove yourself to others, but I also think you're trying to prove something to yourself. That you can succeed without anyone else's help. You can surpass them in business even without the privileges they all enjoy."

I took my time hanging my pants up while I thought about what he'd said. "That's true. But I have other motivations that aren't quite so self-centered. I pursue money because money is powerful. When you have it, you can do many things. You can help those who don't have it. You can direct the course of government. You can access places and policies that people without money have no access to."

"You mentioned Blackwood has a charitable giving arm."

"Ells, a large portion of my income goes to helping low-income kids get out of poverty. I am aggressive at making money because I can use it to help others. This project I told you about in Hell's Kitchen is something I've been working toward for almost ten years. It's the work of my heart."

His eyes widened. "I didn't know. Tell me more."

"The Blackwood Giving Program is our version of the York Foundation," I explained, unbuttoning my own shirt and deliberately not looking at him. He was too tempting with his bare chest and rounded shoulders. If I wanted to keep any rational brain function, I needed to look anywhere but at a shirtless Ellison York. "The new building in Hell's Kitchen will take up an entire city block with retail and restaurant space on the ground floor and a mix of office and residential space above. The purpose of it is..."

I hesitated. I'd always kept my shit close to the vest. Was it really necessary to tell Ellison all of this? What if he used it to keep Ian from signing the building over to me?

"The purpose is...?"

I glanced at him and tried to remember this was the man who'd left his lucrative corporate law job to earn peanuts fundraising for a school.

"My hope is that the ground-floor rents will help support the rest of the building so it can be used to house up-and-coming business talent. People with the skill and drive to become entrepreneurs but without the connections and financial seed money to get their foot in the door."

Ellison sat up. I could see his interest sparked. "What do you mean?"

I tossed my shirt onto a pile of dirty clothes on the floor of the armoire. "The Blackwood Giving Program currently identifies and offers to mentor and financially support underprivileged talent. We usually find them through our contacts with local universities, but sometimes we simply get a tip or an application. It's typically a young person with a big idea. I'm hoping to build a space where we can offer our support to a larger pool of talent and also form a community of sorts. A place where these fledgling entrepreneurs can meet and work with mentors to grow and pursue their ideas while also learning some of the basics necessary to run their own business. Accounting, legal, taxes, etc. We've spent almost ten years running this program and have determined that one of the indicators of success is being in proximity to necessary resources and support."

"Wow." Ellison was clearly impressed. "This... I love this. Hang on, so... you're creating an incubator of sorts to help people like you. Like where you were fifteen years ago. You had the drive and the ideas, but you didn't have the contacts or money to get started."

I nodded and stripped off my socks. "Exactly. This is it. Everything I've been working so hard toward, and I'm this close. There isn't anything I wouldn't do to make this work."

"It sounds amazing. I need to put your person in touch with my sister," he said excitedly. "We have several students who might be good candidates for that kind of thing."

I turned to him and closed the armoire door. "We only accept underprivileged kids. Not private school kids who come from money."

He let out an incredulous laugh. "You... you're implying all private school kids come from money. I told you that half of our students at the academy are on full-ride scholarships. It's the whole reason we started the program in the first place. To offer an elite, private school education to kids who wouldn't normally have access to it."

I climbed into bed but stayed out of touching distance. This conversation was unexpected, and I didn't want to interrupt it with my greedy fingers on his irresistible body.

Ellison had mentioned the scholarships before, but I hadn't thought through how that meant the school had to find a way to fundraise to cover it. And that was the job Ellison had left the city to do. Fundraise to offer underprivileged kids a private school education like the one he'd had.

Ellison York had started a school for underprivileged kids. To offer them a better education. To give them a stronger start where they'd have a better chance at getting into a good college, meeting families with connections to better jobs, and—because it was a boarding school—getting out of some bad living situations as well.

I eyed the man next to me. What else didn't I know about him? What other damaging assumptions had I made about him?

"I misjudged you," I admitted in a rough voice.

He snorted. "No shit, really?"

I reached for his hand. "I'm sorry. Will you tell me more about your school?"

Ellison looked at me for a few beats as if assessing me. "Yeah. I'd really like to. I love talking about Warrington. The kids are amazing. A few of them remind me so much of you. There's this one girl—she's from a mining town in West Virginia—and she's like a sponge. She was taking notes for me in a meeting with one of our nonprofit attorneys who was trying to explain some legal options for a project we're doing, and I could sense her taking it all in and biting her tongue against giving her opinions. It reminded me of the time you caddied for Norman Heath and Bob Kelty when they were discussing their assessment of a new investment opportunity. They were trying to decide how much to invest, and your ears were rotating on hinges. I could see how badly you wanted to ask them questions and participate in the conversation."

I huffed. I couldn't believe he'd noticed me paying attention to that. I couldn't believe he'd noticed me at all.

"Those idiots didn't even consider the regulatory issues involved. At the time, the state senate had a bill in the works to significantly curb expansion of..." I stopped myself and met his eyes. "I like to get a man in the mood by discussing regulatory permitting of road projects. Is it working? Is this turning you on?"

I pulled Ellison's hand up to my lips and kissed each knuckle softly, lifting my eyebrows seductively until he collapsed with laughter. "Leave it to Grey Blackwood to look sexy talking about the state senate and roadwork."

After tackling him down onto the bed, I lost all trains of thoughts that had anything to do with legislation, scholarships, venture capital, golf, or the past. All I wanted taking up space in my brain was the seminaked man underneath me and the fact that we had all night together to touch each other and make each other feel good.

Even though we'd only been here for a day and a half, I already felt more relaxed, more at ease with the man I'd clearly misunderstood. I felt stupid now for judging Ellison based on who he was one drunken night at the club. But now we were finally past that. I could finally explore who he was *today*.

I leaned in to kiss him, tasting the faint traces of wine and whiskey on his breath. Ellison's arms and legs wrapped around me, and I felt so good, I wanted to laugh. When had I ever felt so happy? So turned on?

I kissed him everywhere, batting his hands away when he tried to get me to move faster. He began his usual litany of begging which made me feel like a damned superhero, like I held all the power to bring him pleasure. He hadn't had a single moment of being unsure of having sex with another man, which was another area in which I'd judged him unfairly. Instead, he was open and willing, verbal and hungry.

We humped and groped and sucked and kissed until both of us were a sweaty mess and half the sheets had come unmoored from their corners. The room was full of the scents of sex and sweat, and I couldn't get enough of it. I wanted to press him down on the bed face-first and fuck him into the mattress, but I also wanted to slide into him again plain old missionary style so I could see the complete abandon on his face when he gave up his release to me.

"Want you," I grunted into the skin between his shoulder blades. "Want to fuck you."

I vaguely remembered he'd mentioned topping me. Was I ready for that? Did I feel any differently about it now than I had before?

"Grey," Ellison breathed, humping the bed. I held one of his hands up above us, and his other hand reached back to clutch at my hip. "I can't... I can't keep... I want to come. I want..." He sucked in a breath as I slid a lubed finger into his ass again and reached for his gland. His words after that were unintelligible.

"Want me inside, sweetheart? Want me deep inside this ass until you feel me fucking you everywhere? Or do you want to change things up and fuck me this time?"

His eyes rolled back, and he made another choked sound of need.

"Going to have to use words, Ells. Tell me what you want."

I pressed my hard dick against the back of his thigh while I continued stretching him with my fingers.

"Want you." His voice was muffled by the wrinkled sheet under him. "Want you so much. Can't think. Please."

He was too far gone and clearly happy with the direction things were going. I grabbed a condom and rolled it on quickly before slathering it with the rest of the lube on my fingers and bending one of his knees up to give me easier access.

When I slid inside of him slowly and carefully from behind, he groaned deep and long into the sheets. Our fingers twined together and clasped each other tightly.

"Grey," he breathed between gasping breaths.

"I'm here. Tell me you're okay." I wrapped my free hand around his front and held him close. My body lay along the back of him, connecting us from head to toe. My lips pressed kisses behind his ear and down the back of his neck. I murmured nonsense into his ear about how good he felt, how tight he was, how fucking gorgeous he'd been all night.

"I watched you," I admitted in a low voice. "Couldn't keep my eyes off you. Wanted you. Wanted to pull you into a corner and touch you, rub my hand up your shirt to tweak your nipples the way you like and slide my fingers inside the back of your pants to finger this tight fucking ass."

"*Nghhhh.*"

"I didn't want anyone else to touch you, to even look at you," I said, not caring anymore that he knew the truth. "You're mine. I wanted everyone else there to know it. Do you understand me?"

"Oh god," he whispered. His fingers tightened around mine as I fucked in and out of him from behind.

"Want you to come," I said, finally withdrawing one hand from his so I could jack his cock. He gasped and threw his head back on my shoulder.

Ellison's faint sound of agreement almost made me smile. His body's hot, tight clench on my dick made me see stars. If he didn't come soon, I was going to beat him there. "Fuck, babe. Fuck. Please," I said. "You feel so fucking good on my cock. Need you to come for me. *Fuck*."

Ellison reached back and grabbed my hair before groaning out his release. I felt the hot pulse of his dick in my hand, and it was all I needed to let go of my shaky control and thrust deep into him one more time until my own release hit hard and fast.

We lay there entwined together as our heartbeats slammed and our breathing stuttered. The bed was in ruins around us, and one of the bedside lamps lay tilted halfway off the table.

"Maybe I'm gay," Ellison said weakly after a few minutes spent trying to catch our breath.

I laughed and reached for the condom before pulling out of him. Ellison made a whimpering sound of discontent, so I pressed a firm kiss to his shoulder. "Wait here."

When I returned with a wet cloth, he'd rolled onto his back and lay studying me with one arm behind his head. The pillows were nowhere to be found.

"Why do you let me get close to you when we're having sex but not when we're talking?" Ellison asked after I finished wiping him down.

I shot him a look. "Are we going to talk about our feelings now?"

"Yes. Buckle up, buttercup. It's going to be excruciating." His grin was pretty fucking enticing, but I kept a decent scowl on my face to discourage him.

"I don't get close to people as a rule."

"No shit?" He faked shock for two seconds before rolling his eyes.

I gestured for him to get off the bed so we could replace the sheets. Thankfully, I'd noticed the extra set on a shelf in the top of the armoire. The cleaning crew was going to give us the stink-eye after noticing we'd sexed up yet another set.

As we worked together to fix the bed, I thought about what he was asking. "I didn't trust you," I admitted. "I didn't want to give you more ammunition to disappoint me with."

Ellison nodded. "That's what I thought. What about now, though?"

He leaned across the bed to smooth the sheets. His naked body still called to me like a damned snake charmer even though I was spent from our earlier activities. "Now, I'm willing to try and open up a little more, but it's not like a switch I can flip."

"Old habits die hard," he suggested.

I nodded.

After we finished making the bed, he followed me into the bathroom so we could brush our teeth. "Will you tell me about what happened after that night at the country club?" he asked when we were finished at the sink.

I met his eyes in the mirror. "I cursed everyone associated with Crosbie Country Club, the York family, Heath and Kelty, and all those fucking drunk assholes who dared you to fuck with me. Then I vowed revenge on your dad, Norman Heath, Bob Kelty, and Paulina Benson."

Ells turned his back to the sink so he could face me for real. "Why Mrs. Benson?"

"She came and found me the next day and propositioned me. Said if I would show her a good time—and who even uses that phrase anymore?—she'd make sure her husband hired me after graduation."

"You're kidding!" Ellison looked so disappointed, as if he couldn't wrap his head around the fact some people were simply shitty humans.

"No. I even considered it. A job at Benson Investment Partners would have been even better than the one I had lined up at Heath and Kelty. But how the hell would I have worked for the man after sleeping with his wife?"

I saw the storm brewing on Ellison's face, so I reached out to pull him into my arms. "Don't be mad at me for considering it. I was desperate. I didn't want to go back to flipping burgers and delivering dry cleaning."

"I'm not mad at you," he snapped. "I'm mad at those fuckers who screwed you over. I'm mad at my dad, at Bob and Norm, at Will Dinsmore for starting the dare, but most of all, I'm mad at myself for not speaking up right away. For being a fucking chickenshit. For not looking out for you. For not making it right."

His voice cracked at the end. I leaned in and kissed him gently before pulling back. "Do you remember Justin Nottely? He won the tournament that night with his dad."

Ells nodded. "Of course I remember him. He's the one who took your job at Heath and Kelty."

"Do you know where he is now? Besides working for me since I took over the firm?"

"He's... I think he's a VP or junior partner by now."

I took Ellison's hand and led him back to bed, pulling down the covers so he could climb in. Once we were settled in bed, we lay on our sides facing each other. "He's a junior partner. He makes five or six hundred thousand dollars a year."

Ellison's forehead crinkled. "Yeah? So?"

I ran my fingers through his messy hair. "If that night in the club hadn't happened the way it did, that's where I'd be right now, working for someone else and making a fraction of what I make now. I'd be begging for a seat at the decision-making table instead of sitting at the head of that table. Do you see what I'm saying?"

He clenched his jaw and exhaled through his nose. "Yes, but you had to work way harder for it."

I nodded and leaned back on the pillows. "I heard about this guy at Yale during our senior year who'd applied for a patent. He'd come up with a new method of coating termite bait pellets so they wouldn't break down in the digestive tract of other animals like dogs and cats. He'd spent all his money on running the experiments, compiling his data, and applying for the patent, so he needed outside funding to help him create a professional presentation and enough samples to give potential clients the ability to do their own testing. I knew it would be big, and I wanted to be part of it. The guy said he'd cut me in if I could help him scrape together the money. I talked to my mom, trying to brainstorm ideas, and she offered to sell her car. We gave the guy five thousand dollars, and I spent another thousand I had in savings on drafting an airtight contract giving me a share of his future profits."

"And it paid off."

I glanced over at him. "Hardicoat, the chemical coating company that started with that product, is valued at three hundred million dollars today. Unfortunately, I had to sell him back most of my shares early on because I needed the cash. I paid my mom back, obviously with interest, and then used the money to invest in two other opportunities. One failed terribly, but the other was Lumeniar, which hit paydirt. From there, it was a matter of grinding, working my ass off to research and select the best opportunities."

Ellison sported a satisfied grin. "I love that story. I want you to come talk to the students at the academy about working hard and taking risks. Succeeding without connections."

"Well, I wouldn't have gotten into Yale without the connections I made working as a caddy at Crosbie," I admitted. "One of the members wrote me a personal recommendation, and another nominated me for one of the scholarships I needed."

He frowned, but I could tell he was getting sleepy. "Turn on your front," I murmured. "I'll rub your back while I tell you about more of the companies I invested in early on."

It didn't take long before he was asleep. I lay there a little while longer, enjoying the feel of his skin and the newfound realization that we had a lot in common.

Ellison York was a good man.

And it was time to admit the truth.

I was falling for him. Hard.

20

ELLISON

I woke up in a mental bed of hearts and flowers and in a physical bed of six-plus feet of hot, muscular male octopus. Grey was all over me with his hands and mouth, and I wanted to scream cheesy epithets like "I win!" or "Fuck yeah!" Instead, I ended up in a sloppy, sleepy sixty-nine, which I decided was just about the best way to start a day off on the right foot.

"You're getting better at that," Grey said, idly stroking patterns on my thigh with a fingertip after we'd both come. "Little more practice and you'll just about have it."

I yanked his leg hair until he yelped. "I need to talk to my dad after breakfast," I said, killing the mood entirely. I was both nervous and excited to move the ball forward on this real estate deal. I wanted to get York settled back with my dad, have Grey able to move ahead with his project, and be able to return to Vermont to get to work on fundraising at the academy. I had a feeling I'd accidentally landed a new donor last night during my conversation with Grey.

Grey sighed and moved off the bed. "Count me out for that conversation," he grumbled. "I tried talking to him again last night, and he walked away. I don't blame him, and honestly, I was happy not to have to fake it. But it doesn't bode well for..."

He was so predictable. Grey's entire body tensed up as he realized what he was about to say.

"Doesn't bode well for what?" I asked as innocently as possible.

He cleared his throat as he disappeared into the bathroom. "Running into him in the future."

I grinned. The only way he'd run into my dad in the future and be forced to talk to him was if he was with me at a family event. Which meant he expected to be with me at a family event.

I floated through showering and dressing alongside Grey. Once we changed the subject away from my parents, he seemed to relax. I asked him more questions about the Blackwood Giving Program and saw him light up as he described some of the programs it supported.

We made our way down to breakfast, still talking happily about the common interests we'd discovered the night before. I had a million questions I wanted to ask Grey about whether or not he'd be interested in pursuing an actual relationship when we got back to town, even though I'd be returning to Vermont while he stayed in the city. Would he want me to stay and work at York next week before returning, or would he let me out of our "deal" now that things weren't antagonistic between us?

Was he feeling the same way I was, or was there a chance he saw this as a temporary physical thing rather than the start of something more?

I pushed down the nerves that tried to sneak into my gut. Why did I even need to settle these issues so soon? I didn't. I simply needed to enjoy what I had in the moment and stop worrying so much about putting a label on it.

Once we were settled at a breakfast table with full plates of food,

Cate came up with a couple of the women she'd introduced me to yesterday at lunch. "Can we join you?"

Grey stood and pulled out a couple of chairs for them with pristine manners that had obviously escaped me. I murmured an embarrassed apology and hid behind my coffee mug. Grey let out a soft laugh and leaned over to press a kiss to my cheek.

The ladies were wide-awake already, trading stories and jokes. I didn't pay much attention until one of the women seemed to be addressing me with a goofy smile on her face. "Y'all are just so sweet. My cousin is gay, so I get it."

Grey's hand tightened where it had been resting on my thigh.

"I don't understand. You get what?" I asked, truly not following. I still blamed being under-caffeinated.

"Your struggle. You're so brave. I love seeing two men not afraid to show their affection in public."

I tried to determine if I was mildly offended or majorly offended. I looked at Grey as if he might hold the answers. His expression was ice-cold. *Ah. We're majorly offended. Good to know.*

I smiled benignly back at the lady. "If you think this is brave, you should have seen me giving him head on the beach yesterday in broad daylight."

Cate and Grey both choked on their coffee. I couldn't hold back a laugh. "Just kidding. But we did have sex in the tennis house after the tournament, and I'm pretty sure Mrs. Gilbert was spying on us through the windows."

I could tell everyone thought I was joking again. Only Grey knew the truth, and his face was dangerously red. I leaned over and whispered, "Sorry I never told you about Mrs. Gilbert, but at least now you know why she's been flirting with you ever since."

"I'm going to murder you in your sleep," he promised in a low voice.

"Are people always this rude about the gay thing?" I knew the answer to the question, of course, but I wanted to acknowledge, at least between the two of us, how sorry I was about it.

"Pretty much."

After that, Cate's friends didn't really know how to respond to us. One of them seemed to suddenly take an interest and began flirting with Grey. The other looked everywhere but at either one of us. It was fine by me. All I wanted was to talk to my dad and get past the remaining challenges.

Cate and her friends eventually drifted off to get ready for the croquet tournament Binnie had organized for this morning's activity. It was probably the promise of mimosas that drove the ladies' excitement more than the promise of mallets and wickets. I told Grey he should join them on the lawn and get started without me.

"Not for a trillion dollars," he promised. "Besides, I need to hop on a video call in about twenty minutes, and Binnie offered to show me a quiet study I can use. Do you mind if I leave you for a bit? This is a company I'm working with in Paris. They're making a big announcement first thing in the morning tomorrow, and I wanted to review the messaging first."

"That's fine. But..." I tried to figure out the best way to approach the subject. "Are we good with the York Capital thing? Our deal? I mean... if Ian agrees to sell you the building, you'll really give my family back the York Capital name?"

Grey looked at me skeptically. "Why are you asking this now?"

I could tell he was fighting the urge to think the worst of me, so I rushed to reassure him. "I plan to talk to Ian about everything, but I wanted to check in with you first."

"Don't talk to Ian without me."

"No, I—"

He cut me off. "Ells, seriously. I want to be there."

How could I tell him I'd already talked to Ian about it? And how would he feel if he discovered the truth about my father's involvement in the building Grey needed for his project?

"Don't you trust me to manage my own godfather?" Great, now I just sounded petulant.

"I trust you to remember this is my project on the line," he said carefully. "I don't want it managed for me behind my back. I want to be involved. I'd like to be able to explain my plans to Ian and address any issues or concerns he has."

"I think he's going to agree to sell it to you. But I need to know if he does... if he does, you're going to sign York back over, right?"

Part of me worried this was part of Grey's revenge. I wouldn't blame him for being tempted to renege on the deal. Well... I wouldn't blame him if it wasn't *me* he was dealing with. I had a hard time believing he'd betray me and our agreement that way. Still, I needed to know before I could get my father to agree to let Ian sell the building.

"Yes. I will return York Capital, and with the handful of original assets as you requested. All assets acquired after your father's hire date will be transferred to Blackwood Holdings."

I let out a breath and smiled at him. "Good. Perfect. Thank you."

I could tell he was still wary, but I hoped to give him good news within a couple of hours that would remove his doubt forever.

After we stood up, I pulled him into a hug and squeezed him tightly.

"What are you doing?" I could hear the reluctant smile in his voice.

"Being brave enough to show affection in public," I said with a dramatic sigh. "Not all superheroes wear capes, Grey."

I knew I was making light of a serious issue. We wouldn't always be in the safe environment of a private house party. I wasn't naive about the risks involved in showing affection to him in other places, but I also wasn't experienced with it. Hopefully I could find a time to talk to him about it and ask questions to overcome my own ignorance.

His strong hands pressed up along my back until one gripped me by the back of the neck. "You're an inspiration," he said dryly. "Maybe do something better with that mouth than spouting bullshit."

I leaned forward and kissed his smirk, relishing in the chance to show him how I felt about him, even though it was too soon for pretty words. I could only imagine how Grey Blackwood would react to a giant emotional confession. He'd probably shudder in revulsion and then change the subject to avoid getting any messy feelings all over him.

When we finished kissing, I met his eyes. "Thank you," I said again. "Really. You're a good man, Grey. I'm sorry for everything, but I'm not sorry we had a chance to reconnect and get past everything."

"Can we not?" He lifted an eyebrow in challenge. "I'd really rather play croquet than talk about this again if that tells you anything."

I nodded and agreed, but not before kissing the fuck out of his face again. "Go make your video call. I'm going to look for a Honeycrisp apple even though they're not in season yet. A girl can dream."

While Grey left to take his video call, I made my way to the kitchen and had to settle for a Gala apple. It was a bad omen.

I crunched on it unhappily on the way to the room my parents were staying in. They were enjoying a breakfast tray at a small table in their much larger room. The television played Fox News at a low volume while my mom scrolled on her iPad and my father buttered his toast.

When I entered the room, my mom stood up and gave me a hug. "I loved catching up with you and Cate yesterday. That young lady is a delight. And so smart! She said you were going to escort her to the Ballard Ball in November. I think that is absolutely wonderful, dear. I don't know why you don't pop the question and let us plan an engagement party for the holidays."

I stared at her. "Uh, because I'm dating Grey?"

"But your father said that was all a fabrication. A ruse. Isn't that true? Warren?"

My father shifted in his seat. "Marianne, let me have a talk with him. Why don't you go ahead and hop in the shower?"

Mom shot Dad a pointed look before leaving the room to take her shower and get ready for the day. Clearly, she was trusting him to "fix" this misunderstanding.

"Have a seat, Ellison."

I sat down across from Dad and poured myself a cup of coffee from the carafe on the tray. When Dad finished eating his toast, I began. "Tell me about Marlette Venture Partners."

He looked surprised, but he controlled it well. "What about it?"

"How long have you had it? Who else is involved? What's the asset value?"

"Why are you asking? How did you hear about it?"

I took a sip of coffee and tried calming down. "I'm asking because I want Marlette to allow Ian to sell the building in Hell's Kitchen, and he says he can't do it without your approval."

He frowned. "Why does he want to sell the building? And what does it have to do with you?"

I'd finally reached the point where I had to trust I held enough cards in this deal to win the hand. Once he knew Grey was involved, my father would fight tooth and nail to fuck him over. But I couldn't think of another way to explain my interest in the deal. I tried anyway.

"The company that wants to acquire the building has plans to create a charity incubator that's closely aligned with the mission of my own programs at the academy. If they can succeed in building this place, I'll have another pathway to success to offer my students."

"Why this building in particular? We have a client with specialty fittings in their office space. It would take a large investment to recreate in a new space."

"The purchase offer would include compensation for that."

My father was suspicious by nature. He knew there was more here than I was letting on. He took his time, glancing out the window at the sun rising higher over the water. "Who's the purchaser?"

"A group called BGP."

He faced me again. "And the *B* stands for Blackwood?"

I ground my back teeth together and nodded.

Dad grinned. "Then obviously the answer is not only no but hell no."

It was time to play my trump card. "What if I could get York Capital back in exchange for you allowing the sale to go through?"

He tilted his head. "Grey would agree to give us back York Capital in exchange for my signing off on the sale? What's the catch? He'd be better off finding another real estate plot for his project."

"It wouldn't be the full value of the company. He would take the assets, all except the original ones from before your tenure, and give us the name and history back. We would have to rebuild the assets with new investments."

Dad let out a derisive laugh. "With what money?"

"How about with your Marlette money?" I snapped. "Or the money from the sale of the house I got back for you?"

His eyes narrowed at me, revealing a familiar cunning that made the hair rise on my skin. "What's in it for me?"

"Your family business. Your legacy. Generations of history."

Instead of sentimentality, all I saw on my father's face was disgust. "What's the point of a family business when there's no family to take it over from me?"

His words hit me like a boulder to the gut. I hadn't thought of that. Why hadn't I thought of something so damned obvious?

"No," he continued, tapping his chin. "I might as well let it die now and focus on Marlette. And, as a bonus, Grey Blackwood can suffer the consequences of his own actions." He sighed happily. "I really love to see a liar and a thief get what's coming to him."

He reached for another piece of toast like the conversation was over, but it couldn't be over. Grey and I had made a deal. I wanted him to have this building, to be able to pursue his lofty goals with the project. I wouldn't be able to stand it if my father's ego and spite screwed Grey over yet again.

I couldn't let that happen.

"What would change your mind?" I asked, hating to take the first hit in a negotiation that I'd come in here thinking I had in the bag.

"Hmm. I'd reconsider it if I had my son by my side at York the way it was meant to be."

My fingertips went numb, and the fuzzy, tingly feeling began moving its way slowly up my arms. "Me? At York?"

He nodded with smug satisfaction. "Under contract again. Give me another ten years. You love the city. Why move out to the country when you can stay in your own apartment and use your connections at York to keep fundraising for your little pet project? Hell, I'll even agree to bump up the foundation's contributions as long as we get York Capital in the black again."

I couldn't give him ten more years at a job I hated. I couldn't.

I shook my head. "No. It's too much."

He misunderstood me. I'd meant it was too much sacrifice to ask of me, but he'd thought I'd meant ten years was too much.

"If you're willing to give up the extra foundation money, I'll accept a five-year commitment. Give me five more years to change your mind. Hell, Ellison. When you take over York, just think of the money you could steer toward your charity projects. You'd do a hell of a lot more good for those scholarship kids at York than working on-site at the school for peanuts."

In theory, he was right. As long as I worked for York, I could direct corporate giving to the programs. But I couldn't develop alternative funding sources to replace York's contributions as long as I was working nights and weekends at my job.

I'd be dependent on my father. Under his thumb. Again.

My father watched me carefully. I shook my head again, feeling like the most selfish asshole on earth. If I truly cared about Grey, I'd do this. Five years and plenty of money for the academy? Why wouldn't I agree?

Because I hate it there. I hate the law. I hate working with my father. I hate working to make rich people richer.

Five years and Grey's project could launch incredible new ventures. Five years and my father might retire and put me in charge of the foundation.

It was only five years.

"I'll start an internship at York Capital you can offer to one of your students each year," he said, sweetening the pot. "Hell, I'll offer one at Marlette too."

I considered it. It was a small price to pay to get the approval Grey needed for the building. Besides, it would give me five years in the same city as Grey. It would give us a chance at developing a real relationship without the challenge of long distance.

But the real deciding factor was the memory of his face last night when he told me how he felt about the project.

"This is it. Everything I've been working so hard toward, and I'm this close. There isn't anything I wouldn't do to make this work."

I hadn't been able to make things right for Grey back then, but I could sure as hell do it now.

"Okay," I said, exhaling a big breath. "You'll agree to sign off on Ian's building sale if I come back to York for five years."

"And agree to stop seeing Grey Blackwood socially," he added casually.

I let out a harsh laugh. That was one thing I was definitely not willing to sacrifice. "No fucking way. Try again."

Dad shrugged and stood up. "That's a condition of my offer. Take it or leave it."

I stood up and moved toward the door. "Easy enough. I leave it."

Dad made a sound of disgust. "Fine. Jesus, fine. But he's not going to stay with you once he learns you've gone back to work for his enemy," he called as I walked out. "You'll see."

My dad sounded so sure of himself, even I wondered. It was true that Grey was going to be royally pissed at me.

When I reached the end of the hallway and began descending the back staircase, I dropped all pretense of control. I wanted to scream and cry, bang my fists on a wall and throw things. My father was a selfish ass. It wasn't a surprise but a continued, devastating reality that seemed to rear its ugly head up more and more often the older I got.

Or maybe I just saw it more clearly now.

I made my way into the first empty room I came to on the main floor. It was Ian's office. I slumped down in a chair in front of the empty fireplace again. I hated my father.

A few minutes later, Cate came rushing into the room, looking frenzied. "Oh! I was looking for Uncle Ian or Aunt Binnie. Have you seen them?"

I shook my head. "Want me to help look for them? Is everything okay?"

She nodded, then shook her head. "I don't really know. My aunt down in Florida just had a bad fall and was rushed into surgery. My parents want to get there as fast as they can since my dad has her medical power of attorney. I was hoping to find us a ride to the airport."

I stood up, thinking Ian and Binnie were most likely preparing to host the rest of their guests on the croquet lawn. If I had to sit here and wait until Grey's call finished, I'd drive myself crazy. Might as well run them to the airport and help kill time in the process. "I'll drive you. The housekeeper has keys to Binnie's SUV."

We rushed to get everyone and their luggage loaded in the SUV. I tried finding Grey to tell him where I was going, but when I found the small office Binnie had put him in, he was in full business mode, explaining something technical I didn't dare interrupt. Instead, I asked the housekeeper to tell Grey where I'd gone as soon as she saw him leave the study.

The drive to the airport was frustrating as hell. I'd forgotten to grab my phone off the charger in the rush to get out the door, so I didn't have a navigation app to warn me about a traffic jam on Main Street. I apologized to the McArthurs, who were clearly stressed about the delay. When I finally got them there, I wished them well and headed back.

On the long, silent drive back to the house, I tried to remind myself of what I'd be gaining rather than what I was giving up. This project meant everything to Grey, and that meant a lot to me. I would think about all of the kids his project would help, all of the opportunities that were going to be created by his generosity. I was privileged to be a part of it in some small way.

But how was I going to tell him that the deal was done? He'd asked me to wait for him, but wasn't there a saying about it being better to ask forgiveness than permission?

It turned out my fears about how to explain things to Grey were for nothing because I finally arrived back at the house, I learned my father had taken care of it for me.

And Grey Blackwood was gone.

21

GREY

"Do not interfere with an army that is returning home."
~ Sun Tzu, *The Art of War*

Maybe I wouldn't have taken everything the wrong way if my call to the team in Paris hadn't gone to shit first. But when I got off the video conference, I was in a foul mood. I walked out of the private study in search of the one person who could possibly lift my spirits, but when I got back to our room, I noticed all of Ellison's things were gone.

At first, I'd thought I'd walked into the wrong room, and I'd quickly backed out of it. But then I'd spotted my own leather business card holder on the small desk next to my sunglasses, exactly where I'd left both items.

I crept back into the room and opened the armoire. Sure enough, my clothes hung there just as I'd left them, but the other half of the space was full of empty hangers. After I moved to the bathroom and discovered his toiletries missing, I pulled out my phone to text him.

Me: *Where are you?*

I worried something unexpected had happened to call him away urgently. Surely, he would have interrupted my call to tell me or at least sent me a text informing me of his sudden departure?

I checked my texts and found nothing from him. I tried texting Marcel to make sure my phone was working properly. He responded right away.

Before I knew what I was doing, I was out the door in search of anyone who might have information about what had happened. I found Binnie out at the croquet course, but she claimed not to know anything. I looked everywhere but couldn't find Cate. Finally, I had no other choice but to look for Ellison's parents.

The butler directed me to Ian's office, where Warren York was sitting at Ian's desk. "There you are," Warren said. "Finally. Ian has drawn up some papers for you. I thought you'd like to take a look at them."

"Where is Ellison?"

Warren smiled in a way that made my skin crawl. "He left. Said now that we all had an agreement, he didn't want to spend another minute in your company. I told him the polite thing to do would be to at least stay long enough to explain things to you, but he was in too much of a hurry to get back to his precious school. You know how he feels about that place."

I could tell he was lying, but I couldn't figure out why or what his game was. "What agreement?" I asked.

"Didn't you talk to Ellison about giving York Capital back to us in exchange for getting Ian to sell you the Hell's Kitchen property?"

I froze. Where the hell was Ellison, and what had he told them?

"Where is Ellison?" I asked again.

"He's gone," Warren said. "He'd left some work undone at school when he raced to the city to deal with everything last week."

Ellison had definitely mentioned needing to finish up some work tonight for the academy, but I hadn't realized it was anything he needed to be in Vermont for.

I glanced at Warren. "And Ian has agreed to sell me the building?" He must have been closer to Ian than I'd been led to believe if he had that kind of sway over him. But then again, they'd known each other for decades and were close family friends. It made sense.

He nodded. "As long as you put York Capital back in York hands. I understand you'll be transferring the bulk of the investment assets out first."

I felt like I was being played, only I couldn't see the pieces on the board and I didn't know the rules.

"What did Ellison tell you?" I asked, stalling for time.

"That he did what it took to get you to make us a deal," Warren replied easily. "And you're a man of honor, whatever the hell that means, and wouldn't renege on the deal."

He was right. I wouldn't. Even if what Warren was implying was true. But I didn't believe it. Ellison wouldn't have...

I remembered him giving me a hug this morning at breakfast.

"Thank you. Really. You're a good man, Grey. I'm sorry for everything, but I'm not sorry we had a chance to reconnect and get past everything."

My blood slowed, and I felt myself pulling away from the conversation Warren was trying to have with me about legal terms and contracts.

"Are we good with the York Capital thing? Our deal? I mean... if Ian agrees to sell you the building, you'll really give my family back the York Capital name?"

What... what exactly had he been asking me?

"I think he's going to agree to sell it to you. But I need to know if he does... if he does, you're going to sign York back over, right?"

The truth of our last encounter rang in my head with clanging cymbals. I'd asked him not to talk to Ian without me, but he'd clearly done it anyway. Just to be sure, I asked, "When did Ellison talk to Ian about this?"

"Yesterday afternoon. At least that's what Ian told me."

And Ellison hadn't mentioned it to me even last night when we'd had our heart-to-heart. I thought about how open I'd been with him, how vulnerable. And he'd known the whole time he'd gone behind my back to talk to Ian about the building project when all I'd ever asked him to do was introduce me so I could talk to Ian myself.

I hated being managed.

I glared at Warren. "And you? When did he tell you about getting York back?"

"This morning."

So that was that. I'd told Ellison how important it was to me to talk to Ian myself, and he hadn't taken the opportunity to confess he'd already talked to him. Then he went one step further and talked to his father, my absolute nemesis, about it without me as well. So much for trusting him.

You knew better than to trust a York.

I turned to leave.

Warren called after me. "Where are you going? I have legal paperwork for you to sign!"

I turned to face him, angrier than I'd been in a long time. "As if I'd trust your attorney to draw up the paperwork. No. Your son was right when he said I won't renege on the deal. I want that building, and I'll give York back to get it. But I'll have my own damned lawyers put together the contracts. Expect to hear from them tomorrow. In the meantime, don't ever fucking contact me again. From now on, I will only speak to you through an attorney."

I strode back up the stairs and packed my things as quickly as I could. The sooner I got out of here, the sooner I could wash the stink of this entire scheme off me.

I dialed Marcel.

"Hey, boss."

"Get me out of here as fast as you can," I said, hearing the rough anger in my voice. "Bonus points for finding a way to block Ellison and Warren York from ever being able to contact me directly again."

"Oh, shit," Marcel said softly.

"Yes. Oh shit, indeed. And before you say a word, this didn't have a damn thing to do with my lack of faith or...or... baskets of fucking apples. It had to do with Ellison York fucking me over for the second and final time. Text me back when the car is out front."

While I waited, I found a few touristy postcards in the desk drawer and chose one to use. I wrote as polite a thank-you note as I could manage to Binnie. I hoped like hell she was ignorant of all these machinations, but I didn't know for sure. Suddenly, every interaction I'd had at this party was suspect, and every friendly smile felt like manipulation. Either way, it wasn't polite to leave without a goodbye, but I couldn't stand the idea of faking nice in front of any of these people.

Instead, I snuck out like a thief and asked Henry the butler to give the postcard to Binnie for me.

It wasn't until the car was pulling out of the driveway that my brain processed what Henry had mumbled under his breath as he'd held the door for me.

"Don't be an idiot."

Well, if he had been talking to me, it was too late. I was already a colossal idiot for trusting Ellison York again. I didn't believe a word his father had said about him using me just to get the deal done. I'd seen the genuine happiness in Ellison's face when we'd been together. He couldn't have faked that.

But I'd trusted him to let me handle the real estate deal without going behind my back and involving his father. Why in the world would he have even told his father my business? There was no explanation. If there had been, Ellison would have texted me back.

When I got to the small airport, Marcel's text directed me to wait for my own plane to land. I was annoyed he'd sent the plane instead of chartering a helicopter, but I did as he'd said. When the plane landed and I climbed on board, I saw Marcel himself. He and Luca were sitting in two of the wide leather seats wearing Hawaiian shirts and sipping fruity drinks.

"There he is!" Luca said, holding his drink up in a toast. "Thank you for getting me out of yet another baby shower."

Marcel's expression was full of maternal angst toward me. I chose to look at Luca instead. "What are you two doing here?"

Luca swallowed a sip of his drink. "We're Greynapping you and taking you to a private island in the Caribbean. Don't argue. You know how this one gets." He thumbed in the direction of my personal assistant.

"I do, indeed," I said softly, finally looking at my friend and right-hand man.

"Come to papa," Marcel cooed, holding his arms out. Normally, I would have batted his hands away and bitched at him for teasing me, but this time I didn't do either of those things. I walked into his arms and held him tightly, trying my hardest not to cry like a goddamned baby.

I sensed Marcel exchanging glances with his husband over my shoulder, but I was too far gone to care.

"Can I get you a drink, sweetie?" Marcel asked when our hug came to its natural end.

"God yes," I groaned, dropping into the seat across from theirs. "Anything but a Persnickity High-Hat."

22

ELLISON

"Do not press a desperate enemy."
~ Sun Tzu, *The Art of War*

When I returned to the Duckworths' house, I secretly hoped to spend the rest of the morning flirting wildly with Grey over croquet. The two of us would snicker about the old-fashioned game, but we'd secretly enjoy the time outside together with each other on such a beautiful sunny day. He would be downright giddy knowing the building sale was in the bag and the project could move forward.

But that's not what happened.

"Where's Grey?" I asked Henry when I didn't find him in our room.

"He left." I could tell he wanted to say more, but he didn't.

"What do you mean, left? Where did he go?"

"A car picked him up. He had his luggage. I presume he was headed back to the city. Maybe by way of the airport?"

I stared at him and almost laughed. "I just came from the airport." Then I realized I wouldn't have recognized him in a strange car on the road, even if I'd passed him. "Why? Do you know why he left? Are you sure?"

"He was picked up by a local taxi, and he had his bags. That's all I know for sure."

"But..." I tried to decide where to even begin. *My phone.*

I raced back up to the room and searched for it, but I discovered immediately that the room was completely empty of all our possessions. I turned around in circles before going back downstairs to find Henry again.

"Is Binnie playing a trick on me? Am I being pranked? My things are missing."

Henry looked annoyed and nervous, an odd mix. "I believe they are in your parents' room," he said in a low voice. "And, unrelated to anything at all, Mr. Blackwood spoke to your father before he left."

Anger overwhelmed me. I nodded my thanks to Henry before asking if he knew where my father was currently.

"Avoiding croquet by wandering down the beach, if I'm not mistaken."

I stormed out of the house and down the boardwalk before kicking off my shoes and aiming at the man fifty yards down the beach. Thankfully, he was alone.

"What the fuck did you do?" I yelled.

I could see the smug satisfaction on his face when he turned to look at me. "I told him the truth."

"What truth?"

"That you used him to get York Capital back."

"He already knew that," I snapped. "He agreed to it."

His smile turned crafty. "Really? Because he seemed sort of surprised when I told him you were back in the fold and had happily agreed to spend another five years at York. "

Damn it. "Grey knows I wouldn't have agreed happily." Didn't he?

My father shrugged. "How many times have I told you, Ellison? The truth doesn't matter nearly as much as what *appears* to be true."

So my father had lied. He'd manipulated. The only surprise was that I was surprised.

"My goodness, you should have *seen* the look on his face when I told him you'd already spoken to Ian, also." He paused and gave me a sad smile as the wind off the water ruffled his hair. "Or actually, maybe it's best that you didn't, son. I've never seen someone so angry. Like you'd managed to ruin him *twice*, in a way, isn't it?"

No, it wasn't like that at all. But had it seemed that way to Grey, who'd barely begun to trust me?

Yes, I could easily believe my father had made it seem exactly that way.

I felt like a mouse under a lion's paw. Like he was toying with me just because he could. And I'd always known my father was an asshole, but I hadn't realized just how callously, needlessly cruel he could be until that moment.

I really wished Grey was there so I could ground myself in his calm presence, the antidote to all my father's lies.

"You know, Ellison, I feel like it's my duty as your father to say that if Grey *truly* cared about you, he would have known you didn't have the balls to manipulate him that way, even if he deserved it." He sighed. "He really doesn't know you at all, does he?"

But he *did*, I wanted to scream. He knew me better than anyone. And he cared about me.

Or at least I thought he had.

"You know..." Dad snapped his fingers like he'd just had an amazing idea. "It's not too late to put a stop to this business. My assistant has already sent his lawyers a draft contract, but we can rip that up if you'd like. Grey Blackwood can keep York Capital, Ian can sell Marlette his building, you can go back to your precious school."

"You're going to hold me to the employment contract? Even after all this? After you ruined everything?" I huffed out a laugh that was not at all amused.

"Of course." He shrugged. "A deal's a deal."

For half a second, I thought about it. About going back to Warrington and pretending this whole week hadn't happened. But then I thought about Grey's face when he talked about how much the Hell's Kitchen project meant to him.

"Yeah, no. We're going through with the deal."

Dad shook his head with fond exasperation. "See what I mean? No balls. But don't worry. Now we have five more years to work on it." He winked. "And now that you know about Marlette, I could use your help in that arena too. Desi's a brilliant researcher and moneyman, but the man lacks vision."

"Desi," I repeated, stomach plummeting. Grey had said Desi was investing in an LLC outside of York, though the man had denied it in our meeting. "You and Desi Martinez own Marlette."

My father nodded excitedly, practically rocking up and down on the balls of his feet in the soft sand now that he'd gotten his way. It turned my stomach. "We were trying to shift York's most important clients over to Marlette before my brother Mark did something stupid! But it wasn't easy. No one knows who Marlette is, and we couldn't tell them. So we had to start small."

"You've been undercutting York's clients."

"I've been creating a backup plan. Something to protect our family against ruthless raiders like Grey Blackwood."

I snorted. I knew exactly what ruthless looked like.

"I have to go. Where are my things?" I needed to find Grey, to explain. I didn't believe for a second that he had simply left without trying to talk to me. He was better than that, more honorable. My father thought he could get me to believe it because it was something *he* would have done. But Grey was a better man.

He wouldn't have believed my father's lies. How could he have, after everything I'd told him about my father using lies to manipulate people? Didn't he trust me at least enough to stick around and *ask* me?

"I packed them for you and put them in my room. I knew you'd want to head back to Vermont today and close things up there before heading back to the city."

I turned to leave, walking like a zombie until I hit the steps of the boardwalk. After getting my bags from my parents' room, I searched through them for my phone. The power was off, so I turned it on. After a second, a text came through with a ping.

Grey: *Where are you?*

The tears I'd been fighting since the beach came then. Thank god he'd texted instead of leaving without trying to reach me. I swiped at my cheek with the back of my hand and pushed the button to call him. The phone rang once before diverting me to voicemail.

"It's me," I said, trying to sound normal. "Will you call me, please?"

I ended the call before saying anything else. Then I arranged for a car to pick me up to take me to the station, where I planned to take the train back to the city. I didn't need Vermont. I needed Grey. There was no doubt in my mind where I would go when I got to the city.

Grey's apartment. We needed to talk.

It took several hours to get there, and when I finally walked into the crisp, clean lobby of his building, the doorman stopped me. "Mr. York, sir, I'm afraid you're no longer on the allowed list. Let me call up for you."

I'm not? I stared at him as my entire body vibrated with nerves and shock. "Yes, please."

A few minutes later, Jenny stepped off the elevator, looking nervous. "Ellison, what happened?"

"I don't know. I need to talk to him. Can I come up?"

"Honey, he's not here. Marcel said they were headed out of the country. He won't be home for a couple of weeks."

I let out a burble of laughter. This was a joke. It had to be. "Can you get him on the phone?"

Jenny twisted her fingers together and shook her head. "Marcel said he's going somewhere with no reception. I assumed you were going with them. It sounded like a resort in the middle of nowhere. I know Marcel has been trying to get Grey to take some time away. He kept saying he would agree after the York deal was done."

I laughed again, only this time I couldn't stop. I laughed until I cried.

And then I cried for three straight days until my anger at Grey

Blackwood finally surpassed the pain of the broken heart he'd left behind.

23

GREY

"The good fighter will be terrible in his onset, and prompt in his decision."
~ Sun Tzu, *The Art of War*

It was amazing how many contracts you could sign by good old-fash-ioned fax machine. At least that's what Marcel told me. In truth, I was fairly sure he was hiding a satellite hotspot in his room, but I didn't care. As long as all of the York business was behind me and I could safely claim lack of cell reception as the reason I hadn't heard from Ellison, I was fine.

Well, that and about twenty gin and tonics a day.

"For the third time, you can't fax your mother a fruity drink," Marcel said without looking up from his Kindle.

"Who assed you that?" I slurred. "I didn't ass you that."

"Mmpf." Marcel's eyes flicked up to land on Luca's teeny-weenie bikini. Again.

"Didn't you get enough of his teeny-weenie last night?" I asked, reaching for my drink to take another sip. I got a face full of ice instead. Stupid glass probably had a hole in it. "You two were so loud, I thought your villa was going to untether and float away."

"The villa is on land, sweetums. Not over water. And his weenie ain't teeny."

"Huh. My villa is over water." I tried getting more drink out of my glass, but it only gave up more ice cubes.

"No it isn't."

"Get terribly seasick on it."

"That's not seasickness." He looked back down at his Kindle. "And we're moving villas. If I have to listen to you sing along to 'In Your Eyes' one more time, I'm not going to be able to get it up anymore," he muttered.

"I need a boom box," I said, looking around as if one would present itself here on Nothing-to-do Island.

"I think you should sober up so we can talk about your boyfriend."

"Luca's your boyfriend," I corrected, trying not to think about Ells.

"Actually, he's my husband. But I was talking about Ellison York. I may have acquired some interesting intel about him that you might like to hear, but you'll have to be at a net-zero gin and tonic before I'll give you such important information."

I didn't understand any part of that except Ellison and husband. "He's not my husband," I muttered.

Marcel sighed and made some kind of hand gesture to the cabana boy before going back to reading his Kindle. Three or twenty-five minutes later, the cabana boy brought me a huge glass of gin and tonic.

"Epic," I said, lifting it with two hands. I grimaced when I took the first sip. "This is really watered down."

"Water usually is," Marcel muttered. "Drink up," he said a little louder.

I did as he said and fell promptly to sleep. Sometime later, I awoke with a raging headache and a tongue the size of a blowfish.

Marcel was still sitting beside me, reading his book. "I had the cabana boy slather you with sunscreen. You're welcome."

"No you didn't," I grumbled, sitting up slowly under the huge umbrella that hadn't been there before.

"No, but I thought about it. Instead, I had him do me."

From the lounger on the other side of Marcel, Luca murmured a sleepy "You wish."

I rubbed my face with my hands and tried to shake off the fuzzy feeling. Hangovers sucked. I'd hoped to keep a nice buzz around the clock to avoid getting one.

"Did you say you had information about Ellison, or was that a fever dream?" I asked, assuming the latter.

He set his Kindle down on the table next to him and turned to face me. "I talked to Ian Duckworth."

I groaned and lay back down on the chaise. "Never mind. I don't want to hear this."

Marcel ignored me as usual. "Obviously, we've been in touch about the contracts. He said something the other day, but I didn't realize its importance until this morning when I was talking to Luca about it."

"What did he say?"

"Ian said he was disappointed in you for leaving Ellison. He also said that Ellison was upset when he got back from taking Cate to the airport on Sunday morning. He was looking all over the property for you."

My head was pounding. "When did he take Cate to the airport? And why the hell does he think I was the one who left Ellison?"

"I don't know. But he told me that he and his wife really thought the two of you were serious. They were shocked when you left without saying goodbye. They asked me if Ellison found you before you left the Hamptons."

None of that made sense. "He left first," I said, and it maybe came out a little more hurt and accusatory than I would have liked. "I told you that."

The first night on the island, I'd gotten drunk and spilled all the beans about Ellison and me. Marcel and Luca had listened with big hearts and even bigger opinions, but I hadn't been in the mood for listening.

"That's what I said to Ian, but he said no. He said you left first, and then Ellison got mad at his dad, but neither one of them ever explained why to Ian. I assumed he simply got it wrong, so I didn't think much of it. But then I remembered the thing about taking Cate to the airport."

"No. If Ellison had been upset, he would have called me. He would have tried to get in touch with me. Explain to me why I haven't heard from him all week."

That *definitely* came out more hurt and accusatory than I would have liked, but all the gin and tonics in all the land couldn't have kept me from noticing how empty my arms were when I went to sleep without Ellison at night, or how hopeless the days seemed when I woke up alone.

Marcel's jaw dropped. "Are you kidding? You told me to block his number. You told me to make it so neither York could get in touch with you directly!"

"And you did it?" I asked. Sitting up quickly required me to grab my pounding head before it exploded. "Jesus Christ, Marcel! Since when do you do what I ask?"

Luca leaned forward and shot me a glare. "Watch it, asshole."

I sighed. "It doesn't matter. He still went behind my back to arrange everything with Ian when I asked him not to."

"Is that bad enough to lose him over?" Marcel asked.

No. Definitely not. But my trust had been razor-thin to begin with. It hadn't taken much to scare me off, and Ellison would have known that.

He should have come to me, dammit.

"Also," Marcel added, "an interesting detail came up while I was talking to Ian. One of the tenants in his building needed help refitting their new office space. We negotiated additional funding for that."

I didn't want to talk about this right now, but it took less energy to close my eyes and ignore him than to argue.

"In the process of dealing with that, I got a list of the current tenants. The largest one is Marlette Venture Partners."

"Don't know 'em." But something about the name was familiar.

"No, me neither. However, I looked into them the way I always do—"

Luca hummed. "My baby hides his nosiness under a mantle of respectable diligence. Adorable and conniving."

"*Anyway*," Marcel said. "Marlette is owned by Desi Martinez and Warren York."

My brain started churning against my will. "Wait."

"Right," Marcel said, leaning forward and poking me in the shoulder. "Marlette is Marianne York's maiden name."

It was like he was constructing a story in several different languages and expecting me to follow it. "What the hell does this mean?" Did Ellison know? When I'd left him alone to question Desi, had he already known about Desi's involvement in another company with Warren?

I blinked at Marcel. "Why would Desi and Warren own a completely separate investment company?"

"I don't think that's the important part of this."

"Then what is? I don't understand anything you're saying." I looked around for the attendant and waved him over to order a Coke and some food. Maybe that would help my brain snap out of its haze.

Luca sat forward to meet my eye over his husband's shoulder. "I think his point is, there's more to this than we realized. Maybe Ellison knew that. Maybe he had to do some negotiating in the background to make this work for you."

Marcel added, "Or maybe he didn't know, but he found out about it and tried to smooth it over for you."

The attendant arrived with the icy soft drink. I took a deep gulp and swallowed. "Or maybe Ellison was part of it all along."

Marcel rolled his eyes and flopped back on his chaise. "There's the Doom-Bringer I know and tolerate. At the risk of making too much sense for your hungover brain to handle, Grey, you won't know the truth unless you ask him." Under his breath, he muttered, "Not that this has ever stopped you from rushing to judgment before."

"Mpfh."

I took a few more sips of Coke before remembering the recording on my phone from Ellison and Desi's meeting. In all the craziness of that week, I'd never gone back and listened to it.

Marcel was wrong. I *could* find out the truth without talking to Ellison.

After picking my way through a sandwich and fries, I excused myself to go back to my villa and find my phone.

Hearing Ellison's voice made me regret eating the sandwich. My stomach tightened with nerves. I missed him so fucking much. It was pathetic how used to him I'd gotten in such a short time.

I found the voice recording and hit Play.

"Hey, Desi, come on in. Grey had to run something downstairs. How are you?"

"A little frustrated if you want to know the truth. What the hell happened?"

Ellison sighed. *"Uncle Mark happened, I guess. I'm worried about some of our clients. What if Grey pulls their funding or changes the way we support our investments?"*

The sound of a chair squeaked. *"They'll be fine. I have confidence in the contracts you set up for them."*

"Thanks. I guess you're right. I'm worried about Dad too, though. I kind of wish... well, never mind. It is what it is."

Desi hesitated before speaking. *"Don't worry about your dad. He's a smart man. He knows how to look out for himself. We all do, don't we? It's never a good idea to have all your eggs in one basket."*

"What about..." Ellison paused and lowered his voice to a whisper. *"Investing personal money in some of our clients? Have you ever considered that? It's just... I worry about these clients. And I have a little money to invest..."*

"Me? No, of course not. But if you were interested... I could probably help you find some ways of going about it." The smirk was clear in Desi's voice. *"There are ways to get around the rules."*

Ellison blew out a breath. *"Okay, yeah. Thanks. I'll think about it."*

"What do you know about Blackwood? Your father told me you have a

history with the man."

There was a beat of silence before Ellison's voice took on a different tone, a lighter one as if he was smiling. *"He's pretty amazing, actually. I know everyone is worried about how he'll manage the company, but... so far it seems like he knows what he's doing. I've followed his career for years. He's thorough, smart, and deliberate. Did you know the first VC company he acquired was on the cusp of collapse? He structured the takeover before the owners could take their money out of their clients' projects prematurely. If he hadn't taken over Innor VC when he had, their collapse would have led to the grounding of Aerocepte's entire fleet for months. The commercial airline industry would have suffered a major setback. The man's a fucking genius. No wonder he's a billionaire."*

I continued listening to Ellison describe my corporate successes in a way I'd never heard before. Not only had he followed my career, he'd been impressed with it. And he hadn't been afraid to tell Desi Martinez, one of his father's toadies, about it.

That wasn't the voice of a man out to get me or a man with a hidden agenda to take me down. But I'd already known that, so what the hell was my problem?

Stone-cold fear.

I crawled onto my bed and lay back to stare at the ceiling. A rattan paddle fan rotated lazily above me, and the distant lapping of the water on the beach through the open sliding doors provided a rhythmic backdrop to my jangled thoughts.

Cate had been at breakfast with us that morning. If he took her to the airport Sunday morning, it had to have been while I was on the call with the team in Paris. But then why had his clothes been missing from our room? Had he intended to go somewhere with her? Had he taken his things to the airport but changed his mind and returned?

It didn't make any sense.

I thought back through my time with Ellison in the Hamptons, the fight we had on the beach especially.

"What happens if you walk away from me again?" I asked.

Ellison pinned me with his glare. "Need I remind you that so far this past week it's been you who's walked away from me? I've laid myself at your fucking feet, begged you for more, introduced you to people who matter to me. Do you want promises? You know I can't make them, and you also know you yourself wouldn't make them this early on. But I'm here. I'm not walking away from you. This is me fighting, dammit. And I want to break through this infernal fucking wall you have built up and see the real Grey Blackwood. I hate when you get that stoic look on your face and act like you don't have a heart. You do. I know you do, so fucking show it to me!"

Fucking fuck.

How many times had he accused me of running off instead of talking to him? Had I done it again? No, I'd texted him. I'd tried calling him.

But then I'd blocked his number and left the damned country like a fucking coward when he hadn't called me back within an hour.

I jumped up and raced next door, not caring that there were clearly sex noises coming from Marcel and Luca's villa. "I need to go to Vermont," I yelled through the door. "I need your help."

Luca's voice was clear and unhappy. "Fucking Christ. *Go away.*"

"On it, boss!" Marcel said with a laugh, before letting out a long, debauched groan. I put my fingers in my ears and raced back to my own villa to take a quick shower.

I needed to get to Ellison and convince him it had all been a mistake. I would beg him on my hands and knees if necessary.

After all these years, it was finally my turn to do the groveling.

When my plane landed at the small airport closest to Warrington Academy, I was nervous enough to consider puking just to get it over with.

"Breathe, Grey. Vomiting on a man is not considered a declaration of love in most cultures," Marcel reminded me.

Love? Jesus. I swallowed hard.

"Not helping," I muttered. By the time I walked into the administrative office of the school itself, I was pouring sweat.

The receptionist looked up at me with a smile. "May I help you?"

"Yes, I'm here to see Ellison York, please."

She frowned. "He's not here. Ellison lives in New York."

I turned to Marcel in confusion. "But he works here. In Vermont."

Thankfully, Marcel took over with his usual charm. "We were under the impression he'd moved here to work full-time in development for the school," he said with a smile.

"Well, yes. He did, but then he went back to work for his family business in the city. He's a lawyer, you know."

My hands started to shake worse than they'd been before. "That's not possible. He hates the law. He quit York Capital."

She frowned. "Well, yes, but then..." She glanced over my shoulder. "Maybe you should talk to his sister... Gigi? These men are looking for Ellison."

I turned to see a woman who looked completely different from Ellison in coloring but had the exact same searching gaze. I recognized her as an older version of the pretty girl at the country club. "Gigi, I'm—"

"Grey Blackwood," she said in a flat voice. "You'd better come into my office."

She let us into a small office to the side of the reception desk and closed the door behind us. Marcel and I took seats in front of her desk while she took her chair on the opposite side. "Why are you here? What do you want?"

"I want your brother," I said, without meaning to say it like that. Even though it was really very true.

Marcel put a hand on my arm and leaned forward. "He means he'd like a chance to talk to Ellison. We believe there may have been a big misunderstanding."

She lifted an eyebrow at him, and I wanted to laugh. I'd been on the receiving end of that look many times from her brother. "And you are...?"

"Grey's keeper. The man who's trying to untangle the giant mess he's made of things."

Finally, Gigi's face softened. "Thank god someone's trying. Maybe while you're at it, you can find out why he decided to go back to work for our dad, something he swore he'd never do."

"You don't know?" I asked.

She shook her head. "I tried talking to him about it, but he just said it was complicated. I thought maybe he wanted to stay in the city because of you, but clearly that's not the case. You haven't talked to him?"

"No. I thought he was here."

"He was. For several days of intense heartbreak recovery. He cried *a lot*." She shot me with a glare that went straight to my gut and twisted it, hard. The thought of Ellison in tears over *me* nearly broke me. "But then he said he had to go back to the city. Something about honor and 'a deal's a deal'? He packed up his things and took off."

I stood up. "Then I need to get back home and find him. Thank you."

She narrowed her eyes and gave me a thousand-watt smile. "If you'd *really* like to show your gratitude, you could donate to our program. Ellison would be very appreciative."

Marcel barked out a laugh and produced a checkbook from his messenger bag, then handed it to me to fill out.

When I gave the check to Gigi, her eyes widened in shock. "My god. You really were grateful. Th-thank you very much for your generosity." Then she looked up from the check. "Did you want a portion of this to go toward the Blackwood Scholarship fund?"

"You don't need to fund a scholarship in my name," I said, standing up. "Use it however you see fit."

She blinked in surprise, and then her eyes danced like she knew something I didn't. "The Blackwood Scholarship fund was established over ten years ago, Mr. Blackwood. It was my brother's pet project and one of the reasons we started this school in the first place. Half of our students are here on a Blackwood Scholarship."

The sound of Marcel's sigh faded as the room around me wobbled and dipped.

I sat back down in a graceless heap.

24

ELLISON

"It is easy to love your friend, but sometimes the hardest lesson to learn is to love your enemy."

~ Sun Tzu, *The Art of War*

It had been ten days since I'd left the Hamptons. Ten days of accepting my new reality and getting to experience all the punishment of my decisions and little of the reward. Ten days of coming to terms with the fact Grey Blackwood wasn't the honorable man I'd thought he was.

"Dude, your sister is on line one," my assistant, Skyla, said through the intercom on the conference table phone. "She said she tried you on your cell first."

I pulled out my phone and looked at it. Sure enough, two missed calls and a text. My head was in the clouds these days. I was overlooking stuff left and right. After slipping my phone back into my pocket, I picked up the conference room phone's handset. The meeting wasn't supposed to start for another few minutes, and people were still trickling in and helping themselves to coffee on the sideboard.

"Hey."

"Yeah, so, ah... we just got a huge donation from BGP."

"Awesome," I said, reaching for my pen and flipping it through my fingers. "I'll process it when I get home tonight." It wasn't like I had anything else to do. A few friends had invited me out for a drink, but I kept putting them off. Pretty sure going out with someone this mopey was about as exciting as staying home to iron clothes.

"Grey Blackwood is a specimen of a man," she said with a sigh.

I sat up. "Wait. BGP like Blackwood Giving Program?"

"That's the one."

My heart tripped over itself, ramping up to a speed it hadn't seen in approximately ten days. "He was *there*? He went to Warrington? What for? No, wait, never mind." It didn't matter. I didn't care. "Define huge," I prompted in a low voice. Maybe I cared a little.

"Like, I've never seen this many digits on one check before." The smile in her voice was obvious. "It's... pretty amazing."

"And did... did he say anything? Was it... did he say how he wanted it spent or... how he was doing?" I was pathetic, but my sister already knew that. She'd been the one to greet my sorry ass when I'd finally turned up in Vermont and promptly burst into tears on her doorstep.

"Nope." She paused. "But I did mention putting some of it toward the Blackwood Scholarship fund."

I groaned. "Please tell me you didn't."

"Oh, but I did. And Ells? I think you're going to need to get in touch with him and thank him personally."

"Hah! Yeah right. Like that's going to happen. No. No way. This one's on you, sis. Not happening on my end. Nope."

I couldn't even wrap my head around seeing Grey right now. He would be all... corporate and stoic like he'd been when I'd first seen him in this same damned conference room a couple of weeks before.

Like that guy who'd just walked in. Broad-shouldered and

wearing a perfectly tailored suit. Blond hair styled just so and blue-green eyes that...

I blinked. "Oh shit," I whispered, staring at the vision in front of me. "I've finally had a psychotic break."

"What do you mean?" my sister asked through the phone.

I blinked again, but Grey Blackwood's image was still there. My heartbreak and anger had finally combusted together to form an actual hallucination.

"I think I need medical help," I pleaded in a whisper. "He's here."

Before she could ask who, I continued. "Grey. Grey is here. Grey." I couldn't stop saying his name. I loved the way it felt on my tongue. Saying it out loud made it real.

He pinned me with his stare, and I dropped the handset with a clatter. The noise got everyone's attention, and the room went silent.

"Wh-what are you, um..." I swallowed and glanced around, desperate for someone to tell me what the hell was happening right now. "What are you doing here?" Was that a little squeaky? Too squeaky?

Somehow, my squeaky voice seemed to make him relax. His shoulders dropped away from his ears just a little, but his eyes grew even more intense.

He took several slow steps toward me. "I'm here for you."

"*Pfft*," I swallowed again. Had my throat ever been this dry before? No. Surely not. "That's... *pfft*."

The corner of his lip curved up, which made me *mad*. And suddenly I remembered how very fucking *angry* I was.

"Get out," I said, finding my voice. "You don't have a right to be here anymore."

"I know," he said softly. "But I need to talk to you."

I shook my head a little frantically. "*Pfft*. No. No way. Not happening. *Pfft*." Why did I feel like a broken record?

He took another step forward and dropped to his knees right in front of me. He reached for the arms of my chair and swiveled it until he was kneeling between my knees. I glanced nervously at my coworkers, who stared in shock at the unexpected scene.

Grey put his hands on my thighs and moved them up to my hips and then around my waist. "I'm so fucking sorry," he said in a rough voice. "I'm so, so fucking sorry."

I swallowed again. *Be strong. Do not fall for this shit.* I shook my head emphatically.

"You can't say no, sweetheart," he said softly. "Because I love you, and I'm not taking no for an answer."

What? What did he say? What?

I shook my head again, only this time it was in a desperate attempt to keep my eyes from filling with tears. I would not get mushy and emotional in front of my colleagues.

"You don't," I croaked. "You can't."

He raised a hand to cup my cheek. I closed my eyes to savor the familiar warm caress before I realized what I was doing.

"I do. I will. Forever. I was wrong to leave. I was wrong to believe what your dad told me. And I was so very fucking wrong not to give you a chance to explain."

I nodded. "Yeah," I breathed. "You were. Asshole."

He chuckled in that deep, vibrating voice that made my insides dance and twist for him. His smile dropped. "But I was scared. So scared of my feelings for you."

I leaned down and rested my forehead against his. I just wanted to go home with him and fall asleep in his arms, take a time-out from hating him so I could love him for a little while.

"I hate you," I said with all the love in my heart.

He cupped the back of my head. "I know, baby. And I deserve it. But I'm not going away this time. That's how I realized I'd fucked up. You said you wouldn't walk away. I should have believed you."

I heard someone sniffing behind me and turned to see Nessa and one of my attorney friends both waving hands over their faces to fight back their own tears.

"Kiss him, you idiot," Nessa said.

I turned back to Grey. His face was full of love. I couldn't pretend he didn't mean what he'd said, even though there were so many things left to say.

"Kiss him, you idiot," Grey said softly. Even though he was smiling, I could still see the fear of rejection in his eyes.

I leaned forward and kissed him for several long moments, not noticing until I came up for air that everyone else had finally left the conference room to give us privacy.

"Did you get the building?" I asked. His face lit up, and he nodded.

"Yes, but I don't want to move ahead on the project without your help. Hopefully, you can leave this place and come work with me. Unless you want to go back to Warrington."

My excitement dropped several notches. "I can't. I'm... contractually obligated to work for York Capital for five more years."

His forehead crinkled as he moved back to sit in a chair he'd pulled in front of me. He clasped my hands in his. "Why?"

"It's a long story," I said, not wanting to get into it and risk upsetting him.

"Do you want to be here? I thought you didn't want to be a lawyer anymore."

"I don't. But I signed a contract."

"With York or with your dad, specifically?"

"With York. It's an employment contract."

Grey frowned again. "Then let yourself out of it."

The man knew how contracts worked, so why was this so confusing. "I can't."

"But you own the company. You're under contract with yourself."

"No, my dad..." I saw the smile overtake Grey's frown. I was missing something. "My dad owns York Capital."

"Does he?" Grey asked. "Or does Warren York *LLC* own it?"

His hands tightened on mine, and he winked at me. "How much do you want to bet Warren York doesn't actually own Warren York *LLC*?"

Oh my god.

"Who does?" I whispered, already guessing the answer.

"His son. If I recall correctly, the deal was getting York back in the family for legacy reasons. I saw no harm in saving everyone the paperwork by transferring it to the younger generation a little early, so I went ahead and passed it down to you. You know, for legacy reasons."

I let out a laughing groan and tackled him, nearly tipping his chair over in the process. Grey's arms came around me and held me tight while I kissed his face off.

"I love you too," I confessed softly when we both finally stopped laughing.

"I know. I feel it. I'm only sorry it took me so long to believe in it."

Grey kissed me again as tenderly as if I was his most precious treasure. I lost myself to his kisses as usual and didn't pay any attention to the world around us. When we finally pulled back to take in a breath, I noticed Grey looking a little sheepish.

"What is it?" I asked.

He shifted over to reach for the strap of his messenger bag. "I dropped this when I came in, so I hope I didn't screw things up." He dragged the bag closer, and I moved my butt back into my own chair but stayed as close to him as I could.

He opened his bag and pulled out a brown paper bag with a familiar logo on it. Sunday Orchard. I opened it and peered inside to find half a dozen perfectly ripe Honeycrisp apples.

I looked up at him with way too much emotion pressing on my chest for a simple bag of apples. "This kind isn't usually ready till late September," I said softly.

"I know. Gigi said if I wanted to grovel, I needed to splurge on the good stuff. So I drove up to the best orchard in the area and begged the guy to work a miracle since I knew Honeycrisp was your favorite variety. He walked me out to the trees and spent an hour searching for a few that were good enough to pick."

The man in front of me, who owned several multinational companies, a private jet, a penthouse on Fifth Avenue, and millions of dollars sitting idly in a "just in case" fund had bought me the one thing that cost very little but meant so much.

"How did you know Honeycrisp was my favorite kind?" I asked, even though I knew the answer already.

"Because you told me. And I always listen when you talk," he said, leaning in to kiss the spot on my neck he seemed to like best. "Sometimes it just takes a minute for what you say to really sink in."

I shuddered.

Here was a man who acted like a stoic, unfeeling bastard intent on conquering the corporate world one hostile takeover at a time, when in reality, he was the kind of man who paid attention to the people around him. He looked out for them, cared about them, and listened.

The men I'd grown up with were callous fools who used people and things, then discarded them. But Grey took things over so he could make them better. Make them stronger.

That's what he'd done for me.

Grey Blackwood made sure I had running shoes when I wanted to move, extra food off his own plate when I wanted to eat, and strong arms around me when I needed reassurance. The boy who'd never quite fit in had grown into a man who'd cleared the obstacles from my path and taught me what love truly meant.

I'd spent the last fifteen years daydreaming about a practical stranger, and now I was wide-awake, living my dream with the love of my life.

"I hope you didn't want me to share," I said, teasing him but really hoping he didn't want any of my perfect apples.

Grey's eyes danced as they met mine. "I'll trade you back your father's 1968 Cobra for a bite of one of your juicy apples..."

I laughed and held the bag close to my chest. "Hell no. Why would I agree to that when I can have both?"

He leaned back in his chair and watched me with that sharp gaze and knowing smirk that had made powerful men tremble—and made me tremble, too, for an entirely different reason. "Who says I'm going to give you access to that car, Ellison?"

God, I loved this man. Every day with him was going to be a challenge, and I couldn't fucking wait.

I braced my hands on the arms of his chair, leaned in, and whispered against his ear. "Well, Mr. Blackwood, I have certain... assets you might not have considered."

"Is that so?" Grey's breath caught.

"Mmm." I let my nose trail down the side of his jaw, inhaling his unique scent. "A wise man once told me negotiations are all about emotions. That a successful negotiator will consider what might bring his opponent the most... *pleasure*. I'd be willing to make you a deal."

"By all means, Mr. York. Let the negotiations begin."

EPILOGUE

"Those who are able to adapt and change in accord with the enemy and achieve victory are called divine."
~ Sun Tzu, *The Art of War*

I could tell Ells was nervous.

"We don't have to go," he said for the millionth time.

I slid my silk tie through its loop and smoothed it down. The reflection in the mirror behind me showed a very fidgety boyfriend. "It's your sister's wedding. Pretty sure we have to go."

"Yes, but... it's... the reception is at Crosbie Country Club..." He twisted a cotton handkerchief in his hands, the one I'd given him to put in his pocket "just in case" the ceremony got to him.

My baby was a crier, and I loved that about him. He wasn't afraid to show his emotions.

"That's what it said on the invitation," I said calmly, turning around to grab my suit coat off our messy bed. Since Ellison had moved in almost a year ago, the penthouse had undergone a stealthy but unrelenting makeover. Ellison's impact on our home was striking. Suddenly, the apartment had gone from something worthy of a spread in a modern design magazine to a comfortable home that actual real humans lived in. There were colors and soft fabrics, framed photos and quirky artwork. He'd even started hinting at getting a small dog, which I was absolutely not on board with but had gone ahead and asked Jenny to prepare for nonetheless.

The puppy would be coming home for Ellison's birthday in two weeks, and Jenny had already secretly decided his name needed to be Noodles. I suggested Midas instead, or at least Victor. We finally agreed to wait and see what Ells wanted to name his own dog.

"But you don't want to go back there," he insisted.

"Who says?" I shrugged into the jacket, hoping like hell the weather was cooler out in Greenwich than it was in the city.

"Me, okay? Me. I say. I say you shouldn't have to go back there!" He flapped the handkerchief in the air so violently, I reached over to save it.

After folding it and placing it in the pocket inside his suit coat, I smoothed down his lapels. "I'm fine. But I think you might need a shot of something."

"Why are you so calm? I hate that shit."

I wasn't as calm as I seemed. While I didn't give a rat's ass about the elitists at the club, I cared very deeply for Ellison's comfort. "Sweetheart, I am calm because I want this day to go well for Gigi and Ethan. Also? No one at that club holds power over me anymore, with one exception."

"My dad's not going to be there."

"I don't mean your father." But the reminder Warren wasn't going to be there was a nice little bump in my already great mood. He and Desi were busy with their attorneys trying to figure out how to defend themselves against charges stemming from an anonymous tip to Cate McArthur, the attorney in charge of fraud complaints at the SEC. Rumor had it, she was a bulldog and was known for swift, harsh punishments.

Fortunately, Ellison hadn't seen him in months, ever since Warren had shown up unexpectedly at the Yale Club while we were having brunch with Ian and Binnie. Ellison had shocked everyone by ignoring his father completely. Ian and Binnie had gone along with it, showing their unrelenting disdain for the crap Warren had put his son through.

He sighed. "My mom loves you. You already know that."

It was true. When Marianne York had discovered the deceptions Warren had perpetrated on his own son, she hadn't even given him a second chance. She'd left him immediately and filed for divorce. A certain someone had signed the York's Fifth Avenue apartment over to her, as well as settling some of the proceeds of the sale of the Greenwich house on her in a trust. She was happily continuing her life of leisure in the city without much of a ripple in the water of her life.

"I mean you, dollface," I said, using his term.

Ellison's face softened, and he let out a sigh. "Stop being mature and sweet, or I'm going to have to fuck you again just to take some of my power back."

I pulled him into my arms and kissed the spot under his ear I loved. "Promises, promises," I rumbled against his skin. "Although I'm not sure I'm up for bottoming again anytime soon. Marcel asked me why I was limping the other day. I said I'd pulled a muscle, and he made a snarky comment that's too filthy to repeat. Suffice it to say, he seemed to know the real reason. After that, I swear he coughed *power bottom* under his breath several times in the middle of a meeting."

Ellison's grin made my stomach swoop. His fingers reached under my suit coat to grab my ass. "Even your PA knows you're still a bossy shit when you bottom."

It was time to change the subject. "If you're a good boy and stop worrying about me, I'll let you suck me off in the helicopter."

He rolled his eyes. "Your mom is picking us up at the airport. Besides, the flight only takes twelve minutes."

I nuzzled the spot I'd kissed under his ear. He smelled like my apple shampoo mixed with the coffee I'd brought him in bed this morning. "At this rate, it would take me about four minutes to get off," I murmured. "You look incredible in that suit."

He sucked in a breath and tightened his hands on my ass. "Yes, well, it just showed up in my closet the other day. I guess I have Roni to thank for the perfect fit?"

I didn't want to talk about our personal shopper, the tailoring of his suit, or even the short helicopter ride out of the city. There were more important things to say, like a particular question I planned to ask when I got him alone in that storage room again.

"I love you," I said, inadvertently patting my pants pocket where a certain item was ready and waiting. It wasn't time yet, but it would be soon.

"Mm, so you say..." His tease turned into a groan when my hand came down to stroke the front of his pants. "If you really loved me, you wouldn't have committed us to a round of golf in the morning."

"You love golf."

"No. I don't even like it."

"But you played it almost every day that summer I worked at the club," I said, pulling back to look at him. This was a surprise. How did I not already know we shared a dislike of the sport?

Ells threw his head back and laughed. "You're an idiot. I played it almost every day because I was crazy attracted to one of the damned caddies. Couldn't keep my eyes off his delectable ass. And now I get to fuck it. See, Grey? Things work out. You just have to be patient."

"Lesson learned," I said dryly. "Patience pays off. Then you won't mind waiting until we're in the hotel tonight to suck me off."

"I never said anything about sucking you off," he reminded me, pulling out of my arms and reaching for his wallet and phone off our dresser. "But now that we're on the subject, I think I might owe you one in the storage closet during the wedding reception. If you're a good boy and get us out of that tee time, I might consider also letting you have my ass in the hotel room later. You know why? Because I'm a giver."

"Such a giver," I murmured, remembering how vocally he'd begged me to pound his ass an hour ago in the shower.

We made our way downstairs to the car that was waiting to take us to the helipad at Hudson Yards. As soon as Ellison slid into the back seat, he reached up to clap Emery on the shoulder. "Any way you'd want to detour us past the Hell's Kitchen property so I can see the fencing they put up?"

Emery winked over at me. "Mr. Blackwood already told me you'd want to do that way, sir."

Ellison settled back in the leather seat, happily inquiring about Emery's nephew. Ellison reached over automatically to rest his hand on my leg. I winced and hopped away, panicking about him feeling the outline of the ring in my pocket. Ellison stopped talking long enough to slow-pan toward me.

"Does my touch disgust you now?"

I cleared my throat. "I'm just nervous about the club. You know... all the people there. The memories."

"Bullshit."

Quick, think of something, you idiot.

"Uh..."

Suddenly, the car jerked to a stop with a screech of tires. Emery stifled a curse at the car in front of him before easing the car ahead again.

"Terrible traffic," I muttered.

"Grey..."

"Oh look! The building! It's being demolished on Tuesday. You should come. Join me. Watch it with me."

Ells narrowed his eyes at me before realizing Emery had pulled the car over and parked. I distracted my boyfriend by making a big production of getting out and sneaking past the temporary fencing to grab a piece of rubble from the Hell's Kitchen site.

"For you," I said, presenting him a... rock.

He sighed. "'Date a billionaire,' they said. 'He'll lavish you with extravagant gifts,' they said." He looked down at the dusty rock now sifting a few of its charms onto his formerly pristine suit.

"Maybe one day I'll get you a real one," I said, forcing my hand not to go anywhere near my pocket.

Ellison looked at me with that mischievous expression he seemed to get more often than not these days.

"I dare you."

Want to read the story of how Luca and Marcel got together? Click here to sign up for the newsletter and read their free 12k-word short!

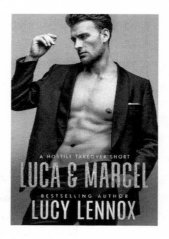

LETTER FROM LUCY

Dear Reader,

Thank you for reading *Hostile Takeover*.

If this is your first Lucy Lennox book, welcome! I hope you enjoyed it. What should you read next? Try *Borrowing Blue*, my award-winning, bestseller gay romance novel with over three thousand five-star reviews on Goodreads! Borrowing Blue is the story of a sudden hot kiss between strangers that turns into much, much more.

All Lucy Lennox novels can be read on their own so find a story that appeals to you and dive right in.

Please take a moment to write a review of this book on Amazon and Goodreads. Reviews can make all of the difference in helping a book show up in book searches.

Feel free to stop by www.LucyLennox.com and drop me a line or visit me on social media. To see inspiration photographs for all of my novels, visit my Pinterest boards.

Finally, I have a fantastic reader group on Facebook. Come join us for exclusive content, early cover reveals, hot pics, and a whole lotta fun. Lucy's Lair can be found here.

Happy reading!

Lucy

ABOUT THE AUTHOR

Lucy Lennox is a mother of three sarcastic kids. Born and raised in the southeast, she now resides outside of Atlanta finally putting good use to that English Lit degree.

Lucy enjoys naps, pizza, and procrastinating. She is married to someone who is better at math than romance but who makes her laugh every single day and is the best dancer in the history of ever.

She stays up way too late each night reading gay romance because it's simply the best thing ever.

For more information and to stay updated about future releases, please sign up for Lucy's author newsletter here.

Connect with Lucy on social media:
www.LucyLennox.com
Lucy@LucyLennox.com

WANT MORE?

Join Lucy's Lair
Get Lucy's New Release Alerts
Like Lucy on Facebook
Follow Lucy on BookBub
Follow Lucy on Instagram
Follow Lucy on Pinterest

Other books by Lucy:
Made Marian Series
Forever Wilde Series
Aster Valley Series
Twist of Fate Series with Sloane Kennedy
After Oscar Series with Molly Maddox
Licking Thicket Series with May Archer
Virgin Flyer
Say You'll Be Nine
Hostile Takeover

Visit Lucy's website at www.LucyLennox.com for a comprehensive list of titles, audio samples, freebies, suggested reading order, and more!

Made in the USA
Middletown, DE
22 November 2021

53154935R00179